Gathering Storms

Kerry McGinnis was born in Adelaide and at the age of twelve took up a life of droving with her father and four siblings. The family travelled extensively across the Northern Territory and Queensland before settling on a station in the Gulf Country. Kerry has worked as a shepherd, droving hand, gardener and stock-camp and station cook on the family property Bowthorn, north-west of Mount Isa. She is the author of two volumes of memoir, *Pieces of Blue* and *Heart Country*, and the bestselling novels *The Waddi Tree, Wildhorse Creek, Mallee Sky, Tracking North, Out of Alice, Secrets of the Springs, The Heartwood Hotel, The Roadhouse*, *Croc Country* and *The Missing Girl.* Kerry now lives in Bundaberg.

Also by the author

Pieces of Blue

Heart Country

The Waddi Tree

Wildhorse Creek

Mallee Sky

Tracking North

Out of Alice

Secrets of the Springs

The Heartwood Hotel

The Roadhouse

Croc Country

The Missing Girl

KERRY McGINNIS

Gathering Storms

MICHAEL JOSEPH
an imprint of
PENGUIN BOOKS

MICHAEL JOSEPH

UK | USA | Canada | Ireland | Australia
India | New Zealand | South Africa | China

Michael Joseph is part of the Penguin Random House group of companies
whose addresses can be found at global.penguinrandomhouse.com.

Penguin
Random House
Australia

First published by Michael Joseph, 2022

Cover photography by Julie Fletcher/Getty Images, sharply_done/Getty Images
and Christopher Meder/Shutterstock
Cover design by James Rendall © Penguin Random House Australia Pty Ltd
Typeset in Sabon by Midland Typesetters, Australia

Printed and bound in Australia by Griffin Press, part of Ovato, an accredited
ISO AS/NZS 14001 Environmental Management Systems printer

NATIONAL LIBRARY OF AUSTRALIA
A catalogue record for this book is available from the National Library of Australia

ISBN 978 176104 690 2

penguin.com.au

FSC www.fsc.org MIX Paper from responsible sources FSC® C009448

We at Penguin Random House Australia acknowledge that Aboriginal and Torres Strait Islander peoples are the first storytellers and Traditional Custodians of the land on which we live and work. We honour their continuous connection to Country, waters and communities. We celebrate their stories, traditions and living cultures. We pay our respects to Elders past and present.

This one is for Nerida and
Thursday afternoons with her harpies.

Chapter One

Lisa arrived in Southbend in mid-November on a day of gathering storms, when the air dripped with humidity and the huge grey-white cumulus clouds were piled like soapsuds above the line of timber fronting the banks of the Rainsford River.

The vehicle approached from the east in a swirl of dust that slowly died as its wheels met the bitumen streets of the town. I was sitting at the table on the verandah, the coolest spot in summer, sorting invoices, and I watched the dusty vehicle slow as it hit the main street, travel slowly along it and then nose into the parking space in front of the pub, just two blocks over from me. A woman got out and hurried inside without pausing to look around her. I couldn't place the vehicle though, and in a town as small as Southbend one soon came to recognise the wheels that belonged there.

When I glanced up again, it was to see the same vehicle cruising towards my place. The woman pulled up beside the Carter's Nursery sign with its garish illustrations of palms and hibiscus flowers. My father-in-law, Angus, who had designed and painted it, had originally gone for overwhelming brightness, despite my protestations that nothing in nature had ever attained those colours. 'You won't think so in a coupla years' time, lass,' he had replied, and I'd had to admit that he'd been right. Deserts anywhere couldn't better the weathering effects of Gulf Country sun on paint.

I waited, invoices forgotten, as both car doors opened and the woman and then a child emerged. They were bare-headed, dressed in t-shirts and shorts, the child loitering behind the woman, her footsteps dragging.

'Come *on*, Lisa,' the latter snapped, seizing Lisa's young shoulder and propelling her forcibly forward.

I stepped to the edge of the shade while they traversed the garden and called to them. 'Hello. I'm Penny Carter. Can I help you? There's a back entrance if you're after plants.'

'I haven't come to buy,' the woman responded. 'Is Angus McCloud here?'

'He's around somewhere,' I said. 'He could be taking a nap.' It was the hottest part of the day, when customers rarely came and the plants were best left alone, with potting and watering being done in the comparative cool of either morning or evening. 'Look, come up out of the sun while I go see. Who shall I say wants him?'

'Tell him his granddaughter's here,' the woman said. Having climbed the steps, she pulled a chair out from the table and sat uninvited. 'I'll wait.'

Astonished, I stopped mid-step and swung back to face her. 'What? His granddaughter? Who *are* you?' I stared at them both. The woman had heavy legs and thick arms and looked about forty. Her hair was scraped back into a ponytail, and she wore frown lines between her brown eyes. The child was a thin, sullen-looking girl with a peaky face, hazel eyes and straggling brown hair. She was pre-pubescent – nine, perhaps ten years old. She glowered at me as the heat rushed into my face and my gaze turned back to the woman. 'You . . . What do you mean, his granddaughter?'

The woman waved a dismissive hand, a hard expression on her face. 'It doesn't matter. I'm Pauline's half-sister, if you must know, and I've been lumped with her kid long enough. And now she's come to visit her grandad. Just for a week. So why don't you go find him and let me get on my way?'

Shocked beyond speech at the woman's effrontery, I went. If the child really was Angus's grandchild, then that made Pauline Michael's wife, which meant . . . Stunned, I clapped a hand over my mouth. Angus wasn't resting; I found him in the open-fronted workshop to one side of the smaller shadehouse where we grew the ferns and house plants. He was seated on an old oil drum engaged in sharpening a handsaw. He looked up at my approach, saying, 'Yeah, I know. But it's too hot to lie around. Cooler out here, so I may as well be doin' something.' And then, catching my expression. 'What's wrong, lass?'

I said baldly, 'There's a woman come. She's brought a child called Lisa with her. To stay, she said. Apparently she's your granddaughter.' It was half a question.

'What?' He shot to his feet. 'What woman? Who is she?'

'According to her, Michael's wife's half-sister. Angus, I know that makes the child your kin but I can't – I won't have her here! How that woman would dare to even think—'

'No, no, of course not,' he soothed me. He stroked his nose, a habit he fell into whenever agitated or thoughtful, as if even after seventy years he still couldn't believe anything so big could belong on his face. 'Bloody cheek! I'll speak to her, lass. They can put up at the pub and I'll go over later and talk to the kid. She's too young to know—'

'Ha! Maybe so, but what about her aunt or half-aunt or whatever she is? You can't tell me *she's* not perfectly aware of the situation.'

'All right, Penny,' he said calmly. 'It's no good upsetting yourself. I'll get rid of her. Make yourself a cuppa, and leave it to me.' Wiping his hands on the seat of his jeans, he settled his battered old hat and headed for the front of the house.

A cuppa. Angus's panacea for everything. Ignoring his advice, I followed him, but found only the child kicking her heels where I had left her. The car and the woman were gone.

The girl was eyeing Angus dubiously. 'Grandad?' Her voice was uncertain. 'She never said you were *that* old.'

'Where's your aunt?' I demanded.

She shrugged. 'Lily? She went. To the pub, I expect. Are you my dad's other woman? You're too young to be a grandma.'

I took a deep breath. 'Yes,' I said. 'Michael McCloud married me seven years ago, so I suppose I am.' I noticed then that a smallish bag lay at the foot of the shallow steps. 'Is that yours?' Without waiting for an answer, I looked at Angus. 'She's just dumped her and gone.'

'Right.' He wiped a hand over his chin and flicked sweat away. The humidity must have been over ninety per cent, normal for this time of the year. He looked at the child and smiled, the wrinkles of his face adjusting to the kindly gaze of his faded blue eyes. He was a slow, gentle man, old Angus. Good for the long haul, as he said himself, though he'd take his own time getting there. 'So, you're Lisa. I don't suppose your father told you about me?'

'No,' the girl said. 'Lily said you were my grandad, so why didn't you come and see us when Daddy died?'

'Because I didn't know about you then.' He pulled a chair out from the table. 'Whew! It's hot. Let's sit down, shall we? How old are you, Lisa?'

'Eleven.' She made no effort to sit, just folded her arms and scowled at him. 'My mum died last year.' The childish face twisted for a moment, then resumed its sullen expression. 'That's when Lily came and got me, but now she's fed up. If she wanted a kid, she said, she'd have had her own. So now you're it. That's what she told me.'

A dreadful certainty filled my mind. I said sharply, 'Your aunt said you were just here for a visit – a week.'

The unchildlike look she cast me contained equal measures of dislike and triumph. 'She says a lot of things. Like she was going to the pub. I bet she never. She'll be long gone by now.' There was no mistaking the satisfaction in her tone.

I swung sharply, craning to see past the corner of Flint's Place on the next street over, and it was true. The pub's parking, a marked area under the poincianas that edged the lawn around the building, was bare, save for a dust-smeared Toyota, which, at a guess, had come in from some station. And when I looked, the west bound road leading off from the edge of town held a hint of dust. It could have been a willy wind or stock crossing the road, but was likely Lily leaving Southbend.

*

Twenty minutes later, as I nosed my own vehicle back into its bay in the shed, having completed the rounds of the town, I knew that Lisa was right. The woman had gone and, much as I didn't want her, it seemed the girl was here to stay. For the moment at least. There must be somebody, I thought wildly, slamming the cab door and striding back to the house, who could take her, whose responsibility she was. But with her parents dead, and her aunt (half-aunt?) abrogating the task of caring for her, it seemed depressingly likely that Angus was her only remaining relative. Her father, Michael, had had no siblings and presumably if there had been any on Pauline's side, it wouldn't have fallen to a mere half-sister to take the child in.

'Well,' Angus said reassuringly, meeting me at the door, 'we'll sort something out, lass. Come and sit down, have a cold drink. It's thirsty weather.'

Lisa piped up behind him. 'I'm hungry. Lily said I could wait till we got to the pub, but she didn't buy anything and we came straight here.' She sidled behind the old man and I was suddenly ashamed of myself. I had been less than welcoming. And how traumatic was it for a child to know herself a burden and then be summarily dumped on strangers in surroundings far different from any she had known?

'All right. I'll find you something.' I turned towards the kitchen. 'Come with me. You can call me Penny. I didn't know when I married your father that he already had a wife. I'm sorry your mother died. Of course you can stay and visit your grandfather. You'll like that, won't you, Angus?'

'Too right,' he agreed heartily. 'Mike never told me he had a kid. What about your mum's dad – do you see him at all?'

'He's been dead forever. I never knew him,' Lisa said, glancing around at the cupboards and benchtop as she entered the room. 'Don't you have air-conditioning?' She wiped sweat from her lip.

'No, but there's a fan.' I switched it on and we all enjoyed the rush of air against our damp skins. 'So there's only you and Lily now?'

'There's only me,' she muttered. 'Lily's gone to Darwin. We were going too, Mum and me, but we went shopping that day and she fell down right in the middle of it. An ambulance came and a police lady—' With a great effort she stiffened her wavering voice and repeated, 'So there's only me.'

Pity tore at me. 'I'm so sorry, Lisa,' I said, realising even as I spoke that I was caught and she was here to stay. Angus would insist on it and, anyway, how in good conscience could I condemn her to the dubious mercy of the welfare system? It was inconvenient and, from a strictly selfish point of view, grossly unfair, but she was all that was left in the world of Michael McCloud, whom I had once adored and, even now, could not entirely cease from the habit of loving, despite daily damning his bigamous soul to hell.

Chapter Two

Lisa made the most of the sandwiches I produced and emptied half the jug of freshly squeezed lime drink. She gave monosyllabic answers to most of Angus's questions, but I gathered that she had lived with her mother, Pauline, and Michael (when he was there) in Cairns for all of her short life.

The information was a further jolt of betrayal. Just a couple of hours' drive from our own old home in Atherton . . . I thrust the memory from me. It did no good to dwell on what was past and couldn't be undone, and I reminded myself again that Michael's child could not be blamed for his sins. Though she could be corrected on her manners, I decided, as she announced, 'I'm finished,' and got up, leaving her chair pushed back and her plate and glass on the table.

'It's polite to thank people when they feed you,' I said mildly. 'And put your chair back in, please, before you take your dishes to the sink.'

Lisa threw a scowl my way, said, 'Thank you, Grandad,' and then flounced her way to the sink with the dirty utensils. I suppressed a sigh, reminding myself that it was only natural for her to hate the person she saw as her mother's rival.

'I'll show you the spare bedroom,' I said. 'Got your bag? Have a shower if you like – it'll cool you down. Or a sleep if you're tired. This way.'

I waited near the bathroom door until I heard the shower start. Angus, clearing up in the kitchen, saw me coming and followed me out the back into the moist shade of the fern house where, shaking his head, he raised defensive hands against an expected outburst.

'I know, lass, I know.' His face was troubled. 'Poor little brat! You don't have to tell me it's not fair or what you want, but she's got no one else. It's us or the welfare mob, Penny. She's my own blood, my only descendant, but God knows she needs more care than I can give her. She mightn't know it, but she needs you too.'

'I'm not arguing,' I said tiredly. 'I don't like the way it was done, but of course I can't turn my back on the child. Which is going to be fun, because she plainly sees me as the ogress that's ruined her life.'

Angus rubbed his nose. 'I'll sit her down and explain things to her. And find out what happened to her mother. She was young, so she must've been sick, had a wonky heart or something, to just drop dead, if that's what happened. There's school too,' he said vaguely. 'Kids have to go to school.'

'That's the least of it,' I said. 'Eleven . . . so she's still in primary. She can start tomorrow. I'm sure they'll be glad of another pupil.' Like in all small towns, and Southbend was certainly that, the local school sometimes struggled to keep up its pupil numbers and stay open. 'It will only be short-term because the holidays start next month. High school might be a problem though, seeing as we don't have one.'

It would mean boarding or home schooling. The first we couldn't afford and I hadn't time for the other. Managing the nursery and working with the Department of Primary Industries on its reforestation scheme, which kept us afloat financially, left little enough time for the sideline of coffee and cake for travellers that I also ran.

There was no way I could add home tutor to the mix. And Angus, bless him, wouldn't recognise an algebraic problem if it waved a gun at him.

The shower had stopped when I went back inside. I finished up in the kitchen, then went quietly down the hall but the door to the spare room was shut. Perhaps the girl was sleeping. Wherever she and her aunt had stayed overnight – Georgetown maybe, or Normanton – it was still a very long drive to Southbend. The room beyond the door was silent, so I carried on to my own bedroom and found Lisa there, going through my dressing table drawers.

'*What* do you think you're doing?' I stepped past her and slammed the drawer shut, catching a handful of underclothes and almost her fingers as I did so. 'You're a guest in this house, young lady. Is this how your mother taught you to behave?'

'You're a good one to talk!' Lisa glowered at me, startled but not the least bit abashed. 'You stole my dad, you stinking witch.' She was holding a photo frame she'd taken from the drawer where I had thrust it, face down, when I moved in here, still not ready to follow my first raging impulse to rip up the image. She raised it to her furious face and spat on the glass. 'So there! You're not even as pretty as my mum was.'

Ignoring this and the heartfelt desire to box her ears, I spoke as calmly as I could. 'Lisa, if you're going to live here, and you don't seem to have much option beyond a foster home, you are going to have to accept some ground rules. Respect is one of them. For myself, my property and your grandfather. We, after all, will be feeding and housing you, though there is no obligation on my part to do so. I'm sorry about your mother. I lost mine too, you know, when I was quite young, but trying to hurt others won't help your pain. As for your father's actions – I am as much a victim as your mother was. Now, put that down, please, and go to your room. It's up to you if you want to stay here or not. You can let your grandfather know what you decide.'

Lisa's face twisted stormily at my words and tears gushed from her eyes. 'I hate you!' she snarled, then flung the photo frame onto my bed and rushed past me. A moment later the door to the spare room slammed so hard it shook the walls.

'Delightful,' I muttered and set about restoring the drawers. When I had done so, I picked up the photograph and used a tissue to clean the glass. Then, overcome by memory, I sat on the bed to regard the image of Michael and me on our wedding day. As always, my heart twisted painfully at the sight of him and I damned my weak nature that, after three years and all the trauma of betrayal, I still felt something for him. It would have been so much easier just to hate that crinkle-eyed smile and those steady grey eyes. His brown hair was curly – 'a matching pair,' he had quipped the second time we met as he eyed my blonde head. 'What do you bet our kids'd have curly locks too?'

That was Michael; he'd say anything, while his easy manner and beaming smile washed away any possible offence. He'd been tall and attractive but not flamboyantly so. He'd had . . . charisma, I decided. That special something that drew people to him. I'd wondered at first what he'd seen in me. As Lisa had noted, I wasn't that pretty. Not the sort of stunning girl one would expect a man like Michael to be attracted to. Supposedly all brides had a special radiance about them and, trying to be objective now as I studied the portrait of myself, my happiness *had* shown. My gown and veil were simple, my bouquet a modest size, but there was a sparkle in my blue eyes and a bounce to my honey-blonde curls that gave a lift to my otherwise ordinary looks. My make-up had been professionally applied by a girlfriend who worked in the business, and that was part of it, but love had done the rest.

Sighing, I stood up and slid the picture onto the highest shelf in the wardrobe to await the day when my late husband had left my heart as surely as he had my life.

The following morning, having checked with Sally Price who ran the little school at Southbend, I escorted a reluctant Lisa there. She headed sulkily for the shed bay where we kept the station wagon and the four-wheel-drive workhorse and was frankly disbelieving when I said, 'We'll walk. It's not far. It'll give you a look at the town.'

'This dump isn't a town,' she sneered. 'It's a . . . a whistlestop.'

'Well, it doesn't have any fancy shops,' I agreed, 'but we've a racecourse, a post office, a caravan park, a butcher, a school and a clinic. There's the General Store, which also has a cafe in it, and a fuel depot. Not to mention Carter's Nursery and the pub. Oh, and Flint's Place – he caters for fishermen, and we get plenty of them. I think we do all right for our small population. You'll be the twenty-fifth pupil in the school.'

'Huh!' was her only response.

'It's come a long way in the last twenty years,' I continued pleasantly. 'Back in the seventies, you know, there was nothing but the pub, the racecourse, the hall and a general store. And a one-man police station. The crowds came for the races and the sports days but only about five people actually lived here. Now we have several hundred.'

'Big deal.' We had reached the school gates and she stopped suddenly, hoisting the backpack containing her lunch and drink bottle and very little else, higher. 'If you were pretending to be my dad's wife, why isn't it Macloud's Nursery?'

'Because I've gone back to using my own name,' I said. 'And all the pretence was on your father's side, Lisa. It was a sham marriage. He couldn't legally marry me because he was already married to your mother. That's a crime called bigamy. You can go to jail for it.' I saw her lips press together and said gently, 'I'm sorry, but it's the truth. I know you loved your dad and I did too, so we have that much in common. Now, come along and I'll introduce you to Mrs Price.'

Back home again, I found Angus in the middle of morning chores. We had an automatic sprinkler system for the nursery but, as our water was pumped straight from the Rainsford River into an overhead tank without benefit of a filtration system, keeping the miniature sprayheads clear was an ongoing chore. In summer, potted plants left unwatered even for a day, as I had learned to my cost, seldom survived.

Before the accident that had claimed Michael's life and brought my world crashing down about me, we had run a small but prosperous nursery at Atherton on the Tablelands. Well, I had run it. My lifelong love of growing things meant that I had always been headed for a career involving gardening. Michael had his own job as a travelling rep for a big machinery firm and was on the road more often than he was at home. I had suggested once that he give it up and help full-time in the nursery but he'd shaken his head.

'You *want* the business to fail, Penny? Me, with my black thumbs? Besides, the extra money's useful and I like driving.'

'But you're only here three days out of seven,' I had protested and he'd laughed and kissed me.

'You know what they say, "Recipe for a long-lasting marriage – absence makes the heart," and so on. I have to go, sweet. See you Friday.'

What I didn't know then was that tucked away in a suburb in Cairns was his other family, his real wife, Pauline, and the daughter I had now seemingly inherited, both of them as ignorant of my existence as I was of theirs. Of course, the accident had brought everything into the open, all the quicker because one of the police officers who had attended the head-on collision was from the Tablelands and had recognised Michael's Toyota Camry. Then, when Michael's body had been removed and his effects searched, his wallet was found to contain contradictory information.

I had at first denied that it could possibly be his wallet or his driver's licence. 'See,' I had choked, tears blinding me, 'it's not even his! Oh, he looks a bit like my husband but McCloud is spelt wrong. There is no "a" in his name and that's not our address.' I had stared at the photo of a dark-haired woman tucked behind the licence. 'And that's plainly not me or anyone I know.' Sudden certainty burst in me and I smiled through tears of relief. 'You've made a mistake. It's not him.'

But of course it was. The truck driver from the second vehicle had a concussion and a broken leg. The massive bullbar on the behemoth he drove had largely protected him, but not even the airbag had saved Michael. Later, the police had come back asking further questions related to the shocking disclosure of my husband's other life. Was he suffering from depression at all? Had he seemed worried of late? Was the business in financial trouble? I had indignantly denied it all, even though by now I knew how deep his betrayal of me had been.

'Why?' I demanded angrily. 'He was happy. *We* were happy. If something was wrong, I would've known.'

'But would you, Mrs – er, McCloud?' the sergeant asked. 'You didn't know about the other wife. You see, the truckie's saying it was deliberate. He swears Michael sped up before the collision and then swerved right into the truck's path. There was no way he could avoid him, he said, and the findings of the traffic unit that investigated the accident bear this out. There was no attempt at braking on your hus— on Michael's part. So I'll ask you again, how did he seem the morning he left?'

It ended eventually and I was left in peace. Angus, who had drifted into our lives two years previously, had got me through it. The official inquiry, the police's questions, the press circus. Bigamy in a small town was titillating news. During the course of our four-year marriage, Michael had seen little of his father. Angus had not come to our wedding because Michael had said he had no idea where the old man was, that his father was a drifter, never in the one place for long. 'A bit of a nomad,' was how he had put it. He might be on the opal fields, he told me, or crewing on a trawler, or fencing somewhere out the back of Woop Woop. He'd drifted off after Michael's mother's death, when Michael himself was a teenager, and they'd only run across each other once or twice since.

Michael had been welcoming enough when the old man turned up and it had been his suggestion that Angus should work for me. At the time, I'd thought it endearing of him, believing it to be his way of safeguarding his father's future without offending his pride. But when the truth came out, a cynical part of me admitted that it was more likely an attempt to protect his own lies. It wasn't, after all, a great distance from Atherton to Cairns, and Angus's wandering feet might well have taken him there if not for the job. It had been, I surmised once the truth was out, a risk Michael wasn't prepared to take.

Chapter Three

All of that was old history, and I had more to think about just now. I had come back to Southbend because I couldn't bear to stay on the Tablelands where, by then, everybody knew my story. Nothing spreads faster than gossip in a country area, especially that of a salacious nature. I had put the business on the market and, with Angus's help, moved across the state, following my memories back through the years to the point of my beginnings in the district, to bury my past.

The town, once little more than a pub and a cop shop, had grown amazingly as the bitumen, and the concurrent explosion of tourism, had spread across the outback. The opportunity was there, I thought, and I, or at least my name, was known in the area. That counted. I would be seen as belonging and accordingly face none of the distrust that outsiders – 'blow-ins', whom the locals cynically expected to pull up stakes and leave at the first setback in a land where setbacks were common – usually had to contend with.

But I was one of them. I had spent the first ten years of my life here, the only child of Imogen and Walter Carter, owners of Bracton Park, the small cattle station thirty kilometres west of the Rainsford. It had been sold since and in the twenty years that ensued, I had neither seen nor spoken to my father. Our relationship, poisoned as it was by my mother's disappearance, had resulted in an estrangement that could never be bridged. I had no desire to do so and I neither knew nor cared what his feelings were on the subject.

The town had welcomed both me and my business. The hard years of the seventies when cattle prices had crashed to disaster level, followed by the eighties with its costly disease-eradication drive that had decimated an industry already on its knees, had now morphed into the more hopeful nineties. Stock shortages arising from the drastic culling of herds had raised cattle prices again, while the ever-increasing outback tourism had expanded the small towns, opening opportunities for those willing to back their beliefs. New roadhouses had sprung up along lonely highways, and campgrounds flourished; the Southbend pub had moved in half-a-dozen demountables to serve as extra accommodation, and a man around my age who went by the name of Flint had come to town soon after I did, to open a combination craft shop and fishing charter business. That said more about Southbend's potential than anything. It was the right time for new ventures and so far Carter's Nursery had done far better than I'd dared hope.

I couldn't have managed any of it without Angus though. My ex-father-in-law had become my business partner. 'Because I need you,' I told him when I had first brought up the idea. 'I can't do this alone, Angus. I have the money, so your experience and strength will be your capital in our arrangement.

I do really need you.' It was the simple truth. Setting up the infrastructure, shifting the heavier pots around, building the various shadehouses, putting in the complicated watering systems – all were tasks beyond my own know-how and muscle. Even digging the trenches for the water lines was beyond me. Southbend was black soil country – heavy, immovable earth that set like concrete when dry, and once wet became a nightmare of gluey mud. Angus's old but wiry body had literally saved me thousands of dollars in plant hire alone.

He had also finagled our contract with the Department of Primary Industries for the reforestation program they were currently running. Growing the thousands of native seedlings that lived in the larger of the three shadehouses was the backbone of our business. We were paid to produce them, and paid again when they were either sold or we planted them out in areas designated by the DPI. We had Prime Minister Bob Hawke's tenure of office in Canberra to thank for this and his election promise of a million trees for the environment.

'Our bread 'n' butter, lass,' Angus had said. 'Nothin' like a bit of government sponsorship.'

When they were large enough, the young saplings were used in degraded areas of river bank to control erosion and flood damage, or sold to graziers wishing to replace timber that had been clear-felled in earlier, less enlightened times. Salinity on some of the coastal properties was a growing problem that could only be lessened and ultimately controlled by replanting the native scrub.

I had been lucky, I thought as I lingered by a row of gutta-percha that would soon need potting on, if only in that respect. Angus was the best thing to come out of my sham marriage. He, unlike his son, had stayed faithful to our agreement. Increasing age might have contributed by curbing his restlessness, but I also think he felt some responsibility for Michael's actions, and standing by me was his way of making amends.

'Maybe I wasn't much of a father to him,' he had said once the funeral was done and I had begun to put back together the shattered remnants of my life. 'I took the easy way, always movin' on and looking for the new when I got tired of things, and it's what he did too. Maybe I never taught him right from wrong.'

'No,' I said. 'Don't blame yourself. He was honest enough in other matters, just not love. What he wanted he had to have. If I'd agreed to simply live with him . . .' I had sighed, remembering the times I had wrestled with myself over this. 'But he was a traveller.' And, I had thought, I knew the cost of unsecured love. People left you. I might have been in love with Michael but I wasn't prepared for it to be open ended. If I gave my heart, I wanted – I *needed* – security. My mother had walked away from me with nothing to bind her except the love she had professed. Which, in the end, obviously hadn't been a strong enough tie. It had made me wary, but as things had transpired, even the precaution of marriage vows had not saved me.

'There you are, lass.' I jerked out of my reverie at Angus's approach. Sweat dampened the light cotton shirt he wore; he pulled a hand down his face, flicking moisture away, and lifted his elbows away from his body. 'Whew! Hotter 'n hell already. Gotta rain soon. I been wonderin' how we can get the word on young Lisa's background. Got any ideas?'

I stared at him. 'Well, her mother's dead. She told us that much. What else did you want to know?'

'What killed 'er would be a start. And whether she was rentin' or owned a house, if there was a will – that sorta thing. The kid's got nothin' but that pitiful bag she came with, Penny. There must've been some money in the bank, or how did they live?'

'They couldn't have owned a house,' I said. 'How could Michael have afforded two places? It was only my savings that swung the deposit on ours. As for anything in the bank, don't forget the aunt housed Lisa for over a year, so that'd be gone.'

He rubbed his nose. 'Thing is, we don't know. Maybe Pauline had money herself – from her family I mean. We don't know nothin' about that Lily woman. If there *was* anything, she could've conned the kid out of it, and it's maybe why she took off. Well, I'll not be havin' that. So how do we find out?'

'We could talk to Greg?' I suggested doubtfully. Sergeant Banner was the law's representative in Southbend. I knew him only in passing and saw him, as I did most of the town's inhabitants, at the various social events. A quiet, morose man with a drinking problem, he spent more time in the bar than his office and seldom stirred beyond the two places.

'Nah, you'd have to report a crime afore he'd do anythin''. I was wondering about Flint and that computer of his. Supposed to be able to find anythin' on them, ain'tcha?'

'I believe so.' Carter's Nursery had its own computer for bookwork, but no internet. The desktop model worked reluctantly whenever the temperature went above thirty-eight degrees, often freezing the screen or shutting down. Evenings gave a better response but Southbend was a long way from the super-highway the politicians liked to talk about. Flint, however – nobody ever called him anything else – had built himself a small, airconditioned office where his stereo system (he was a music nut) and computer lived.

'I'll talk to him,' I said. 'But only if he lets us pay him for his time online. Lord knows how long it'll take, dial-up is so slow. What are you working on here?'

'Huh? Oh, thought I'd head out and fill a trailer. Start on the next batch of pottin' mix. Them young trees in the first bay are about ready to pot on.'

'Want a hand?'

'Nah, you go see Flint. Sooner we find out . . .'

Angus was really concerned, then. Somehow I had not expected him to fall so readily into his role as guardian and concerned grandfather, but Lisa's plight had plainly brought out the protective streak in his nature.

'Okay. I suppose I should stick around for customers anyway. Have fun.'

We used literally trailer loads of potting mix a year, so we made our own, mixing animal fertiliser, compost, sand, a little red soil from the country upriver where the plains gave way to hills, and the rotting leaves from beneath the bauhinia bushes to render it light and permeable. Preparing it was a tedious chore and you needed to get the quantities right, but it was better than paying for it to be delivered. Freight was the killer out here for any small business. Which reminded me, I needed to check our supply of the black polythene bags we used for the native trees. We'd need at least five hundred on hand once we started potting on. I could fax an order through to Goola and have them brought up on the mail truck.

Spotting a weed poking up through the leaves of a geranium, I pulled it and moved on down the row, removing others as I came across them. I found aphids on the stem of a hibiscus and detoured to locate the spray and deal with them, then had to narrowly inspect all those plants surrounding the affected one. So absorbed was I that I started when a voice spoke suddenly behind me.

'Oh, there you are! You need a cowbell on the gate, Penny.'

I glanced around to see Ellen Howard, a local grazier's wife, her body rounded with her first pregnancy. 'Sorry, I didn't even hear the vehicle.' I glanced down at her distended shape. 'How are you standing the heat?'

'It's not much fun with the bub and all.' Her hands cradled her stomach, huge against her normally lean frame.

'Yes, I can imagine. How much longer?'

She grimaced. 'Another month. Our little Christmas gift, as Tom calls it – I tell him he won't think so when he's up changing nappies at midnight. Look, Penny, I need a hand. I know nothing about plants but I want something fairly unkillable for Gwen's birthday. What would you recommend?'

'Gwen Moroni? Hmm. Bracton Park has very minerally bore water, so not ferns . . .' I let my gaze rove over the clumps of pots. 'There's always geraniums, or what about a desert rose? They're pretty in a grotesque sort of way. Lots of blossoms. It belongs to the succulent family. From Madagascar, so it's actually a desert plant.' I pulled one out to show her, its swollen trunk and stubby branches supporting an amazing number of flowers. 'There're pink ones, red ones and a mixture of the two. I believe you can get a white and a yellow as well, but I don't have them.'

Ellen eyed it uncertainly. 'It's certainly different with that bulbous trunk. And look at those flowers!'

'Yes, it's a double. A bit unusual.' I smiled. 'You get twice as much for your money.'

'How big will it grow?'

'Depends on the pot size. I'd guess if it was planted out it might make a large shrub or a smallish tree. They're very easy care.'

'I'll take it,' she decided. 'Gwen loves her garden but she loses a lot of stuff.'

'That'll be the water.' I shrugged at her surprised look. 'I grew up on the Park. My father used to own it back in the day.'

'Oh, I didn't realise – still feel like we're newcomers to the district, even though we've been at Rumhole eight years. That's a weird name for a property, isn't it? You don't know what's behind it?'

I shook my head. 'A bottle, I should think. Or a truckload of them. It's always been called that as far as I know.'

When Ellen had gone I made myself a cuppa, then hung the *Back in 10* sign on the gate the customers used and drove down May Street to Flint's Place, reflecting that the vehicle was habit – I could easily have walked. Like other businesses in town, Flint's had a double-barrelled approach. The fuel depot had a workshop that did mechanical repairs, the general store served also as the post office and had a couple of tables for tea and coffee, while Flint, besides producing truly elegant woodwork from native timber, ran fishing charters on the river. The walls of his front room, which opened off the verandah and served as his office, were lined with fishing rods and nets and other tackle to do with the sport. Our friendship benefitted us both in that a good day's charter work often brought him to our door with a slab of barramundi, which he would then stay to enjoy. He lived alone but whether that made him single, divorced or widowed, I had never enquired.

He appeared on the verandah at my call, dressed in khaki shorts and shirt with thongs on his feet. He was tall and rangy with sun-damaged skin, the ends of his brown hair, which he wore long, bleached to the colour of ripe wheat. I shook my head at the thought, wondering where the comparison had come from. There wasn't a wheatfield within eight hundred miles of the Gulf.

'Flint,' I said, 'have you got a minute?'

'Penny.' His easy smile flashed. 'Any time. Come in out of the sun.'

'I can't stay. Angus has gone off with the trailer so there's nobody seeing to customers. I wondered – well, Angus did, really – if you'd look into something for him? On the internet.'

I explained as coherently as I could. Flint was one of the few people in Southbend who knew that I had been married. I'd have preferred that nobody did, but he'd picked up a parcel of nursery stuff for me in Goola not long after he'd first arrived. It had been addressed to my married name, and I'd told him the truth that I'd been widowed and wished to put it all behind me by resuming my maiden name. He had never mentioned it since and the rest of the town believed me to be single still.

I had the sudden unwelcome thought that that could change this very day if Lisa decided to spread her version of events among her fellow pupils. It would be an easy way to take revenge upon me and my perceived sins. I shook the idea away, saying, 'What do you think? Is it too much trouble?'

'Course not. I'll have a look tonight. If her death was so unexpected, there's bound to be a mention of it somewhere. The *Cairns Post* would've picked it up for sure. About a year ago, you said?'

'Maybe eighteen months – I'm not really certain. Thank you, Flint. Angus will be grateful. I am too, of course. Now, I must go – there could be customers asking themselves how long ten minutes is.'

'Okay. I'll drop over later if I turn anything up. See you, Penny.'

'See you,' I echoed, 'and thanks again.'

Chapter Four

It stormed that night, a rousing, thunderous downpour with the white flashes of lightning ripping the skies apart and briefly illuminating the soggy garden, where branches thrashed about and the ground ran with water. The temperature dropped by a good ten degrees. I got up to find a blanket and to check on Lisa, whom I found standing in what looked like an oversized pink t-shirt at the window, watching the storm.

Of course she would be used to them, I thought. Cairns had its share of violent weather. I stuck my head through the door. 'Okay? I know it's loud but it's just the forerunner of the Wet.'

She spoke without turning, saying unpleasantly, 'I'm not stupid, you know. I come from the north.'

'Well, if you need a blanket, there's one in the wardrobe.' Pulling a face, I withdrew, shutting her door again, and reflected that living with Lisa was going to get old very quickly. One had to make allowances, but still . . .

Flint had dropped by after closing time, finding me checking sprays in the fernery. Angus had the cement mixer running and was feeding it shovelfuls of the ingredients that went into our potting mix. The task was far too laborious for hand-mixing and the machine achieved a nice, even result. Lisa was inside, hopefully engaged with her homework, though I wouldn't have bet on it.

He greeted me cheerfully. 'Penny, I think you'll find that's wasted labour. It's going to storm tonight.'

'Oh yes?' I squinted at the sky, where the clouds were piled like some mad washerwoman's soapsuds. 'I've heard that one before.' I flicked the tiny spray head I had just replaced and was rewarded with a fine mist of spray. 'So, were you able to find out what happened?'

'Yep. It was in the *Post*. "Shopper collapses into death from mystery illness." That was the heading, but in fact the poor woman died from an aneurysm. An artery burst in her brain and killed her. Apparently she was well known and liked. Her boutique in the mall was popular with the younger set, and she was actually shopping in a Mathers shoe store when it happened.'

So, Pauline had owned a business too. The nasty thought came to me that Michael had chosen women capable of supporting themselves. No doubt it was how he could afford to run two homes. For a mad moment I wondered if there could be a third wife somewhere, but surely not. There were just so many places one man could be. He had always returned from his road trips on Thursday evening and left again on Monday, and I had actually counted myself fortunate that he only needed to work a four-day week.

I thanked Flint for the information. 'I see. Her daughter has come to live with us.' He had undertaken a service for us and deserved to know why, I thought. 'Lisa is Angus's only grandchild and *he* appears to be her only blood relative, if you discount the woman who dumped her here and immediately took off. Lisa's pretty unresponsive to all women at present. Sees me as trying to replace her mother, I suppose.'

His eyebrows climbed and he shook his head. 'Kids! She doesn't see you're doing her a favour? How old is she?'

'Eleven. She's grieving, Flint.' I stifled a sigh. 'Hopefully she'll come round.'

'She will,' he said, 'when she knows you better. So, what happened to the shop? Did it close or is someone running it until the kid's old enough to handle it herself?'

'We don't know. I wasn't even aware it existed. Lisa has said nothing about it or where they lived. I suppose she thinks it's none of my business. We don't know if her mother owned their home or if they were renting. Of course, Lisa might not even know, though kids are pretty clued up these days. Angus is a bit concerned that the half-sister might have ripped her off – the child seems to have nothing but the bag of clothes she brought with her.' I shrugged. 'If there was anything shady going on, I don't see what can be done about it now though. It's over a year since Pauline died, after all, so you can bet that any goods or money are long gone.'

'Eighteenth of March last year,' Flint said, 'so more like twenty months. Look, I'm heading off on Monday with my art stuff. The season's well and truly done here. Tell Angus I'll look into it while I'm on the coast, see what I can find out. If you have the address, then it shouldn't be too hard for me to look the place up and check out what happened. The neighbours will know if it was rented or sold, and if so who bought it.'

'Oh, that would be great – it'd really set his mind at rest – but are you sure it won't be putting you out?'

'Course not. Anything to oblige, Penny.' He sketched an elaborate bow. 'I am wholly at your service. Besides, it won't actually take me out of my way, will it?'

I smiled. 'When you put it like that. But thank you anyway, Flint. You're a good friend.' Townsville and Cairns, especially the latter, were his primary market for the timber art he produced throughout the year. I knew he made multiple turned items for local and passing trade – bowls and platters and spinning tops, tool handles, pen holders and novelty objects – but his art pieces sold for four and five figure sums in coastal galleries. 'You have to go where the money is,' he'd said once, which was sound business sense. Outback tourists spent their cash on fuel and camping fees and inexpensive souvenirs of their travels. We both knew that. Between ourselves we referred to it as the twenty-five-buck rule. Anything priced above that was usually returned to its shelf. 'Of course, if it does storm, you won't be going anywhere.'

'True.' The sun wrinkles about his hazel eyes deepened. 'A day's hold-up . . . what's that in the scheme of things?'

'Spoken like a true Gulfite.'

'Well, I've been here two years now. That ought to qualify me.'

I laughed then. 'You wish. Fifteen years and you'll still be that new bloke who blew in a year or two back. Some of your neighbours are third generation, so you've a way to go yet.'

*

I smiled to myself now, remembering the conversation, and returned to my bed, relishing the sound of the rain on the tin roof. I hoped Angus had put the trailer under cover, for if he hadn't, then yesterday's labour was wasted. Tomorrow would be an ideal time to start repotting root-bound young trees, and highly suitable too for seeding the tiny grow pots with the next generation. There was nothing like rain to guarantee the emergence of seeds that could lie dormant for months in less propitious conditions.

In the early morning with the dew running off the roof, I met Angus coming in from checking the rain gauge, his grey hair sprinkled with droplets from the poinciana growing by the front gate.

'Two and a half inches,' he beamed. He still used the old measurements, having no wish at his age, he said, to learn a new lingo. 'That'll fetch a few creeks up.'

'Yes.' I told him about Flint's plans. 'He'll have to give it a couple of days till the black soil dries; they'll have run down by then. How did the mix fare?'

'She'll be right, lass. I reckoned it'd storm so what the shed didn't stop, the tarp will. He's a good bloke, Flint. Havin' him check for us'll put me mind at rest. Thing is, you just never know what people'll do these days.'

'It was his idea. I told him you were fretting about it and he offered.' I turned to scan the street. 'Just look at that water!' It was lying in long grey pools either side of the road, the surface shivering a little in the breeze so that it gave back a fractured image of sky and poinciana branches. Two plovers planed down beside it as I watched, their clinking calls clear and sweet in the fresh stillness of the morning.

'Yep, and more coming, less I miss my guess.' Angus dragged his boots over the scraper at the front steps, then bent with a grunt to pull them off. 'Wet's not far off now.'

After breakfast, Lisa refused my offer to walk with her and set off to school carrying nothing but her lunch. Whatever books she must have had at Atherton had plainly been abandoned. My questions on the subject elicited nothing but shrugs, as did my wishing her a good day. Tightening my lips as she walked out the door, I supposed it was something that she had carried her dishes to the sink. I would give her time, and perhaps Angus could get through to her. The only remarks she had made throughout the meal had been addressed solely to him.

The storm had put a stop to out-of-town visitors, so Angus and I spent the morning repotting young trees into the next-sized polythene bags and settling them back on their benches.

'We could do with another bench on the far side there,' I said. 'There'd still be room to get between them and have space for a barrow, don't you think?'

Angus considered the idea. 'Just about,' he agreed. 'When we get this lot done, I'll see Barry about hirin' the welder. I reckon there's enough pipe out back to do the job. Might need a few extra steel posts for the stands, but.' Barry Lacey from the fuel depot ran a comprehensive workshop and would probably have preferred the work to hiring out his gear, but we all saved where we could, and welding was one of Angus's many skills. There wasn't, I had discovered, much my ex-father-in-law couldn't do, from working greenhide to baking bread. He'd been an opal miner, a stock-camp cook and a ringer in his day, and the Lord only knew what else. His varied skills were my main asset, for green thumbs, a knowledge of plants and the ability to balance the books were all I could bring to the business.

Clouds boiled up during the day, only to be shredded mid-afternoon by a high-level wind, negating the possibilities of further storms for the moment. When school let out I dragooned Lisa into accompanying me down to the river. We stood in the middle of the bridge, looking down to where the overnight rain had swollen the Rainsford's normally placid waters to a brown torrent in which all manner of debris, washed down from the banks in the storm, bobbed and spun.

'I saw a big fat tree frog here once,' I said. 'He must've fallen in. He'd climbed onto a bit of bark and was sailing along, sitting up like Jacky, watching the world whirl by. I suppose he knew he couldn't live in such swift water. I imagine even frogs can drown.'

'Yeah?' Lisa sounded supremely uninterested. 'Who's Jacky anyway?'

'It's just a saying. It means looking important, bunging on airs.'

Her lip curled. 'Like you. Pretending to be my dad's wife.'

I sighed. 'Yes, it was pretence, but not on my side. I believed your father was single – he told me he was. When you love someone, you trust them, Lisa, but he lived two completely separate lives. Did you know that he used the same surname but spelled it differently for you and your mum, and for me? When he was with me he was Michael McCloud, with a capital "C", and in Cairns everyone knew him as Mike Macloud, with an "a". So the police told me. That's how he got away with it for so long. You probably think I should have discovered what he was doing, but I could say the same thing about your mother. We were both his victims, so hating me is pretty pointless really. Especially if we have to live together.'

She glared fiercely at me but her bottom lip was trembling. 'We were happy,' she choked accusingly. She wanted me to know it, to feel guilty – to show, I suppose, why she would never forgive me. But my words must have got through to her, for a second later she cried, 'Why did he have to do it?' In that moment all the pain and loss of her fractured young life was there for me to see, and pity instantly wiped away all resentment at her presence.

'I don't know, my dear. I really don't.' I moved to hug her but she shook off my touch, her look enough to kill the impulse to physically comfort her.

'I'm not your dear, either!'

Persevering I said, 'He hurt everyone he loved, and I think he did truly love us all, Lisa. I know it's hard to understand, especially when you're young. You hurt *so* much, and you think if you were older it would help – but it doesn't. I thought that too when I lost my mother. I was only nine, and I thought if I was a grown-up everything would feel different, that it wouldn't matter so much, but it still does. Even now when I've turned thirty.'

Lisa's eyes were bright but she had swallowed the threatened tears. She said, 'You're old,' but more as a discovery than in disparagement. 'Did your mum die too?'

'That's what they told me,' I said. 'But I found out later she didn't.' I heard the flatness in my tone recounting the unforgiveable. 'She just left me. Got in the car one day, drove off and never came back.'

'Yeah?' With devastating candour she said, 'She didn't love you then. What did your dad do?'

'He sent me away to live with his sister. He was a busy man, and he had a station to run. The point is, I survived and so will you.' I slapped at a mosquito feasting on my arm. 'Come, we'd better go back. The mozzies are venturing out.'

Chapter Five

The following day brought more wind and a thin line of clouds far off to the north. The water had gone from the roadside, swallowed by the thirsty earth, and a crust had formed over the black soil, making travel possible with care. I saw Flint's loaded vehicle drive out, pause while he locked the gate, then head off south towards Goola and the eastern highway. He'd be on bitumen within an hour, and then it was a straightforward run to the distant coast.

Over smoko I broached the subject of a town trip to Angus. We usually stocked up before the Wet, though not to the extent that the stations did since we had the store in town to draw from, a once rambling old building set opposite the pub. It was now raised on sturdy blocks and refurbished, and, if rumour was to be believed, had at one time included coffins in its stock. It carried enough supplies for most Wets, but it never hurt to lay in a little extra flour and the like, in case of an extended closure of the Southbend airstrip. Bread and other perishables came on the weekly mail flights during the monsoon season, but cyclones and extended rain depressions could close any airstrip. And Christmas was coming. Which this year was going to include Lisa, who would soon be needing more clothes than the few she currently owned.

Angus and I agreed on four days hence. Travel on Sunday, bank business and a day's shopping on Monday and home again, weather permitting, on Tuesday. At this time of year it never paid to linger lest bad weather arise in our absence, making the way home impassable. Lisa could take a note to school tomorrow, for she would have to accompany us – unless Sally Price, herself the mother of two daughters, could host her in our absence? It was tempting but I discarded the notion; shirts and shorts were just a matter of size but the rest of her needs were of a more personal nature. It would be an expense but I couldn't outfit her from a charity bin. Also, my baser nature hinted, buying her a few new things might help soften her attitude towards me. And I was, I silently admitted, ready to take any help I could get in that department.

On Thursday morning Lisa didn't get up when she was called. She was normally less than prompt in obeying so I had got on with making breakfast, and was cutting her lunch when I realised she still hadn't appeared.

'Lisa?' I called outside her closed door. 'Come on, you'll be late.' Receiving no answer, I opened it and found her small shape still hunched under the sheet. 'Lisa!' I put command into my tone. 'Up. Now. You'll be late for school.'

Despite her closed eyes I could tell she was ignoring me rather than sleeping. 'Not going,' she muttered fiercely, opening her eyes to glare.

'Yes, you are. Now, come on, what's the matter? Are you sick?'

She flung back the sheet and reared up, spitting the words at me. 'Yes, I am! I'm sick of you always bossing me around, telling me what to do. I hate you! Why should I even listen to you? You're not my mother.'

'Because I'm the one looking after you?' I suggested. 'Are you running a temp? Let me feel your head.' I reached to touch her forehead and she jerked back, slapping my hand away, an ugly look on her face.

The blow stung and I lost my temper. 'Right, young lady! That's enough. Get up, get dressed and get into that kitchen in the next ten minutes or you'll be going to school without breakfast. I mean it, Lisa! And I'm not telling you again.' With great restraint I closed the door without actually slamming it, and stalked back to my task.

Angus wandered in, headed straight for his chair and reached for the teapot. 'Where's Lisa?'

'She's coming,' I said curtly, adding under my breath, 'She'd better be.'

And she came, her hair unbrushed and a scowl on her face. She muttered a greeting to her grandfather, glared at me and deliberately upset the milk jug when she put it down, passing it off with an unconvincing, 'Uh oh,' and a shrug.

'Right.' I rose for the dishcloth and mopped up. 'Insolence will get you nowhere. I'll be out when you get home this afternoon, but when I get back I'll expect to see all the shadehouses raked up. Your grandfather will show you what I mean. And he is not'—I turned a minatory eye on Angus—'going to help you. Isn't that so?'

'If you say so, lass,' he agreed, hoisting an eyebrow. 'Somebody want to tell me what's goin' on here?'

'Perhaps Lisa would like to. Only she's got about five minutes to get to school, so it had better wait.' I did not need this, I told myself. Why should I be the one to end up landed with a brat of a kid who wanted her ears boxed in the worst possible way? It seemed like some evil gremlin had singled me out for a tattoo that flashed 'PICK ME' whenever a disaster was stooging around looking for a place to land.

'Lisa?' Angus said enquiringly.

She hunched her shoulders and didn't answer him, though I could see the effort she was putting into holding her tongue. Bolting the last of her cereal, she snatched up the sandwiches I'd made and ran out the door, teeth unbrushed. At least she'd taken her schoolbag with her. Seething, I pushed my tea away and drew a deep breath.

'What the hell's goin' on?' Angus asked. 'Looks like both of youse got your knickers in a twist over somethin'.'

'Just see she puts in a solid hour on that rake,' I snapped. 'If she's living here, it's by our rules. I've got to get on.'

I spent the morning working in the shadehouse seeding grow pots with next year's crop of baby trees. The work calmed me and gave me time to think. Perhaps I had overreacted. I was inexperienced with children, but surely it wouldn't hurt Lisa to learn that there were consequences for bad behaviour?

Several customers came to interrupt me. The first storms of the season seemed to bring on bouts of Greenthumbitis in the town, I had found, and I sold two ornamental shrubs and a ground cover, and diagnosed a case of mealy bugs in a neighbour's coleus.

Although our lunchbreak gave him the opportunity, Angus made no further enquiries into the morning's contretemps. At two-thirty I boxed up a cake I'd made and walked across to the hall to join the other members there for the monthly meeting of the Country Women's Association.

Afternoon tea followed the meeting and at four o'clock I walked home, resolving to be patient with my troublesome guest. Life had given her a pretty raw deal and it was natural – however inconvenient – I told myself, that every so often she should have a meltdown. I was the most convenient person to blame and it didn't necessarily mean that she really hated me.

'Lisa?' Dumping the cake container in the kitchen, I walked down the hall to her room but she wasn't there. Continuing out through the back door, I saw that Angus must have kept her at her allotted task for the dead leaves and plant matter in the largest shadehouse had been raked tidily away. 'Lisa?' I called and then I heard rather than saw her in the small potting house. 'What are you doing?'

She was holding the rake reversed, using the handle like a scythe and belting furiously at the minuscule grow pots I had filled that morning, knocking them flying in every direction.

'Stop it!' I shouted. Racing forward, I seized the wooden handle as she lifted it back for another swing. She wrestled furiously with me but I was stronger. I ripped it from her hands and all at once she collapsed onto her knees crying as if her heart would break.

I was practically speechless. The pots were a stiff plastic and many had split apart from the violence of her blows.

Potting mix was spread everywhere, along with the precious, now wasted seeds. Half a day's work in ruin. 'What the hell do you think you're doing?' I yelled. 'Is this because I made you go to school? Well, let me tell you—'

'I'm sorry,' she blubbered. 'I didn't – I couldn't – I want my mum!' The last words were a despairing wail. Grubby hands over her face, she wept unremittingly.

My baffled rage eased at the sound of her sobs and I crouched beside her and gently pulled her hands away. 'Stop crying, Lisa. Stop. Look at me. Now, what's all this about? I can't help you if I don't know. And I do want to help you – we can't be going on like this. You know that as well as I do.'

She raised wet, misery-filled eyes to meet mine. 'It's her birthday today. I know she's dead and I'm never going to see her again, but I want to. I just want . . . and I never will.'

'Oh, sweetie.' I folded her into a hug. I knew that useless, hurtful ache that no balm could cure, the unfairness of being singled out by fate for unimaginable loss, and the oblivious way the rest of the world ignored your pain. 'It's all right,' I said. 'I'm not angry any more. You should have said. You'll never stop missing her but it will get easier, I promise.'

I felt the dampness of tears against my neck but she didn't try to escape the embrace and after a bit, as she calmed down and her breathing evened out, I put her gently from me, and thumbed a teardrop away from her damp cheek. 'Let's go inside. You need to wash up, and I think a drink and perhaps a piece of cake wouldn't harm, hmm?'

Lisa sniffed and wiped her nose on her wrist, her gaze falling on the mess of wrecked pots as she did so. The colour rose in her cheeks, and her eyes darted briefly to mine and then fell.

'I'm sorry.' Her voice was small and ashamed. 'I – I wanted to smash something. I shouldn't have . . . And I don't hate you. I wish I'd never said that. I didn't mean it.'

'I know.' I pushed her gently forward. 'We'll talk about it later. Come on.'

That evening a subdued Lisa surprised me by wiping up the dishes, which I took as a sign that the afternoon's outburst had possibly been a turning point in our relationship. I thanked her with a smile and later, when she went off to her room, I was, along with Angus, wished a goodnight. Another first. I went to bed with the feeling that I was finally making headway with her.

It rained again that night. The ground was quite wet by now and, the storms having started, it was a good time to plant out the young trees. Two physically exhausting days ensued. It was a slow business loading the trees onto the trailer and the tray of the four-wheel drive, transporting them to the badly eroded site at the edge of the river and getting the digger down through the moisture-heavy soil that clung to and stained everything it touched.

The DPI had previously fenced off the ground to ensure that cattle, wild pigs and brumbies didn't trample or damage the young trees before they had settled in, but it didn't help that they had neglected to put in a gate. The trees had nearly three years' growth on them and the polythene grow bags full of soil made them heavy to lift.

'I'll have muscles like Mr Universe,' I panted, pausing to wipe my face with a sleeve. 'Couldn't we just cut the fence, Angus, and fix it again afterwards?'

'I ain't got no wire strainers,' he objected, but after the

second trip he relented enough to untie the wires from several posts and then weigh them down with the trailer wheels. The idea was always to replace the native growth so we had a mixture of eucalypt species: red gum and bloodwood and carbeen; some bauhinia for the higher areas where the water wouldn't lie, and gutta-percha and the odd whitewood for the swampier ground.

With the last sapling planted, we stood for a moment by the empty trailer to gaze across our work. We had staggered the young trees, trying for a natural look. Some would inevitably die and dormant seeds from older trees would eventually sprout, but in ten years' time the whole lot would hopefully meld together as if nature, rather than man, had placed them there.

'Well, that's done,' I said, stripping off my heavy gloves, now rank with sweat and mud. 'Thank God the DPI pay well. I'll make out the invoice tonight and we can post it in town.'

The mining town of Hamilton was five hours' drive away, a change for the better as it had been an all-day trip when I was a child. The roads had improved vastly since, with concreted causeways instead of the many bone-jarring little creeks through the Selwyn Ranges, and the formerly rutted two-wheel track was now a graded gravel highway with wide table drains. Once suitable only for four-wheel drives, it was now travelled by roadtrains and vehicles towing caravans.

After the rain, the road edges were soft, the slippery camber on the curves a trap for the inexperienced driver, which Angus was not. 'Bit of caution and common sense,' he liked to say, 'saves a lot of grunt work.' And the drive in was no exception to his rule. Outside the vehicle the day was steamy and cicada-ridden with stretches of brown water in the table drains and a sky rinsed clear of dust.

In town we found our usual motel and, worn out by the long drive, made it an early night. The next morning we proceeded to make the best use of the Monday, Angus heading off to fuel up and organise the bulk grocery order while I handled the banking and then, with Lisa in tow, headed for the shopping centre. Here, though a little discontented by the lack of variety, Lisa confided her preferences in colour and style and we shopped for school shoes, tops and shorts, underclothes and a simple little sleeveless sundress. That done, I gave her some spending money and dismissed her to browse.

'I'll be in the coffee shop over there,' I said, 'right next to the clock. Come back in half an hour, okay?'

She nodded and left. I had no qualms about leaving her to her own devices. Cairns had bigger shopping malls and she would be used to negotiating them. Lugging our purchases, I ordered at the counter then sank thankfully onto the couch in the corner where I could keep an eye on the passing throng. When Lisa returned we'd go back to the motel for a late lunch, then spend the afternoon on nursery business and Christmas shopping. I needed more stationery for the office, price tags, coir lining for hanging baskets, the baskets themselves if they were available (which they probably weren't) and new gardening gloves. All of these could be had more cheaply from a coastal supplier, but I had learned to pick up what I could from the chain stores on my town trips for the end price was much the same.

When Lisa returned I bought pasties for our lunch and some sweet buns and we took a taxi back to the motel where

Angus had a fair load roped onto the back of the vehicle. Inside, he was boiling the jug.

'Just in time,' he said. 'I was gunna head down to the corner for fish 'n' chips.'

'I've got baked goods,' I said. 'What's the bundle on the load?'

'Ah, I picked up a few steel posts, welding rods, another shovel handle – stuff like that. If I'm gunna finish that bench, I figure me own welding rods'll come cheaper than Barry's. How you girls doin'? Anything left in the shops?'

'I've still the nursery gear to get, if I can find it. If I give you a list, could you pick up the office stuff for me – if you've finished your own jobs, I mean?'

'Yeah, no problem. Want to come along 'n' help your old grandad, Lisa?'

'Okay. I'm going to change first.' She vanished into the bathroom with one of the plastic carry bags and reappeared wearing her new dress. Her body hadn't yet started to develop and her thin arms and flat shoulderblades lent a poignant vulnerability to her childish shape as she pirouetted before the unit's only mirror.

'Yes,' I said, 'very nice. Just your colour. Come and have some lunch while the pasties are still warm. There's a litre of milk in the fridge if you want a cold drink – or do you want tea?'

'Milk, thanks,' she said, and after a moment, 'And for the dress.'

'You're welcome.' I smiled at her. 'You look so nice, Angus will want to be showing you off to all his mates.'

'Too right.' The old man winked at her. 'Pretty as a spotted calf, you are.'

'Silly,' she said through a laugh. 'Calves aren't spotted, Grandad.'

'Wanna bet? You'll see, lassie. They come striped too.'

I hid my satisfaction in a mouthful of pasty. Life with an amenable Lisa was so much more pleasant. I hoped the change would prove permanent.

The trip home was uneventful. The soft shoulders of the road that could have made the going treacherous on the journey in had dried, and where previously water had pooled in the table drains and creeks, only cracked and glossy mud now remained. The sky was building towards more storms, and through the red country the black lancewood trunks stood in sharp contrast to the brilliant green of the fresh grass coming through. We pulled off the road on a limestone ridge to eat our sandwiches and drink thermos tea. Cicadas drilled deafeningly in the still midday heat and the repeated *woop-woop* call of a swamp pheasant echoed through the low scrub.

Angus rose stiffly to check the ropes on the load before we started off again. 'Another coupla hours.' He shifted in his seat, getting comfortable. 'I swear this damn road gets longer every time I travel it.'

'You wouldn't have liked it in the seventies then,' I said. 'The country's come a far way since. Pretty soon we'll have bitumen to the door.'

He snorted. 'I should live so long. You right there, lassie?'

Lisa, who was staring at the passing scenery, nodded as she said, 'Yes,' and then turned to me. 'Did you always live out here, Penny?'

'When I was younger than you are now, I did. It was very different then – and it will be again in a few weeks when the Wet gets here. Not so dry and dreary looking where the rain hasn't been. Lots of grass and birds and butterflies, flowers too, and running creeks. It's like a different place, you'll see. Can you swim, Lisa?'

'Yes. Why, is there a pool?'

'No, but we have the river. There's a good swimming hole down by the bridge. When the water clears again, I mean. You mustn't go in though when there's a run of fresh water and it's all muddy.'

'Yeah?' She sounded dubious. 'What about crocs?'

I said reassuringly, 'This high up the river, there're only the little Johnson River ones; they won't hurt you. But you don't swim alone, okay? Always have someone with you.'

She sniffed scornfully. 'I know that. I'm not an idiot, you know.'

'Well, just remember,' I said mildly and left it at that.

Everything was fine at home. I made a cuppa while Angus brought the loading in, and when we'd finished I went straight out to check the shadehouses. No disaster had befallen them. A few pots from the stack were scattered across the driveway so there must have been a wind, but the sprays had worked and the plants looked okay.

I was relieved. Once, soon after our arrival, we had gone away overnight without chaining the gate and some careless caller had left it unlatched so that Hart's goats had got in and eaten half our stock. The animals had the run of the

Common but never lost an opportunity to break into a garden if they could. Angus had since affixed a very strong spring to the pedestrian gate and a man-sized padlock to the chain on the main entrance, but the devastation that had met us back then was hard to forget, with months of labour and care lost in a few hours.

That evening, Angus loaded the pump and portable tank onto the trailer, along with the many coils of hose we kept for the purpose, and drove off to give the newly planted trees their second and last watering. Lisa went with him. He'd asked if she wanted to help him and to my surprise she had agreed. A hat for her had been among my purchases and I sent her back to get it before she left. 'You *must* get into the habit of wearing it, Lisa.'

She'd sniffed disdainfully. 'I don't care about a few freckles.'

'Maybe not, but sunstroke isn't funny. Neither is skin cancer.' She yanked it on mutinously with unnecessary force then, but when they pulled out of the yard I saw her smile at something Angus had said.

The following day, my first customer was Sue Hart of the goats. The wife of a council worker, she also happened to be Southbend's hairdresser, who used her back verandah as a salon. She was also the current president of the local CWA.

'How was Hamilton?' she asked, surging up to the verandah. She was a large lady of indeterminate years and incurably cheerful. 'Saw you head off 'n' come back loaded down,' she added with a twinkle. 'And I see you have a young guest staying?'

'Lisa. She's Angus's granddaughter. She's come to live with us because her mother died.'

'Poor child.' She sighed with quick sympathy. 'But nice for you.' Sue had always wanted children of her own but it hadn't happened. She shook her head now as if chasing off regret. 'So, Hamilton?'

'Much the same. The road was pretty good; the rain settled it down nicely. Speaking of which, I'm sure we're going to get some more.' The air was thick with moisture, and Sue's face was flushed and dripping from the half a block she had walked from her home. 'How can I help you today?'

'It's the Christmas dance.' She plopped herself onto a chair and fished a fan from the bag she carried. 'Lordy, it's hot!'

'Yes?' I encouraged her to continue. 'I missed part of the last meeting, so what was decided?'

'Plants,' she said. 'The ladies thought it would nice'—she winked—'and simpler, for the supper tables to use plants as decorations this year. They said you'd know which ones. So maybe ten or twelve pots, so big . . .' She sketched a size with plump hands in which her rings were deeply embedded. 'Their idea was to whack a bit of tinsel around the pots and just set 'em out. I fancy it's to save all the usual nonsense with paper and glitter and glue. Mind you, I think that's the fun part, but each to their own. So what's your take on it? Would you have anything suitable?'

'Well, it'd be different – and easier. And I'm bound to have something that would fill the bill, Sue. How about poinsettias? You know them? Red and green – in fact they call them the Christmas plant. I might just have a dozen. Do you want to walk back and check them out?'

Sue heaved herself up. 'I think I know the ones you mean. Very colourful?'

'That's them.' The screen door slammed behind us and she sighed with pleasure as we entered the shaded dampness outside. 'There on the middle row.' The poinsettias were just getting their colour and really could have been designed, I thought, for the festive season.

'Lovely, Penny. Just the ticket. Ooh, I could spend all day here. Look, I won't take them now, but can you bill the CWA for a dozen? Now, the other thing that came up at the meeting is the hall stage. We'll have Barry as usual to run the music, but Gwen suggested we carry the theme through there and make a sort of bower of plants for him to operate out of. So we'd need bigger tubs, sort of leafy, jungly things. What do you think?'

'I'm sure I can find something.' I hesitated, loath to lose a sale but prompted by honesty. 'The bigger pots are quite expensive, though. And to mask the music deck, you'd need more than one or two.'

'That's the cunning bit.' Sue smiled beguilingly; she must have been quite pretty once, I thought, and she still had beautiful skin, her face as smooth and flawless as a child's. 'The ladies hoped you might rent them to us, just for the night. Not the ones for the table centres – we'll buy them and share them out after. But the others.'

'Well, of course. I'll work something out and table it next meeting. How's that?'

'Wonderful. It's Thursday next, so we'll see you there.'

Well pleased with the sale, I went back to work, filling trays of tiny tubes for later seeding. We mostly collected our own, buying only what was difficult or unreliable to obtain.

Bauhinias, with their pods, and conkerberries, with their fruit, were easy, as was the quinine tree and some of the eucalypts, but we had never had success with gutta-percha or beefwood. Some native seeds needed smoke, others just heaps of time, and these we bought as seedlings from the DPI's nursery in Atherton.

Over lunch I told Angus about the dance order and we worked out a rental price to charge.

'They might make a regular thing of it,' he said hopefully. 'There's the Easter dance and the races and the campdraft.'

'Mmm, though we'll hardly make our fortune on those. Now, if there were weekly affairs . . . So how did the watering go last evening with Lisa?'

'Yeah, good.' He rubbed his nose. 'She's just lost, poor kid, but happy enough when she's too busy to remember. She was chattering away, asking all sorts about Annie. Looking for a family, of course.'

'Annie? Oh,' I remembered, 'your wife.' I hadn't known her; she'd died long before Angus had come into my life. 'What about Pauline's parents?'

He shrugged. 'Cactus, both of 'em. He was drowned quite young, rock fishin' I think, and she never remarried. Heart got her in the end, when Lisa was six.'

'Poor child.' I was aghast. 'So much death! What are the odds of that? Parents and grandparents gone, though Pauline's father can't have been that young. What about Lily, the half-sister?'

He shrugged. 'Teenage misadventure, maybe? You said Lily weren't no spring chicken. And when I say young, I'm talking maybe mid-fifties. That's young from where I'm sitting.'

He hesitated before adding, 'She's comin' round, you know, Lisa. She gave me a hug last night when we got back. Just grabbed me, squeezed 'n' ran off, shy like. But still wantin' affection.'

'She misses her father.' I sighed. 'Don't we all?' Though I wondered how I could, three years on, still mourn for Michael and the life we'd had together while simultaneously wanting to kill him. Love was a difficult discipline, hard to navigate when understandably mixed with habit, fury and deceit. If my emotions were still so uneven, who could blame a child for hers?

'I am trying, Angus, and I think I'm getting through to her but I can't force it,' I said. 'She's coming to trust me though.'

He got up. 'Yeah, I seen she's happier lately. It'll work out. Gawd! If that boy of mine was here today, I'd give 'im a bloody good kick up the arse for the trouble he's caused. Believe me, I would.'

Chapter Six

Ten days after leaving, Flint returned, his vehicle smeared with the mud of travel. We'd had another storm that had left a clean blue sky shining brilliantly above the green and scarlet of the poinciana blossoms fronting the pub. Down on the river bank the mill blades turned lazily, and far off to the north, above the line of river figs and Livingstone palms, white cumulus clouds bounced up the sky like huge round balls.

I stood on the verandah watching a flight of black cockies with their discordant cries and saw the opened windows at Flint's Place and the dirty vehicle pulled up on the drive. I was still there, enjoying the morning's freshness, when he emerged in his trademark khaki shorts and shirt and began hosing off the mud.

'Flint's back,' I told Angus. 'Covered in mud. I'm glad we got that trip to Hamilton over when we did.'

'Yeah. Looks like an early Wet comin',' he agreed. 'Wonder what he found out?'

'We'll have to wait and see.'

It wasn't a long wait, however, for Flint turned up during our smoko break in the fernery. 'Have a seat,' I said, nodding at the folding chair leaning against the wall beside the esky. 'How was your trip? You want a cuppa?'

'Wouldn't say no. Black, thanks,' he added as I half rose to get the milk from the esky. 'As for the trip, I've had drier ones. The Lynd was up on the way back, and I had to camp on the bank till she ran down; saw the biggest croc in there too. Musta been every inch as long as my vehicle. The old Port road was a real mess. Looked like a truck went through before me, cut it to pieces. I could barely see through the windscreen for mud.'

'I saw your vehicle. That apart, it went well?'

He grinned. 'I saw you seeing. Yeah, the business part was good. And Angus, I chased up those enquiries for you. Even had a chat with the solicitor who handled the lady's estate.'

Angus put his mug on the ground and sat forward. 'Yeah? How'd you manage that? That stuff'd be confidential, wouldn't it?'

Flint sipped his tea and accepted a piece of date slice from the plate I offered him. 'Thanks. Mmm, home cooking?'

I raised a brow at him. 'Know any bakeries round here? Of course. So, tell us what you found out.'

'Well,' he said, looking at me rather than Angus, 'it seems they had money troubles. Your brother-in-law took out a second mortgage on the house, which Pauline didn't know about. I got this from the woman living next door. Apparently the two were great friends and Lisa's mum regularly confided in her. The neighbour blamed the mortgage for her friend's death. Said she was stressed out of her mind because the business was in trouble too, and – this is her view, not a medical opinion – that's why the aneurysm occurred. Anyway, she gave me the name of the solicitor involved, so I looked him up the day before I left.'

'And he talked to you?'

He read my surprise. 'Well, I laid it on a bit about the kid – motherless, homeless, penniless. Said she only had her grandfather, who was on the pension . . . In short, I pulled out all the stops, and he told me everything had been sold up to pay off accrued debts. His opinion was that it was bound to happen from the moment the bank granted the second mortgage. Lisa and her mother were turfed out of the home and living with some sort of relative, Lily somebody, when the mother died. He assumed that's where Lisa still was.'

'She was Pauline's half-sister,' I explained. 'The one who dumped her here.' I looked at Angus, willing him not to correct Flint's assumption about Lisa's father and thankfully, he didn't. 'Well, it seems she's guilty of nothing but callousness, because there can't have been anything there for her to get.'

'Looks that way,' Angus agreed. 'Thanks, Flint. You done good. That poor woman . . . husband dead, debts to 'er eyeballs and the 'ouse sold from under her. Maybe the stress did kill 'er after all.'

I made some noncommittal reply, my thoughts elsewhere. I was remembering the police officer's question: *Was Michael worried about anything?* And the truck driver's opinion that Michael had driven into him on purpose. Was the accident in fact no accident at all, but a suicide brought on by debts and the inevitable unmasking of his double life? I had discounted the idea, rationalising that of course the truck driver would try to shift the blame. He was the survivor, so there was only his word about what had occurred. But now my heart sank with the stark knowledge that the man hadn't necessarily lied. Michael's death could well have been a deliberate act, it seemed. But it would help neither Angus nor Lisa to voice my suspicion, simply add to their pain. I stood instead and gathered up the empty mugs.

Flint rose with me. 'I picked up something for you in Cairns. I'll run it down for you now. It's a bit heavy to carry.'

'What is it? You shouldn't have,' I protested but he just grinned and left to return ten minutes later in his vehicle with a washing-machine carton strapped on the back.

'It's not what it looks like,' he said as my mouth opened. 'There were a couple of council blokes digging it out of a median strip and I said I'd take it off their hands. I wrapped the root ball in a sack. And I've kept it shaded and watered, so it ought to make it.'

'It' proved to be a mature strelitzia, the large leaves and bold, beak-shaped flowers with their vibrant colours looking no worse for its arduous journey.

'A bird of paradise! Oh, Flint, that's wonderful. Thank you so much.' I eyed him in sudden suspicion. 'Now, you're telling the truth . . . you didn't go and buy it?'

'Scout's honour. If I had, don't you think I'd have insisted on a pot?'

I laughed. 'Of course. Well, thank you for thinking of me. I love it.'

'That's no hardship, Penny.' Then briskly, 'Where do you want it? I reckon it deserves to go straight into the ground.'

I willed myself not to blush and studied the yard. 'There, I think – against the wall. It'll give it protection from the south-easterlies. And I'll bring a few of the larger potted trees over to put around it for shade, just while it settles in. They're a premium flower, you know, for those gorgeous big tropical arrangements. You see them in swanky apartments and posh hotel foyers. The plants themselves cost the earth. They're really quite tough though, like orchids.' I was babbling. I changed the subject while he plucked up a shovel from the tools by the shed door and walked over to the spot I'd indicated. 'So, what else did you do in Cairns? Go snorkelling, see a film, visit the reef?'

'Nope.' He thrust down with his boot on the shovel edge, slicing through the heavy soil. 'Most days were wet, so I did a bit of browsing, found myself a new interest.'

'Oh yes?' I watched the hole deepen. 'What's that?'

'Enamelling. They were running a workshop just a coupla doors up from the pub I stayed at. I just happened to duck in there out of the rain while it was on and got interested.' I must have made some sound for he cocked an eyebrow at me. 'What?'

'My mother did that,' I said. 'She made jewellery. I . . . it's years since I thought about it.' My hand started towards my throat and I stilled it, remembering the day I had destroyed the copper pendant she'd given me, decorated with its tiny enamelled daisies. She had made two, one for each of us, and strung them on black leather thongs. Very chic back in the seventies and the age of flower power, I thought now. I had always worn it – until the day I smashed the beaded enamel petals with a brick, and took a pair of pliers to the copper backing, blinded by tears of rage and loss, before hurling the formless lump away.

'You'll be able to give me some pointers then,' Flint said blithely, reaching for the plant. He settled it into the hole he'd made, gently released the sacking and backfilled. 'How's that look?'

'Great. Thank you, Flint. I'll give it a drink, then get the trolley and bring a few saplings over.'

'Here.' He handed me the shovel. 'You've got a customer. Point me in the right direction and I'll do it.'

I did as he said, thanked him again, then went over to greet the man alighting from a shire vehicle. Council business. I grimaced, but these things could go either way – another fussy regulation to be implemented, or a really useful order. A new family recreation area had been in the pipeline forever and we'd been hoping to benefit from it; long before it was fenced or grassed and the picnic tables went in, they would need trees. Metaphorically crossing my fingers, I went to meet him.

Lisa came home from school with a companion. 'This is Roseanne,' she said challengingly as the pair entered the kitchen. The newcomer was a pretty, plump little thing with dark hair and brown eyes. She glanced quickly at me, twisting her hands awkwardly together, as I smiled at her.

'Hi, Miss Carter. Is it okay that I've come?'

'You don't have to ask her,' Lisa muttered.

'Of course.' I ignored the interjection. 'Lisa's friends are always welcome. You're Marlene's girl from the shop. I've seen you with your mum.'

'That's right,' she murmured shyly, biting her lip. 'Me and Lisa, we're in the same class.'

'That's nice. It's good to make new friends. Now, would you girls like a cold drink and something to eat?' I opened the fridge and pulled down the biscuit tin from its shelf. 'You can take them outside. There's a table in the fern house, the coolest place at present.' They vanished out the back, Roseanne offering meticulous thanks. She had nice manners, I thought and hoped, if the liaison lasted, that they might serve to influence Lisa. Who had probably been quite a different child before her father's death, I reminded myself. Michael had been a polite and considerate man and I couldn't believe that he would have accepted rudeness in his daughter.

It was his politeness that had brought about our first meeting. I had tripped on the post office steps in Atherton and fallen, luckily without injuring myself, though the knee I'd banged on the concrete step insisted otherwise. So occupied was I with the pain that I scarcely noticed the passerby who collected my bag and parcel, then produced a clean handkerchief to mop the blood from the scrape on my knee.

'Are you all right?' His touch was gentle, his grey eyes concerned and he genuinely seemed to care as he gave me a hand up and restored my belongings.

'I'm fine, thanks,' I said, but my first step brought a gasp of pain.

He took a grip on my elbow and said firmly, 'You're not. Do you think you can make it to the cafe there? I'm Michael, by the way, and my time's my own just now, so don't feel that you're putting me out or being a nuisance. You just need to sit down for a bit and catch your breath.'

He led me to a table, bought coffee for us both and we chatted until the smart of my injury lessened and I felt more myself.

'It was my own fault,' I told him. 'Women are supposed to be able to multi-task but that obviously doesn't include reading while negotiating steps. I was trying to decipher the date on my parcel, you see. I've been waiting for it forever.'

'Ah, something important then?'

'In a sense. Flower seeds from Western Australia.' He looked blank and I laughed. 'I run a nursery. I've been waiting to get these in the ground before the growing season ends.' I finished my coffee. 'Thank you again, Michael. You've been most kind and now I really must go.' I picked up my parcel. 'These need to be planted soonest if I'm to sell them this year.'

That was the start of it. Later that afternoon he'd come to the nursery, ostensibly to buy a plant for his office, before sheepishly admitting that said office was in Cairns and he was rarely in it. In the end he'd abandoned the purchase – *I'm rubbish at making up my mind* – and asked me out instead, and it had simply developed from there. He was thoughtful, charming, not bad looking and loved his job.

'I like driving,' he'd told me, shrugging off my query about tiring hours behind the wheel. 'It's a sort of freedom. I'd die of boredom in an office job, and I'm good at selling.' Well, he was certainly that. He'd sold me his footloose, bachelor-looking-to-settle-down story, wooing me with patience and ardour over weeks of chat and walks and coffee that morphed naturally into dinners, until I had become addicted to his presence. I had believed every word he said, and why wouldn't I? He was as sincere and seemingly transparent as a child about his life, his work and his hopes for the future. I had been deliriously happy, like some sappy romantic heroine with Prince Charming come to call.

Now, looking back, I wondered how he had explained his absence to Pauline during our ten-day honeymoon, but Michael was always glib. I had even teased him about his salesman's ability to find an answer for everything.

'Can I help it if I'm smart?' He'd crinkled his eyes at me, making my heart melt, the dark curls falling across his brow as he turned his palms up in helpless supplication to some higher power. 'As Popeye says, *I yam what I yam.*'

'Every maiden's dream,' I had quipped. 'I just wonder how you've made it this far without some woman grabbing you.'

'Because my heart was waiting for you, my darling.' He'd drawn me into his arms then and kissed me, and, God help me, I had believed the truth of his answer and his kiss. A fierce, raw happiness had swelled in me for the fact of his existence and the improbability of our finding each other in a world surely filled with prettier, more interesting girls than me.

'I love you,' I had said, nestling against his chest where I could feel the steady beat of his heart. 'Falling down those steps was the best thing that ever happened to me.'

Or the worst, I thought now.

I had so many memories of Michael. Sharing the verandah swing with him while the moon rose over the town and bats flitted like bits of darkness through the silvery air. Holding hands over a dining table in some restaurant, our eyes on each other while a waiter tried to get our attention with the menu. Him bringing me flowers, bunch after bouquet after potted arrangement ('And I'll keep on until you love me better than them'), and picnicking in the park with the wine decanted into a thermos to keep it chilled in the heat . . .

It had been a small wedding, a few friends and my Aunt Julia, who treated her attendance as a chore she'd rather have skipped. She had never been actively unkind and had done her duty by me as a child, taking me in when my mother vanished, but when at eighteen I'd left her home to make my own way, it had resulted in mutual relief. She'd had nothing but antipathy for her only brother and had never met my mother, and this, on top of not being fond of children, had meant we'd never had a reason to bond.

Perhaps Aunt Julia's supply of humanity, I hazarded, had simply been low. She had been a professional student, endlessly educating herself, while I had found my interest and happiness in the earth, growing and tending the garden she ignored. And when Michael had entered my world, I considered it complete, a shining orb of happiness garnished with a love that would carry us unscathed into old age. Or so I had believed until the day it all came crashing down, like one of those fancy glass balls from a Christmas tree, their perfection instantly changed into a thousand shards that wounded at every touch, their destruction so complete that restoration was out of the question and their fragile magic forever lost.

Chapter Seven

Another ten days passed before the council got back to me about Clarkson Park, the name that had been decided on for the new recreation area.

'Who's Clarkson when he's at home?' Angus asked between mouthfuls of lunch. 'God! It don't rain today, I'm a Dutchman.' Sweat trickled down his face. He palmed it away and wiped his hand on his jeans.

'A pioneer. The first settler in the area. He took up Bobton Downs.'

'Never 'eard of it.'

'Not surprising, seeing it no longer exists. It was a small block at the mouth of the Rainsford. A poor choice on his part – mostly swamp, saltpan and scrub. It was subsumed into Castlereach Station yonks ago. So the government would get its pound of flesh in rent, I expect. I doubt you'd make a living off it – well, Clarkson plainly didn't or it would still exist today.'

'So how'd you find that out?'

'It's on the pastoral maps,' I said patiently. 'Most stations had them so they could see how the boundaries ran.'

I remembered then what he wouldn't necessarily have known. 'When I was a kid, none of this country was boundary fenced, the way it is now. So you needed to know where your property ended and your neighbour's began. My father had his map on the wall in the office. We – I – used to dream up stories about the names. Bobton – only I called it Bobtown – was where the bunnies lived.'

'*Bunnies?*' He gave me an old-fashioned look. 'How'd you make that out?'

'Because they hop. Bobbing up and down, see?' Reminiscently I said, 'I always wanted one for a pet.'

He snorted. 'Huh. You ever seen what rabbits do to land, lass? Bloody plagues of Egypt got nothin' on 'em.'

'Well, anyway,' I said, reverting to business, 'the council's sent a plan for where they want the trees. They haven't said what sort so we can please ourselves.' I pushed the lunch plates aside and spread the paper out. 'I thought if we used African mahogany here for the outer row – they're tough, quick growing and get quite huge – and then we could have a banyan here in the middle next to the shelter. It'd become a king tree in time, simply enormous, and would give very dense shade. Then maybe a few poincianas here and there to fill in any blank spots. They're quick growers but short lived so by the time they die the others will need the space anyway. The irrigation system won't be going in before June, so I included watering in the contract. Not that we'll need to do much of that. By the end of the Wet they won't need coddling.'

'Looks like you got it sorted,' Angus said. 'When do you want to get 'em in?'

'If it storms this arvo, how about tomorrow? The last fig we've got is awfully pot bound, poor thing – it's one of the reasons I included it – and the rest of the saplings are quite big enough to go out now.'

'Right.' Angus thumped the lid back onto the butter as he always did, and as usual I winced, expecting the plastic to split. 'Then how about we grab the stakes and go mark exactly where they want 'em, soon as we finish here? It's too bloody hot for me to be diggin' holes twice if I was to get it wrong.'

Later that day a thunderstorm fulfilled Angus's prophecy and the last of it saw Flint's vehicle pulling up out front. He made a run for the verandah, where he shook himself like a dog, shedding water from his sun-bleached hair. His hat drooped wetly, along with his socks, which he peeled off to lay over his muddy boots before handing me a plastic carrier bag.

'Brought you some red claw. I got myself some new traps in Cairns and they work just fine.'

'Or there're lots of suicidal cray around,' I suggested, smiling. 'Thank you, Flint. What a treat! You must stay for dinner.'

He grinned. 'I was hoping you'd ask. I do get sick of my own cooking.'

'What about a beer?' Angus suggested, then, catching sight of Lisa, added, 'Come and meet our neighbour, lassie. This is Lisa, Flint. My grandkid.'

'Very pleased to make your acquaintance, Lisa.' He nodded and offered his hand. 'You shake, or you reckon that's only for men?'

'Why would it be?' she bristled. 'My mum shook hands. She said it started off because if strangers shook hands when they met, it showed they were friendly.'

'Really?' I said. 'How's that work?'

She gave me a disdainful look. ''Cause it showed they weren't holding a weapon.' The implied 'Don't you know anything?' hung unuttered in the air.

'Is that right?' Flint pursed his lips. 'Makes sense, I suppose. How are you liking Southbend?'

'It's all right,' she said grudgingly. 'Me and Roseanne are gonna help Grandad plant trees tomorrow.'

'If we don't get bogged.' Angus tousled her hair. 'C'mon, Flint, that beer's calling.'

They went inside while I examined my gift, holding one up for Lisa to see. 'You want to help me cook them?'

'Yuck! You're gonna eat that?' She stared at the claws and whiskers and shuddered. 'Well, I'm not. No way!'

'You can have salad then,' I said, 'but you should try just a teeny bit. You never know, you might even like it.'

In the end she did, but only because Flint teased her into it. He treated her naturally, neither talking down to her nor asking laboured questions, but like someone truly interested in her opinion. She opened out under this treatment and began to display a similar interest in him.

'Flint's an artist,' I said lightly, 'and a fisherman.'

She looked at the remains on our plates and sniffed. 'That's not fish.' She turned her shoulder, making it plain she was speaking only to him. 'My dad used to take me fishing.'

'Maybe you can come out with me one day,' he said. 'You and Penny. Everybody should hook at least one barra in their life.'

Her face lit up. 'Really? That'd be cool. When?'

He smiled at her eagerness. 'Not just now. I'm a law-abiding man and the barra season's closed at present. So, after the Wet, before the tourists start. If Penny has the time, of course.'

She scowled, but I said, 'Thanks, Flint. It sounds great. And you must come and help us eat the catch – whatever it is.'

Lisa pulled a face, eyeing the dirty plates. 'Only not *that*.'

We all laughed and, after looking briefly startled, she couldn't quite suppress a pleased little smile.

The following day was a Saturday. Roseanne arrived soon after breakfast and the two girls climbed happily into the back of the vehicle where Angus and I had loaded the trees. Two inches of rain had fallen overnight and puddles dotted the yard, their surfaces shivering in the breeze.

'You don't think you'll bog down?' I looked dubiously at the water lying on the verges of the road. 'It's not like there's been much traffic over there at the park to harden the ground.'

'I'm bloody sure I would,' Angus said dryly, 'only I don't plan on leavin' the bitumen. I'll chuck the barrow on and use it to shift the trees.'

'Well, don't kill yourself. I wish I could give you a hand.'

'And who'd mind the shop then?' He heaved the barrow up, added a crowbar and shut the tailboard. 'I'll be right. You girls wanna ride in the front?'

'No. We like it back here,' Lisa called.

'Right, well see you hang on.' He climbed into the cab and drove carefully away, the back wheels sinking deeply, if momentarily, into the patch of soft ground between the yard and the bitumen.

They were scarcely out of sight when my first customer turned up. I sighed. The nursery wasn't even open and I hadn't yet washed the breakfast dishes, but the vehicle, with its green and gold door logo, came from the fuel depot and was being driven by Muriel Lacey, the biggest nosy parker and gossip in town.

Deciding not to make it easy for her, I said, 'You're very early, Muriel. I haven't opened yet.'

'Oh well, it's only me.' She gave an insincere laugh that sounded forced. 'I thought I'd pop by while it's still cool – well cooler,' she amended, 'to look at some ferns. I knew you wouldn't mind. After all a sale's a sale isn't it? No matter what time of day.' She was an extraordinarily plain woman, in her fifties, I judged, with sun-damaged skin, inquisitive eyes and a large wart on her chin.

'That's true,' I said blandly. 'Well, you know where the plants are. You go and browse while I finish my chores in the kitchen.'

'Oh, but I might need some help,' she answered swiftly. 'Knowing me, I'd wind up with something unsuitable. I don't know how you remember all the plant names, let alone how they grow.'

But you have no trouble holding on to every detail of people's lives, I thought silently. If there was a scandal, Muriel was first to know and spread it. And she could manufacture the most innocuous happenings into something questionable, seemingly without needing to draw breath. Giving up, I said, 'Very well then. What were you after?'

'Mmm, I don't really know. Something for the verandah – but maybe that's too hot? By the way, I hear you've got a young visitor staying. A rellie of yours, is it? That must be nice.'

'No,' I said shortly. 'She's Angus's granddaughter, here for a visit.'

'Oh, lucky him. He'll like that. I never see mine. His son's or his daughter's?'

I said tersely, 'His son's, but I don't really know the extent of his family.' I crossed my fingers mentally as I added, 'Lisa's a nice child and he seems to be enjoying her company. What about this one? Not as delicate as maiden hair, or as aggressive a grower as whaleback. It does well indoors, but it can stand partial sun if you had a sheltered spot on your verandah. Not much care required, just watering and trimming away any dead growth.'

'Maybe – or that one beside it? Oh, I don't know – perhaps just an ordinary plant, a cactus, say? How's your dad getting on, by the way? Do you hear from him much?'

I stiffened, wondering if this, rather than Lisa's provenance, was the purpose of her visit. 'Not much. And he was fine last I heard.' Which would be about fifteen years ago, if anyone was counting, when Bracton Park had been sold. I had read about the sale, but the article had only mentioned his name, not his future intentions.

'He must be getting on,' she mused. 'Still on his own, is he? I expect he never got over your mum leaving like that?' No doubt catching the look on my face, Muriel tutted sympathetically and raised her palms in a placatory fashion. 'Well, it was common knowledge, Penny. We all knew about it. How could we not in a place this size – it was even smaller back then.

But you were only a child – you wouldn't remember much about those times, or me. My father was a drover – Joe Bindle. He'd probably have worked for your dad.'

'No, I can't say I do.' I stared at her with a vague memory of felt-hatted men on horseback who came to lift the Bracton Park cattle each mustering season. The roads had been impassible for big trucks in the seventies, and sale cattle from the Gulf had all been walked to the railhead in Tewinga to be trucked to the coastal meatworks. Had the drover taking ours been her father? I had no idea. 'Well,' I said briskly, 'I must get on, Muriel. I haven't even done the dishes yet. So, which one do you want – the fern or the cactus? Both would do well indoors. Just don't over water them, and see that they have light.'

She took the hint, bought the cactus and left, little wiser, I hoped, than when she'd arrived. Frowning, I returned indoors, dredging through the past, trying to recall old names, but the thing was, if you deliberately put something out of mind, as I had my childhood, then details tended to fade into obscurity. I wondered if Joe Bindle had known my mother. Muriel would've been a young woman then – twenty-ish I thought – and no doubt all over the tale of the runaway wife who had abandoned husband, child and vehicle to vanish from the district. Leaving the vehicle plainly meant that she had fled with someone else, a detail to delight the gossip-mongers, I thought sourly.

I remembered the black look on the face of my father. He was fifteen years older than my mother, hard working with a brooding stillness about him and no softer side, even with his family. I had always feared him and the way his silences were often broken by sudden, inexplicable rages. Comfort and jokes and the sharing of dreams had been within my mother's metier, instant obedience my father's. And once she was gone his face had worn a look of restrained and baffled fury – at her, or at the wild surmise and gossip that I now knew must have been rife in the district?

I had shrunk from him in the two short days between my mother's disappearance and my own banishment, remembering quarrels and shouting behind closed doors, and her surreptitious tears in the days before she left. And after he had abruptly told me she was dead, he ordered me to pack my bag because, he said, I was going to live with my aunt, a woman I had never heard of let alone met.

No further explanation was forthcoming. He didn't take me himself. I and my bag had been bundled onto the mail truck that ran from Southbend to Goola, from whence the station-master saw me onto a train to the coast. It was a terrifying journey for a nine-year-old to make alone. The furthest abroad I had ever been was to Hamilton. I had no money, just a packet of sandwiches the mailman had given me, and no idea how to manage finding more food, or a toilet, or where I would sleep. A friendly woman had helped me, staying with me on the platform once we reached Townsville until the stranger who announced she was my Aunt Julia had plucked me up, like a parcel she'd been informed was arriving.

I hadn't seen or spoken to my supposed father since.

It had taken me some years to understand the meaning behind my parents' rows. I had pieced together the truth from the fragments of fights I had overheard in those final days, before my young world collapsed. I had worked out that

I was, in Walter Carter's words, 'a bloody ring-in. Some other bastard's by-blow'. It didn't mean it was true, I had reasoned – only my mother could know if it was. But *he* believed it, which meant that I did too. I didn't know what my aunt knew. She never mentioned my father to me; their rift was buried somewhere in the irreconcilable past and I had no wish to learn, then or now, anything further of the family I apparently didn't belong to.

The only thing Aunt Julia did tell me, when I was fifteen, was that Walter had lied to me. Imogen Carter hadn't died the day she vanished from my ken. She had simply left me and her old life behind to seek new horizons with somebody else. It was the worst blow of all. Before I had believed myself tragically orphaned, a fate that could overtake anyone. But from that point on, I knew that I had simply been abandoned, like a toy, or a pastime that no longer fulfilled the purpose for which it had initially been chosen.

Chapter Eight

The CWA had accepted my price for the rented pots to decorate the dais for the dance, but the day after the school holiday break-up, Sue Hart called an emergency meeting and those members who could make it gathered in the hall. Most of the station women were missing, the roads too boggy for them to attempt the trip into town.

'I've rung them,' Sue said, 'and they're on board with whatever we decide. I thought the meeting today would give you all the chance to talk it over, but really it's the bulk of our out-of-town members who will be most affected by our decision. Briefly then, ladies, I'd like us to bring the Christmas dance forward. The way the weather is, the longer we leave it the less likelihood there is of it happening at all.'

'When were you thinking?' Marlene asked.

'Well, what about next Saturday? It's been bucketing down, but I notice the wind is southerly today, so we could be in for a bit of a dry spell before it starts again.' Sue threw up her hands. 'I mean, who knows? We can but plan, but I do feel it's now or forget the whole thing, and that means Santa doesn't come and the kids'll be disappointed.'

'Let's do it then,' I said, glancing around and thinking that I'd have to find something to wrap for Lisa. Greg Banner, the police sergeant, usually did the Santa bit for the kids, which was odd considering his morose visage and dour outlook. Perhaps he'd seen too much crime in his former posting, I hazarded, but his heavy frame and drinker's paunch suited the costume, and the little ones were willing to be fooled.

'What about the supper?' Muriel demanded. 'That's not much notice. I mean, it's supposed to be special. Have you even enough left on your shelves for fancy cakes, Marlene?'

'Oh, I think so. And if anything extra's needed, there's always Wednesday's plane.' Roseanne's mother bristled. 'I've certainly got flour and tinned apples.' This was a dig at Muriel, who invariably turned up to all social occasions bearing the same uninspired dish of apple pie.

'Well,' Sue said diplomatically, 'let's decide on a number, shall we, and then work out quantities for supper? Penny's got the decorations covered. Barry will look after the music as usual, and if Greg stays sober enough to be our Santa, we're pretty fixed. Let's say we leave the baking till Friday – we should have an idea by then on what the weather's doing. And if we have to postpone . . .' She blew out plump cheeks and plied the fan she always carried.

'Well, that's what freezers are for,' I said, standing up. 'Is the urn switched on? What if I make us all some tea before we start the lists?'

*

That evening, I sat on my bed going through an old chocolate box of keepsakes looking for something suitable to wrap for Lisa. All the kids would get a gift from our dour Santa, so she must too. In the end I found a string of fake pearls and a bracelet of sparkly beads. They would have to do, and I berated myself for not factoring in the Christmas dance when I was in town. I wrapped up the pearls in a square of Christmas paper and laid the bracelet aside. She could wear her new dress to the dance and the pretty stones would help make it special.

Roseanne heard about the event from her mother and over dinner on Wednesday night Lisa said, 'Are we going to the dance Saturday, Grandad? Roseanne and her mum and dad are. She said all the kids go, even the babies.'

'Well, everyone attends these affairs so the children can't be left behind,' I explained.

'Course we are,' Angus replied. 'You wanna be my partner? Not often these days I get to take a pretty girl dancin'.'

'I don't know how to,' Lisa admitted. 'But Roseanne says it doesn't matter. You learn as you go. She reckons it's fun.'

'Ah, there nothin' to dancin',' Angus said airily. 'The music gets into your feet, see, and they go themselves. Ain't that right, Flint?'

'Well, it's not too wrong,' our guest for the evening agreed. 'We should make up a party. What do you say, Penny? Lisa and Angus, and you and me. It'll save me from being placed in charge of the bar, and it'll keep you out of the kitchen.'

'A proper attitude, that is,' I reproved. But there was a certain truth in his observation. In small communities like ours, the same few individuals judged responsible enough always ended up doing the donkey work, with the unattached and childless forming the front of the queue. 'Still it'd be nice to have the evening off, so thank you. Of course, we don't know yet if it'll even happen.' I nodded at the intermittent bloom of light beyond the window. 'That storm looks like it could float the ark.'

'Nah.' Angus shook his head. 'No thunder, gotta be miles off. Round Seven Hills way, I'd reckon.'

'We can hope.' I looked at Lisa. 'I'll be baking fairy cakes tomorrow for the dance supper. You and Roseanne could help decorate them if you like.'

'Maybe,' she said grudgingly. 'I'll see if she wants to.'

Angus was right and the storm rained itself out. In the morning, the girls presented themselves in the fernery, where I was loading the hand trolley with the pots I had earmarked to dress the stage.

'Mum let me bring her cake book over and I've got some little silver balls too, to put on the cakes we make,' Roseanne said eagerly.

'Well'—I smiled at her—'we'd best get started then. Have you shown Lisa the book yet? There might be time for you to make something special out of it. But we'll have to freeze it before you decorate it – the icing will melt and run otherwise.'

'Oh, yes.' Roseanne's brown eyes sparkled. 'There's a ballerina cake. Could we make that one?'

We could always use it for pudding, I thought, if it didn't turn out. A dollop of custard could rescue a great many culinary failures. 'We can try. I'm about finished here, so I won't be but a minute. Go wash your hands, girls, and we'll get started.'

Lisa lost herself in the enjoyment of cooking, laughing quite naturally as we mixed and baked. The oven made the kitchen even hotter, so once the pans of little cakes were cooking, Roseanne carried the cake book out into the hallway, a natural breezeway through the house, and showed me the picture of the ballerina cake. I studied it doubtfully: a dome formed the shape of the skirt, easy enough to mimic if I used my pudding basin, but it relied on the upper half of a plastic doll inserted in the top to make sense of the design.

'It's lovely,' I said, 'but we don't have a doll. Is there another one, perhaps?'

Cross-legged on the floor, the two girls explored the book, dark heads bent together, exclaiming and arguing over the possibilities. As I ladled out cake mixture and swapped the pans about in the kitchen, I heard the murmur of their voices and gave thanks that Lisa had made a friend. Roseanne would help fill in the long school holidays when the Wet kept us from moving about and there was little to fill the stretched-out summer days.

They settled at last on a clown design that would need two round butter cakes, one for his face and the other to cut up to make his ears and the two parts of the collar of his costume. Both watched me anxiously as I studied the instructions.

'Yes,' I said. 'We can do that. Just let me check what colours I have for the icing. Lisa, you find the pans in the bottom drawer there, and Roseanne, if you could get the eggs from the fridge? And the butter. Put the book over on the table, please – we don't want to spill anything on it.'

Supervising the making was slower than doing it myself but worth it, for Lisa actually called me by name once, something of a rarity. When the mix was in the oven and the clearing up done, I smiled at both girls. 'Now, I think we can steal four of those little cakes for ourselves. I've made some icing. What say you decorate them while I make the tea? I'm dying for a cuppa, and Angus will be too.'

Angus, whose fathering skills might or might not have fallen short, seemed intent upon being the perfect grandparent. He praised the cakes extravagantly and, having listened to their plans for decorating the clown's face, sent them off to the store with a handful of coins to purchase liquorice sticks. ''Cause I reckon they'd make pretty good hair, if you cut 'em fine enough.'

Happy with the idea, they shot off, arranging to return in the late afternoon when the day had cooled, to undertake the decorating. In the meantime, I suggested, they might decide whether they wished to keep the cake or donate it to the dance supper. The lure of a wider audience, I thought, would probably win that one.

The rain held off, and on Saturday morning Marlene, Sue and I gathered at the hall with Barry Lacey to set things up for the dance. Flint had offered his services to transport the heavy tubs of plants for the dais and was an enormous help in patiently shifting them around to provide just the right decorative screening for the music bench. He and Barry heaved the collapsible tables out of storage and set them up in the supper room-cum-kitchen, while I and the other women washed the crockery and cutlery that had sat unused in the cupboard since the last dance back in August.

'We ought to do this more regularly,' Sue mused, rubbing industriously at a tea stain in a cup. 'The Tewinga branch have monthly dances.'

'Only because they've got a larger population,' Marlene said. 'The stations are smaller down there, so there're more people in the district.'

'But the town is smaller too,' Sue argued. 'If you can call a pub and a store a town.'

'Maybe they're just mad keen dancers,' I said lightly. 'Anyway, we get a good roll-up when we do have them. Where are the tablecloths?'

'Should be sealed in plastic, somewhere,' Marlene said. 'Let's hope so, anyway. The geckos will have made a right mess of them otherwise.'

They were in a box beside the sink, the garbage bags that held them intact and firmly tied. We dressed the tables with the poinsettia pots and colourful paper napkins, and then Flint wheeled in the final plant I had brought, a young native pine.

'Where do you want it, Penny?'

I looked at the two women. 'This one's on the house – a Christmas tree. I've got a box of old decorations and I thought the girls might like to dress it this arvo. What do you think?'

Sue clapped her hands, beaming. 'It's a great idea. We should've thought of it ourselves. How about the end of the stage there? In full view and unlikely to be bumped into.'

'Good idea.' Marlene surveyed our efforts. 'I think we've done us proud. I just have to find the cashbox now. Stan'll be manning the door, and I took the Santa costume round to old Grumbleguts yesterday.'

'Who?' Flint asked.

'Sergeant Banner,' I said. 'He *is* inclined to complain.'

'Oh, right. How do you know he'll be sober?'

'He'd better be,' Sue declared. 'He'll catch an earful from me if he isn't.'

'Right,' Flint repeated. 'You all finished, then? If so, I could run you ladies home.'

Marlene accepted the offer, so she and I climbed into Flint's vehicle. Sue, who never walked anywhere she could ride, had brought her own. We drove the short distance to the shop and I waved to Stan before reminding Marlene to tell the girls, who were at her place, to come home to collect the decorations for the tree. Back at my own gate I paused, holding the door handle, to thank Flint for his service. 'You were a great help. Angus and I would have really struggled with those big tubs.'

'It was no trouble. I'll pick you up about seven tonight, then?'

'Oh,' I hesitated. 'I was . . . that is, I assumed we'd just meet up at the hall. Angus can run me over.'

'No trouble,' he repeated. 'He's taking Lisa, remember? Don't steal her thunder. She'll love being his date for the night.'

She would too, I thought, and it would only strengthen the bond forming between them. But did that mean that I was to be considered Flint's date? I felt a worm of uncertainty stirring in my stomach. He was a good friend, and I liked him, but that was it. I liked Stan Bentley too. And I couldn't imagine going on a date with him.

'Well, thank you,' I said helplessly. 'I'll be ready.'

Angus, foregoing his afternoon nap, took the girls across to the hall and stayed with them to lock up again after they'd finished with the tree. I packed the now iced clown cake, along with the smaller ones, into plastic carriers, then returned them to the fridge. The liquorice-strip hair on the cake was a brilliant touch, as was the red plastic bottle cap they had used for the nose. The finished product really looked too good to eat, I told the girls, who beamed with pleasure, then rushed to the door, yet again, to check on the weather.

Southbend, backed by the river, faced south onto a flat, open plain fringed with thin timber, and you could see for miles; as far at this moment as the heavy black line of clouds on the distant horizon. They bore the glaze of heat but were changing even as we looked, the skirts of rain thinning away to a grey nothingness as the build-up began to drift apart.

'Is it going to come in?' Roseanne asked anxiously.

'Not today,' I said, 'it's breaking up, but soon. It might be a very wet Christmas.'

Lisa was too excited to eat much of her dinner. She had washed her hair and let me plait it back into two neat ridges on the crown of her head, finishing with a little bob on the nape where the ends were gathered in. The new dress, patterned in pink and sage green, looked fresh and pretty and brought a smile to her face when I gave her a gentle push towards the long mirror in my room.

'There. Don't you look nice? Oh, and there's this – every girl needs a bit of bling.' I handed her the bracelet I had dug out, asking curiously, 'Don't you have anything of your own?' It seemed odd that she wouldn't have at least a cheap necklace.

'I had a heart locket on a gold chain and a gold brooch, but Lily took them. To look after, she said, but she never gave them back. And she said my bangles were rubbish and threw them out.' Lisa looked mutinous for a moment, but then her face relaxed as she turned her wrist so the light caught the glass facets. 'Are you giving me this,' she asked suspiciously, 'or do you want it back?'

'It's yours to keep. Now, off you go and knock your grandad's eye out. He'll be skiting about you all over town.'

She giggled, ran a few steps, then halted briefly on one foot. 'Thanks, Penny,' she said stiffly. 'And for this.' She held up the arm with the bracelet, gave me something that was almost a smile and shot through the door.

It was nearly seven. I pulled off the housecoat I'd donned following my shower and dressed hurriedly in a light sundress with narrow shoulder straps, and a pair of heeled sandals dusted with rhinestones. I brushed my curls, put on matching rhinestone earrings and sprayed scent onto my throat and the hollows of my elbows. Grabbing a clutch purse, I rushed into the kitchen and got the last of the packed cake boxes onto the table just as Flint's voice called from the front door.

'Come in,' I called breathlessly. 'You can help ferry stuff out.'

'Evening, Penny.' He came in and swooped on the boxes I was picking up. 'Here, I'll get those. You look lovely and cool. Nice shoes.'

'Aren't they?' I pointed a toe. 'Not much occasion for them out here. You look very smart yourself.' He was wearing dark slacks and a pale blue, short-sleeved shirt. 'No khaki?'

He grinned. 'I do have a bit of town clobber. Doesn't get much of an airing though, bit like your shoes. Is this the lot?'

'Yes, I've got this one. It's the girls' special cake.' I hurried ahead of him to hold the door. 'I'll leave the verandah light on. Those can ride on the floor, but I think I'd better nurse this one – it's a bit fragile.'

'So how's the taming of the interloper coming along?' he asked as we rolled down the street.

'Don't call her that.' I smiled at him to soften the reprimand. 'And the answer is slowly but steadily. Every now and then she softens towards me, so I'm making progress – I think.'

'Takes time,' he agreed. 'I've found patience gets you most things. Here we are then.' He pulled on the handbrake and killed the lights. 'Straight to the supper room with this lot?'

'Yes. I'll come too – maybe I can find room in the fridge.'

Music swelled from the cone of light coming from the open doors. Stan Bentley, wearing a cowboy shirt and string tie, was posted at the foot of the shallow steps rattling his cashbox good-humouredly at all comers. The headlights of vehicles speared the dark from two directions as the station contingent began to arrive, and the muggy air held a mixture of scent and cologne and woodsmoke from the kitchen stove where the boilers would be heating for the many litres of tea and coffee served with supper. A couple danced past the door in a swirl of skirts and polished boots and my pulse leaped. If there had been a floor underfoot, my toe would have been tapping. Flint must have shared the feeling.

'Come on, let's get this done. There's good music going to waste here.'

Chapter Nine

It was a pleasant surprise to discover that Flint was quite at home on the dance floor. 'Thistledown,' he murmured as we danced together in the Pride of Erin.

I twirled under his arm, murmuring, 'You're not so bad yourself. Where did you learn?'

'Saturday lessons after footy. That was the deal with my mum. She said I'd thank her one day. What about you – bush hops?'

'No, proper lessons.' Dancing was something Aunt Julia had neglected in my growing years. We had practised the waltz in the school's gym during half-a-dozen lessons prior to the senior formal but that was all. Literally my first personal expense when I'd started work was to enrol in a dance class, and I had loved it ever since. Michael had also been a good dancer. I thrust the thought aside and looked about for Lisa, finding her wrong-footing the steps in the corner with a patient Angus. Roseanne was making only a slightly better job of it with another schoolmate, and I made a mental note to offer lessons to both girls. There would be plenty of opportunity, for business would be quiet to non-existent once the Wet set in.

The press of moving bodies increased the heat despite the overhead fans' best efforts. Sue had borrowed an industrial-strength standard fan from the pub and set it up in the supper room to make regular sweeps across the crowded tables, a blessed relief amid the noise and close proximity of sweaty bodies. The CWA ladies had excelled themselves as usual in producing the supper, and to their obvious delight, the girls' clown cake was passed the length of the table to be admired before being cut. Catching Lisa's eye, I gave her a thumb's up and for once she responded with a wholly uncomplicated grin.

'I think you're winning,' Flint murmured. He reached out to lade a variety of eats onto his plate and stood up. 'What say we find somewhere cooler outside and I'll get us something cold from the bar. You like beer?'

I wrinkled my nose. 'No. White wine, please – or a soft drink. I'm too hot for tea.'

'Come on then.' He shuffled one leg over the long bench, freed the other and reached out a hand to help me up.

The night air was muggy but blessedly cooler than inside. I sat on the front steps out of the direct spill of light and the parade of insects drawn to it, while Flint went off to the bar. He returned with a stubby, and wonder of wonders, a glass of chilled chardonnay.

'Thanks.' I took a mouthful and sighed with pleasure. 'We should air condition the hall but I don't suppose the council would hear of it.'

'Can't see it,' he agreed. 'Last time I went along as an observer to a council meeting, they were all tied up in knots about the cemetery. That Reilly woman from Wildhorse Creek reckons they should be rescuing the area's history. She was quite vehement about it too. Apparently she wants a beautification program for it. A new fence for starters, a board of some sort erected with a list of names and dates for the tourists, and a "contemplative area" where they can sit and think about it all.'

No corpse had been buried in Southbend's plot for at least forty years, and the cemetery was derelict, a forgotten tangle of broken and slanting headstones amid a sea of weed and rusted wire.

'That sounds like Fiona,' I replied. 'She's married to Simon Reilly. Both their families go way back in the town's past. And it's actually not a bad idea. There *is* a lot of history in the district.' I wrinkled my brow trying to remember. 'Some rellie of hers – a great uncle, or maybe it was her grandfather, I'm not sure which – had the first store in Southbend back in the days when most of the graziers were part-time carriers. They used to haul the wool clip in from properties on the Barkley, to the old Port on the coast, and cart out the supplies that those same boats brought in for the stations.'

'You mean there really was a port? I thought that was just a shortened name. You know, like Rumhole. Portwine, maybe? Grog seems to be a feature of the north.' He offered the plate. 'Here, have something.'

I took a macaroon and nodded in thanks, my mouth full of sweetness. 'No such thing. The Port was the original settlement in pioneer days. There was a meatworks too, back in the eighteen hundreds. I think bits of the old works are still up there on the saltflats. You see, Fiona's right. If even the residents don't know our history, the council *should* be preserving what's left. So, she wasn't getting any support for the idea?'

'Uh-uh. The Works Department want another grader. And they're still wrangling over this new water set-up for the town that's apparently been on the agenda forever.' He emptied his beer and burped gently. 'I guess social issues like the cemetery come in a long way behind the practical ones. Might've been good for your business though, Penny, if they'd gone for it.'

'Oh, yes? We dig a lot of holes, Angus and I, but only for trees. We're not about to start fencing, or realigning headstones.' A thought struck me. 'Actually, that old fence was falling down back when I was a kid. I think my father might've been tendering for the job of patching it up – he did fencing in his spare time, you see. I know he worked on the old bridge. If he did win the tender, that makes the cemetery fence over twenty years old. And he mightn't have replaced the whole thing anyway, so the wire could've been there for sixty or seventy years. In which case the state it's in is no surprise.' I selected a lamington and bit into it. 'Ooh, these are good.'

He gave me a confused look. 'Wasn't he a property owner, your dad?'

I laughed shortly. 'So were all the men who carted to the Port. Land keeps you poor, Flint. That much hasn't changed, whatever else has. My father did a bit of droving, a bit of fencing – whatever came up that fitted in with working the property. That's why he helped build the original bridge.'

'I see. But getting back to my remark, I meant if the cemetery project were to go ahead, I could see a plan for the odd seat and some shade trees from your nursery. Tourists aren't going to hang around in the blazing heat.'

'That's true. Well, more power to Fiona's efforts then. She's a very determined woman. It's mainly down to her that we got the new hall, you know.' I dusted coconut from my fingers and sipped at the wine with a sigh of content.

'Did you miss it?' Flint asked abruptly. 'When you left the property, I mean, when you were a kid? You must've had a pony and dogs – all that. Why did your father sell up?'

I said reluctantly. 'Oh, he didn't – not immediately. That happened five or six years after my mother left. I expect he got tired of it. I was living with my aunt when the Park changed hands, and I only heard it third hand anyway. It's complicated, Flint. My parents didn't get on.' I remembered the shouting from behind the bedroom door, *Some other bastard's by-blow,* like an echo in my head. 'I think,' I hazarded, fabricating rather than admit to the fault of my existence, 'that my father wanted a son, because I never meant much to him.' It could well be true. 'And when my mother left, he couldn't wait to farm me off to his sister. I was nine at the time, nearly ten. So I remember facts I'd picked up about the district, like the old meatworks, and that most of the graziers' forebears had been carriers, because we learned about our own district in Social Studies. And I didn't forget the old names, of course, because some of the station families are third and fourth generation now, and all over the maps anyhow.'

'I've noticed – Pages Hill, Clarks Creek.'

'Yep, they're the ones.'

'So, no Carter Range or Knob or whatever?'

I smiled. 'We were latecomers – everything was already named.' I was glad of the question; it gave me a chance to deflect the conversation. 'What about you? Where's your family from?'

'Horsham. That's on the Wimmera, north-west Victoria.'

'Good heavens! You certainly left home then,' I quipped.

'Years back,' he agreed. 'Came to Queensland, liked it and stayed. My grandad had a blacksmith's shop – lots of farm horses to shoe back then – and my dad got his boilermaker's ticket, but I was more into wood. I was apprenticed to a cabinet-maker in Horsham and then'—he shrugged—'I just wandered.'

'Do you ever go back to see your family?'

'Not since Mum died. One of these days, though. I hear from Dad occasionally. He's living with my brother now, and there're plenty of grandkids to keep him busy.'

'No sisters?'

'Nope, just Ben and me. He runs the stock and station agency in Horsham. The Wimmera's farming country, you see.' He hesitated delicately, 'So, your late husband's people – there's just Angus now?'

'That's right. Angus has spoken of a couple of second cousins – his father's brother's offspring – but he hasn't seen them for fifty years. They could be dead. It's why he's so taken with Lisa, of course. And speaking of which . . .'

'Yes.' A vehicle was pulling up across the road. The headlights died and from within the hall children's voices, led by a couple of women, burst into 'Jingle Bells' as I scrambled up. 'Here comes Santa. We'd best go in.'

Greg Banner made his entrance through the supper room, sweating under the white foam beard, a large red sack slung over one plump shoulder. A cheer arose from the children scattered about the bench seats as they all rushed forward to stand before the dais, the littlest accompanied by their mothers. I saw Roseanne urging Lisa, who was hanging back until Angus leant sideways to murmur something. A couple of older station boys were shrugging off attempts to have them join in and remained seated among the men until their names were called. Then they slunk forward, red-eared with embarrassment, to accept their gifts. One boy, I noticed, succumbed to curiosity and opened his, while the other two thrust theirs aside, determined to prove they were beyond such childish matters.

The names were called alphabetically by surname. Bentley therefore was near the head of the queue, but Roseanne waited until Lisa's turn came, then they retired together, flushed and giggling, to open their presents. Reaching the end of his chore, Greg rose to make a speedy departure. The heat must be killing him, I thought. Sally Price, forever the teacher, marshalled the kids into another verse of 'Jingle Bells' as he left, and then the two girls, led by Roseanne, were scampering over to where Flint and I sat, to show off their presents.

'You'll have fun with that,' I said, admiring the box of eye make-up Roseanne held. 'What did you get, Lisa?'

She looked at me, her dark eyes unreadable. 'You don't have to pretend, you know. I'm not a little kid any more.'

'I know,' I said equably. 'I was much younger than you are when I stopped believing in Santa and reindeer. I just didn't want you to feel left out.'

'Thanks,' she mumbled, and then in a burst of candour, said, 'It's better here than with Lily. It's a lovely necklace. Would you do it up for me, Penny?'

'Of course.' She turned her back and I clipped the string of pearls in place. There was something so vulnerable about the thin neck of a child; it looked as fragile and precious as a flower stem, and as easily damaged. As I closed the little catch, I had the sudden desire to hug the girl but patted her shoulder instead. 'There you go.'

I watched them hurry off as the music started up again, thinking that this was something else Michael had deprived me of. We had been married three years but he had always maintained we shouldn't hurry to start a family, but instead make the most of there being just the two of us. I had acceded, thinking it sweet of him to want me all to himself, and never wondered that he was home so little to take advantage of the fact. It only added insult to injury, I thought acerbically now, though I hadn't known then, that when he was away from me, he had been spending the time with his own child.

I had dreamed, as I imagined most young wives did, of a bassinette in a light and airy room, and a chubby toddler's hand in mine. There would be nappies and teething rings and those special breaking smiles as the baby came to recognise my face. And I would be tired and harassed and my body would ache, and I would love my burden more than life itself. Those starfish hands that patted my breast, those tender arms tight about my neck, the little voice that whispered, 'I love you, Mummy.' All those things I had imagined and witnessed with other young women and their babes that I had missed out on and might now never know.

We should put the baby plans on hold, Michael had said, for five years. It would still leave us plenty of time, he had maintained, and the intervening period would be just for us. 'Because, call me selfish, but I don't want to share you yet,' he had murmured with that crinkly eyed, coaxing smile.

I grimaced now, remembering, wondering what excuse he would've invented once the five years were up. Looking back, it seemed obvious enough now that Lisa was the reason he didn't want a child with me.

As deeply as I felt the unfairness of my loss, perhaps it had been for the best. When my world collapsed, wouldn't a child have made matters so much worse? They would've been fatherless too, like me, with no claim to the name of the man responsible for their existence. Illegitimate and Lisa's half-sibling – just how would that have worked out? A little shiver goose-fleshed my arms as Flint's voice broke into my thoughts.

'Do you want to skip this one, Penny? You look a little tired.'

'No, no. It's fine, I'm fine.' I flashed him a smile and pushed at my curls. 'Sorry. I was miles away. We should be going soon, I think. You don't mind? Only Angus must be tired and it's past Lisa's bedtime.'

'Whenever you're ready,' he agreed. 'It's been a good evening. I've really enjoyed it. The music, the company and'—he grinned—'the eats. The women round here sure can cook, and that includes you, Ms Carter.'

'I'll pass the compliment on at the next CWA meeting,' I said. The music swung into a faster beat and couples around us began forming circles. I grabbed his hand. 'Come on. One last go on the floor. It's the Mexican hat dance. Get us into a ring. And after this, my good man, you'll be the one looking tired.'

Chapter Ten

We went to bed that evening to the growl of distant thunder and the intermittent flare of lightning along the horizon. Another day and the dance would never have happened, I thought, and the following morning proved me right. I woke to coolness, to a heavy grey sky and the patter of rain on the iron roof.

'Thank gawd for a day off,' Angus declared, settling onto a verandah chair. 'I ain't goin' out in that. A man'd find himself rusted solid.'

'Why, you think your joints are made of metal?' I asked.

'Times they feel like it,' he retorted, eyeing the broom and bucket I held. 'Where you off to, lass?'

'Hall clean up. I'll be back for smoko. You want to come, Lisa? You don't have to,' I added, heading for the vehicle.

To my surprise she followed. 'May as well. Do you have many dances here?'

'A few each season. Next one's at Easter. Did you enjoy yourself last night?'

She lifted a shoulder self-consciously. 'It would've been

better if I could dance properly. Grandad had to keep telling me when to turn. He said I'd pick it up soon enough, though.'

'I know all the dances, so I could teach you, and Roseanne, if you like,' I said. 'Music and practice, and a bit of space – that's all it takes.' I tossed the broom and bucket onto the vehicle's tray and unlocked the cab. 'Hop in. Oh, wait a bit.' I'd forgotten tea towels. 'There'll be lots of washing up,' I explained on my return, holding them up, 'and sweeping, and mopping. The morning after's always a bit of a drag.'

Sally Price, Sue, and Roseanne's mother, Marlene, were already at the hall, and Roseanne herself arrived on foot a few moments after us, carrying the broom her mother had forgotten. Raindrops dewed her hair like a spray of tiny diamonds, her cheeks were prettily flushed and she was out of breath from running. She was on the cusp of puberty, I thought, and beside her Lisa looked the child she was. The two girls greeted each other and went into a huddle, then Roseanne declared they would wash up.

'That's great,' Marlene said. 'Mind you heat the water well, love. You want me to light the stove?

'*Mu-um!*' the girl protested. 'I'm not a baby.'

'If you're sure.' One of our tasks would be cleaning out the wood stove after last night's use, but there was a little gas camper in the cupboard for just such contingencies as washing up. One day the CWA might afford solar hot water. I said as much and Marlene nodded. 'We can hope. Or the council could do it.'

'Yes . . . I don't think that's likely though. Flint was telling me that Fiona Reilly's trying to get them to fix up the old cemetery, and having no luck.'

'It needs doing,' she agreed. 'If my bones were in that old wreck of a joint, I reckon I'd walk right out. Maybe straight to Bob Page's door to rattle a few ribs at him,' she added. Bob Page was the chairman of the shire council, a pompous, self-satisfied man from Seven Hills Station, who was very loath to spend public money on anything but machinery.

Sue, flushed and perspiring, stopped sweeping to lean on the broom. 'What if we were to do it ourselves – make it our next project, I mean? I expect we'd need council approval, but we could have a plan drawn up and get quotes for the work. Fiona's right, you know. We *should* be looking after our historical sites. Lord knows the whiteants have eaten most of the district's old buildings. There's nothing left of the pub at Captains Creek, for instance, or the fever hospital. As for the old meatworks, what the termites haven't taken the salt has. Nothing lasts unless it's steel or stone.'

'I think that's a wonderful idea,' Sally said. 'Could we do it? Has the CWA the finances for it? What would it cost, anyway? And if we did, wouldn't we need a full-time caretaker for the graves? There's no point weeding unless you keep it up.'

'I should think if we'd done the work and spent the money that the council could take it on,' I said. 'They already pay a man to pick up and mow and keep the centre strips tidy. I expect he'll be looking after the new park too, when it's finished. The cemetery wouldn't be much extra.'

Sue released the broom to clap her hands decisively. 'Ladies, we have a possible plan. I think that's a brilliant use of our resources. I'll raise it at the next meeting. We've, what – close on twenty-five members, counting the station women? One of their husbands can surely take a look at the fence and give us a quote to replace it. Maybe Fiona could organise a working bee from among them to straighten crooked headstones and lift the fallen ones? What do you think? They do the work on the sport's ground for us so they'd probably agree. We should take a look first, I suppose, to see how bad it is before we ask.' She paused to mop her face, plainly bursting with ideas. 'We could plant trees for shade, and Sally, you could draw a plan to scale, couldn't you? Teachers always seem to be able to draw. Just something to take to the meeting for the ladies to study.'

'And so Muriel can't immediately object that we don't know what we're taking on,' I added dryly. Muriel was the member that every organisation has and none of them want, protesting every suggestion and finding endless reasons why whatever was being proposed wouldn't work. Vocal as she was, she also rarely volunteered to clean up after events. 'Or,' I said, not to be difficult but just to raise another option, 'we could spend the money on a solar system for hot water in the kitchen.'

Marlene shook her head. 'To wash up half-a-dozen times a year? That won't help the tourist trade. Or posterity. My vote goes to the cemetery.'

Both Sally and Sue agreed. 'It's a blot on the town the way it is,' Sue said briskly. 'But the meeting can vote on it, Penny, if you think—'

'No,' I said quickly, 'I was just having a Muriel moment. I'm with Fiona – history and tourism every time.' I handed over my broom. 'Here. I'll clean the stove out. No point sweeping the kitchen until the ash has gone.'

*

The Wet, having hinted at its proximity, decided to ease itself into full production. It rained heavily again that evening and then continued in sparkly afternoon showers that fell to the right while the sun was shining to the left, or moody morning mists that turned to a fine, all-day drizzle, interspersed by the occasional downpour. The grass grew exponentially, the ground steamed, the river rose and fell, and every mosquito in Queensland seemed to have migrated to Southbend. Cool, muggy or steaming hot, the days rolled by past Christmas and the new year, while the rainfall total steadily rose.

Flint came for Christmas dinner and a week later I held a New Year's party on the front lawn for half-a-dozen neighbours and friends. Mosquito coils and personal protection having proved inadequate, Angus produced several buckets of smouldering cow dung, which did the trick, though the eye-watering smoke was a trial to all.

'Old bush trick,' he said complacently. 'They had wet seasons back when I was a boy, you know, and there wasn't none of these fancy candles and roll-on stuff then. You made do with what was and, as you see, it works.'

'How's the campaign for the cemetery going?' Flint asked as we hovered on the edge of the smoke, holding our glasses or, in his case, a bottle.

'It's in the works,' I said, 'which is to say it's inching its way along the chain. The CWA's behind it, but the council has still to hear the proposal and agree, and they won't meet again until March at the earliest.' Half the council was drawn from the station folk and we wouldn't see them in town until the Wet was over. 'However,' I said, grinning at him, 'behind every councillor is a CWA wife, so I think it might happen. They've got a couple of months in which to wear them down, so I'm hopeful.'

He shook his head. 'You women. And they say it's a man's world.'

'You have the brawn and power,' I said lightly, 'so we have sneakiness. At the end of the day, things have to balance out somehow, so that's fair enough.'

I had expected a facile answer to my throwaway observation, but he shook his head, his expression unexpectedly serious in the dim light of the coloured bulbs Angus had strung for me. 'I'd have thought you of all people, Penny, would know that fairness doesn't come into it. Life just happens, and there's bugger all we can do to change it.'

'Why?' I asked baldly. 'What has it done to you?' And then in one of those lightning moments of comprehension as my mind leapt from Flint's reference to my situation to his obvious meaning, added belatedly, 'You're married. What went wrong?'

'Not any more. She's gone. We lost our little girl and it put too much strain on us, on the marriage.' He shook his head. 'We were both too young. Alice was only nineteen when Sam was born. She—' He broke off. 'Ah, what the hell,' he said, and lifted the bottle to his lips.

Shocked, I reached to touch his arm. 'I'm sorry, Flint. I had no idea. I—'

He shook his head. 'I'm the one that's sorry, Penny. I dunno why I brought it up. At your party too, for God's sake! It must be the drink.'

'Yes,' I agreed dryly. 'A couple of beers will do that every time. I would never have . . .' I trailed off. 'But it does explain why you're out here – someone with your talent. I have wondered.' It went through my mind then that I didn't even know this man's first name. He had introduced himself to me as Flint and it was what everybody called him.

Now, he shook his head at me, his expression severe. 'Whoa, now. Don't be saying that. Southbend's not a bolthole for failures. That was a lifetime ago and I'm here because I like it. It's a great little town and it's where I want to be. For the peace and quiet and the people—' He slapped at his neck, then looked from his blood-smeared fingers to me and suddenly the old Flint was back. 'And of course the mozzies. Biggest, hungriest models ever made. Can I get you another drink?'

'No, thanks. But I think it's time to bring out the dessert, if you want to help me and the girls carry dishes?'

'Who could refuse?' he said. 'Just lead the way. I'll bet it's delicious.'

After that, the evening went back to normal but later, lying in bed, I puzzled over Flint's admission. It was so unexpected, though tragedy could, of course, visit anybody's life. Perhaps the party and a drink or two had served to bring back memories, causing him to say what I was sure he now regretted. To meet Flint, one would think he hadn't a care in the world. He was capable, kind, possessed of a rare talent – all enviable attributes that cloaked a difficult past. But to lose a child! I wondered what had caused her death. 'Our little girl,' he had said, but how little? Did that make her a baby, a toddler or primary-school age? Not that it mattered, I supposed. No parent would ever get over such a thing, they just learned to cope and it seemed that Alice, his wife, hadn't.

Well, I would respect his confidence as he had mine, and follow his example, because in the end what else could you do? Life did its worst and you picked up your load of sorrow and regret and stumbled on with it, while the trauma slowly receded behind you, although the ache stayed in your heart. Looked at objectively, it was a good thing that the shock of the blow anaesthetised the pain for the time it took one to get one's bearings back. Nature's way of helping the body and spirit cope, perhaps? Flint had apparently learned to do so, but then, I thought, yawning, he'd had longer to deal with it. If Alice had been nineteen, then he probably wasn't much older, maybe twenty? Call it ten or twelve years then, for I'd long since put his age in the early thirties. I was deciding between thirty-two and thirty-four when I fell asleep.

The following Wednesday brought in a dawn with the clouds so low and dark that I slept past my usual six o'clock waking time. It was misting by breakfast, a thin grey veil that spangled leaf edges and clotheslines with silvery drops, but barely wet the already sodden ground.

'Won't be no plane comin' today,' Angus observed. 'You weren't waitin' on the mail, were you?'

'Not particularly,' I said. 'What have you planned?'

'Not much. Might fix that bust downpipe later, supposin' I can find a joiner.'

Angus never threw anything out. Half the shed was filled with what I termed junk and he called spare parts, though I had to admit that occasionally they came in handy. The polythene downpipe had come apart in the last heavy downfall.

Angus had trimmed the broken edges but had not yet joined the two bits together.

'Well, wait till it clears,' I said. 'We don't want you catching pneumonia.'

'From rain?' he scoffed. 'It's a bug, ain't it? Don't worry about me, I'll be right.'

'Famous last words.' I stood up to clear the table. 'What about you, Lisa?'

'I'll help Grandad till Roseanne gets here.'

'Make sure your room's tidy first.'

'Okay,' she said calmly. We had settled into a mostly amicable relationship, and since Christmas she'd seemed to have shed the angst she had displayed on her arrival. I was teaching her to dance, I let her cook, and we talked about things that interested her as I tried to give her the sort of guidance that girls approaching puberty needed. She was respectful, occasionally grateful, and even showed rare flashes of liking me, but her love for Angus was absolute. It was a natural reaction to her only blood relative, I thought, glad for her sake that he was there. Family mattered, and the old man doted on her. Part of me was relieved but I also couldn't help feeling a twinge of hurt to be so plainly superfluous to their mutual fulfillment.

I had finished the dishes and tidied the kitchen before Roseanne arrived, banging on the front door and shouting a cheerful, 'It's me, Miss Carter,' before letting herself in.

'Wipe your shoes,' I called. 'Lisa's out the back.'

I carried on, turning out the contents of the linen chest, which needed tidying and to be checked for mildew. Prolonged overcast weather and high humidity encouraged the growth of mould on linen, cotton, paper and leather. During the Wet, no book or sheet or shoe was ever safe from its presence. I had just decided that it wasn't an issue at present when there came a crash from the back, followed by a startled cry as somebody hit the ground.

I froze where I stood, my heart plummeting, then revving into overdrive at Lisa's panicked shriek of 'Penny!'

Chapter Eleven

'Dear God!' I flew through the back door to discover Angus on the ground with the girls struggling to lift the heavy ladder that straddled his body.

'What happened?' His face was white and screwed into a grimace of pain. I helped heave the weight off him. 'Is it your leg? Your hip? Where does it hurt?'

Lisa was standing very still, eyes enormous and fearful. She was panting for breath, the knuckles of her right hand stuffed hard against her mouth as if to hold back a scream. Roseanne hovered, solemn and still, beside her. Lisa said, 'Grandad?' in a wavery voice, and to me, 'His foot slipped and he grabbed at the ladder and it fell on him. Is he going to be all right, Penny?'

'I'm sure he will be. Come on, Angus. Let's get you up, and see what the damage is.'

I went to lift his arm, but he shook his head, eyes squinted almost shut. He unclenched his teeth and, without moving anything but his hand, flapped it at Lisa. 'It's okay, lassie. I've done me back in, that's all. Just gotta lie for a while.'

I'd seen this before. Like most men of his age who'd

laboured for a living, Angus had back problems. I said, 'Okay, but we have to get you inside. Lisa, can you run and tell Flint what's happened? Ask him to come. And Roseanne, is your dad home? Could you bring him?'

The girls sped off and I crouched beside Angus to feel his legs and ankles, turning them gently for signs of pain. 'You're sure it's just your back?'

'There's no bloody *just* about it,' he snapped. 'But yeah. Felt it go when me foot slipped. Now, see here, Penny, I don't need no doctor and no hospital. Some painkillers 'n' a bed, that's all, and I'll be fine. In time,' he added dourly.

'I know. But,' I said firmly, 'I'm still going to check with the doctor. Ah, this'll be Flint.'

He'd driven over, Lisa sitting anxious in the passenger seat beside him. 'How's it going, old fella?' he asked, coming to squat beside Angus. 'I've brought a board along. You want to try standing, or will we carry you in?'

'Would I be bloody lyin' here if I could get up?' the patient snarled ungratefully.

'That's a no then,' Flint said cheerfully. He looked up. 'Here's Stan. We'll have you inside in a jiffy.'

I hurried in to clear the way and pull the cotton cover off Angus's bed. Luckily the toilet was next to his bedroom. I knew from past experience that he was not a good patient. Last time he'd hurt his back was before the move to Southbend; I'd borrowed a walker from the local hospital to help him shuffle about, and I wondered if the same would be possible here. The town only had an unstaffed clinic to which the flying doctor made monthly visits – wet seasons excepted, of course. Surely, though, it would have such staples as crutches and walkers.

I phoned the doctor while the two men were getting Angus into his room and received the expected advice of Panadol and bed rest. 'Give it a couple of days and check back,' Doctor Branson advised. 'If it's happened before, then your patient will be familiar with the pattern recovery takes. It won't be an overnight fix, but he'll know that.'

Later, with Angus settled, Stan removed himself, declining a cuppa. Leaving Lisa hovering over the patient, I went out to put the ladder away and found Flint up it, fixing the two ends of the pipe in place.

'You shouldn't have bothered,' I protested. 'I wish Angus hadn't either.'

'It needed doing, Penny. First decent downpour and you'd find yourself with a creek under the house, gullying out your foundations. How's the old boy doing?'

'He'll be okay. Lisa's the one who . . . She was absolutely terrified when it happened.'

He climbed down and folded the ladder's A frame flat. 'Understandable. He's her last family member. I mean, if healthy young parents can die without warning, you're not going to think your grandad's immortal, are you?'

'I suppose not. Poor child. I'll talk to her, convince her he'll be fine.'

'Will you be?' he asked bluntly. 'How will you manage, Penny?'

'Oh, easily. There's nothing much *to* manage while it's raining.'

'Well, if anything comes up needing muscle, just give me a call.' His gaze sought mine and held it. 'Promise me you will?'

A little startled by his intensity, I said, 'Yes, of course.

Thank you, Flint. You and Stan are both good neighbours, and I do appreciate it.'

He opened his mouth, then apparently thought better of it, grinned instead and picked up the ladder. 'Must be my boy scout training showing. Okay then, I'll just shove this in the shed. Remember, sing out if you need a hand. That's what neighbours are for.'

Angus's recovery was slow, as the doctor had predicted. It took a couple of weeks and he was every bit as cranky a patient as I remembered. Lisa kept him company playing endless card games, everything from Snap to, I was amused to discover, poker. Once she got the hang of it, she became a ruthless opponent and I frequently saw the bulk of the matches they played for heaped on her side of the wheeled medicine trolley, which, like the walker, was on loan from the clinic.

Angus, shaking a doleful head, would mutter, 'I shouldn't never 'ave taught 'er to bluff.' Which, of course, delighted Lisa.

Flint came to visit, dropping in with a couple of cold beers or a paperback novel and staying to chat, sometimes lingering on the verandah afterwards to ask if I needed a hand with anything. The Wet was his time for his woodwork, when he carved his art pieces or created the high-end furniture that was so popular with the eastern galleries. I had seen his workshop out the back of his home, where an impressive collection of timber milled into slabs was stacked for drying. He had bandsaws, a drill press, something called a router whose purpose I couldn't guess, and even a steam press for curving wood.

We talked the small news of the town, of neighbourly spats and complaints to the council, of the state of the river, the rise and fall of which controlled travel to some properties, and the rain reports from further north and west, whose effects were also felt in the height of the Rainsford. He was interesting company at a time when nothing much was happening, and sometimes spoke of ideas presented to him by each piece of timber he worked. 'You see the potential in the grain,' he explained, 'and you just want to bring it out. Like a shape waiting to happen.'

He'd also started experimenting with enamelling, fishing in his breast pocket one day to show me his first pendant, a smiley face on a round disc of copper. 'Second attempt,' he said. 'Didn't get the heat right first go and the glass rod melted all over the place.' He'd punched a hole in the disc and bent a fine bit of copper into a loop to take a chain. 'I thought maybe Lisa would like it?'

'I'm sure she would,' I agreed, 'and even more if you made another for Roseanne. The pair are at that stage where they share everything.'

'I can do that.' He grimaced. 'Lord knows I need the practice. It's a bit harder than it looks.'

'You'll improve,' I told him. 'And, like anything, there're tricks of the trade. You can buy the findings, you know.'

'The what?'

'The little bits that hold things together, like the loops to string a chain through, and the backings for brooches and earrings, when you get round to them. It's a wonder your workshop didn't cover that.'

He frowned. 'It was more about the chemistry side. And

they were making bigger things anyway – decorative pots and stuff. So how come you're such an expert?'

'Well, I'm not,' I protested. 'I told you, I watched my mother making things, that's all.'

'Ah.' He nodded. 'That's right, I remember you saying. You must've been only a bit of a kid when she died.'

It was on the tip of my tongue to agree and change the subject, but something compelled me to answer honestly – perhaps the fact that he'd been honest with me about his own tragedy. 'She didn't die, Flint, though that's what I was told at the time. I found out years later that she left us. Just got in a vehicle one afternoon and drove away. We never saw her again.'

His brows shot up. 'Drove away where?'

I sighed. 'Here – to Southbend. Bracton Park is thirty kilometres west of the Rainsford. My father found the vehicle down by the river, so she must've met somebody here and gone off with him. That was the theory anyway. Nobody saw her, or noticed the vehicle. Apparently they thought she must've drowned – that's what they told me.' I could still hear our plump cook's motherly voice, shaky with unshed tears. 'Your mother's gone to heaven, darling, to be with the angels, but she'll always watch over you.' Winnie had cooked at Bracton Park for as long as I could remember, which in truth, I reflected now, was probably only four or five years. I had been left in her care that afternoon while my mother drove herself to Southbend. It wasn't far – no distance at all for the bush.

'Back by smoko time,' she'd called, but I was sulking and hadn't answered or even looked up, because she'd said I couldn't go with her. So I had missed out on seeing her one last time. Later, when I'd believed her dead, my behaviour that day had brought me almost as much grief as her absence. I would torment myself by thinking that if I had only looked up, smiled, waved, then maybe she wouldn't have drowned. She'd have thought of me instead and gone straight to the store and returned without stopping at the river bank. How such an accident had occurred, I couldn't imagine, and it was only after I went to live with Aunt Julia that a boy at school asked me straight out what I hadn't known people were thinking.

'Is it true your mum killed herself?'

'She did not!' I had flown at him, too shocked to worry about getting hurt in the scuffle that followed. 'It was an accident!'

And then, when she judged me old enough to know, Aunt Julia told me the truth. Not an accident, not suicide, but the worst of all – abandonment.

Now I looked at Flint and mustered a small smile. 'It's old history. I suppose my father – at least the man I called that – wanted to spare me the truth. Though he was gone too, within the week. Well, I was. He parcelled me off to live with his sister and I haven't seen him since. It was years before I learned what actually happened, that my mother just cleared out and left us.'

He shook his head. 'Penny! You poor kid. What do you mean *the man you called that*? He wasn't your biological father?'

'Apparently not. My parents' marriage wasn't a happy one, and maybe that's why. My mother was afraid of him. Sometimes she'd have bruises, you know, or maybe a swollen face or a sore arm. I heard him shouting at her in the bedroom one night not long before she left. Maybe even that same day – the time's all messed up in my head, so I can't be sure, but perhaps that's what finally drove her away. Anyway, I heard him say it – yell it, really.' I shrugged. 'Then, when she'd gone, his actions made it plain it was true.'

He frowned, hazel eyes abstracted as if, behind them, his brain was busy. 'So, you're assuming she ran off with someone? Who – your real father, perhaps?'

I literally gaped at him. In all my hurtful gropings through the mystery of her disappearance, trying to decide what I had done that was so bad she would leave me without even a goodbye kiss, I had not once considered that. My biological father had never been more than an unspecified shadow in my subconscious. Some children in my position, I knew, wove elaborate stories about their unknown progenitor, determined to find what was missing from their life, but not me. Walter had been a scary enough presence in my life that I had neither imagined what my real father might be like, nor felt the slightest desire to meet him. One experience with fatherhood was enough. For whatever reason he had left her, just as she had left me, and consequently I wanted nothing to do with either of them.

I realised I was staring at him, as I digested the idea. 'Seriously? After nearly ten years – eleven, if you count the pregnancy. Why? I mean, really, Flint, isn't that a bit of a stretch?'

'Well,' he said, scratching his jaw, 'was there someone – a particular friend you can remember? It needn't be a man, you know. If she was afraid of her husband, a woman might have helped her get away.'

'And leave her child? I don't think so. Besides, none of the district women could've just upped stakes and gone for most of a day, which is how long the trip to Hamilton used to take, and that's only one way. They'd have been missed, or seen, either coming or going. You know how hard it is to keep anything private in the bush. People notice and they talk.'

'That's true. Word would've got around. Were the police involved?'

I shrugged. 'Maybe. I don't know. Look, I was nine years old – I daresay I knew less than half of what happened. Only that Walter was more scary afterwards, and Winnie, our cook, kept hugging me and saying it would be all right. She got the rough edge of his tongue too, when she told him what she thought about sending me away.' I sighed, wondering how we'd got this far down a track I'd never wanted to revisit. 'Like I said, it's old history.' I stood, a gesture of dismissal. 'The girls will be back any moment.'

'Yes, I must be off as well.' He rose too, then hesitated. 'You've whetted my curiosity, Penny. You mind if I poke around on the internet a bit, see what I can turn up?'

'Have at it,' I said dryly. 'But I think you'll find that opting out of a marriage isn't very newsworthy.'

Chapter Twelve

That evening, sitting in front of the TV, my thoughts returned to the conversation with Flint, and I wondered why I had been so forthcoming. Not that it mattered – my mother's history was hardly a secret. Everyone in Southbend must have known it, since any newcomers would unfailingly have learned of it from the old hands once I returned to the area. Family stories clung on through the generations. A grandparent's youthful peccadillo was recounted with just as much relish as in the first retelling.

It had to have been known throughout the district that my mother was abused by her husband, though it wouldn't have merited much attention in the seventies, of course. Walter Carter was known as a hard man, as tough in his dealings as he was on his wife, but that was his business. In the bush you had to get along with your neighbours, but you didn't have to like or approve of them. And station life was hard on women, who, back then, often only had basic amenities, little social interaction and weeks alone when their husbands were working away from the homestead.

But that, I thought, was no excuse for what Imogen Carter had done. Running may have been her only option, but why hadn't she taken me? She knew that I was afraid of the man she called my father. He had never touched me, but I had still feared his harshness, his size, his hard stare and the way the little muscles of his jaw worked when his temper was engaged. I had been as wary of him as I would have been a savage dog. She had known this and still she had left me.

'You watchin' this rubbish, Penny?' Angus asked.

'What? Oh, not really.' I glanced distractedly at the screen, where somebody covered in stone dust was dismantling a wall in one of those home makeover shows. 'Switch it off if you want. How's the back tonight?'

'Gettin' there.' He was using the walker and it was the first night he'd made it into the kitchen for his dinner. 'I'm sick of lyin' around.'

'I know. Maybe you could bag and label some of those dead finish seeds tomorrow? I noticed the pods are starting to split.' We'd collected a corn bag full back in October from a bore site on Seven Hills Station.

'Anything,' he said, and cleared his throat. 'You seemed to be havin' a mighty long confab with Flint this arvo. What was that about?'

'Ancient history. I happened to mention my mother and he asked about her, that's all. Angus, you know she ran off with someone . . . Do you suppose – it's just something Flint assumed but – do you think it could have been my real father?'

His look was suddenly fierce under his bushy brows. 'Now why would you be worryin' about such a thing?'

'I'm not,' I denied. 'I never once imagined . . . but the more

I think about the whole scenario, well, doesn't it strike you as odd? When would she have had a chance to meet somebody, let alone hook up with him? And how did they organise her getting away? There weren't any phones back then, just the radio, which'd be an awfully public way to arrange an assignation, don't you think? And they must've been in touch to meet up at the river the way they did. The timing had to be pretty tight, because her vehicle was found that same evening, and she only left home after lunch.'

'It ain't worth worryin' about,' he said. '*He* ain't. He got your mum in the family way and dumped her. Why would you even want to know a man like that?'

'I don't. I never did. It's just a puzzle. I've just never thought about how it could've worked, and now I have, it seems queer, that's all.'

'Ain't nothin' so queer as folks,' he said sententiously. 'And you can pin that in your hat.'

'It doesn't matter, anyway.' I cocked my head. 'Is that rain?' There was a whisper of sound like ghostly footsteps on the tin roof.

'Sounds like it. The sprays off?' Those in the fern house had automatic settings; the rest were controlled manually.

'Yes. I think I'll turn in. You can manage okay?'

'I ain't helpless yet,' he grumped and began the painful business of getting himself upright.

In bed, I stretched luxuriously and lay listening to the hushing sound the light rain made. As a child, the violent storms the Gulf sometimes hosted had scared me, nights when it seemed the roof would lift off with the force of the wind, when rain had lashed the windows like shotgun blasts, and the ferocious cracks of lightning had split the horizon with dazzling light. But the misty benison of gentle rain was different, bringing a sense of snugness, like I was a bird in a nest sheltered by a canopy of leaves. I curled onto my side and slipped easily into sleep, still thinking of that child. And inevitably I dreamed.

'*But I want to come,*' I wailed, tugging at the woman's dress. '*Why can't I, Mummy? Why can't I?*'

'*Not today, Tuppy.*' The old name I hadn't heard since floated naturally into mind. I was Penny the coin, not Penelope as most assumed, and therefore my pet name was 'Tuppence'.

'*But why not?*' I whined.

'*Now, that's enough.*' Her hand touched my cheek and I jerked angrily away. '*It'll just be a quick drive, straight in and home again. You'd be bored to tears. I'll be back by smoko time.*'

I dropped my head sulkily, watching from the corner of my eye as she got into the Land Rover and slammed the door hard. It was the only way to make it catch. The sound boomed like a warning shot and terror suddenly had me by the throat. I forgot my hurt feelings; all I could think of as she waved to me and smiled was that something awful was going to happen.

'*Don't go, Mummy! Don't go!*' I screamed the words and ran as fast as my nine-year-old legs would take me, chasing the dust cloud into darkness that had come from nowhere to overwhelm the bright day. But the vehicle vanished. Its tail light winked as she braked for the gate but though I ran and ran until I felt my heart would burst, my legs got heavier and slower and then the gate and the vehicle were gone, and there was nothing but the sound of my sobbing and a desolate cry of '*Mummy!*' that came out as a whisper as I woke.

*

At dawn there was half an inch in the rain gauge and, the girls said, arriving back mid-morning from a jaunt down to the bridge, another rise in the river.

'Bigger fall upstream then.' Angus looked up from his task of extracting the seeds from their pods. 'Lisa, you want to fetch me them paper bags from the kitchen? In the cupboard by the stove. And could you bring the pegs from the laundry too, lassie?'

'Okay.' She dumped the towel she'd been carrying and returned with the items. 'What are those things?' She picked up a seed, rolling it in her fingers.

'Them's baby trees. We plant some and sell the rest of 'em to the government nursery. Shove a handful of 'em in a bag, that's right. Now, fold the top 'n' peg it. They're dead-finish seeds, so write the name on the bag.'

'Dead finish. You're having me on, aren't you?' Lisa said suspiciously.

'Nope. Cross my heart, lassies, I swear it's true. Some folk call 'em prickly wattle too. Right,' he said approvingly as she wrote it down, 'That's the ticket.' He gave Roseanne a wink. 'You can help too if you want. No charge.'

The girl giggled and agreed. 'We were going to go swimming, but the water's too dirty. Mr McCloud, have you seen that tree trunk high up in the big fig tree by the bridge? Do you know who put it there?'

'The river did,' he said. 'It was carried there in a flood and got caught up in the fork of a branch. When the waters dropped, it stayed there.'

Roseanne's mouth fell open. 'No way! It's metres and metres up.'

'Yep. About the same level as the pub bar, which is where the water got to that year in the flood. Have a look sometime – it's marked on the wall there with the date.'

'Truly?' She cast a glance out the door as if expecting to find us suddenly islanded by a malevolent stream. 'Could it happen again, do you think? Would our shop get flooded?' It was built on the same level as the pub.

'Not unless we get a really bad cyclone,' I interposed cheerfully. 'Because it's been raised up. And even then, I think you'd still be quite safe. Your shop's a lot higher now than it was when the pub flooded. I expect we're all too close to the river really, but back when the town started, everyone looked after their own water so they needed to be near the Rainsford. Anyway, big floods are pretty rare. There was one when I was a little girl. It washed all the stock clean out of the old store. Tins and bottles and washing tubs and tyres – everything was in the river. But that was twenty-five years ago. Probably the same flood that put the tree trunk up in the fig.'

It had been my first school year, so I had been five at the time. I remembered seeing the river banks stripped bare of their pandanus and the bridge barricaded with debris: tree trunks and flood wrack and even the dried-out form of a mummified cow, the hide now wet and sloppy, washed into the river from wherever it had died. I had poked at it curiously with a stick, asking, 'Why's it all stretchy and funny, Mummy?'

'Because it's rotting, Tuppy. That's what happens when things die. Now, come away before you get the smell on you.'

Four years on, when I was told she had drowned, those words had haunted me. However tightly I clenched my eyelids,

I could still see her skin, spongy and soft as it disintegrated in the water. Not my mother at all, just some stinky horrible *thing*, nothing like the image that Winnie had painted of her smiling down on me from a place called heaven.

One hot January day, Southbend received quite unexpected visitors. Unexpected because travellers simply didn't arrive in the Wet, let alone in a horse-drawn conveyance painted over with flowers and with an actual chimney sticking out of its roof.

It was Lisa who spotted it first. She came running into the house, calling, 'Grandad! Penny! Come and see.'

'What is it?' I followed her out to the front verandah, Angus, who no longer needed the walker, stumping along behind.

'Look.' She pointed. 'I've watched and watched. They've been coming forever, like they were swimming through the heat haze. At first I couldn't work out what the horses were. Are they from a circus, do you think?'

'At this time of year? Surely not.' I stared at the painted vehicle with its two horses standing in the shade of the poincianas at the front of the pub. The wagon, if that's what it was, was the length of a fair-sized caravan, though the details were hard to make out through the shimmering air, and were further blurred by the shapes of two more horses standing behind it.

'It's like a little house on wheels,' Lisa said. 'And look, there are the people.' A woman, who sat on the seat at the front, twisted around to face the door-shaped aperture behind her. And the tall thin form of a man was just leaving the pub.

He pulled himself up beside the woman and, a moment later, the rig moved ponderously off, the heads of the front horses nodding as they crossed the street, while the two behind, I saw, were hooked on to the back. The wagon wheeled slowly to the right to head through town.

'Be makin' for the Common,' Angus said as they passed behind the houses. 'Jeez, it'd be forty years since I've seen a workin' wagonette. Wonder what the story is there?'

'What do you call that religious colony in America?' I asked. 'You know, the ones who don't have electricity or cars? The Amish. Yes! Could they be them, I wonder?'

'Looks like travellers to me,' he said. 'I remember 'em from when I was a kid. They used to come round the farms, sellin' stuff, doin' odd jobs.'

'I'm gonna go tell Roseanne,' Lisa said, leaping down the shallow steps. 'Will we get to meet them, do you think? I wonder how long they'll stay.'

'Well, whoever they are they'll be a point of interest for the town,' I observed, watching her thin form vanish down the street. 'It's a strange time of the year to be travelling though. I imagine you can bog a cart just as easily as a car.'

'Wagonette,' Angus corrected. 'A cart's got two wheels. They musta stuck to the main roads and waited on the creeks to run down. Might be lookin' for work, I suppose.'

Lisa eventually returned to say that the strangers had made camp in a paddock out the back of town. They had rigged a tent beside their vehicle and the horses had been turned out to graze, but there was no sign of their owners.

'You could go and visit them, Grandad,' she urged.

'Me? Why?'

Lisa scowled. 'Well, I would've gone and knocked on the door, only Roseanne made such a fuss. Said her mum would kill her. She wouldn't even let me climb through the fence.'

'And a good thing too!' I exclaimed. 'Really, Lisa. Didn't your mother teach you about stranger danger?'

'Of course!' she flared, scenting criticism. 'But it's different out here.'

'It's not. Anyway, people are entitled to their privacy. I'm sure we'll learn all about them before long.'

The following day proved me right for, chatting with Marlene when I dropped into the store for some baking powder, and pausing as always to admire the orderliness of the revamped old building, I learned that the newcomers had been in before me.

'Stan ran them back to their camp,' she said. 'It's an awfully long walk with a bag full of groceries. It took them fifteen days to get here from Goola – can you imagine?'

'So who are they, and why did they come?'

She wrinkled her nose in indecision and pushed at her fair hair, which was falling out of its clip. 'It's a couple and their teenage daughter. As to why they're here, who knows? They look like a couple of hippies fallen out of the seventies, so maybe they just travel, go with the flow as the mood takes them, you know? They're a bit worn looking, sort of used-up. Not too much money, I expect. She had hair to her waist and his was on his shoulders. Both of them brown and skinny-looking. Patched jeans and a long skirt with a rip in the hem. The girl was pretty.'

'Was she? What're their names?' I had learned that questions needed repeating with Marlene. She always had so much to say that the thread of conversation was easily lost.

'Zim,' she said, 'and Fodo. She's Fodo.' She raised her brows, presumably at the unusual name. 'The girl is maybe thirteen. Home schooled, shy. She didn't speak at all. Apparently they've been on the road since she was born.'

'Really? Where are they from, I wonder?'

'He's foreign, quite a thick accent. She sounds English, very posh. But they could be made up, the names – remember flower power and the Summer of Love, when girls were giving themselves names like Misty and Sioux Moon? No,' she added with a laugh, 'I don't suppose you do. Well, I don't either, to be honest, but my mum told me about it and I loved the music.' She hummed a bar of 'San Francisco', then reverted to business. 'Zim's looking for work, asked me to put the word around.'

'What's he do?'

She opened her hands expressively. 'Anything and everything, according to him. Good with horses. He can build and paint and weld. And,' she added, 'I'm pretty sure he mentioned milking cows too. Oh, and curing ham and bacon.'

'I'll bear it in mind,' I said, picking up my purchase. 'See you, Marlene.'

Chapter Thirteen

The following day, I met Zim myself when he came to the nursery, pulling off the cloth hat he wore and giving a little bow as he introduced himself. I hadn't heard his approach but a glance across the garden showed the wagon – wagonette, I corrected myself – pulled up beneath the sign with someone on the seat holding the reins.

His name, he said, was Zim Cilovic – '*Seelovich,*' he pronounced carefully, as if accustomed to people getting it wrong – and he was much as Marlene had described. Thin and brown with ropey arms, greying hair in a ponytail, worn clothes and canvas shoes rather than boots. His eyes were dark, his face lined and weathered. He spoke quickly, his accent thickening the vowels. He was pleased to be in our fine town, he said, and he was hoping to find work.

I shook my head. 'It's not a very good time of the year for work. The stations aren't hiring now, and the council workers are mainly doing maintenance – because of the wet season,' I explained carefully, wondering if he understood about the monsoon. 'All the outside work stops then.'

'But I work inside too,' he said. 'In the shed, in the garden. I fix the motor, mend the door. Anything you need, I do.'

'I'm sorry, I've nothing for you. But perhaps one of the other businesses . . .?'

'Yes. I try them all. I am not lazy man – I like to work. My wife also. She teaches the pupils, she cooks.'

'You could try the pub.' I remembered then that he'd been there yesterday, adding, 'And the council office. I really doubt they'll have anything though. They lay off their outside staff over the Wet. Come, I'll show you where to go.'

I felt sorry for him and wondered if his earnestness hid a desperate need. I hadn't a doubt that in three months' time, when the stations' season began, that he'd find work – his wife too, if she really could cook – but three months was an eternity if your need was immediate. He followed me to the road, nodding at my directions, which I couched as simply as I could.

'Thank you. You are most kind lady. I would buy the little tree for gratitude, but there is no place to put it, you know?' He smiled and I glimpsed a rakish charm that momentarily eclipsed the damage that weather and the years had done.

'That's all right.' I turned to watch him swing himself up onto the wagonette seat where the patient figure holding the reins waited. It was the girl Marlene had mentioned, a slim young thing, as pretty as a picture, with a cloud of dark wavy hair and wide grey eyes. Marlene had called her a teenager and I thought she was bang on – an early developing thirteen, maybe fourteen, with the blessing of unblemished skin. Already her face had the interesting planes of puberty, and small breasts peaked the front of her kaftan type top worn over jeans and sturdy ankle boots. I smiled at her. 'Hello. I'm Penny. What's your name?'

'This be my daughter, Meadow,' Zim said. At least that's what it sounded like, though maybe I had the spelling wrong. She smiled shyly, showing a glimpse of pretty teeth. She would be a stunning young woman, I thought, with those eyes and cheekbones and that gorgeous hair.

Zim clicked at the horses and they plodded forward, broad white faces bobbing as they walked on. The vehicle itself was a work of art, its closed sides and rounded roof of timber painted a rich cream with red and green edgings. The panels that made up the walls of the miniature house were a riot of intertwined flowers and vines that flowed around the sides and back, interrupted only by the front where the driving seat was set before the entrance.

Back inside, I told Angus about the encounter. 'Do you think he's a Romani?'

He shrugged. 'Who knows? Not sure how he'll go for work, but maybe Bev'll put him on at the pub. He's been talking for the last six months about running concrete paths between them new dongas, and puttin' up a shelter roof over 'em. First cyclone'll have it down, of course. But he's pretty good at that, old Bev – talkin'.'

'It's a good idea though,' I said thoughtfully. 'At present, those buildings do look like they've just been dumped there, and the ground's either dust or mud, so a decent path would improve the place. And shade anywhere never hurts.'

'Like I say, he's talking about it. If the labour turns up, he might even do it.' Bev Candle, the local publican, wasn't exactly a go-getter but his wife, Agnes, who was of Chinese and Aboriginal heritage, kept him moving forward. She was rumoured to have a formidable temper and Bev, it was said, knew better than to rouse it. Legend had it that she had once taken a .22 rifle to him, hunting him along the river bank with carefully placed shots designed to miss. Bev had apparently neither reported her misdemeanour nor stepped out of line since, and the business continued to flourish. As the only pub in town, it would be almost impossible for it not to, I thought. It was the heart of Southbend, the first building erected back in the days when the pioneers had carted wool to the now defunct port, and civilisation was so far over the horizon as to be unglimpsable from the lonely north-west.

'Well, maybe Zim'll be in luck, after all,' I said.

Angus had guessed correctly. School began again the following week and by then we had become accustomed to the sight of Zim each morning, jogging past bareback on one of the big bays that pulled the wagonette, on his way to work at the pub. According to Flint he was levelling the ground and boxing in the paths in preparation for pouring concrete. 'Which,' he added, buttering a scone, 'is likely to be held up till God knows when if this cyclone comes in.'

There was a low in the Gulf of Carpentaria that the Met office was following closely. A cyclone watch had been declared and every news bulletin showed the ominous swirl of cloud located north of Mornington Island. It could go east to the Cape coast, or west into the Territory – or it could roar straight south, in which case Southbend was bound to cop it. The temperature had dropped and the heavy skies kept releasing quick little showers that gusted away a minute later, though heavier falls had been recorded upriver and the Rainsford had risen accordingly.

We could only wait. Angus plodded about, securing loose items in the yard and fixing extra tie-downs to the corners of the shadehouses. If the eye of the storm came through, it would probably strip the foliage from most of our plants, but flooding wouldn't be a problem. Only the largest planters stood on the ground and, while they might be toppled, their weight should prevent them being swept away. And plants were resilient; given time they'd recover. In any event, there was nothing we could do about it.

In the meantime, Lisa had her way and she and Roseanne had contrived to meet Zim's daughter. I had seen them pass in the street, the three heads bent together, the two girls apparently conducting their new acquaintance on a tour of the town.

'Her name's Meadow – like, you know, a field,' Lisa informed me. 'She's nearly fourteen and her mum used to be a teacher. Her dad grew up in some country in Europe. Bose or Bosie – something like that. He's been out here forever though.'

'Bosnia?' I suggested.

'That's it. Oh.' Her eyes narrowed in sudden comprehension. 'That place on the news where the war is now?'

'Uh huh. So, nearly fourteen – Meadow must be in high school then?'

'Yeah.' Lisa rolled her eyes. 'And before you start, she *is* doing school, Penny. Her mum used to be a teacher, in America. Then she met Zim and came to Australia with him.'

'Teacher, eh? A good career if you're moving about a lot,' I said. 'Hairdressers, cooks, teachers – they can always find work.'

Abruptly, Lisa asked, 'What's going to happen with me next year? I can't do high school here.'

'We'll figure something out,' I said, having no idea what. 'Will Roseanne be boarding?' Most of the north-west's youth attended boarding schools in Charters Towers.

She shrugged. 'I suppose. There's nowhere else, is there? I'd sooner get a job.'

'And to do that, you need an education.' We'd had this talk before.

'Yeah, yeah. Or I could just plant things like you do.' She shot me an uncomplimentary look. 'Dead easy. You don't need years of dopey school for that.'

'But you do for the bookwork involved in the business. Damn,' I said, pausing our conversation. A heavy shower was sweeping towards us across the roofs of the town. 'Quick, help me get the washing in. It's nearly dry.'

The shower passed. I folded the towels and put the dry ones away and by then Lisa had gone too. Flint came by, knocking the fresh mud from his boots before dropping into a chair on the verandah. His shirt was damp and the fine hair on his forearms misted with droplets.

'You all set for a blow?'

I shrugged. 'I think we're as prepared as we can be. Nobody's ever cyclone proof. What about your place?'

'All locked down. I could nip up and check your roof and gutters, if you want. I've re-screwed mine, just to be on the safe side.'

I hesitated. It was something neither Angus nor I could do, and he was offering, but I didn't want to put him out. However, he took the decision out of my hands.

'I'll get the ladder and fetch my drill.'

The clump of his boots overhead and the whine of the drill eventually brought Angus into the kitchen where I was browning meat for a casserole. 'What the hell's all that racket? Who's up on the roof?'

'Flint. Doubling up on the screws. Were you napping?'

'Resting me eyes,' he said with dignity. He scanned the heavy blanket of clouds beyond the window. 'If that lot drops its load, we'll want a bloody boat, not a roof. Where's Lisa?'

'Out somewhere. She and Roseanne have made friends with Zim's daughter.' Another light shower blew over and I filled the kettle. 'Go tell Flint I'm putting smoko on. He'll be getting soaked up there.'

'Bit of water never hurt nobody,' Angus grumbled, which was quite a reversal from his former stance, but he went anyway. I turned the gas down and added the vegetables, thinking that I should also cook the slab of brisket in the freezer. If we lost power it would keep longer without refrigeration than dishes made of fresh meat. We had a rainwater tank but it wouldn't harm to fill a few vessels with water as well. Tanks, even full ones, could be damaged. And one thing was certain, the town water would be undrinkable, and that was supposing the council didn't pull all the pumping equipment from the river once the flooding started. If they did, the town would be waterless. That there would be a flood, I had no doubt. Lisa had already reported that the bridge was under water and the cyclone hadn't even made landfall yet.

I carried the tray out to the verandah just as the girls came pelting down the road in front of a heavy shower. Laughing and panting, they hurtled up the shallow steps and I saw that Meadow was with them, hanging back a little as if unsure of her welcome.

'You just made it,' I said. 'Hello, Meadow.' I had to raise my voice as the rain thundered on the tin roof. 'Lisa, would you bring some glasses and the jug from the fridge? I expect you could all do with a drink. There're more cakes in the big tin – you can bring some of them too. And, Roseanne, do you want to get the extra chairs from the kitchen? I'm sure Meadow will help you.'

Murmuring assent, they left as Flint sprinted to join us, wet as a drowned duck. He bent to unlace his boots, saying cheerfully, 'Just finished that in time and no mistake.'

'Yeah. I'd say this lot's good for an inch or more,' Angus agreed. Metric measurements didn't exist for him.

'You want a towel?' I made to rise but Flint shook his head and I subsided again as the girls trooped out with their burdens. He looked up with a smile of greeting that froze on his face and the hand he had raised to wipe the moisture from it fell, as limp as a puppet with its string cut.

He said hoarsely, 'Who . . .?' He'd gone as white as a sheet and I saw the movement in his throat as he swallowed.

Alarmed, I said, 'What's wrong? Are you okay, Flint?'

He nodded, dazedly. 'Yeah. Fine. I just . . . Sorry, Penny.' He looked at Lisa. 'So, you have a new friend?' His colour was coming back, but he breathed as if he'd been winded.

'She's Meadow,' Lisa said proudly. 'Isn't that the coolest name?'

'Unusual,' he agreed.

'Meadow Cilovich,' the girl said politely. 'How do you do?'

'*And* she lives in a wagon,' Lisa interrupted with an air of triumph, as if inviting him to beat that.

'I've seen it,' he replied. 'Nice to meet you, Meadow. I'm Flint. That's my shop across the way.'

She gave a shy smile. 'I know. The girls said. They been showing me around.'

'That's nice. So where're you from?'

'Everywhere. We go all over.' The dark hair rippled about her face as she lifted her head. 'And I do do school. My mum's a teacher.' Plainly it was a question frequently asked of her.

'Well, sit down, Meadow.' I gestured at the glasses and plate of extra cakes. 'Help yourself. Your father knows about the cyclone, doesn't he – that it's likely to affect us, I mean?'

She nodded. 'The man at the pub said. But we'd already heard it on the radio. I've never been in a cyclone before.'

'Well, it ain't somethin' to be wished for,' Angus said. 'Look at what happened to Darwin.'

'A couple of decades ago,' I reminded him. 'A bit before their time, Angus.'

He shrugged. 'Just sayin'.'

The girls finished their refreshments, thanked me and took themselves off to Lisa's room while the rain continued to thunder down, bending the tree foliage with its force and spreading pools of water in the yard. Angus pottered off to his current task and Flint eyed the downpour and then his wet boots.

'Wait till it stops,' I urged. 'Are you sure you're all right?' He had hardly spoken after his few words to Meadow and his ready smile was still missing.

'I'm fine. It was just the shock,' he said. 'Zim's girl – she's the living image of Alice, my wife. As she was, I mean. She was about sixteen when we met for the first time, and for just a moment it was like seeing her ghost.'

'Meadow's thirteen,' I said, 'but I'll grant she looks older. So you grew up together, you and your wife? She must've been very pretty.'

'She was beyond pretty, plain beautiful. We were just kids when we met. I was only a year older and I fell for her like a ton of bricks – me and half the boys in the district. We got married when she turned eighteen.' He shook his head. 'God, you think you're so bulletproof at that age! There's no way to guess where you're heading and you wouldn't believe it if someone told you.'

'I'm sorry,' I said, without knowing the cause, though I remembered him saying she'd left him. 'What happened?'

'We lost our little girl.' He drew his hands down his face, pulling the skin taut over his cheekbones, and I saw the deep sadness in his eyes. 'Well, I told you that. She was just two years old, the image of her mother.' He gave a bark of laughter. 'Parents say that, don't they? I mean, she had Alice's hair and her eyes, but who can tell how that would have changed as she grew? Maybe more like me? She'd be twelve now, my little Samantha. But we lost her, and Alice . . . Alice couldn't cope. There was hope at first, but once that was gone she killed herself.'

I gasped in horror, but something wasn't making sense. There couldn't be hope if the child had died – and then a memory burst, like a shell, in my head. 'You're talking about Sammy Flint! Little Sammy was *your* daughter?' It had been a media frenzy for weeks, the child snatched from her stroller in a busy supermarket and never heard of again. Her mother turning her back for less than a minute as she paid at the checkout. 'Oh, Flint, I'm so sorry! I never connected it to you because you were always just "Sammy's father" in the media.'

He nodded wearily. 'I don't advertise the connection. It's the easiest way to escape the press. They always want to bring up the past – the first anniversary, then the fifth and the tenth . . . With unsolved cases, that sort of thing can run on forever.'

'So the police never found who took her?'

'Some paedo.' He closed his eyes briefly. 'They told me afterwards that she was probably dead within twenty-four hours. That's the pattern, apparently, with very young children. I think in her heart that Alice must've guessed it too.' He shook his head. 'My poor little love. She was never very strong.'

'That's so dreadful!' No wonder he'd moved from wherever he'd – they – had lived and wound up in the back of beyond at Southbend. Or that he called himself only by his surname. He was right about the media. They exploited tragedy the way vultures did carrion. It was plain that hope no longer figured in the equation; ten years on, he had accepted his loss, for he hadn't said that his daughter was missing but that she was gone. Vanished, irrecoverable, never to be returned to him. An event like that would hang a shadow over your life forever, so how, I wondered, did one ever find the strength to surmount it?

Hesitantly I said, 'You don't believe there's any chance she's still out there? That somebody took her because they just wanted a child to love? It is possible, you know.'

'No.' His tone was definite. 'In the beginning I did – I clung to it. I was like a madman, peering into strollers, following women with young children. It's a wonder I didn't get myself arrested. But the police didn't encourage the theory – and they're the ones with the experience.'

'It *could* happen though. It has before.' I was surprised to find myself so invested in convincing him. 'Your little girl might still be out there with a false name and a fake family—'

'Don't, Penny.' The words and the harsh tone stopped me in full flow. He sighed and shook his head. 'Sammy's gone. Even if she was out there, as you put it, and that's a pretty big if, she's still gone. She was two. How would I recognise her ten years on? And how would she remember me? It's best to just let it go.'

The conviction in his voice silenced me. We sat there while the rain drummed on the iron roof, falling so forcefully it overshot the gutters. Inside, Lisa's door must have opened for I heard one of the girls laugh and winced on Flint's account. His face looked weary all at once, older and full of regret.

He raised his hands, palms up. 'Shit happens,' he said. 'That's life. You can't change the past, so the only thing to do is to accept it and move on.'

Chapter Fourteen

The downpour continued through the afternoon and into the night. It rattled monotonously on the roof and sheets of water cascaded across the yard. At nightfall I went out, shrouded in an old greatcoat of Angus's, to check the shadehouses, righting pots that had fallen over and moving others from beneath the direct overflow of flooded gutters. The slippery black soil clung to my shoes like glue and the shadecloth bowed under the weight of the deluge.

At news time the TV screen showed only speckled dots, but the radio, between bursts of static, told us that Cyclone Fern had crossed the coast and was heading into the Gulf Country, where the little township of Southbend lay directly in its path.

'Sounds like we're in for it,' Angus said gloomily.

'It might break up yet. They do, sometimes, once they get ashore,' I said hopefully. 'On the bright side, we'll not be watering anything for a bit. So that's money for nothing.'

'Yeah, well, maybe that'll pay for some of the damage it's gonna cause,' he grumped.

Dawn came in grey and cold. Lisa arrived rugged up at the breakfast table, her eyes bright with interest. 'Holy cats, Penny! It teemed *all* night. Have you seen the yard?'

'I know, it's a bit wet. More to come I'm afraid.' Outside, the wind had developed a whine and the brown water running down the bitumen was dotted with torn-off twigs and leaves. 'I think you'd better stick at home today.'

She shivered. 'It's too cold out, anyway.' A booming noise sounded and we both rushed to the window to watch a loose oil-drum bowl past, its impetus slowed by the water. I heard a distinct creak from the poinciana by the gate and eyed it, mentally chalking it up as our first likely damage. They were brittle trees and it was very top heavy just now, with its summer foliage.

I rubbed the goosebumps on my arms as I turned back to the table. 'Listen to that wind.'

It got worse as the day progressed, a shrieking gale that hurled the rain like shrapnel against the house, which seemed to rock on its foundations. Odd wind gusts blew water in through the front door, but it was important not to seal the place, Angus said. 'Gotta equalise the pressure, see, or she'll lift the roof. An' keep away from them windows, in case they blow in.'

I was happy to obey. The power was still on, and so far we had water, but it would only be whatever was in the town's reserve. The pumps must have been pulled from the river bank by now, for the river itself had become visible in brief glimpses between the cascading rain that blotted everything from sight until an extra strong gust blew it horizontal. The surging brown waters had reached the top of the dip that led down to the bridge, which put it about ten metres from the pub's back lot and, I calculated, maybe five over the bridge itself.

'That last group of trees we planted will be under water,' I fretted. 'And probably washed out of the ground by now.'

'We can't do nothin' about it, lass.' Angus switched on the light, dispelling the gloom, and snapped the pack of cards in his hands. 'Who's for a game of euchre? Help pass the time.'

The rain just kept coming. 'It's like a cloudburst,' Lisa said later in an awed tone, as she watched the brown torrent surge across the yard beneath the house. One of the corner posts on the biggest shadehouse had partially collapsed, its footing undermined by the relentless current, dragging the shadecloth down across the young trees. 'I hope Meadow and her family are okay,' she added anxiously as a sheet of iron, torn from somebody's roof, fled past. 'And the horses. They've got no shelter, poor things.'

'They'll be right,' Angus comforted. 'They'll get into the trees an' turn their rumps to the blow an' wait it out.' To me he added quietly, 'I dunno 'bout that wagonette, but. She'll catch a lot of wind with them high sides.' He didn't add what we both knew – that the tent would be long gone.

The room rocked to a particularly vicious blast that came with a roar like a freight train, and I gulped in fright trying to stay calm. If this continued, the tent mightn't be the only casualty. And, as if the thought had caused it, a mighty crash sounded from the front yard and I knew that my earlier prediction had come true. The poinciana's roots had been torn from the sodden soil and the great mass of the tree was down, crushing the gate it had fallen across in a welter of snapped branches and smashed greenery.

Then the lights went out.

'Right.' Angus squinted at the clock. 'S'only five, but I reckon we should eat, Penny. While we can still see what we're feedin' our faces.'

'Good idea. And no showers tonight, because the water'll be next to go.' We had a stock of candles and a torch for emergencies, but who knew how long before the power would return? That depended on what the cyclone had damaged to cause the outage and whether it was replaceable. Southbend wasn't on the grid; the town made its own electricity and was responsible for its own repairs.

The evening wore on with more ferocious windblasts rocking the walls. The rain torrented down and it grew colder. We rugged up and I lit a candle, but the shifting airs in the house continually snuffed it out until I found an empty pickle jar and fixed the candle inside it. The light it threw was dim but better than total darkness.

'There, that's better.' I put my arm around Lisa, who sat between us on the couch. 'What do you think – bedtime?'

'Can't we just stay here a bit longer? I'm not tired yet. And it's sort of cosy with the light.'

She was frightened and I couldn't blame her. But there was strength in company. I said, 'Do you want to sleep in my room tonight? It'll save on candles.'

'Could I?'

'In a little while then. Listen.' I sat up suddenly. 'What's happening?'

'Wind's droppin',' Angus said. The dreadful roar that had filled the world was easing at the same time as the heavy thunder on the roof lightened off.

'Is it over?' Lisa asked.

'Nope,' Angus said. 'She'll be back. Where's the torch, lass? I'll just nip out an' see how it's lookin'.'

'Well, get a coat first, and the gumboots. I don't want you catching your death.'

When the wind stopped I took the opportunity to light another candle, and Lisa and I shifted her mattress onto the floor of my bedroom. I went around the darkened rooms inspecting the windows for leaks and found none. The verandah chairs, which I'd forgotten about, had blown away, but I could look for them tomorrow. A light was bobbing up the road towards us and presently, through the rush of water, Flint sang out from the street.

'Penny, Angus! You okay?'

'We're fine,' I called, lifting the bottled candle. 'Mind out, there's a tree down over the gate.' I heard him swear, then the sounds of a struggle, and eventually he came wading through the debris of branches up to the verandah. He wore boots and a yellow oilskin, but his head was bare.

'How're you doing?'

'We're okay. Angus is checking out back. I think we've lost a shadehouse. What about your place?'

'Satellite dish has gone, but the rest is okay.'

'I never thought of that,' I confessed. 'Maybe ours has too, because the TV wasn't working. I just thought it was the storm. Look, come in, I'll make some coffee. Lord knows how much rain we've had. I'd have put out a bucket, only it would've blown away. The gauge must've been overflowing for hours.' I cocked my head suddenly. Now the wind had stopped, it was like my hearing had returned. 'What's that noise?'

'The river,' Flint said grimly. 'I'd reckon Bev and his missus are getting the pub stools up on the counter about now. And anything else they can lift as well.'

Lisa ghosted to the door and was caught in the edge of his torchlight. He said kindly, 'How's it going, kiddo? You okay?'

'It was awful.' Her voice shook. 'I thought the roof would blow off. Is it finished now, Flint?' Her voice begged for him to say it was, but he shook his head.

''Fraid not, but you're safe here with Penny and Angus. I screwed that roof down myself and I guarantee she won't be lifting.'

'Thank goodness you did,' I said with a smile. 'You'll have coffee?' To Lisa I added, 'I think there might be half a packet of marshmallows in the fridge door. Have a look and I'll make you some chocolate.'

Angus came back in then, shedding his coat in the laundry and shaking the wet from his hair. 'How's it looking?' I asked, bringing him a towel.

'A right bloody mess. All the shadecloth's been ripped off the shadehouses and the big 'un's collapsed. Trees an' pots all over the bloody place, an' the shed roof's mostly gone.' He spoke with a sort of weary relish in an effort, I thought, to counteract dismay.

'Oh dear.' I grimaced. 'Well, there's nothing we can do about it right now.' I mentally ran over the contents of the shed where, apart from the vehicle and Angus's tools, we kept our nursery supplies. They were bagged in heavy-duty plastic and should survive a drenching – save for those already opened. A light patter sounded on the roof, growing steadily in volume as we consumed coffee and cake at the kitchen table in the flickering candlelight.

'Good idea,' Flint said, nodding at the jars.

'Yes, well, maybe I'll get a pressure lamp for next time.' Rain, sounding like hail, rattled against the window and the wind was working up to its earlier fury.

Flint stood up. 'Here it comes again. I'd better get back.'

'Don't leave us, Flint,' Lisa begged, just as I said impulsively, 'Why don't you stay? You'll get soaked if you go out now. You can have Lisa's room, because she's camping in with me tonight.'

He looked down at the child and, catching his eye, I nodded over her head. She obviously felt more secure with him here, which I supposed was normal in the absence of the man who would have been her natural protector.

'Well, if you're sure,' he said. 'I'm actually not that keen on another drenching.' His glance suddenly took in his boots and the mud he had tracked across the floor, bringing a look of comic dismay to his face. 'God! I'm sorry, Penny. I never thought—'

I took up the candle. 'A bit of mud's neither here nor there right now, so don't worry about it. I'll just get this young lady settled and be right back and we'll work out something for you.'

In the absence of a mattress, this turned out to be the large cushions off the couch and all my spare blankets.

'That's fine,' Flint said, when we'd piled them into a broadly rectangular shape on the floor. 'Many's the time I've slept on worse. Waking up with a stiff neck in front of the computer, for instance. Which reminds me, Penny.' He sat on the bedding and patted the space beside him. 'You got a minute?'

'What is it?' I perched beside him, the candle jar on the floor between us, the shadows flickering over the damp hair on his shoulder. 'You should have a towel to dry your hair.'

'It's fine,' he said. 'I've been meaning to tell you, I did a bit of browsing on the net. You were right – there's nothing about your mum, but what is interesting is just how many people have died suddenly or vanished over the years from this neck of the woods. Somebody compiled a list. There were four disappearances that were never explained and during the same time, another four blokes killed themselves.'

'Really? That seems a lot. Over how long a period?'

'Oh, they go well back – thirty-odd years. The first to disappear was Sven somebody, a Swede. Apparently he took a shortcut walking through the Big Scrub on Seven Hills Station. They never found his body. Next one was some stockman on Rainsford Downs, Harry Lucas. That was twenty years ago. An accident of some sort, the report said. Searchers found his horse but not him; happened in the ranges somewhere, so pretty rough country, I'd imagine.'

'Hang on.' Closing my eyes, I tapped my forehead. 'I think I heard something about that. Wasn't he a headstockman? Thought to have perished?'

'The site wasn't big on details, so I'm not sure,' Flint said. 'After that there were a couple of shootings. A bloke went crazy in the pub and they found him the next morning down by the river. He'd blown his brains out. And some station owner offed himself as well. Then there was the young nurse, Colleen . . .' He scrubbed his chin. 'I forget the surname. Her case was a bit like your mum's. She'd been working as a cook at Mount Ixion and left one day to drive to Hamilton, but never arrived or returned. Nobody ever saw her again.'

'If she was a nurse, why was she working as a cook?'

Flint shrugged. 'Who knows? Wanted a change, or a bit of adventure, maybe? There was a police investigation but they never even turned up her vehicle, which was a bit odd. If she'd broken down and started to walk to look for water, say . . . But the vehicle – it was a Land Rover – should still have been found. The consensus was she must've changed her mind and turned off into the Territory at Camooweal, instead of heading south to Hamilton. That was just a few months before your mum went. Then some grader driver hung himself at Skopje's Hut on Seven Hills, and a druggie overdosed on a trawler out in the Gulf about ten years ago. They brought the body in and flew it to Hamilton, so whoever was compiling the list counted him in too.'

'Well,' I said, 'it's interesting, and maybe a bit unusual considering how small the population is out here. But it's probably on a par with the rest of the country. People do kill themselves, and sometimes they get lost and perish, and if a body wasn't found before the Wet came, it probably never would be. And all this was on the internet? Why? I mean, who put it there?'

'God knows. Just about anything you want to know is there to be found if you look long enough. As to who does it – search me.'

'I can't imagine having the time even if I knew how to do it.' I rose, picking up the candle. 'I hope you'll be comfortable. Lisa's asleep, so if you'd really rather your own bed . . .'

'And go out into that?' He cocked his head and for a moment we listened to the roar of wind and rain. 'I'll be fine. Off you go, Penny. I'll see you in the morning.'

'Goodnight, Flint.' Carrying the candle before me, I went.

It was a long night. I dozed and woke, each time hearing the roar of the wind until the sound lulled me again into sleep. The rain continued, lightening off towards morning and by the time the first grey light crept through the window, it had finally stopped. Leaving Lisa sleeping, I dressed, had a quick wash and went out under a louring sky to discover just how bad things were.

Flint was there before me. I found him out the back righting the heavy pots that had blown over. Their contents were in a sad way, branches crushed on some, foliage completely gone on others; in some cases the pots themselves had split or the soil washed out. Most of the smaller plants were in the mud, the two ruined shadehouses stark as skeletons in the grey morning. The shed rafters gaped at the sky, their buckled sheets of iron decorating the street a block away. Lifting my gaze beyond the fence, I saw stripped trees, damaged houses and a trampoline frame wrapped incongruously about a power pole. Water lay like a blight on the land, filling the road verges, pooling in yards, covering lawns.

'Morning,' I called as Flint looked round. 'How's the river?'

'High,' he said. 'The pub's surrounded, cemetery's under, and the main road into town is flooded. I've been out along it to check. I'd guess Cutaway Creek has breached its banks higher up. The river's still rising. Not by much. Be worse downstream though, with the water from Cutaway coming in.'

'And the Manning,' I reminded him, but the junction of that creek was ten kay further downstream. Cutaway, which ran only in the Wet, joined the Rainsford right on the northern edge of the town.

'Yeah.' He rumpled his hair as he gazed around. 'It looks bad at first glance, Penny, but nothing we can't fix. Shed roof's easy. We can bang the iron back into shape and screw it on. Might leak but that can be patched. You're going to need new shadecloth, but a bit of work'll see the frames right again. As for the plants, well, you'd know best, but I reckon a lot of 'em will recover. And you've still got your sat dish. Probably needs aligning before you'll get reception though. Then there's the tree out front and your gate – nothing really major. Oh, and I've checked the power lines. They seem okay, though the head's been blown off the pub's windmill.'

'I don't think they use it any more. And it's thanks to your foresight that we still have a roof,' I reminded him. I glanced across at the corner where the torn leaves of the strelitzia flapped in the breeze. 'Your plant made it through. How's your place?'

'Pretty much okay. Trees down, of course, and junk everywhere – not mine. There was a toilet seat blown onto the verandah, if you can believe it.'

I laughed, the sound strange against the background murmur of moving water. 'Weirder things have probably happened. How did you sleep last night? Those cushions can't have been too comfortable.'

'They were fine. How's Lisa?'

'Still out to it. She was terrified, poor child. Thank you for staying, I think your presence reassured her.' I tilted my head as a cupboard door banged in the kitchen. 'That sounds like Angus is up. Breakfast's on the way.'

'I'll bring my chainsaw after,' he promised, 'and we'll get that tree off your gate. I imagine there'll be plenty of work for it elsewhere too.'

'First things first,' I said practically. 'And that's food.'

Chapter Fifteen

We were halfway through breakfast when a clatter of hooves interrupted it. I said, 'What in the world . . .?'

The others followed me in a rush to the front door just in time to see Zim flying past bareback on one of his bally-faced bays. The horse's heavy legs and large feet sent the spray flying wherever the bitumen dipped enough for water to have collected, but the rider looked fixedly ahead, only veering off the road to jolt to a stop outside Flint's Place. He was yelling something we couldn't make out as he dropped the reins and vaulted the fence, heading for the front door.

'Hoy!' Flint jumped off the verandah and jogged into the open, waving his arms and yelling, 'Over here! Zim!' The man's head whipped around and a moment later he was scrambling back onto the bay, driving him headlong towards us.

'He's lookin' for you,' Angus observed. 'Something's up.'

'I never woulda guessed,' Flint said dryly. 'Question is, why?'

That became obvious the moment Zim arrived. Dismounting in a rush, he ploughed through the wreck of the poinciana as if it wasn't there, heedless of the branches tearing at him. Arriving at the foot of the steps, the words poured from him. 'Mr Flint, you have the boat. Please, you have to help! My daughter – she is in the water. Carried off. Me, I cannot swim. For the love of the good God, you help me please?' He was desperate, his voice choked with tears.

'Take it easy, mate,' Flint said. 'Of course I'll help. What happened?'

The explanation came in a frantic rush. 'She finds the horse to ride him home, but he is too close to the bank and it . . . Whoosh!' He waved his arms to simulate a cave-in and sobbed again. 'I see them in the water, I hear her scream and I run but she is gone and the horse. Swept away, and you are only man I know has boat so I come. We must go now. Now! Before she drown.'

'Can Meadow swim?' I asked.

'Yes, yes, but hurry! Water is fierce, strong. She is only weak girl. Please, we go now!'

'Right.' Flint gave a peremptory wave of his arm. 'Come on, then. We'll need the tinny and the outboard. This happened in Cutaway – the creek near where you're camped?'

'Yes, yes. Is big water. Black banks – they crumble, they fall.'

'You'll need an extra hand to steer,' Angus said. 'I'll come.'

'You will not!' The thought of him bouncing around in rough waters horrified me. 'I'll do it. No argument, Angus. You'd probably injure yourself just getting into the boat. Go, Flint! Pick me up on your way past.'

Fifteen long minutes later, the three of us were manhandling Flint's tinny into the turgid waters of Cutaway

Creek. The boat, fortunately, had already been on its trailer and, leaving the bitumen at the Common boundary, Flint had put the Toyota in low range four-wheel drive and gunned it across the short distance to the creek's side at such a speed that it hadn't had time to bog down, although it sank deeply into the sodden soil the moment we stopped.

Fodo, whom I had yet to meet, was waiting there when we arrived, pacing and wringing her hands, her state bordering on hysteria. It was with difficulty that I stopped her climbing aboard too. In the end, Zim had yelled at her in his native tongue and she'd burst into tears but obediently stepped back.

'Look,' I said hastily, throwing the blanket and towels I had snatched up into the boat, 'go to the shop. You know Marlene there? Wait with her. We'll come back there when we've got her.'

There was no time for more. I slid down the greasy bank, grabbed Flint's hand and was hauled into the rocking boat. He lowered the engine, started it, spun the prow to face downstream and we were off.

Looking out from the boat, my heart sank. I hadn't had time to notice until then how wild the water looked. It roiled past, high, fast and dirty brown, crowned with tannish-coloured foam and with the occasional branch bobbing into view in the current. We barely needed the outboard's power as we were whipped along in the grip of the stream. I had never appreciated quite how wide a creek Cutaway was and doubted that any swimmer, let alone a child, could survive in the rush and volume of its waters.

Zim sat rigidly beside me while Flint steered. He scanned the banks, one clenched hand moving to the motor's beat, his gaze wild and frantic.

'We should spot the horse,' Flint muttered and I understood the unspoken message that we were very unlikely to find an unconscious body in waters as muddy as these. Meadow had drowned, I thought – she must have. At the barest minimum she had been in the water more than half an hour, and a person could drown in what – three minutes? She might not even have survived the initial immersion if the horse had fallen on top of her. All four of Zim's animals were big brutes. I hoped Flint wasn't going to take us beyond the junction into the Rainsford itself. Cutaway was barely manageable but taking on the Rainsford in flood would be grabbing the tail of a tiger. It—

'There! There! Look, is horse!' Zim started to his feet, pointing, and the boat swayed alarmingly as I grabbed his arm and hauled him back down.

'Got it,' Flint said tersely. 'Sit, mate! Don't stand.' He leaned on the tiller and the boat swung sluggishly, fighting the current to angle across to the left, where a horse lay supine on the greasy bank with someone kneeling beside it. My heart leapt before I'd consciously noted the figure was too large to be Meadow. It was a woman though, doing something with a rope. I was shocked to see we had come already to the northern reach of the town and I was looking at the back lot of the fuel depot. Which made it Muriel Lacey with the horse. A tractor idled somewhere behind her and, as we watched, chugged slowly into view, its big wheels making heavy weather of the mud.

'Meadow?' Zim shouted.

Seeing us, Muriel stood up. 'What's up?' she called loudly. '*Penny*, is that you?'

Flint's voice cut through the chug of the engine and the subdued roar of water. 'Have you seen the girl? She went into the water with the horse.'

Muriel shook her head. 'No. Just him. Saw him in the water, then he washed up here. He's about done, just made it to the bank. Gotta get him on his feet – creek's still rising – dangerous!' she shrieked, as if telling us something we didn't already know.

We didn't wait for the rest. The water had already widened in line with her news. Cutaway had broken its banks here so that the junction of the two waterways, which lay just ahead of us, had broadened to include a section of pandanus and young river figs. We swept down towards them at a shocking pace, my fear mounting with every passing metre. There were falls not all that far downstream. The flood waters would have levelled them now but in normal times they presented a wall of white water with some quite nasty rocks below. I didn't see how Flint could stop the boat unless he steered it towards the line of flooded timber, which might help stem the pull of the current. I stared at them, calculating our chances, for even Zim, it seemed, had now grasped the danger and was gripping the side of the boat with whitened knuckles.

And that's when I saw the girl. I blinked, looked again to be certain, then cried out, pointing. 'There! In the pandanus, Flint! It's her.'

The sodden bundle was indeed Meadow, barely conscious and lodged firmly in the tangled trunks and branches of the saw-toothed pandanus, which she must have grabbed at, or been swept against as she hurtled downstream. Zim gave a great cry and half rose before remembering, helped by my urgent grab at his arm. Flint, calculating angles, began to turn the tinny, a fraught manoeuvre for it had to be completed before the combined currents of the two streams grabbed us. I saw at once what he intended and, from the tense line of his body, how difficult it was likely to prove. Any miscalculation would either see us overturned or carried out into the Rainsford to very likely meet the same end.

He had brought a rope. When, moments later, we were lying with the nose of the boat pointing back upstream, he changed places with me, keeping his weight low. Zim, meanwhile, was calling to his daughter until she slowly lifted her head to look at him.

'Keep it straight,' Flint said, relinquishing the tiller into my grasp, 'and be ready to give it more throttle if you feel we're losing ground. I'll get the rope on her first. Zim'll have to balance the boat. I just hope to hell he keeps his head.'

Moments later, I saw what he meant when the man leant towards his daughter and the tinny began to list. 'Back!' Flint yelled as he crouched forward. 'Lean back.' Zim raised his hands and nodded, and as his weight shifted slightly the boat righted again; the two men must weigh about the same. The incident must have impressed itself on the distraught father, for after that he stayed stoically in place until Flint had completed the difficult task of securing the rope without dislodging the girl from her precarious perch, then half dragging, half lifting her into the boat, which rocked crazily, threatening to capsize.

'Daddy.' Meadow fell into Zim's arms and began weakly to cry. Tears ran down his face as he stroked her hair and comforted her. She was a mess. It wasn't called saw-toothed pandanus for nothing. The skin on her face and arms was ripped in myriad places, some of the wounds seeping blood. I passed him a blanket and used the towel to dry her hair and wrap the worst of the lacerations. They were only shallow and would, I thought, heal without scarring. A bit of antiseptic cream would be sufficient when we got back – which I feared was going to be the more difficult journey.

Flint was looking grim and with a frightened lurch of the heart I said quietly, 'Something wrong?'

'Extra weight,' he said briefly. 'The motor's already working flat out.' It sputtered as he spoke as if threatening to quit, then caught again. 'Dammit! And I'm not sure how much fuel we have left.' He glanced at the bank and made up his mind. 'I'm gonna beach her soon as, while we've still got power. Once the engine stops—'

He didn't need to complete the sentence, and my anxious gaze sought the right-hand bank, looking for a place where we could land. The creek bank, undercut by the effect of past monsoons, ranged between steep and sheer, save for the section where the horse had foundered. It must have been a watering place for animals and it was this we made for, me clenching my hands and willing the motor on during every painful second it took. The horse was gone, either rescued or washed back to its death in the water. The former, I thought, or we should surely have seen him. The engine sputtered again as Flint gave us our orders.

'Straight over the side soon as we touch. Then grab onto the boat and hang on before the current takes it. Here we go – Shit!' The expletive was for the sudden cessation of sound as the engine died for good. We were still a metre short of the bank. 'Go!' Flint yelled and Zim leapt, sweeping Meadow along with him. The boat rocked from the thrust of his leap and I almost fell. Flint half caught, half pushed me and I found myself in water midway to my thighs. It was cold and shockingly strong, shoving against my body. I clung to the boat, feeling it begin to pull me, then Zim's strength joined my own. The weight of it lightened as Flint splashed overboard and the three of us wrestled the cumbersome shape through the greasy mud to the shore, the engine braking our attempt as the propeller dug into the flooded bank.

Flint swore and hauled himself back into the canted boat to lift the motor. He then made a giant stride back over the side and went straight down on his face in the mud. I reached for his hand as he swore again more imaginatively, and I helped pull him up till the greasy ground claimed him once more, this time dragging me with him. Lying in a heap in the slush beside him, our arms and clothes coated with black mud, I began helplessly to giggle, recognising it even as it happened as relief, a release of adrenalin in reaction to the strain of our rescue efforts. Careless of my hair, I let my head sink onto the bank and laughed like a loon.

Flint's lips curved into an empathetic smile. 'Just as well it's you and not Angus,' he murmured. 'Rolling around in the mud wouldn't do his back much good.'

'No.' I sobered at the reminder. Up close there were little gold flecks in the irises of Flint's eyes. There was a dark ring about each one and I noted the curve of lash and brow and a tiny sunspot at the corner of one lid. There was an intimacy in gazing so closely, reading so deeply of another and with a jolt I recognised the warmth of his regard, intuiting his intention in time to drop my gaze and scramble up, my heart jolting.

'Ugh! I must be a sight.' I turned my back, flicking off as much of the sticky mud as I could. 'Maybe there's a hose at the house we can wash under?'

'We could certainly use it.' Flint planed his hands down his body, spreading rather than shifting the mud. Our glances met briefly and I looked quickly away, my colour heightening.

'I'll go ask.'

'My horse!' Zim exclaimed just as Meadow, who'd hardly spoken till now, gave a little cry and, with the amazing resilience of the young, sprang up and ran towards the huge creature that had caused all the trouble.

'Joey-boy. You're safe!'

Chapter Sixteen

The horse was standing, washed free of mud, but it was only as we straggled up to join Meadow that I saw Muriel on his far side, engaged in strapping up his hairy fetlock. She slapped a familiar hand on his wet shoulder. 'There, boy. That'll help a bit. Good God, Penny! You're safe – but what happened?'

I said stupidly, 'You got him out of the creek – how?'

'Winched him out with the tractor. Well, Barry did.' She ran a hand over the horse's huge wet body and the bay hide shivered under her touch. 'He's a bit sore where the rope bit in, but it was the only way.' She took in our bedraggled appearance. 'You got the girl then?'

'This man,' Zim said dramatically, 'my life is his! He save my daughter.'

'She was on the horse,' I explained, 'and the bank gave way under them. They're both lucky to be alive. Is there somewhere we could wash, Muriel? And maybe Barry could run us back? The boat's out of fuel.'

'Yeah, 'course. I'll give him a yell.' To Flint she added, 'And we can fix you up with some fuel.'

'Not right now, thanks. The tinny's secure where it is. I'll collect it later.' He looked down at his filthy form and mud-caked boots. 'But a wash would be great.'

'And could you ring the shop?' I asked, remembering. 'Zim's wife should be there. She'll be frantic. Let her know Meadow's safe.'

Meadow was fussing and petting over the horse, his whiskery chin resting on her wet head as she bent to feel his leg. 'Thank you for saving him,' she said shyly to Muriel. 'I was afraid he'd drown.'

'Ah, he's a fine big lad, and the leg'll get right – he's just pulled something there, that's all. Speaking of drowning, my girl, you're damn lucky to be alive,' she said severely. 'Don't you know better than to trust a creek edge in flood? You could all have been killed.' She gave the horse a final pat and turned to us. 'Well, come over to the yard. You'd best hose off while I make that call.'

'How come she knows about horses?' Meadow asked as we stood on the Toyota's tray, hanging on to the head rails while Barry drove us to the store. My clothes were too wet and dirty for the cab and the others had also refused Barry's half-hearted offer to ride with him.

'Her dad was a drover. I expect she learned from him.' The vehicle pulled in at the shop and I cast an eye at the heavy clouds. 'Just in time. Here comes the rain again.'

The girl squealed as the first drops hit us, as if she wasn't already soaking, then jumped down and ran. I followed more slowly, watching Fodo, who gave a cry at sight of her bedraggled daughter and met her halfway, squeezing her into a hug. Roseanne and Marlene watched from the shelter of the shop's awning. Lisa was there too, I saw.

She eyed me critically, saying cheerfully, 'You look dreadful. And yuck! Your hair's all muddy.'

'I know,' I answered curtly. 'Let's get home – it's going to pour.' I caught Marlene's eye and lifted my hand in a brief wave. She would hear all about the rescue from Zim. Flint glanced our way and looked ready to follow, but I kept walking, breaking into a jog as the rain fell more heavily. 'You might have brought the brolly,' I complained.

'Why?' Lisa tipped her head back and stuck out her tongue to catch the drops, closing her eyes against the sting of them on her face. 'This is fun. Besides, it wasn't raining then. So is the horse dead?'

Leaving her questions unanswered as we reached our house, I kicked my muddy shoes off and hurried into the shower. It wasn't until the water was blasting down, echoing the battering on the roof, that I let myself remember that moment on the bank when Flint had been within a whisker of kissing me.

I would have to find a means to discourage him, I thought, scooping shampoo onto my hair, though how to do it without losing his friendship, which I really valued, wasn't clear. I was a blind idiot. His frequent neighbourly visits weren't for the sake of Angus's company. And he didn't clean gutters and screw down roofs for the reward of a home-cooked meal. I hadn't seen it because I hadn't wanted to. Yes, I liked him – he was a good friend – but I was well and truly over trusting my emotional wellbeing to others. Twice my love had been betrayed and I had no intention of allowing it to happen again.

I rinsed out the shampoo, scrubbing my fingers vigorously through my wet curls. It made it harder somehow that he was widowed, never mind the loss of his child. But I wasn't responsible for his happiness, I thought defensively, nor did I intend to risk mine again. *Was* I even happy? I was . . . settled, I decided, uncapping the conditioner bottle. I stared at the pool of water about my feet, wondering if being settled equated with being content, and all of a sudden I realised what I was doing and snatched at the taps. God! I'd probably used up three days' supply of the precious stuff. How could I have been so thoughtless?

The rain continued all week. We were sitting under a low-pressure system that had been dragged inland in the wake of the now defunct cyclone, or so the wireless informed us between bursts of static. The power stayed off for three more days and by the end of the week mould was starting to grow on any damp surface it could colonise. Angus and I worked on salvaging what we could of the damaged pot plants and re-covering the mended shadehouse frames with the heavy netting we had in stock, stitching it into place with nylon fishing line from Flint's shop. Ever since the episode by the creek, I had been less forthcoming with invitations to meals, though Flint still stopped by to have the occasional beer with Angus, whose arthritic hip, he claimed, was preventing him from going to the pub.

By now the Rainsford was back inside its banks and council workers had cleared the debris from the bridge. Meadow seemed none the worse for her near shave and was often with the other two girls. The town was recovering from the blow, though odd bits of household stuff would likely continue to litter the Common, where Flint's vehicle still sat waiting for the ground to dry, for some years. And despite all the excitement the flood had created, the river hadn't quite reached the heights of the previous one responsible for the flood wrack in the old fig, though it had come close.

'When can we swim again, Penny?' Lisa asked one afternoon. She was bored, like the rest of us. There was nothing much to occupy her. She had helped with the repotting in the nursery but that work was mostly done; now the plants just needed time to recover and for new growth to replace the broken stems and branches.

'When the water runs clear.' It would be a while. The tap water, filtered and settled in the town tanks, still had a brownish tinge, but at least we could shower as much as we wished, and in the steamy, overcast days that counted for something. We had rainwater from the roof for drinking and cooking, and Cyclone Fern was already history, having blown itself out, though it had brought welcome rain to parched areas far down into the heart of Queensland.

'There's nothing to do,' she complained.

'You can come for a drive with me,' I offered. 'Just upriver a bit. I want to see how many of those trees we put in are still there. Mind, we'll have to walk the last little way. I'm not taking the vehicle off the tar.'

'It'll be hot,' she said discontentedly.

'It's hot here,' I pointed out, 'but suit yourself.' I backed the vehicle from its bay in the shed and at the last minute she came flying after me to tumble into the cab. 'Got your hat? Where's Roseanne?'

She pulled a face. 'She went home ages back. She's got a tummy-ache.'

It was the first time I'd seen the results of the flooding, which even the subsequent rain hadn't quite washed clear. The ground along the river frontage, where the fenced-in area we'd planted lay, was badly scoured, the young timber festooned with flood wrack and leaning in the direction the water had flowed. Most of the grass had gone and all the shrubbery – the conkerberry, turkey bush and native hibiscus – were either broken or lying flat, coated with mud. The cemetery seemed to have fared no better. I had a quick glimpse of debris amid the headstones and made a mental note to check it on the way back. It might be that the flood would prove a more persuasive argument towards refurbishment than the combined voices of the CWA.

Once we were level with the fenced plantation, I pulled to the side of the road and we walked. The ground was slightly higher here; for the first bit of the way there was only the thigh-high grass to contend with, but this soon gave way to a scoured area that looked like a herd of buffalo had tramped through it. The mud-coated grass was slick enough to turn an ankle on, but the fence when we reached it was still standing, though the bottoms of the corner posts had washed out and the wires were festooned with debris. I stood, grasping the top one while cicadas shrilled in the stillness, and ran my eye over our plantings. The bulk of them still stood. The trunk of a dead tree had evidently washed through the plot, for it was now wedged against the downstream posts. Its passage was marked by broken saplings, while a staggered line of gutta-percha closest to the river had vanished altogether. All up, I estimated that around seventy per cent of the trees had survived undamaged, which, given the circumstances, wasn't bad.

'Will you plant them again?' Lisa asked. 'I'm thirsty, Penny. Can we go now?'

'Yes,' I said absently. 'Just let me make a quick count of what's missing first. There's water in the vehicle. Go back and wait if you want.'

She left and was sitting with the door open when I returned, pulling faces at herself in the mirror. 'Are we going home now?' she asked as I turned the vehicle round.

'After a quick stop at the cemetery.'

She brightened. 'Why? What's there?'

'A lot of weeds and history. I want to see how it fared in the flood. The CWA want to fix it up, you know. Make it an interesting place to visit.'

'Roseanne didn't show it to me.'

'It's an overgrown dump. People don't even remember it's there, that's why. We'll have to walk again, because there's only a dirt track.' I coasted to a stop, switched off and got out. 'You coming?'

'How far?'

'Just over here.' We were a kilometre from the edge of town, not far from the knee-high stumps now smothered in grass and vine that were all that remained of the old fever hospital. The site, when we reached it, was actually clearer than before the cyclone; it seemed the flood had either flattened or swept away much of the growth that had almost buried the smaller headstones. It had also toppled more of the larger monuments, though the mud seemed to have cushioned their fall so they hadn't broken. Staring about, I realised it wasn't going to be as simple a task to align them again as we had imagined. Black soil shifted. It cracked foundations and heaved up posts so that no fence line in it ever ran true – and that was without a flood.

Tutting, I trod carefully between the graves while Lisa hunkered over the fallen stones, attempting to read them through the mud and discolouration of decades. 'There's a little baby here,' she called, 'and its mum. Way back in 1902. Imagine being dead that long! It doesn't even have a name – it just says "Baby Mosten". It died the same day as the lady.'

'Mmm. Probably when it was born then,' I said, stepping carefully through a tangle of rusty wire. Part of the fence. The weight of the water shoving against the debris-laden wires had obviously pulled it down. The one corner post that still stood had a drunken lean to it, the water having gouged a great hole at its foot. I bent to push it upright and froze in disbelief. An icy hand clutched my heart and I felt the hairs spring erect on my arms. Then I sprang backwards with a little scream and my foot caught on the edge of a plinth that had supported a broken urn. I went down in the tangled growth and mud, banging my elbow painfully against the concrete edging. I heard Lisa calling my name, but I ignored her and lay covering my mouth to still the whimpers of horror escaping from it.

Chapter Seventeen

Lisa arrived big-eyed to stare down at me. 'What's wrong?' she demanded shrilly. 'Was it a snake? Did it bite you?' Her head was on a swivel, gaze everywhere, and inevitably her eyes fell on the thing the flood had uncovered.

'Don't look!' I cried sharply, but she already was, bent over and peering in fascination at what the post's fall had disclosed.

'Holy cow! Is that a skull? It is, and it's all broken.' She sounded awed but not at all frightened. 'Penny, it's a person! Or it was. But why's it there, under a post? Shouldn't it have a proper grave?'

'Very likely.' I rose, holding my arm, which ached fiercely. I had hit it right on the funny bone and was going to have a massive bruise. 'Come away. We have to go to the police right now.'

'Why?' She looked at me blankly. 'It's a dead person – in a cemetery. So?'

'Yes,' I said grimly. 'A cemetery where the corpses belong in boxes, not under posts. Come on, we're going.'

The police station was closed. A glance at my watch showed

it to be twelve thirty – lunch time then – so I shifted my attention from the tiny office building to the house beside it, but had no better luck. Southbend only had Sergeant Banner in residence; his constable had been involved in a serious motor accident in early November. He'd rolled the police vehicle in the ranges and lain pinned beneath it for half a day until a passing traveller raised the alarm. Greg had been alone at the station ever since. But the blinds were all down in the house and the screen door firmly locked. It was possible that Banner was away, but unlikely, given the boggy state of the country, and a quick look around the back confirmed this. His vehicle was in the shed. Perhaps he was drunk and sleeping it off? I hardly knew the man but given the rumours about him, it was possible. I gave up and returned home to find Flint and Angus making sandwiches in the kitchen.

'Wondered where you'd got to.' Angus looked up from slathering mustard over corned meat. 'We finished 'er, lass. Wanna step out back an' have a shoofty?'

'That's great.' I did as he asked and admired the completed shed roof. 'Well done, and thank you for your help, Flint. Have either of you seen Greg Banner this morning?'

'Not me.' Flint stacked sandwiches onto a plate and I winced as usual as Angus banged the lid onto the butter tub. 'Hi, Lisa, what do you want in your sandwich?'

'We found a dead person, Flint. In the cemetery. Penny screamed and fell over when she saw it,' she replied with ghoulish relish. 'It was buried under a post. Penny wants to tell the cop.'

'No kidding?' Startled, he looked at me. 'What – the flood uncovered a coffin? Bit of a health risk, that.'

'This corpse was never buried. Not in a grave, anyway. As Lisa said, it was under a post that the water gullied out.' I sat down shuddering. 'It was horrible!' I felt faintly sick and the smell of the food was making it worse. I pressed a hand to my mouth. 'Could you put that meat away, please? You do realise it has to be—' I wanted to say a murder, but not in front of Lisa, and compromised with 'an illegal death?'

'Christ! What . . .' He cut the words off. 'You okay, Penny? It must've been a helluva shock.'

'It was,' I said baldly. 'And no, I'm not. I feel sick.'

'What were you doin' messin' around down there, anyway?' Angus demanded.

'Looking at the damage.' Flint poured and handed me a cup of tea. 'Thank you. No, nothing to eat, thanks. So it's a police matter now, only the wretched man seems to have vanished.'

'Probably drunk. I'll go over when I've eaten.' Flint shook his head in wonder. 'How unlucky can you be, eh?'

'I don't suppose whoever it was *chose* to be killed. Where are you off to?' I called as Lisa, sandwich in hand, skipped out the door.

'Just to Roseanne's.'

'Well, don't—' I started, but she was gone. I shrugged. 'She'll tell them. It'll be all over town. Everybody will be out there rubbernecking.'

'Not your concern,' Flint said. 'And what I meant about unlucky – you kill a bloke, bury him good and deep and then somebody comes along and digs a posthole on top of him, just ready to be washed out in a flood. In a cemetery, at that. You wouldn't read about it.'

'I suppose not.' I shivered, saying hesitantly, 'I only saw the skull, so the whole body must be just bones. Unless there's something left on the feet.' I shuddered slightly at the thought. 'So it must've been there for years, decades – maybe even longer.'

'The cops'll sort it out,' Angus said comfortably. 'Not that useless shower Greg, but. Murder'll fetch someone outta Hamilton, you see if it don't.'

Ultimately Angus's words proved correct. Flint left and some half-hour later I caught a glimpse of the police vehicle heading out of town tailed, ten minutes later, by a couple more. Sightseers, so the word had got around. Then Marlene arrived, full of questions.

'Is it true?' She cocked her fair head, a little wrinkle of concern marring her forehead. 'I know Lisa believes it, but I wondered if she'd got the wrong end of the stick. A skeleton, yes – it *is* a cemetery – but *murder?*'

I sighed. Well, I'd never thought the child stupid. To divert Marlene, for I didn't want to dwell on the subject, I said, 'How's Roseanne? Lisa said she had a stomachache?'

'She's got her first period, that's all. So she's feeling bit sorry for herself, but Lisa got her out of bed. The pair of them have gone off to see Meadow, to tell her, I suppose. So why were you out there, anyway? And how did you come to find the body?'

I said rapidly, knowing she wouldn't be put off, 'We were upriver checking our last planting, and I just thought I'd see how much damage the flood had done at the cemetery. The water pulled the old fence down and it toppled a few more headstones. Pretty near the only post left had half fallen over and I don't know why, but I went over to stand it up again. And I saw the skull. That's all.' I watched another vehicle drive out to the edge of town and jerked my thumb at it. 'And now everyone's heading out for a look-see. Talk about a circus!'

'So it really could have been a murder,' she marvelled. 'I thought Lisa might have got it wrong – that maybe a coffin had been washed out in the flood, but . . .' Marlene's indrawn breath made a little whistle. 'I wonder who? However would you tell, though, from just the skeleton?'

'Work out who's missing, I suppose, but for that you'd have to know when it happened and, really Marlene, he could have been the first pioneer in the country. Well,' I amended, 'the second. Somebody else had to be there to kill him and hide the evidence.' I gave a wry smile.

She took the words literally and wrinkled her nose. 'A hundred-odd years? Would bones last that long up here? It's a wonder they haven't been washed out years since.'

'I don't know, but'—I paused, struck by a sudden thought—'can't you just see Fiona working this angle with the council? The notoriety it will garner is a gift for tourism. Learn all about the Gory Deeds of the Gulf! See the very spot where murder was unveiled!' Abruptly I changed the subject. 'What do you and Stan plan to do about Roseanne's schooling next year? Boarding school?'

She sighed. 'I suppose, though God knows how we'll pay the bills. I know they're pretty steep, but even if I had the time, I can't home school her. I didn't finish Year Ten myself, and I wasn't any sort of scholar. What about Lisa? I mean, how long are you keeping her?'

'Angus is her only rellie,' I said, 'so it'll be for the duration. And I frankly have no idea what we'll do about it.' Wistfully I added, 'You think we could get Fiona to lobby the Education Department for a high school in Southbend?'

Marlene laughed. 'Pigs'll fly sooner than *that* happening. But it would be great if the two of them could go off together, being such friends. If my mother was younger . . . but she's got arthritis, and it would be too much worry and responsibility – it wouldn't be fair on her. Not that there's a high school where she lives, anyway.'

'Well, we'll just have to wait and see,' I said. 'Maybe something will turn up.'

But the only immediate change came with the return of Flint an hour or so later.

'So what's happening?' I asked, emerging onto the verandah. 'Where did you find Greg?'

Grimacing, he looked up at me. 'Sleeping it off in the house. I wouldn't say he's exactly sober yet.' He wrinkled his nose. 'The man could hardly walk straight. When I finally got him listening, he insisted on me showing him where the bones were. I told him I hadn't seen 'em myself. Sorry for dobbing you in, Penny – it means he'll want to interview you, probably when his headache wears off . . . Anyway, by the time we got out there, young Lisa must've spread the word because half the town turned up.' He gave a crack of laughter. 'Paid for it too. Greg made 'em dig the bones out. I reckon he had a helluva hangover; he was shaking and sweating like a pig and looked properly sick.'

'So where are they now – the remains?' Every vehicle in the North automatically carried a shovel, I reflected, and it was just like Greg Banner to co-opt assistance for jobs he didn't fancy himself.

'In the clink. They collected the bones onto a tarp and he's locked them up in the cell. Gonna report it, so I expect they'll send somebody out from Hamilton. I got the feeling that he'd rather the body had stayed undiscovered. He's not one for putting himself out.'

It was true enough. 'Maybe he should just bury them again,' I suggested. 'I mean, how will they ever identify the person?'

Flint shrugged. 'That's their worry. Chalk it up as a mystery, I say, and forget it. After all, some faiths bury their people sitting in a hole rather than flat in a box.'

Even so, I mused as he left, it was doubtful there were many such believers in the Gulf. To me it still smacked of murder and, as unrealistic as it seemed at this late date that the culprit would ever be caught, it ought not to go unpunished.

Greg turned up later that evening. He'd either recovered or taken a hair of the dog to steady his nerves for, apart from looking a little pale, he seemed his normal morose self. I explained yet again how I had happened to discover the skeleton while he made a few notes, presumably to let his superiors know he was on the job.

'And what reason did you have to be there in the cemetery? Funny place for a walk, isn't it?'

I exhaled, saying patiently, 'I wasn't walking as such, Greg. You must know about the CWA's intentions to refurbish the cemetery as a tourist attraction of historical interest. I was passing and I thought I might as well see how much more damage the flood had done. That's why. Call it an impulse of the moment.'

'Right.' He flipped his notepad shut. 'Well, that'll do for now. The place is a crime scene, so don't be going back there, okay?'

'Seriously, sergeant? You're going to find fifty-year-old fingerprints or other clues the flood hasn't swept to glory?'

'Police business,' he said shortly. 'Just stay away.'

The following day dawned clear. It was good flying weather and, sure enough, about ten o'clock we heard a plane come over the town and the diminishing sounds of it throttling down to land.

'That'll be the copper come to get the victim,' Angus said when it first appeared as a flash of silver against the sky. It wasn't a difficult guess – mail flights came on Wednesdays and the flying doctor clinic wasn't due for another three weeks. 'Don't reckon he'll be hanging around too long, not with them clouds building to the north.'

Southbend had a bitumenised airstrip now, in place of the old gravel one that had served back in the seventies, but weather still mattered to the pilots of light aircraft.

'At least they'll have somebody able to tell how old the bones are. Look, while it's fine and the ground's still wet, why don't we replace those trees upriver that the flood took? It'll be harder going after the Wet.' The grass would be waist high then, and the black soil would have set like concrete.

'Okay. I'll get the trailer out. You know how many we need?'

'Yes – and which ones. I'll just change into boots and what say we have our smoko first?'

By the time we were ready to leave, the police vehicle was ahead of us on the road, bearing out Angus's guess. They took the turn-off into the cemetery. It would be the detectives this time, I thought, come to view the scene where the body was found and sift through the dirt for clues to its identity. Angus muttered, 'Bit game, ain't they?' But possibly the extra day or two had hardened the ground enough that they wouldn't bog down. It was their problem anyway. We sailed past, got as close as we dared off-road, then began the laborious task of humping the young seedlings from the trailer to the plantation. It was noon before we straggled back to the vehicle, sweaty and worn out.

'Whew.' Wearily I waved my hat before my hot face and collapsed into the vehicle. 'I hope to God there isn't another flood. Home, my good man, and as quick as you like. I need a shower.'

The police vehicle was still at the cemetery. 'What on *earth* are they doing?' I asked. 'How long can you look at an empty hole?'

'Bet they're bogged.' Angus's foot lifted on the pedal. 'Think we should go see?'

'No.' I was longing for the shower. 'Greg told me it was out of bounds to us ordinary folk. Let them dig themselves out, or walk back. It's not far.'

It was mean of me, but I didn't want to hang around; also we'd have to unhook the trailer before we went off-road. It was police business, Greg had said, so let the police handle it. Somewhat ruefully I realised that I had grown as touchy and parochial as my neighbours, who expected to own every happening within their remit and didn't welcome outside interference. Small town syndrome or a healthy curiosity? I was too tired to care.

Chapter Eighteen

Their vehicle had become so thoroughly stuck that it had taken Barry Lacey's tractor to pull it out. This upset the visiting police's schedule sufficiently that the party stayed overnight in Southbend, which we learned from Flint, who had been first port of call for Greg when he'd slogged it back to town. Flint had obligingly taken a cable out to the stranded four-wheel drive but it had proved unequal to the task. Barry Lacey had been called in and while the hapless sergeant was left to assist him, Flint brought the two strangers back to town – to call on me.

I was mildly annoyed. Detective Kent was in plainclothes and nobody had given me his rank and the man with him was dressed in blue overalls smeared with soil, so I kept them both on the verandah where the (now recovered) chairs could be hosed down and the tracks of their muddy boots scrubbed off the boards. Nothing stained like black clay. Flint, who'd slipped off his boots, snagged a chair and pulled it back against the wall, tactfully removing himself from the conversation.

'Look,' I said, 'I've already talked to Sergeant Banner and

answered his questions. The post was leaning, I went to push it up and the skull was right there under it. I can't tell you anything else.'

The detective nodded. 'And then you reported it, Mrs McCloud?'

'Yes.' I thought about adding that I'd have done it sooner if Banner hadn't been drunk, but his words caught up with me. 'What did you call me?'

'You don't remember me? Well, they were distressing circumstances for you. I was the one who broke the news about Michael McCloud's accident.'

'I don't remember you.' Though in truth, now I looked more closely, there was something familiar about him.

'Understandable.' Detective Kent glanced at the sign out front. 'I see you're in the same business still?'

'Yes,' I said stiffly, then realising what he was angling at, added, 'I go by my maiden name now. Was there anything else? That man could have been there for fifty years, you know, and surely that's too long to worry about?'

'Murder's murder,' he replied. He had watchful eyes, I decided, and his face was like wood, giving nothing back. 'Incidentally, what made you think the victim was a man?'

'Wasn't he? Well, I just assumed . . .' I trailed off, before starting again. 'So it really was murder?' I had wondered if the post might have damaged the skull, but that still left the question of who had buried the body.

'Death by blunt force trauma, according to my companion here.' He nodded at his mute offsider. 'Though the manner of the corpse's disposal plainly makes it an unlawful death. And actually it was a woman.'

'Really?' I said blankly. It seemed inconceivable. 'There can't have been that many around half a century ago. Not to be unaccounted for, I mean. Surely there'd be records if somebody disappeared?'

'We'll be investigating.' He tipped his hat, a brand new, uncomfortable-looking felt. 'Thank you for your time.' Flint got up but the detective waved a hand at him. 'And your assistance. It's fine, we can find our way from here, thanks.'

'Bet he's done an orienting course,' Flint murmured as we stood watching them leave. 'See? He even knows which direction the cop shop is.'

I rubbed my arms. 'Where's Greg, then? Detective Kent was very free with his information. I thought police were a one-way street. Information in, nothing out. And who was the strong silent type in the dirty overalls?'

'Forensic officer, I gather. At least he was grubbing about in the mud, collecting bits of rag and stuff and bagging them. The victim's clothing, I guess, rotted to pieces. You couldn't tell what it had been – well, I couldn't – so I can't imagine it being much help in establishing an identity.' He hesitated a beat. 'The detective . . . why did he say "Michael McCloud's accident"? Why wouldn't he just say "your husband's"?'

The question came so suddenly I was unable to frame an answer that wasn't the truth. And in the instant way those thoughts come, I saw that I owed that to him. He had been too good a friend to deserve to be lied to. 'Because he wasn't my husband. Michael was a bigamist, but I didn't know. It was only when he died that I learned he already had a wife when he married me.'

Flint was silent for a long moment. Then he nodded to

himself saying, 'And Lisa – she's his daughter, isn't she? Angus called her his son's girl. I assumed that meant Michael's brother, and that the old boy had had a bloody rough trot to lose two boys, but bad things happen in life . . .' He shook his head. 'And you're picking up the pieces for them both, Penny.'

I said honestly, 'I've grown fond of the child. And it's not her fault. Michael, he . . .' I started, but I had no wish to explain the joy his love had brought me, or the pain of betrayal that followed. 'It hurt Angus too, you know. Helping me is a sort of atonement for what he sees as his failings with his son. And Lisa's all he has left. I couldn't turn her away. Besides, she's a part of Michael—'

'So you still love him.' It was more statement than question.

'I don't know, Flint. Today I could wish I'd never met him, but we were together, if not married, for four years. Sometimes I want those years undone, even though I've probably never been happier than I was then.' Without realising it I'd folded my arms, clasping them tightly with my hands, a classic defensive stance. 'I suppose his death, and the revelation it brought, taught me not to depend on others. They all leave you in the end, so you're better off alone.'

'No.' He cleared his throat. 'That's not true. But words are easy said. It's something you have to work out for yourself. Loneliness isn't life, Penny.' He spoke with feeling.

I didn't ask, saying instead because I might as well clear the air between us now, 'It's why I don't . . . I haven't . . .' I stopped there, fighting the urge to blush. What if I was wrong and he wasn't interested? I would present as beyond egotistical, but he saved me from further speech.

Smiling gently, he said, 'It's okay, Penny. I told you, I'm a very patient man. Be seeing you,' and with that he left, jumping lightly down the steps and striding off.

Meadow came by later, just before school let out. She was riding and slid off the tall bay at the front gate to tie him to the fence. Seeing her hesitating there, I stepped out onto the verandah to greet her. It was the first time we'd met since her rescue.

'Meadow, how are you? Is that . . .' What had she called him? 'Joey? His leg's better then? And your cuts are all healed up.'

'Hello, Miss Carter. Yes, thank you, I'm fine. And, no, Joeboy's still a little lame. This is Baron. Can I come in?'

'Well, of course. How are you? No ill effects from the accident?'

'No, really, I'm fine.' She twisted her hands awkwardly together. 'I never thanked you – you and Mr Flint for saving me. I thought I was going to die so many times. I could hear that tree I was holding on to creaking, you know? Like it was going to break. You were so brave, both of you, to put a boat into that water.'

'Well, your dad was there too, and at least Flint and I can both swim. Have a seat, Meadow. Would you like a cold drink?'

'No, it's okay, thanks. My mum sent me.' She flushed in that vivid way I remembered from my own teens every time my words had come out wrongly. 'I mean, of course I wanted to come – to thank you. She didn't send me for that reason. But she wants me to ask if you could come to tea tomorrow afternoon? If it's not inconvenient, of course,' she added hastily.

'I'd love to. Is there a particular time?'

'About two? I'll have finished school by then. We start early,' she explained. 'Mum's very organised and it's good, you know, because then I have lots of free time. It helps when we're travelling.'

'Mmm. Do you enjoy that, the travelling?'

'It's all right, I suppose,' she said slowly. 'I like seeing new places and that. But it would be nice to have a real home.' Her gaze went to the open door and the hallway that led through to the back, where there was a glimpse of washing on the clothes-line strung between two of the shadehouses. 'Like yours,' she said wistfully. 'And friends. I make new friends like your niece and Roseanne from the shop, for a month or so, but then we move on and I never see them again.'

'That would be a drawback,' I agreed. 'But Lisa isn't my niece, you know. She's Angus's granddaughter.'

'Oh,' Meadow said blankly. 'She told me her mother had died and she lived with her aunt.'

'Did she? Well, I suppose it's close enough. You sure you won't have that drink?'

'Thank you, but I'd best be going.' She flipped back the dark mass of her hair and smiled at me. 'It's been nice talking to you, but Baron hates to be tied up for long.' She wasn't wrong there. The horse had started to paw at the earth, bending his great neck and snorting restlessly through distended nostrils.

'He looks awfully big,' I said. 'How on earth do you get on him?'

She laughed with a glimpse of small white teeth and merry smoky-grey eyes. 'I use a fence, or a log – whatever's handy.' A few moments later she demonstrated by turning the bay side-on to the fence and launching herself athletically from its top onto the horse's broad back. 'See you,' she called brightly before cantering off.

Zim had made a stile from cut-up tree trunks at the fence for pedestrian use because there was only a bogan gate into the Common, a cumbersome thing of wire and posts, heavy to drag about. Having left the vehicle on the edge of the road, I nipped over the stile and found Fodo waiting for me at the entrance to a fly-rig where a table of tea things and a couple of folding chairs had been set up. She wore a long gathered skirt of several different colours and a red blouse, the neck held together with a ribbon. With her waist-length hair hanging and tanned skin, she exactly fulfilled my notion of a gypsy, an idea that the cut-glass precision of her vowels instantly dispelled. She had, I saw, been very pretty, even beautiful in her youth, with her high cheekbones and straight patrician nose.

'I'm so glad you could come. We've never been properly introduced. I'm Fodo Cilovich.'

'Penny Carter,' I replied.

She smiled, her eyes netted with wrinkles. She was probably only in her forties but life on the road had not been kind to her skin. 'I would have asked you sooner,' she apologised, 'but the paddock's been a sea of mud till now.'

'I don't doubt it.' The grass remained lying flat as the flood had left it, with the new shoots now showing through and

I could still see the path that Flint's vehicle had ploughed, both coming and going. 'Black soil is the pits when it rains. It was kind of you to invite me. Did you suffer any damage from the cyclone?'

She grimaced. 'The tent went – could be anywhere between here and the coast, and a few other little things that don't matter much. But please, have a seat. We're out here because it's too hot and crowded in the van. I wanted to thank you, Penny, for helping save my daughter's life. If it hadn't been for you—'

'Then it would have been my business partner, Angus,' I interrupted. 'But he's an old man. The thought of him in the boat was enough to get me there instead. Anyway, no thanks are necessary, Fodo. It's a sort of pass-it-on society out here. We help each other out because we never know when it'll be our turn to need a hand. So please, say no more. Besides, it was all down to Flint, really.'

'Yes, Zim thinks he's wonderful. And a very talented man, I hear?'

'He's that,' I agreed. 'An artist in wood. He makes furniture in his spare time. So, tell me about yourself. You have a very different life; it's not every day you find someone still travelling by horse-power. When Lisa first saw your van, she asked if the circus was coming to town. Do you enjoy the life?'

'I did,' she said. 'I think it's growing a bit old now, for me, and Meadow both. Now she's turned fourteen, she's reached that stage where she wants stability, friends she doesn't have to leave behind, and a bit more social life.'

'She sort of hinted that,' I agreed. 'It must be lonely for her. Even though they're younger, she seems to really enjoy

Lisa and Roseanne's company. When I was a teenager, primary school kids were like annoying siblings – brats you didn't want to be seen with.'

Fodo poured the tea into two unmatched cups of fine china, though the sugar basin was plastic and the milk came in an old-fashioned bottle. 'Just powdered,' she apologised. 'I only have a small fridge so the bottle fits better than a jug.'

'Heavens, we all use powdered milk,' I said lightly, 'except Sue Hart. She keeps goats. So, tell me about your name. It's very unusual.'

She laughed, the dainty cup incongruous in her roughened hand. 'It's a nickname. My father, bless his classical mind, named me Theodora. It means "beloved of God". When we were little, my younger sister called me Fodo because she couldn't say it, and it's just stuck. Zim's from Bosnia and I assure you *his* full name is quite unpronounceable, so we just use the first bit. Simpler for everyone.'

'I see. And is your sister out here too? I can hear that you're English.'

'Good Lord, no!' She sounded quite shocked. 'Sally's in the wilds of Hampshire, part of the county set. She would die at the very idea. No, I was the family rebel. Troublesome and unconventional and'—she was obviously quoting now—'bound for a bad end.' She shrugged. 'But life's for living. I knew it even then. Skipped out from under at seventeen before I made my debut and I haven't missed it a bit. What about you, Penny? Are you a blow-in like us, or a local?'

'I was born here,' I said, 'but I left as a child and only recently returned. It's a hard country to live in given the isolation and the weather, but there are compensations.' I grinned.

'No pedestrian deaths, and not too many break-ins, for instance.'

'There's that,' she agreed. There was grey, I saw, in the wings of hair about her brow, and her eyes twinkled. 'The people seem nice too. I think I'd happily settle here if we could find permanent work.' The corner of her lips quirked and she winked at me. 'The truth is, even rebels have to domesticate in the end. It just may not be here.'

We chatted a little longer. Talking to her was fascinating; she had travelled widely overseas, had trained and worked as a teacher in America where she had met Zim and, after a brief incursion into the African continent, they'd come to Australia where they'd fallen naturally into their present existence, not the least hampered by the birth of their daughter. When I eventually left, it was with a feeling of rapport. She was everything that I was not, daring to a degree I couldn't envisage ever being, and with an openness to the challenges of life that I realised I had abandoned in my determination to save myself further loss.

In my position that day, I thought, she would have kissed Flint as we lay together in the mud, rather than shying away like some Regency virgin. Her life, at least the wagonette part of it, couldn't all have been rosy. There must have been other weather events and accidents and hard times. She didn't have the appearance of a pampered woman. My own carefully calculated existence suddenly seemed lacking by contrast to the freedom of hers. Driving into the yard to garage the vehicle, I suddenly felt less than satisfied with what I had created. Could it be that it wasn't, as I had thought, a future I was building myself here so much as a prison in which to hide from it?

Chapter Nineteen

We had a few more dry sunny days, during which the town cleared away, shored up and patched the damage wrought by Fern. The mail plane, which had missed last week's run, got in and there was fresh bread again. The shop had sold out its stock of frozen loaves and we had been making do with pancakes and scones as I hadn't yet got around to broaching the emergency yeast tin.

Other tidings had arrived with the mail but it was Muriel who delivered these, arriving late on Wednesday afternoon as I was preparing to accompany the three girls down to the river for a swim. The fury of brown flood water had run itself clean again, the river slipping demurely back within its scoured banks as though it had never misbehaved, and the swimming hole was once again crystal clear. I was, however, surprised that Meadow would wish to enter the water after her ordeal, but perhaps it was companionship more than the actual chance to swim that brought her along.

Seeing Muriel's vehicle pull up out front, I grimaced to myself. 'You girls start walking,' I told Lisa, 'I'll catch you up.' I couldn't imagine what Muriel wanted. We knew each other through the CWA – and because everyone knew everybody in a town as small as Southbend – but she wasn't a regular customer. Curiosity had brought her the first time but she'd simply looked without buying. The recent cactus for the verandah was probably her sole purchase. So four-thirty of a Wednesday afternoon seemed an odd time to repeat the process.

'Penny, have you got a minute?' she asked as I stepped out to meet her on the verandah, pulling the door firmly shut and tucking my towel under my arm to indicate that I was in the process of going somewhere. I wore my swimsuit under a top and shorts.

'It will have to be just a minute then,' I warned, pointing at the girls vanishing around the corner of the street. 'They're waiting on me.'

'I've heard something and I just thought I'd better have a word.' She actually looked a little unsure of herself, but I stifled a sigh, expecting some juicy detail of gossip I'd rather not hear.

'Is it important, Muriel? Because really—'

'I think so,' she said abruptly. 'I've had Greg Banner round quizzing me. I suppose he thinks I'm the only one who goes back far enough – short of the station mob, I mean, and apparently the phones are still out there. Telstra hasn't got around to us yet.'

'The sergeant?' I knitted my brow. 'What did he want?'

'He was asking what I knew of anyone going missing from round here, about twenty years ago.'

'And?' I prompted impatiently.

'Well, I told him about your mum. I couldn't think of anybody else. He didn't say why he was asking, but I thought I'd better let you know.'

I frowned. 'I don't see the relevance. As far as I know, my father never went to the cops about it. Why would he if she went off with somebody? Thanks, I suppose, though I can't see . . . Anyway, I've got to go, Muriel. If he asks you anything else to do with her, tell him he should chase up Walter Carter and talk to him. Bye now.' I hurried off, allowing her no time to say anything more. But I couldn't help wondering why a decades-old domestic upheaval should suddenly be of interest to the police.

I found out the following day when I looked up from potting-on tube stock to see the sergeant coming up the drive. I pushed my sweaty curls back from my face using my wrist and stripped off my gardening gloves. 'Greg. Good morning. What brings you here? Are you after a plant?' He must have heard the disbelief in my voice for he shook his head vehemently.

'Couldn't make meself heard from the front. Figured you must be round here.'

'As you see. Something I can do for you?'

'Just a bit of a chat. Of course, I've only been in town a coupla years so I'm not up on the history. I asked around and it seems your mum went missing from these parts twenty years back. That right?'

'You know it is,' I said thinly. 'Muriel Lacey told you so. My parents had an unhappy marriage and one day, just out of the blue, she cleared off with another man.'

'Yeah? He got a name? You ever hear from her again?'

'No,' I snapped. 'And I never knew who he was. I was nine years old, for God's sake. My dad told me she'd drowned in the river. I suppose he thought it was better for me to think she had died so I wouldn't be hankering after her. Then he sent me off to live with his sister. It was years before I knew she'd just left us.' A little frisson of foreboding went through me. 'Why the sudden interest?'

'Well,' he started. His muddy brown eyes stared at me from bloodshot whites, the skin beneath them baggy and dark. 'Seems your bones aren't fifty years old at all. How'd you come by that number, anyway? Scientists reckon the woman's body's been in the ground no more 'n' twenty years.' He pulled a plastic bag from his pocket and held it before me. 'You wouldn't happen to recognise this, I suppose? It was in the soil under the bones.'

I stared at the object within the evidence bag and felt the world rock beneath my feet. Despite the sweat dampening my neck and brow, I was suddenly freezing cold. The object had been cleaned, and the copper disc shone like new, the little enamelled daisies brilliant in the morning light. There was even a scrap of leather thong, blackened by age and immersion in the soil. I had a sudden vision of myself, blinded by angry tears as I destroyed my own smaller pendant. I remembered the savage rush of satisfaction as the enamel had splintered beneath the pressure of the plier's jaws and the passionate hatred I had felt for the mother who had abandoned me. And all the time she'd been dead, dumped in a hole to be forgotten, while lies were spread about her . . .

Banner's voice broke against my ears, the satisfaction in it evident. 'You do recognise it then?'

'I can't – I . . .' My head was filled with a roar like a waterfall. I couldn't listen or think and as the water rushed into my mouth, I ran a few paces before nature took over and my stomach heaved convulsively, ejecting my breakfast. My nose and throat burned and I could feel tears on my cheeks. My diaphragm cramped again and I retched and spat bile. Greg said something but the words made no sense. I wanted Angus. He would know what I should do. I started towards the workshop, then belatedly remembered that he had taken something, some part of a pump, to Barry Lacey to see if he had a replacement.

Ignoring Greg, I ran down the drive and onto the street, my feet fumbling for each step as if I were blind, the images tumbling through my head. *Back by smoko*, she had said, and the vehicle driving off and vanishing into nothing – only that had been the dream where I had run after her. But I hadn't; I had whined and sulked that she wasn't being fair, and then there was Winnie, with her voice all funny, telling me about heaven, and my mother – who had loved me after all and had not abandoned me – watching me from there. And all the time I had hated her and thought . . . I gave a great sob. All those years she had been there alone in the darkness, waiting for somebody to uncover the truth and I had never guessed. I should have known. If I had truly believed in her love, I *would* have known.

'I'm sorry. I'm sorry!' Somebody was mumbling the words. My nose was running, and the breath came short and clogged in my swollen throat. I stumbled against a kerb, felt myself falling and was suddenly pulled to a stop by an arm that caught me around the shoulders. 'I'm so sorry,' I hiccupped. 'I didn't know.'

'Penny! What's up? What's happened?' Blinking bleary eyes, I saw Flint through the wetness, his features wavering out of shape, and the relief of it, of finding somebody I could tell the awful truth to, was so great that I collapsed against him, still apologising.

'Shh,' he said. 'I've got you. It's all right, Penny. I've got you. You're safe, love. Everything will be all right. Shh now.' He rocked me against him and I clutched his shirt and cried as if the tears pouring from me would flow forever, to match the twenty years' worth of sorrow and guilt that burdened my soul.

I was vaguely aware of moving, of being nudged forward and guided until he said, 'Mind the step,' and a door closed behind me. I was inside, the storm subsiding. Suddenly back within myself, I wiped uselessly at my face with the back of my hands until a piece of cloth was pushed into them.

'Here,' Flint said. 'Sit, Penny.' A hand on my shoulder pressed me into a seat. 'Now, can you talk? What seems to be the problem? Is it Angus, Lisa? Are they okay?'

'Yes.' I gave a final wipe to my eyes, then blew my nose and looked at him. 'I'm sorry, Flint. It was the shock. I —' I swallowed, then said raggedly, 'It was Greg. He told me . . . He had my mother's pendant.' All the blood from my head must have pooled in my fingers; I could feel the thud of my pulse in their tips. 'The bones from the cemetery,' I said starkly, 'they're hers. Twenty years and I never knew, never guessed . . . She was murdered, Flint! And I hated her! I hated her for leaving me.' The tears started again and I mopped angrily at them. 'There never was another man. And she never left me. Somebody killed her and buried her and planted the vehicle so people would think she'd cleared out.'

'You're sure of this?'

'Yes,' I said vehemently. 'I'd know that pendant anywhere. I had a smaller identical one and we always wore them. It was . . . was like a pact between us.' I hadn't seen it as a child, but now it was blindingly obvious. 'It was to make us one – against him. Our secret. I was afraid of Walter and my mother was too, I see that now. She was always happier when he was out on the run. And I'—a tear leaked down my cheek—'when I thought she'd left me, I broke my pendant, twisted and hammered it and threw it away. I wish I hadn't. I wish—'

'Ah, don't, Penny, don't,' he said as I sobbed again. It took an effort to halt the tears but presently when I was composed again, he proffered a mug. 'Tea. I could kick that cop. He's an arse. He should have made sure somebody else was there before springing that on you. Where was Angus?'

'At Lacey's,' I said, sniffing. 'He wanted some part for a pump.' I sipped the tea and pulled a face, finding it too sweet.

'Drink it,' he said sternly. 'The sugar's for shock.'

'You must have used a tablespoon,' I muttered. 'It *is* a shock,' and to my own consternation gave a watery giggle, then instantly sobered. 'What about Walter?' It was how I always thought about the man I'd called 'Father'. 'Will the police pass on the news that he's a widower, do you think? Not that I imagine he'd care after all this time.'

'The Hamilton lot, once they know, will want to talk to him, so I'd say yes.'

'They've got to find him first. I have no idea where he is.'

'They'll work it out fast enough. He'll have a vehicle, or be on the electoral roll. They'll want to interview him, and every man in town who was here twenty years ago. Somebody killed her, Penny. They'll be getting their ducks in a row and launching an investigation the moment Greg gets off the phone to them.'

'Of course.' I gave myself a mental shake. 'I hadn't really considered . . .' I had been too busy, immersed in the horror and my own guilt for the feelings I had harboured against my mother. What I felt now, I realised, was anger at the person who had taken her from me. Murder was unforgiveable, a crime from which there was no return, for you could never give back the life you had taken, or undo the harm to those the murdered one had loved. How different would my own life have been had my mother never crossed the path of her killer?

Putting the mug aside, I shook my head at Flint's frown. 'Truly I can't drink that. But I'm okay now. Sorry for falling to bits on you. Now I'm over the shock, I just can't help wondering *why*. Who could have hated her so much to do that? It can't have been premeditated, not unless she really was meeting someone that day. Don't you think?'

'It does seem more like a crime of opportunity, as they say on the cop shows,' he agreed. 'But as far as finding the one responsible . . .' He shook his head, lips downturned. 'Well, I wouldn't get my hopes up, Penny. It's twenty years. The killer could be anywhere. He could've left the country. He could be dead.'

'Or he could still be right here,' I said hotly. 'That's what we have cops for. It's up to them to find out who did it, and if I have to call Greg every day to remind him there's a murderer to be brought to book, then I will.' I stood up, handed him back the damp cloth and turned to the door. 'In fact, I'm going to see him right now.'

He rose also. 'Do you want me to come with you?'

'It's okay,' I said, 'but thanks.' Moved by a sudden impulse, I leaned across and kissed his cheek. 'You've been very kind, Flint, and I do appreciate it. We'll talk later, but I have to sort this first.'

The corners of his eyes crinkled with his slow smile. 'That's a good start then. Anytime, my lady. Just remember, I'm always here for you.'

Chapter Twenty

Going down the steps with those words in my head, I suddenly thought of Fodo's attitude to living. I felt shaken out of myself by the morning's events, as if the landscape of my life, or at least the fixed positions of that landscape, had been tumbled together and rearranged. So much of the past that had defined me as a person had been subtly realigned with this new discovery that now I hardly knew where, or who, I was any more. My mother was still dead, but this new knowledge changed everything in ways I had yet to explore. Who could have thought that just knowing she hadn't left me could make such a difference to everything? It was as if I had thrown off invisible chains I hadn't known I was dragging. The guilt of past feelings still lingered, but that would pass, exorcised by the memory of her love for me.

I went home but Angus had not yet returned so, after washing my face and drinking a restorative cup of tea (without sugar), I walked across to the police station. Nothing was very far from anything else in Southbend, except perhaps the fuel depot and the cemetery, both sensibly sited on the very outskirts at either end of the town.

Greg was in the tiny office and looked surprised to see me. 'Something you want to tell me, Ms Carter?'

'I'd like another look at that pendant,' I said. 'Technically it belongs to me, so when can I have it?'

'It's evidence,' he said, 'so I dunno. After the trial is the usual answer, so your guess's as good as mine. Frankly, this long after the event, the chances of finding out who killed her aren't great. There may never *be* a trial.'

'But you will try?' I pressed. 'Whoever's responsible, he musn't get away with it. She was my mother!'

He looked uneasy. 'You aren't gonna start crying again, are you?'

'No. Was there anything else found with her? She would've been wearing a wedding ring. And what about shoes?' Try as I did, I couldn't remember what she'd had on her feet, but leather wouldn't have completely rotted away, would it?

He consulted a thin file on his desk. 'Nope, nothing about shoes. No sign of any ring. They could've missed it, but it isn't likely. There was this, though.' He delved into a drawer and brought out the pendant along with another plastic bag, which contained two pieces of metal wedged together at the top by two little knobs. I turned the bag about, puzzling over it until it hit me.

'It's the frame of a coin purse. She must've had it with her because she was going to the shop. Shouldn't there have been some coins too? Or did her killer also rob her?'

He shrugged, pursing his lips and wiping sweat from his jowls. 'Might've just carried a cheque book. Not many stations got cash on hand, even now.'

'I suppose,' I admitted, unable to contradict his reasoning.

I gazed through the plastic at the little daisies on their copper backing, wishing I could carry it off with me. 'What will you do now?'

'We'll proceed with our enquiries. Which will be police business, Ms Carter, so if there's nothing else?'

I left unsatisfied, but common sense reminded me that the man was right. So much time had elapsed that it was unrealistic to suppose the killer would be caught. I might, I thought, make a list of the local men, and work out who would have been here twenty years back. But it wouldn't include the station workers who drifted in and out of the district each season, any or none of whom could have been the murderer. And if the police had found the pendant, shouldn't they have also found the ring? You would expect it to still be on or very near her hand, so somebody must have taken it – and what about her shoes? The heels at least should have survived. Had she lost them running from her killer, or had they fallen off when he carried her to her grave? So many questions, to which realistically I might never be able to find an answer.

Angus arrived home on the heels of a storm. Over lunch, while the rain thundered on the roof, I filled him in on the events of the morning. He rubbed his nose furiously, searching for words, his old eyes troubled.

'Well, at least you know now, lass,' he said, 'that it weren't her fault. That bloody copper! Don't they teach 'em nothing about empathy for victims in their training? He wants a good kickin'.'

'That's what Flint said. It was an awful shock and I admit I went to pieces, but now . . .' I stopped to analyse how I felt, and nodded. '. . . now I feel sort of lighter somehow. Yes, it's horrible but, in a way, better. Because it wasn't her decision to leave. Does that make sense, Angus?'

'Yeah.' His gnarled old hand came down to briefly clasp mine. ''Cause you weren't abandoned. Makes all the sense in the world to me. Mind, I wouldn't hold me breath waitin' for 'er killer to be found. Bloody impossible task, I reckon. So the next step'll be arrangin' a funeral when the cops're finished with 'er bones.' He winced apologetically. 'Well, you know what I mean.'

'Yes.' I looked at him. 'She should be buried here. I wonder if we could get permission for that. You occasionally hear about people being interred on the stations, so it wouldn't be so different. I suppose the council would be the place to start?'

He nodded. 'I reckon. But I wouldn't hold me breath,' he repeated. 'Though, come to think on it, council elections are comin' up. Maybe we could get a few other ratepayers to lobby for it too? That might swing it.'

'You're a genius,' I said. 'I'll write up something and take it round. See if I can get a few signatures.'

By the time Lisa got home from school, the rain had stopped and I had carried out part of this plan, taking my petition to Sue, to Marlene at the store, and to Agnes at the pub, all of whom expressed shocked sympathy at the news and immediately agreed to sign. I returned home via Flint's Place, finding him in his workshop, sanding a half-finished design with Meadow hovering in attendance.

'Hello.' I was surprised. 'Fancy seeing you here. How are you, Meadow? How's your mum? I did enjoy my visit the other day.'

'Oh.' She seemed taken aback by my appearance, and rather put out. 'All right, thank you,' and then, blurting it out in that disastrous teenage way I remembered, 'What do you want?' She immediately turned bright red at the gaucheness of the demand.

I ignored her flustered efforts at repair and smiled at her. 'Just a private word with Flint.' I glanced at my watch. 'I think the girls should be home by now.'

'Better run along then,' Flint suggested, sending an absent smile her way. He rose from his work and came to me, voice warm, hazel eyes concerned. 'Are you okay, Penny? What can I do for you?'

Meadow gulped, cast a wounded look at Flint and practically ran from the workshop.

'Oh, dear,' I said ruefully. 'Does she come here often?'

'Pretty regularly of late. I suppose she's bored. Not much for kids to do this time of year.'

'Well, I shouldn't smile at her then, if I were you,' I said bluntly. 'She's got a crush on you, Flint. It's only natural; she's fourteen now, old enough to begin to experiment with the opposite sex, and you saved her life.'

'No way!' He looked astonished and then disturbed. 'She's just a child.'

'And when did you have your first crush on a girl?' I demanded. 'Age isn't any barrier, you know. I was madly in love when I was twelve.'

His eyes widened, then crinkled into a laugh. 'You were? Who was the lucky guy?'

'Oh, stop it,' I said. 'If you must know, he was a boy called Siegfried. He was blonde with blue eyes, the captain of the school cricket team. He didn't know I was alive. It was,' I said, remembering that distant angst, 'extremely painful.'

Flint rubbed his jaw, laughter forgotten. 'Shit!' He looked rueful. 'I never thought anything of her turning up here, apart from suspecting she was at a loose end and wanted someone to talk to. She's a nice enough kid.'

'And,' I suggested carefully, 'maybe she reminds you of Sammy?'

He looked guilty. 'Yeah. That too. Christ! It never occurred . . . Okay, maybe I'll lock the door from now on when I'm out here and she'll get the message. Or,' he said, brightening, 'you could have a word with her mother for me?'

'And of course Meadow's going to heed that? Just think *Romeo and Juliet.* Teenagers thrive on opposition.'

He flung up an arm with a rueful laugh. 'I bow to your superior knowledge. So, you wanted a word – how can I help?'

I explained and showed him my petition.

'Good idea.' He eyed me, asking abruptly, 'How are you feeling?'

'I'm okay, thanks. It's strange. When I learned the truth it was like a dam bursting. And now I feel . . . peaceful, I suppose. I want her killer caught, but at the same time it's like a weight has lifted off me. And doing something positive, like getting her a proper grave, helps too.'

'That's good.' He held out his hand for the petition. 'Got a pen, then?'

'Here.' I gave it to him and as he scrawled his signature, I stepped over to the workbench where the fan was blowing to see what he'd been doing. 'Oh, that's beautiful, Flint. What's it to be?'

'You like it?' He came to my side to lift a large circular frame that he'd cut and fit together so neatly I had to strain to find the joins. The edges of the deep frame were bevelled and the space between, about a handswidth, was filled with a twined design of leaves and bottlebrush flowers, the occasional honey-eater's head and long thin beak peeping out between. More than half the design had been completed, enough to see how the finished article would look.

'Like it? It's wonderful! So much detail.' I ran the pads of my fingers over the intricate carving. 'It's like silk! How long has it taken you? And what will you put in it?'

'I've been working on it a few weeks,' he said. 'It's for a mirror. Can't be finished till I find a glazier to measure it up and cut the glass for me, though.'

'Well, it's almost a relief to know there's something you can't do,' I said, looking at him. Flint grinned, showing a tiny cleft in his chin, and I had the sudden absurd desire to place my fingertip in it. 'What's the timber, and how do you get the images so . . . so precise?'

He shrugged. 'Practice. You draw it on and with the proper tools it's not that hard. The timber's a bit of silky oak I picked up on my last trip out. Doesn't grow up here, as you'd know, but it's great for carving.'

'It's so realistic – I can see every feather on the birds, and each little spike of blossom. Beautiful!'

'I'm glad you think so. I don't decorate many pieces. The timber's mostly best left to speak for itself. But this was sort of crying out for something. Coffee?' I nodded and, laying the frame carefully aside, he lifted a thermos from the back of the bench, turning the fan towards us as he did so. 'Come, sit for a bit and cool off, and tell me what you remember about your mum.'

When I left half an hour later, Meadow was across the road, sitting in the shade on the kerb in front of the pub waiting, I assumed, for Zim to finish work. Or, the thought intruded, to see how long I stayed with Flint? The way she turned her head at the sight of me, to avoid my gaze, practically guaranteed the latter case. I sighed, hoping for her sake that Cupid's arrow hadn't wounded too deeply.

Chapter Twenty-one

Of course, the news of the skeleton's identity was now all over town, due not least to my efforts with the petition, and by the time I got home where the girls were apparently waiting for me, Lisa's first words were, 'Mrs Bentley told us. Is it true, Penny? Was it really your mum who was murdered?' She and Roseanne looked both fascinated and horrified.

'Yes. It's true. I identified the bones by the pendant they found in the hole with her.'

'You mean like the one Flint made us?' Lisa asked, big-eyed, and I nodded.

Roseanne's soft voice said, 'It's so weird that you found her, you know? Like it was meant.'

'I think it's horrid,' Lisa stated flatly and, without warning, launched herself at me, grabbing me in a hug. 'It's awful for you. I'm so sorry, Penny.'

I was deeply touched by her action. I hugged her back, saying, 'Thank you, sweetie. It was a dreadful shock, but now that I know what happened, it's a sort of relief. I won't have to wonder any more.'

Letting go, she nodded, brown eyes serious with the knowledge of grief. 'Yes,' she said quietly. 'You think Sergeant Banner will find out who did it? He doesn't seem very smart.'

Ignoring this observation, I said, 'I doubt it. It's a very long time ago. But I am going to try to have her buried here. I've got a paper to take around town to collect signatures. It's for the council, so they can see it's what the people want – supposing they all sign, that is. I don't know if it'll work, but it's worth a try.'

'We'll help,' Lisa said, 'won't we, Roseanne? We could start now.'

'Well,' I temporised, 'that depends. If Roseanne's mother gives permission . . . and if you stick together. Look, hang on and I'll give Marlene a call.'

A few minutes later, Marlene having given her consent, the girls set to enthusiastically to make a list of streets. 'So's not to miss anyone out,' Lisa told her friend.

'We could get Meadow to help,' Roseanne suggested, while I privately wondered how that would work out.

'Oh, let's just start,' Lisa said impatiently. 'Let's do May Street first, then come back down Condon. That way we can get everyone in the pub on our way home.'

'Not the pub,' I said firmly. 'Angus can ask the drinkers, next time he's there.'

'Oh, but—' Lisa began.

'No way. It's illegal for anyone your age to be in a bar. And,' I added as a clincher, suspecting that she'd likely disobey, 'the sergeant's bound to be there.'

The girls left and I turned my attention to the evening meal. The earlier storm had cleared and cooled the air, but it wouldn't last, I thought, eyeing the distant clouds rising in the north. I heard the clop of hooves and looked out to see Zim jogging home on his huge mount, Meadow sitting behind him. The bay's hide shone in the westering light, his broad haunches as wide as a small table, his feathery fetlocks flashing white beneath him. The flying foxes were beginning to leave the river in a vast swarm of leathery wings, their cries coming faintly through the dusky air as the evening settled gently over Southbend. Spying Angus plodding down the road to the pub for a drink before supper, I withdrew again to the kitchen. All was well in my world.

It stormed again in the night. The air was still and hot as I prepared for bed, and I tossed uncomfortably on the warm sheet, feeling the trickle of sweat where my head touched the pillow. I got up to turn the ceiling fan higher and saw the crowded sky lit with lightning flashes, too far off at present for the thunder to be audible. I dozed off then, but my sleep was fitful with unquiet dreams that made no sense, and I finally woke to a crash that sounded like the roof coming down.

An icy wind swept through the window, flaring out the curtains, and behind it came the rain, thundering down like a river in spate. It sprayed across the room and I jumped up to close the window, then went through the house shutting the rest. By then the yard was already awash, the lightning flashes revealing the bent heads of trees bowing before the storm, and the temperature had dropped ten degrees. Towelling off my wet arms, I returned to bed, pulled the covers up, and lay listening to the racket. It sounded like a hurricane and I was again grateful for the precautionary work Flint had done on our roof.

Daylight revealed broken branches, pots blown over and a litter of leaves shredded from standing trees. One of the poincianas in front of the pub was down. It had survived the cyclone, but last night had been too much for it. Most of the litter came from it. There was three inches in the rain gauge, according to Angus. 'An' about as much again blown straight across it, I reckon. That was some wind. Musta shifted anything that wasn't nailed down.'

'It's certainly messed up the plants,' I said. 'A good thing the house broke most of the storm's force.'

'I didn't even wake up.' Lisa sounded disappointed.

'Well,' I consoled, looking at the dripping morning and the puddles across the yard, 'you can be sure that isn't the last of it.'

Our damage proved to be minimal, but others weren't so lucky. The pub had lost a sheet of roofing iron that, we later discovered, had allowed the bar to flood. Bev Candle, climbing up to fix it, subsequently lost his balance and fell off the roof.

The first I knew of it was a message from Flint delivered by Zim, who leapt off his mount to run and hammer at my door.

'The hell's up with that bloke now?' Angus grumbled. ''E's got a burr up his arse 'bout somethin' and no mistake.'

'Hush,' I commanded. 'Yes, I'm coming, Zim.' I yanked the door open. 'What is it? Your family . . .?'

'Is Mr Flint. He say come now. Is accident at the pub.'

My heart lurched unpleasantly. 'Is he hurt? What happened?'

'Boss fall down. Missus of boss very upset. He say you come.'

'Oh, right.' I sprinted through the house to the vehicle bay and backed rapidly down the drive. I reached the pub before Zim and ran towards the sounds of hysteria coming from the far end of the front of the building, where I found a harried-looking Flint trying to calm Bev's wife, Agnes. She was scrunched down beside her unconscious husband, screaming and sobbing while trying ineffectually to lift his upper body.

'Penny, thank God!' Flint exclaimed at sight of me. 'Can you take her? And phone the flying doctor. Tell him his patient fell off the roof and knocked himself out. No bleeding to speak of, but his right arm looks broken and I dunno what other damage he may have done. Landed flat on his back. He's breathing okay but it's ten minutes now and he hasn't come round.'

'Okay. Come, Agnes. We have to get the doctor for Bev. Come on now. He's safe with Flint, but he needs the doctor.' Holding her arm and continuing to talk, I got the woman to her feet and tugged her away. She was hyperventilating, the sobs coming out as gasps, and I rubbed her back as I urged her onward, hearing Flint behind me giving directions to the hovering Zim.

Once inside, Agnes gave a great gasp and collapsed in a huddle on the floor and continued to sob, moaning, 'Oh God, what if he dies? What'll I do?'

'He's not going to die. He might have broken a bone or two, but they mend,' I said bracingly. 'Where's your phone?'

She ignored the question, rocking on her knees and continuing to cry, so I found it myself in the passage behind the bar and put the call through. The RFDS number, as was usual, was pasted up beside the phone and I got an immediate response, identified my locality and passed on Flint's observations.

'Right,' the male voice responded. 'How long since it happened?' I gave him an estimate. 'And he's still unconscious? I see. You haven't moved him? No, well it's very important that you don't. He could have neck or spinal damage. Keep him warm and we'll be there in a bit over an hour.'

I relayed the message to Flint, found a cotton blanket to lay over the unconscious man, and coaxed Agnes into drinking a cup of heavily sugared tea. She had calmed down enough by then to be amenable to packing a hospital bag for Bev and another for herself.

'I'm going with him.' She glared at me as if I had attempted to stop her. Half Aboriginal, half Chinese, her life could not have been easy and there were those in town, I knew, who thought she had latched on to Bev as a meal ticket, but I didn't doubt her feelings for him.

'Of course. What about the pub? Is there anything . . .?'

'Zim can mind it. He's already helping in the bar.' She nodded, her head busy while her hands continued to scoop things into a toilet bag. 'I'll take the cash to bank and do the re-ordering while I'm in town.' Her voice started to shake on the last words and she burst into renewed sobs.

I put my arm around her, saying soothingly, 'He'll be all right, Agnes. The doctor's on his way.'

'And what if he isn't? What if he dies? He's the licence holder, not me. He should never have been on that bloody roof in the first place!'

'No, well . . . men, you know. Look, I'm sorry, Agnes, I know how worried you are, but don't give up on him just yet.'

She wiped her nose and looked at the wall clock. 'He should be here soon. Zim had better go out to the strip to pick him up.'

'Can he even drive? Zim, I mean?'

'What?' The blank stare she gave me changed as my words sank in. 'Well, you go. I can't leave Bev.'

I waited at the airstrip to collect Doctor Bronsen, his nurse and the pilot and brought them back to the pub, giving them a quick rundown of the situation en route.

'He's probably conscious by now,' I said optimistically, only to find on arrival that I was wrong. Zim had erected one of the outdoor table umbrellas over the patient to shade him and Flint from the growing strength of the sun. Bev lay supine beneath it, his skin grey and clammy looking, his breathing stertorous.

Flint nodded at the doctor. 'G'day, Doc. He doesn't seem too bright, or sound it either. We haven't shifted him from where he landed.'

'Good. That's good.' Bronsen squatted beside the comatose man. They had brought one of those stretchers in two pieces that clipped together under the patient. I watched as they secured a collar around his neck, then lifted him a few inches, one side at a time, to get the stretcher beneath him. An oxygen mask was fitted and with minimum talk between the men he was loaded onto the back of a Toyota belonging to the pub. The doctor was curtly efficient. I thought he looked worried. He was noncommittal with Agnes, who demanded to know when her husband would awaken.

She scrambled onto the vehicle's tray beside the stretcher, with Bronsen on the other side. The nurse, whose name I hadn't heard, climbed into the front with the pilot and, with a shrug at me, Flint got behind the wheel.

Zim and I waited together for his return. 'Did she tell you she wanted you to look after the pub?' I thought to ask.

'Boss Missus? Yes. Also I fix roof.' He was busy dismantling the umbrella.

'Well, mind you don't fall off too.'

He bridled. 'Me, I am the cat. I do not fall. Boss is too fat for roof, not strong.'

'Not fit, you mean? That's true enough.' Bev bordered on obese; his weight would have worsened his fall. Glancing around, I saw the finished concrete work and commented on it. 'The paths you've made look very nice, Zim.'

'I am good worker,' he said complacently. 'No boss ever complain. I am sad at first when is done, but he give me other jobs and now'—he folded his arms and stood four-square, looking at the pub—'now I am boss here.'

'Well, some good comes from everything,' I said. 'Listen, there's the plane taking off now.'

Five minutes later, Flint returned and garaged the vehicle.

'Hop in,' I said, returning to mine. 'I'll give you a lift back. How did you come to get involved, anyway?'

Flint pulled the door shut and reached automatically for the seatbelt. 'Zim. Seems I'm his go-to guy for emergencies now. Agnes's panic had him just about paralysed, and I knew neither of them would manage a coherent phone call, so I sent him to get you. Hope you don't mind. You did a good job with Agnes, by the way.'

I pulled in before his place. 'Happy to be of service. Do you think he'll be okay?'

'He was still out to it when they loaded him. I dunno, but I reckon that's not a particularly good sign. More like a coma than just being knocked unconscious. And it was a hard fall, Penny. The man weighs a ton. He must've hit the ground like a load of bricks.'

I sighed and switched off the motor, twisting sideways in my seat to face him. 'What a year we're having. First the cyclone, then finding my mum, and now this. Poor Agnes. I know she's a bit of a taskmaster when it comes to Bev, but honestly he was born lazy. He *needs* someone to drive him. Doesn't mean she doesn't love him.'

'It comes all shapes,' he agreed, 'as we both know. Do you want to tell me about Michael – that was his name, wasn't it?'

'Yes.' I felt his eyes on my face as he waited through my silence. Eventually I heaved another sigh and met his gaze. 'He deceived me, but I did love him, even after I found him out. Michael was . . .' I searched for the truth amid the mix of hurt, bruised pride and residual anger in my heart. 'He was fun. And very loveable. I hadn't had much of either in my life until then. Not since my mother lef— died. He gave me joy. The fact of his death was as devastating to me as the things it uncovered. I cannot fathom why he did it – married me, I mean – because he seemed to have loved his real family, but I truly believed in his feelings for me.' I traced my fingers over the steering wheel. 'It was so hard for so long after I found out how he'd deceived me. You know they say that ignorance is bliss? They're right. I was happy. And then when it all unravelled . . . Half the time I wanted to die and for the rest—'

Flint's hand captured my wandering one. 'You wanted the satisfaction of killing him yourself.'

'Yes,' I admitted. 'Not very appropriate thoughts for a widow. Only, of course, I wasn't that. I was never more than his mistress.'

'And now?' He hadn't released my hand. Instead his own fingers wandered over my knuckles and drew tiny circles on the back of it sending little shivers through me. 'How do you feel about him now?'

I stared at his face, from the dint in his chin to the straight gaze of his hazel eyes. His hair, carelessly pulled back at his nape, had loosened, the sun-bleached ends fringing his jaw-line, and there was a slight dent in the centre of his nose, as if to match his chin. 'Different,' I decided. 'Now I'm more angry at myself for being conned than at him.' The shivers had reached my spine. 'And somewhere along the way I've stopped loving him. I always wondered, you know, about abused women who wouldn't lay charges against the men who beat them up. Maybe they were afraid to, but there seem to be any number who claimed they still loved them. Even if they'd put them in hospital. So I suppose by their lights I'm less than loyal, but for me, love equals trust.'

'As it should, Penny.' He carried my hand to his lips, pressing them against it. 'Can't see anything wrong with that. Makes you normal. Can you hop out for a tick?'

'Yes, I . . . Why?' But he already had his door open and didn't answer. I opened my own and stepped down as he came around the bonnet to me.

'Because kissing in a vehicle's for teenagers,' he said. Then his arms came around me and his lips were on mine, a gentle caress that deepened into something more. I closed my eyes and kissed him back, opening my lips, my hands tangling in his hair until he eventually drew back.

'Wow!' He was smiling. 'That was worth waiting for. Come in for a cuppa?' There was a twinkle in his hazel eyes.

I said feebly, 'I'm not even sure if Angus is on the job,' but I knew I was going indoors with him for whatever the cuppa delineated, and I seriously doubted it included teabags. 'But I'll risk it.' I reached for his hand and he laughed and pulled me close, so that over his shoulder I caught a glimpse of Meadow across the road behind us, halted in midstride and glaring daggers at me.

She wheeled about in an instant, running back up the street, and I bit my lip. 'Oh dear, I think we may have just broken a heart. That was Meadow. You can look now, she's leaving.'

'Good,' he said ruthlessly. 'If that's what it takes. I'm getting tired of hiding in my shed. This way, my lady.'

Chapter Twenty-two

It was lunchtime when I got back to the house to find Angus peering helplessly into a cupboard, the makings of a sandwich spread across the benchtop.

'Where've you been?' he asked, adding crankily as he shut the cupboard, 'An' where the hell do you keep the chutney?'

'Next door over, bottom shelf. Did you hear about Bev?' I asked, ignoring his first question.

'What about him?'

'He fell off the pub roof and he's in a bad way. The doctor came for him – you must've heard the plane?'

'That was the doc, was it? Yeah. What was a great fat bugger like 'im doin' up on the roof anyway?' He unscrewed the lid and spread chutney liberally on the bread.

'It was leaking after the storm, and I expect Agnes nagged him into it. She's flown in with him, frantic with worry, poor thing. She's left Zim in charge. Do you want a cuppa with that?' I turned to the jug, feeling a sudden flush of heat at the word.

'You bet.' He pulled out a chair. 'What about you? Ain't you eatin'?'

'Yes.' I was ravenous all at once and set about making myself a sandwich.

'So what was the doc's verdict?'

'He didn't give one but he looked concerned. Bev was still unconscious; his arm was certainly broken and he could've had head or spinal injuries. Put it this way, I doubt he'll be home within the week.'

I spoke more truly than I knew, for the evening news carried an item on the flying doctor's emergency trip to evacuate a patient from the little Gulf town of Southbend. The man, rendered unconscious in a fall, had presented in a coma and was subsequently flown on to Townsville for lifesaving surgery. His condition was described as critical.

'Poor old Bev, he doesn't sound too good,' Flint observed. He had dropped in after dinner, his smile and the brush of his lips against my cheek making my body tingle.

'What will happen at the pub?' Lisa asked. 'Can Mrs Candle run it by herself?'

'She's not there, sweetie,' I said. 'She flew out with her husband, but Zim's going to look after things. It's only for a bit. I expect Agnes will come back when Bev's out of danger.'

'Did you see him? Roseanne's mum said his neck was broken.'

'I did see him, yes. He looked very poorly. But I don't think his neck was broken, the doctor just put a collar on it. It's a precaution, that's all, something they always do. In case there is an injury. Have you got homework?'

Lisa sighed. 'Yeah, yeah, I know. I'm gonna do it. Right now,' she added as the signature tune for the news sounded.

'That's my smart lassie,' Angus encouraged, heaving himself up. 'I'm outta beer. Might look in on Zim – see how he's goin'.'

As the front door closed, Flint slid an arm around me. 'Think he's just giving us room?'

'Maybe, you can never tell with Angus. On the other hand, he *is* out of beer.'

'Any excuse,' Flint murmured, planting a line of kisses along my jaw. He reached my lips and I kissed him back before pushing him gently away.

'Not now. Lisa's just through the wall. I'll come over to yours tomorrow.'

He settled back, hoisting an eyebrow at me. 'Are we keeping us a secret then?'

'She's an impressionable young girl, Flint. I need to talk to her first,' I said. 'It's difficult – you must see that. She's only just stopped hating me for being her father's other woman, so she wouldn't be too impressed to find me in your arms.'

'It's been three years!' he protested.

'Since Michael died, yes, but she idolised him. It takes time for children to accept change. You do understand?' I said anxiously. 'I'm responsible for her wellbeing, so I can't just think about what I want.'

His expression softened and he sighed. 'Of course. Very well, my lady. We'll be as discreet as you wish, though if it was up to me I'd stand on the pub's roof and tell the whole damn town. I'm crazy for you, have been ever since we first met. You know that, Penny, don't you?'

'I'm getting the idea,' I said gravely, reaching to push

a strand of hair back from his face, and he laughed and kissed me again.

The following afternoon, I heard Lisa arrive back from school. 'Is that you, girls?' I called from the kitchen. Receiving no answer, I turned from the sink to find Lisa in the doorway, regarding me with a set face. 'Hi, is it just you? Well, there's lemonade in the fridge. Where's Roseanne?'

'Not here.' She dropped her schoolbag and, folding her arms, took a pace forward to confront me. 'Meadow said you're having it off with Flint. Is it true?'

I winced. 'Really, you girls! Flint and I are friends. Close friends. And I cannot see that being any of Meadow's business. Or yours.'

'Yeah? You were "close friends" with my dad too, weren't you? Have you asked Flint if he's already married before you go wrecking someone else's life?'

'He's a widower, Lisa,' I said patiently. 'His wife died. And he and I are both adults. Within the limits of the law, we can do as we please. Remember that little talk we had about respect and privacy? What I do or don't do is no concern of yours.'

Her face went scarlet and tears of temper sprang to her eyes. 'And what about me?' she yelled. 'You go off with him and what happens to me and Grandad? He's old and he's got nowhere else to live. It's not fair. I hate you!' she screamed in impotent rage. 'You can't . . . You're just doing it again! Wrecking lives—' She was sobbing angrily, the tears choking off her words as she gasped for breath.

I went to her and tried to hug her, but she fought me off, still yelling.

'Listen!' I said, 'just listen, Lisa! Nothing is going to change. I'm not leaving town, or you, or your grandfather, or the nursery. We will all be together, you and me and Angus, no matter where my friendship with Flint takes me. Is that clear?'

Lisa quietened mid sob, her brown eyes brilliant in their dampness. In a small voice she said, 'You promise? You're not just saying that?'

'Cross my heart.' I did so, adding frankly, 'You can be a royal pain but I've got fond of you, you know? Maybe I even love you a bit, so you're stuck with me. Better get used to the idea.'

'Yeah, well, I was,' she said hardily, but her bottom lip quivered. 'And when Meadow said she'd seen you kissing him, I thought you'd do it again. Take him away and leave us—'

'Never! And I didn't take your father, you know. It was his idea. He asked me to marry him.'

'Yeah, well, you didn't say no,' she sniped.

I sighed. 'We've been through this, Lisa. As far as I knew then, I was free to say yes. I thought you understood that.'

'I'm sorry,' she said stiffly. 'It just seemed—' Sniffing mightily, she swallowed and tried again. 'I was scared. I like it here. I like you and Grandad, and Southbend. But Meadow knows about love and stuff—'

'She thinks she does, Lisa,' I said patiently, 'but thinking's a long way from knowing.' I was appalled to realise that Lisa had believed I would abandon her. I hugged her fiercely and to my surprise she let me. 'Be kind to her – to Meadow. She's very upset. She's got a crush on Flint and that can be very painful. And yes, she did see us kissing, so she hates me right now, but time will fix that. She's only fourteen, and though she doesn't think so, and you mightn't either, that's very young.'

Lisa wrinkled her nose and sniffed again noisily, applying her usual candour to the subject. 'But how can she fancy him? He's old. Older than you.'

I laughed and kissed her cheek, the first time I had done so. 'I know. Tragic, isn't it?' I straightened up. 'Have a cold drink. I'm making a casserole. You can help me with the veggies if you want.'

Two days went by without news of Bev, though it didn't stop people asking one another if they'd heard how their publican was getting on. Zim, according to Angus, was as much in the dark as the rest of us.

'It must be serious,' I said to Flint. 'Agnes wouldn't normally just abandon the business. I mean, not a word on when she's returning?'

'It's only been two days,' he pointed out.

'But what does Zim know about running a pub?'

Totally relaxed on the bed, arms clasped behind his head as he watched me dressing, he said, 'Enough to keep the bar functioning. This time of year, that's all that matters. Are you going already?'

'I must,' I said regretfully. 'I have a business too, and the lunch hour can only stretch so far.'

It was just as well that I had stayed no longer, for the police vehicle pulled up before my front gate only moments after I'd passed through it. Turning back on the verandah, I shaded my eyes to see Greg Banner and a stranger wearing ordinary clothes – khaki pants and a polo shirt with a flat-brimmed Akubra looking rather incongruous above it.

'Ms Carter,' Greg called, 'a moment of your time, if you would.'

'What is it, sergeant?' I nodded at the stranger. 'Hello. I'm Penny Carter.'

He extended his hand. 'DS Wently.'

'Oh. Do I have to guess?' I asked flippantly, 'Dave, Des – what?'

He didn't crack a smile. 'Detective Sergeant. I'm told you're the one who identified the item on the body from the cemetery. Can we go inside, Ms Carter? I'd like to ask you some questions.'

Once again I found myself recounting the story, not just of watching my mother drive off to her death, but as much as I could remember of the weeks leading up to her disappearance. A lot of his questions I simply couldn't answer and said so frankly. 'Look, I've told you I was nine years old – just a child. I simply don't know.'

Wently had a round hard face and eyes like gimlets. Under the hat, his hair was receding; he would be bald in a year or two, I thought. His hands were large and freckled, the left one sporting a thick gold band. 'You'd be surprised what children know,' he said. 'It's just they don't put it together because they haven't the worldly experience to marry it all up. For instance, how did your parents get on? Were they a close couple? Was your father kind, loving?'

I gave an involuntary shiver. 'No. He was very strict. I was scared of him. We weren't close at all, probably because he wasn't my real father. At least that's what he said.'

'What – he told you that?' Wently fairly quivered with eagerness.

'No, it was something I overheard. They were rowing, in the bedroom; he and my mother. He shouted it at her that I was . . . that I wasn't his.' *Some other bastard's by-blow* rang in my head.

'So they fought then, your parents. Only the once, or all the time?'

'Whenever Mum did something wrong.'

'Wrong? What do you mean wrong – like what?'

I shrugged helplessly. 'I don't know. We'd be happy, she and I, and then he'd come home and something wouldn't be how he liked it, or maybe she hadn't done something right and he'd start to shout. She always sent me to my room then. I think he might've hit her, but I don't know. She never said.'

Looking down, I spread my fingers, remembering the touch of her hand as she smoothed the hair back from my brow afterwards, whispering, 'It's all right, Tuppy, everything's fine.' I closed my fingers into a fist. 'I know now that he was a control freak. He was much older, I think, and I suppose he had rigid ideas . . . She was very'—I searched for a word—'pliable. Always trying to please him. Left to herself, she was happy, carefree – when she could be. I think that's why I believed the talk, that she'd run off with someone else.'

'And the day she left, what did she take? Did she pack a bag, for instance? If you saw her drive off, you should have seen anything she put in the vehicle.'

'She had her purse. It – well, the metal frame of it – was found with her. Because she was going to the shop and Walter – that's what I call him now, not Dad – always said you had to pay for what you got. He didn't believe in credit. Of course, I didn't know what that meant then, and I remember thinking he was silly because you couldn't buy stuff without paying – it was how shops worked. I suppose notes would've rotted away but if there were coins they should have been found. Unless the murderer took them, of course. Like he took her wedding ring.'

'Did he? How do you know?'

'They didn't find it and she always wore it.'

I heard her voice again in my mind. 'Because you make a promise, and the promise is in the ring,' she had told me one day, twisting it about on her finger. I had, I remembered, asked why ladies wore them. 'A ring is a circle, Tuppy. And a circle is forever; it has no beginning and no end. You just stay inside it.'

I hadn't understood her but now I remembered the way I had stared, fascinated at the golden band. 'Is it magic, Mummy?'

She had given an odd little laugh that came out wrong, though I couldn't work out why. Laughing meant happiness, and she hadn't sounded happy. 'You could say so, Tuppy. Like a spell that holds you fast to the end of time.'

Chapter Twenty-three

They left finally and Flint, hearing the details at a later date, had nodded sapiently. 'They'll be after your dad.'

'He's not that,' I said sharply. 'But you're right. That was the next thing Wently asked about. I couldn't help him. The last time I saw Walter Carter was the day he put me on the mail truck. I haven't spoken to or heard from him since. He could be dead for all I know.'

'Sorry, love.' He kissed a knuckle on the hand he held. 'How old do you reckon he'd be now?'

I considered. 'Well, his hair was greying twenty years ago, just round the ears and the front of his head, you know. So he was maybe in his forties then. He seemed quite old to me, but what do nine-year-olds know? He'd have to be in his sixties now, at least, maybe even his seventies, but I couldn't begin to guess given the way this climate ages everyone, then add years of hard yakka on top. How old do you think Bill Howard is?'

Flint raised his brows. 'The bloke that owns Rumhole? Oh, fifty easy. Why?'

'Wrong,' I said. 'Ellen got me to pick up a birthday card for him last time I was in town. He'll be forty-one in March.'

He nodded. 'I see your point. So, what else did they want to know?'

'Only who was at Bracton Park when she left that day. Walter had a couple of men he employed for mustering, but I don't remember their names, or even if they were there then . . . So I could only tell him about our cook, and she was just Winnie to me.'

'Not a lot for them to go on, then. And, incidentally, picking up on your observation, I don't see any signs of premature ageing in you, my lady.'

'No? That's sweet of you. But I haven't been back here very long either.'

He grinned. 'So you'll be old and haggard in another ten years? Is that what you're saying?'

I smacked his hand, smiling fondly. 'Idiot.'

Flint had barely left – in fact, I was still on the verandah watching his tall form walk away – when the gate clicked and I looked around to see Fodo coming up the path. A braided headband held the hair back from her face and she was dressed in her swirly collection of bright colours with a red tasselled belt.

'Hello, Penny,' she called in her incongruous accent. 'Is this a good time for a visit? I can leave if you're busy.'

'Oh, no,' I disclaimed. 'As you see, it's hardly a hub of industry here. This time of year, my customers are too busy fighting off plant growth to be thinking of buying more.'

'I get that. I've never seen grass grow the way it does here.'

'Well, come in. What about a cold drink? It's a long walk from the Common.'

'That would be lovely, thank you. As for the walking, I'm accustomed. We mostly walk. Too much packing up involved in taking the wagonette.' She looked about appreciatively as she followed me into the kitchen. 'This is nice – spacious and light. Windows aren't practical for us.'

'Have a seat and I'll pop the kettle on, though we might take the tea out onto the verandah when it's made. Cooler there. So, has Zim heard from Agnes about how Bev's getting on? Do you know if he's even regained consciousness yet?'

Fodo shrugged thin shoulders. 'Zim hasn't heard, so I can't say. I believe we might learn something soon though. Agnes rang last night to tell Zim that she wished to speak to me at five today, so I thought I'd take the opportunity to call on you as well.'

I raised my brow. 'Oh, I see. I wonder why? I mean,' I added hastily, hearing how that sounded, 'does she have trouble with Zim's accent? I suppose if the line isn't good . . . Or she could just prefer to deal with a woman. I have noticed Agnes doesn't hold a high opinion of men.'

'Zim did mention that she was the force in the marriage.' Fodo smiled. '"The Boss Missus wears the boots" was how he put it. He never can get his head around our sayings.'

I laughed with her, piling the mugs and teapot onto a tray and leading the way outside. 'Come. It's a bit early for Angus, he's a creature of habit when it comes to meal times, so it'll be just us girls.' I arranged and poured, then sat down to pass the biscuits. 'How's Meadow?'

She rolled her eyes. 'Being a teenager. Moods and sulks and "What would you know anyway?" I suppose I've a few more years of that to get through.'

'Luckily Lisa hasn't reached that stage yet, though I must say I'm not looking forward to it. Of course, I'm not her mother – which may or may not help.'

She considered this, head on one side. 'But you're close to your niece?'

'She's not actually my niece,' I admitted. 'It's a bit complicated. She lost both her parents and Angus is her only relative, but he can't raise her himself. So, as I'm here . . .' I left the rest unsaid, adding, 'I'm really glad she thinks of me that way, though. We didn't have the best start, but we're learning to rub along.'

Fodo smiled. 'I think you'll find it's more than that. She's always quoting you and telling us all the things you know about growing stuff.'

'Really?' To hear that was a gift I had not expected. 'It's so hard to know if I'm getting it right, you know? Having none of my own, I have no experience with children, so it's a case of by guess and by God, and hoping I'm doing more good than harm.'

'Kids are more resilient than you think,' she said comfortably. 'I remember when Meadow was six . . .'

We chatted until Angus, whom I'd quite forgotten, came in looking for smoko. 'Oh, don't go,' I said impulsively as Fodo rose. 'I'll make a fresh pot. Talk to Angus while I boil the jug.' So she had stayed on until Angus took himself off again and then, with a glance at the sun, rose from the table.

'I've really enjoyed myself,' she said, flashing her wide smile.

'I don't get that many opportunities to have another woman's company. Thank you so much, Penny. It's been lovely.'

'Well, come again soon,' I said. 'I'm always here. And if there's news of Bev . . .'

'Yes, of course, I'll let you know,' she promised and I stood watching the graceful sway of her skirt as she walked away down the path.

The following morning, Lisa had not long left, walking by way of the shop where Roseanne would join her for the short journey to school, when someone tapped at the screen door. I called, 'Come in,' and, drying my hands, went to meet the visitor. 'Oh, Fodo. You're abroad early.'

It wasn't quite a question but she saw my surprise and said quickly, 'I'm not stopping. Zim dropped me off so I could pass on the news. We're moving into the pub. Agnes has given him the job of manager.'

I raised my brows. 'I thought that's what he was already doing.'

'No, I mean, a more permanent arrangement. Agnes doesn't know when or even if she'll be returning. Certainly not in the short term. So she wants us to take over while she sorts the business out. That phone call last evening – she was quizzing me about my knowledge of book-keeping, and apparently it's satisfactory.'

'I see. So, what's the prognosis for Bev? It can't be anything good if she's talking that way.'

'It isn't. She's known for a little while now. He broke his neck in the fall, and his arm and pelvis. The last two will mend but'—she grimaced—'he's a quadriplegic. Can you imagine, Penny? That poor woman. First she thought she'd lose him and then to learn that he's completely paralysed . . . It's too awful for words.'

'Pretty devastating for poor Bev, too,' I observed. 'Well, it mightn't be how you wanted it but the change will give you windows, and space. What does Meadow think about it?'

'She's excited,' Fodo admitted. 'It's like I've suddenly got the real Meadow back. She's already planning her room and asking if she can get a job in the pub too. I told her maybe cleaning the rooms when guests come, but she's not working the bar. It'd be illegal, for starters, at her age.'

'What will you do with the wagonette? I suppose Bev's rehabilitation will take months, if not years.'

'Zim's towed it up to the pub – he dropped me here on the way. The horses will stay where they are for now.'

'You may never need them again,' I said lightly and she pulled a face.

'It's a big change for us. Zim has a restless nature, so it will depend . . . He's getting older, but aren't we all? And permanent work.' She blew out a breath and laughed a little, plainly excited too, by the turn their lives had suddenly taken. 'No point worrying. I'll just enjoy the change and see what happens.'

And the novelty of that change, I thought as she bade me goodbye, might give Meadow something other than Flint to think about.

There had been no rain now for two days, so it seemed a good time to finish collecting signatures for my petition. The girls had done a sterling job with the closer streets but they hadn't got as far as the northern end of town. And while I was on the job, I could pop in on the Haddons. Jim Haddon was the shire clerk. I barely knew him, but my request to allow my mother to be interred in the old cemetery would go through him to the council, so getting him on side, if I could, would help.

I told Angus what I was up to and drove to the end of the unimaginatively named River Street. Leaving the vehicle, I continued on foot, hallooing from the pavement where dogs were involved and making my way to the screen doors where they weren't. I also took the opportunity to canvass opinion on whether or not those I spoke to thought cleaning up the cemetery for the tourists was a good idea.

The answers differed from 'Why bother?' to energetic agreement, and one red-eyed man, barefoot and wearing nothing but his boxers, whom I'd obviously woken, snarled, 'Who wants to bloody know?'

'It's a CWA poll,' I said, trying for a winning smile and with one eye on my line of retreat. He looked hungover and stroppy, and in no mood to sign anything.

'Time-wasting bunch of bloody old women.' He slammed the screen shut and I heard him swear as he tripped in turning away.

The fuel depot was the last in the street. I glimpsed Barry working on something in the open-fronted workshop, which was set back from the huge, fenced re-fuelling area that contained space enough for semi-trailers to manoeuvre in. I walked around the back to the house where the ground sloped down to Cutaway Creek, and banged on the screen door, calling out as I did so. 'Hello-oo, Muriel?'

She came to the door, broom in hand, which she set aside at sight of me.

'Penny! Well, and I was just thinking I should pay you a visit.' She wore an old-fashioned full-length apron over her clothes and beckoned eagerly. 'Come in. I've got a slice in the oven so you're just in time for a cuppa. What brings you here, anyway?' She waved a hand at the wide window sill, where the cactus she had bought was flourishing in a squat ceramic pot glazed in an eye-watering shade of blue. 'There's your cactus. Looks good, doesn't it?'

'Yes, it's doing well.' I saw she also had window boxes filled with herbs, though the mint looked rather chewed over by grubs, I thought as I followed her into the kitchen. 'What I came about, Muriel, was a petition I'm getting up, for the council when it meets next. I'd like to see my mother's remains interred here, in the old cemetery. I will need their permission, and there might be other legal hoops as well to get through, but I thought if I started with the council . . . So I'm trying to get the town behind me, if you like. I won't be asking Barry – after all, he's a councillor, and I wouldn't want to put him on the spot – but I wondered if you might sign?'

'Why not? Mind you, if the scheme to upgrade the place doesn't go through, you might want to reconsider.' She grabbed an oven mitt to pull the slice out onto the bench and decanted it onto a cooling rack. 'There,' she said, replacing the tray and bustling to the sink. 'I'll just get the jug on, and we can be comfortable. I'm glad you've come. I think there's something you need to know.'

My heart sank. I desperately didn't want to become party to whatever bit of salacious gossip she had to impart but, short of walking out, there was little I could do to prevent it. A flood would be easier to stop than Muriel in full flow. Resigning myself, I said as disinterestedly as I could, 'Oh yes, and what's that?'

Chapter Twenty-four

Satisfied at having secured if not my interest then my attention, Muriel was in no hurry to impart her information. She set out the cups and sugar bowl while the jug boiled, then made the tea and cut the still-warm slice into pieces, which she arranged on a plate decorated with pansies and forget-me-nots.

'There.' Satisfied, she sat herself opposite and with one large hand gently turned the pot from side to side to help the tea draw. She was big all over, Muriel, as tall as most men with thick grey curls springing from her head. She wouldn't, I reflected, have ever been pretty but she was certainly capable, as her rescuing of Zim's horse had shown.

The thought brought the words to my lips. 'The horse is fine, you know – the one you saved. The girls tell me his limp's finally gone, so his leg's right again.'

She nodded as if it was no more than she expected. 'My dad always said I was good with animals. They'll let you help 'em if you go about it right.' Apparently satisfied with her ministrations to the pot, she poured and passed me a cup, and when she had offered the sugar, milk and eats, got down to business.

'The detective in town – he's been to see you, I imagine?'

'The unfunny Mr Wently?' I was surprised. 'He's not still here, is he? I did see him, but I thought he went when the plane did.'

'No.' She rubbed her chin. 'He stayed on, looking into things, asking questions from those of us who've lived here longest. Even been into the council records, so Jim Haddon said.'

'Really? Why? Does he think Bob Page is a wrong 'un?' I spoke flippantly, but I felt a deep unease at whatever she was working around to disclose and wished to distract her.

It didn't work; she replied seriously, 'Of course not. His old man, Billy, was chairman back then anyway. Bob wasn't elected till '85. No, Wently wanted to know about the men who were in the district back in the seventies. He was particularly interested in your dad, and I happened to mention, you see, how the little properties found it pretty tough to survive the seventies, with the Beef Crash and all, and how men like Walter took on outside work. Like fencing, and small droving jobs. I remember one year,' she said reminiscently, 'he walked the buckjumpers into Hamilton for the rodeo, and another time he brought the new herd bulls for Rainsford up from the railhead. Little jobs like that it didn't pay the real drovers to touch, but was extra cash for the battlers like your dad. He—'

'What's all this got to do with anything?' I broke in impatiently.

She looked at me with something of regret in her gaze. 'I'm sorry, Penny. I didn't think. Not that I bear any liking for Walter Carter but he is your father . . . I told the copper that he took fencing contracts too. And afterwards I remembered that it was him who did the repairs on the cemetery fence. When Jim told me Wently had been to the council office looking at the records, I just knew he'd be after the name of whoever got that contract. Because, you know, if your mother had already been buried there, whoever dug that posthole – and it must've been your dad – would have found her.'

It made sense. I swallowed hard. He wasn't my biological father but if it was true then I bore the name of a murderer.

'He came home late that day,' I said. 'And he was in town because he knew my mother was missing – he saw her vehicle.' *By the river,* he had said, *so she musta drowned.* 'Have you told Wently this?'

'He already knew. He found the payment records for the work. He asked me about it.' She spread her large hands helplessly. 'There wasn't any point in my lying, Penny.'

'No,' I agreed flatly. 'I wouldn't expect you to. Well, I imagine everyone's aware that when it comes to murder the police's first suspect is always the spouse. The whole district would've known that my parents didn't get on. And that's a motive in itself.'

'Most people felt sorry for your mum,' Muriel agreed. 'He was a hard man, Walter.' She hesitated. 'Of course, there doesn't have to be anything in it – he wouldn't necessarily even have met her that day, not if he was working. But that Wently's a proper ferret, a real copper's copper—'

'And?'

For once she actually seemed reluctant to continue. 'Well, he was asking about the Gaiter girl too.'

I stared blankly at her. 'Who?'

She shook her head, clicking her tongue in annoyance.

'I keep forgetting you were only a child. There was a young woman who vanished a month or two before your mum did, Colleen Gaiter. She was the cook at Mount Ixion. She left at the end of the season, supposedly for Hamilton, but she never arrived. There was a search but nothing came of it and in the end it was assumed she'd changed her mind. She had her own vehicle, you see, and it was thought she'd headed off west – to Darwin maybe, or the Alice. Even Perth. She was a bit of a free spirit by all accounts, up for anything different. She was a nurse but she'd chucked all that training to come out here and give station work a go. And you can't really blame the cops, because if there'd been an accident or foul play, the thinking was that the vehicle would've turned up, eventually. Nothing stays hidden forever.'

I could have cited a few instances to dispel this myth, but didn't. 'And Wently's assuming – what? That Walter might have dug another posthole for another body? That's hardly credible. What reason would he have if he didn't even know her?'

Muriel shrugged. 'It's probably rubbish. Except we don't know that he didn't know her – or so Wently said. He's like a ferret,' she repeated, 'that's tasted blood and wants more. Doesn't mean there's anything in it, but I thought you should know.'

I got up. 'Thanks, I think. For the tea anyway. It's . . .' I couldn't decide what I wanted to say, so I left it and was halfway to the door when she called me back.

'Here. You forgot this.' She handed the petition to me. 'I hope it works out for you. I'll have a word with Barry about it.'

I nodded numbly and left.

*

Later that night, Lisa in bed, I repeated Muriel's words to Angus, the two of us sat under the kitchen fan, Angus sipping at his beer while I squeezed a fresh lot of limes for tomorrow's drinks. The Tahitian lime out the back, the first tree I had planted on arrival in Southbend, was more than generous with its bounty.

Angus, rubbing his nose, said, 'Gotta say I reckon any copper could make a case for your dad bein' dead guilty.'

'He's not my father,' I corrected tiredly, 'and I agree. But I don't think there's a chance of tying that other woman to him. I mean, why would he do such a thing? Okay, I can believe it of him about my mother. He was a violent man and, however innocently, she did seem to anger him – but a stranger? Why would Wently even think it? If, of course, he does, and it's not all in Muriel's head. Maybe it's a case of her just liking a bit of drama?'

'He's glory huntin'.' Angus crumpled his empty can and burped on a gust of beery breath. 'Wants the kudos for solvin' two deaths in one, see.'

'We don't even know that the woman is dead.' I looked around as a tap sounded on the screen covering the open window, followed in quick succession by others, a tiny repetitive knocking at odd intervals. Getting up, I saw it was dotted with small, shield-shaped bodies and became aware of a faint, repulsive smell. 'Oh, God! The gidyea bugs are swarming. I suppose I'll be sweeping them up for a week.'

Hurriedly I finished with the limes, swept the table clean and placed the squeezed juice into the fridge before shutting the window. 'We'd best get the lights out or the room will be full of them.' I had never worked out how bugs and insects got through fly-screening, but they did. That was another thing about the Wet. The plagues of Egypt, as Angus might've said, had nothing on the wildlife that the Gulf Country seemed able to produce at will – everything from flying ants to locust swarms – and I had learned that all one could do was to wait out the visitation and clean up afterwards.

February slipped over into March and a week of dry weather followed. It dried the topsoil and put a yellow tinge in the grass tops where seeds had formed. The days were still and hot; the monsoon, according to weather reports, had retreated northwards, but there was no saying it wouldn't be back. March could host the heaviest rain of the year or conversely, the Wet could already be over with only intermittent showers to come. After so long with grey skies and heavy cloud, it was good to feel the sun again and see the blue arching above the river timber.

I heard no more from the police. I had no way of knowing if they had located Walter, and Wently seemed to have left town again.

'It'll be on the news if they arrest him,' Flint said. 'And if they do catch up with him, I reckon he'd need a pretty good story to stop 'em doing so.'

'Mmm.' I brooded on what facts we had. 'If they do and it comes to a trial, I suppose they'll call witnesses – Muriel, for instance. Maybe Bob Page – he mightn't have chaired the council back then, but he'd have been on it. And of course he'd have known Walter.'

'They say murder will out.' Flint brushed a hand down my arm. 'Let it go, love. How about taking a trip upriver with me – you and Lisa? I did promise her a day's fishing. It'll be perfect for it now. The river's clear and if the Wet is ending it'll give me an opportunity to check out my best fishing spots – see if the flood changed them, or brought timber down. Don't want to be smashing a prop while I've got my first customers on board.'

I sat up, pretending indignation. 'So you're saying it doesn't matter if it happens when it's just me?'

He grinned. 'Little spitfire. Can't think of anyone I'd sooner be stuck in a boat with, miles from anywhere.'

'Yes, well, Lisa would be there too.' I let him draw me to my feet. 'So, we'll need lunch then? I'll pack it.' It was a Saturday. Angus could keep an eye out for callers, and tomorrow would be time enough to catch up with work in the nursery.

Lisa was at a loose end. Roseanne, she said, was helping her mother in the store. They were turning over the stock and making lists of what was needed for when the road opened. 'She gets *paid* for it,' Lisa revealed, and I couldn't work out if she was envious or simply amazed.

'Well, get your hat and sunscreen if you're coming. And if you put some freeze blocks in the esky, we could take some cold drinks. I'll just grab my camera, then we'll go.'

It was peaceful on the river, with no sound but the birds and the quiet throb of the outboard. Flint had backed the tinny into the water, loaded the rods and bait and put out a steadying hand as Lisa and I stepped aboard dry shod. We stowed the food and seated ourselves as he started the motor, steering us upstream.

He smiled at me. 'Bit different to last time.'

'And thank heavens for that.' I gazed around, remembering our hazardous trip down Cutaway Creek. 'This is so restful. Like drifting through a green tunnel.'

The banks were thick with growth, the pandanus thickets like prickly soldiers forming a fence below the taller tropical growth of river fig, myrtle and wild plum, with weeping melaleuca, heavy with blossom, drooping between them all. Sunlight, dispersed by the greenery, danced on the moving water with fleeting glints of light as we puttered through sweet drifts of scent. The river ran so clear that every stone in its bed was visible and we had barely started when Lisa let out a strangled squeak of excitement.

'I saw a fish! And there's some more!'

'Angler fish, for a bet,' Flint said. 'Do they have black spots?'

'Yes. How did you know?'

'They're everywhere. Little pipsqueaks – they like the shallower water and the banks under the low-hanging leaves. It's where they get their tucker from.'

'How far are we going?' I asked.

'Depends. Let's just see how it goes.'

When the water deepened, he gave me the tiller to hold and got a rod out and baited up for Lisa. 'For when we stop. Ever cast before?'

'No. Dad and me used handlines.'

'I'll teach you,' he promised, 'when we get to the spot.'

We motored on past black and white shags drying their wings on dead tree branches and white herons perched amid the living ones. Very occasionally the bank growth cleared to stony rubble, where cattlepads wound down to the water's edge, and once we saw a family of wild pigs rooting along a muddy bank. They fled at sight of us.

'After mussels,' Flint said. The water had changed to a darker green. 'Getting deeper,' he said. 'Number Two fishing hole coming up.'

'What are the cliffs?' I pointed upstream where the edge of rocks could be seen above the timberline. 'I never knew they were there.'

'It's the beginning of the gorge. Only a short 'un; deep hole coming up. The river bed drops, you see, so the cliffs look higher than they are, because the timber starts lower – if that makes sense? We'll have a look later, after we've tried the rods out here.' Flint cut the motor and let the current drift us bankwards, where the top of a fallen tree provided a handy tie-up point. 'A new one,' he said, slapping the wood. 'It's come down in the flood.'

It wasn't the only damage visible. As the river had narrowed, I'd noticed the gaps in the pandanus and seen the torn vegetation and piled debris along the banks. The watermarks on the melaleucas bore testimony to the height the waters had reached, and in places whole sections of the bank growth had been felled, as if a bulldozer had pushed through it. Creepers, the sappy growth of young Noogoora burr and a purple flowering convolvulus vine were taking advantage of the sunlight, already crowding into the space where the trees had been.

Flint baited a line and worked patiently with Lisa, teaching her how to cast and handle the rod. 'What about you, Penny?' he asked but I shook my head.

'Carry on. I'm happy as I am.' The boat moved gently in the current, tugging on its painter as Lisa, scowling in concentration and biting her bottom lip, tried to follow Flint's instructions.

'Gently,' he said. 'Don't jerk it. It's a smooth action.' She wound in and cast again and he said, 'Better. You're getting the hang of it.'

I raised the camera and took pictures of the two of them, backlit against the river's sparkle, just as Lisa gasped and the line sprang tight, curving away through the water.

'Flint, I got something,' she squeaked. 'What do I do?'

'Let it run a bit. Now, brake. Good, that's good – it'll set the hook. Now, wind it in. Slowly.'

The line was thrumming as she leaned back, her thin arms tautened against the pull. Flint stepped behind her, holding the rod firmly.

'Feels like a big 'un. Wind her in, that's the way. Rest when you need to, then wind some more.'

She struggled gamely on and finally, red-faced from exertion, with the tip of the rod bowed almost to the water, she brought the fish to the boat's side. It leapt once and I gasped at the flash of silver. Flint cheered. 'You've got a beauty! Get him a bit closer.' He leaned over, grabbing the nylon just above the waterline to heave the catch into the tinny, where it flopped about their feet.

'What'll we do with it?' Now it was caught, Lisa looked uncertain, stepping hastily back from its gyrations.

'We'll stick it in the bucket,' Flint said. 'Can you dip it over the side, Penny?'

I did so, hauling the dripping vessel back, and he slipped the now-freed fish into it, saying, 'Good job, Lisa. Best-sized bream I've seen in a twelvemonth.'

'That's dinner,' I said. 'Another one like it and we'll have a feast. Well done, Lisa!'

She flushed with pleasure. 'I never knew they were so strong.'

'Well, have a rest,' I said. 'It's past midday, Flint. Shall we have our lunch now?'

'Good idea.' He winked at Lisa. 'Get your strength up for the next battle.'

She laughed and bent over to look in the bucket where the fish now lay recovering. 'Don't be lonely,' she told it. 'You'll have a mate pretty soon.'

Chapter Twenty-five

We ate our sandwiches and drank the tea and cold juice I'd brought, watching the birds that twittered about us or skimmed down to drink. A shag surfaced beside the boat, startled at its mistake and promptly vanished again. High above us came a flash of white wings, the wrong shape for a heron, and I looked at Flint, who had also noticed it. 'What's that bird?'

'Fish eagle. There's a pair that live about here. The tree we're tied to used to have an eagle's nest in it. Could've been his. Feeling strong again, Lisa? Wanna try for the next one?'

She agreed eagerly but a fruitless half-hour saw her interest wane.

'Time to move on. We'll try the gorge hole,' Flint said, slipping the painter free and starting the motor.

We chugged forward as I handed Lisa the sunscreen. 'Slap a bit more on. Good heavens, look at the banks here. They've been stripped bare!'

'They certainly have.' Flint slowed the boat and pointed at the southern cliff face that rose in a sheer ochre wall, now without benefit of cover. 'There was no big timber along here, the banks are solid rock, but there was a covering of vines and creepers. The flood's ripped 'em all out. See the watermark up there?'

'God! No wonder it reached the town. It's a miracle we weren't all swept away,' I gasped, awed. 'The river must've come through here at ninety knots.'

'Yeah.' Flint reached to shut the motor off. He tipped it up and unshipped the oars. 'We'll just go a little way. Could be anything down there.'

'I thought you said it was deep?'

'It is in the middle. Not so much here.' Even as he spoke, an oar clunked solidly against an obstruction below and we all peered over the side, our eyes defeated by the depth and not helped by the shadow of the gorge wall.

'Is it a tree?' Lisa asked.

'Bloody big one if it is.' Flint prodded about with the oar, which kept hitting the object. He pulled the boat forward and tried again with the same result. Whatever was there was about a metre below the surface. 'I'll have a look.' He kicked off his footwear, removed his hat and slid over the side, setting the boat rocking. We saw the pale soles of his feet as he duck-dived, then the expanding ripples where he'd been.

Long seconds passed. Lisa said, 'What's he doing?' and bent to peer over the side.

I was getting a little anxious myself. I stared at the spot where he'd vanished, wondering if his clothing could have got caught in submerged branches. How long had he been gone? I assumed he was a strong swimmer – he spent half his working life in boats, after all. Then, just as I was about to stand up to do something, his head broke the surface some three metres ahead of us.

'There you are!' I exclaimed as he swam towards us and grabbed the gunwale. 'I was getting worried.'

'Boat's drifted,' he said. 'Reckon you can man the oars and pull it back a bit?'

'I suppose. What did you find?'

'I'm not quite sure.' He sent the wet hair from his eyes with a violent shake of his head. 'Can you hand us the fish donger from under the seat? And see what you can do with the oars.' He took a great gulp of air and then another and swam off. A few moments later his soles flashed again as he dived.

Rowing was not as easy as it looked. I persevered clumsily, hitting the water wrong on every second stroke until I thought we were about in the right position. Lisa, meanwhile, peppered me with questions I had no answer for.

'Just be patient.' I was watching the shore, which seemed to be shifting so I dug the oars in again. The current didn't look much, but the occasional leaf or blossom that rode the surface floated by quite quickly. Then Flint bobbed up beside the boat, holding up the donger I'd given him and a short piece of what I saw was buckled metal. I took it from him. 'What . . .?' I turned it over and recognised the enamelled figures, and the torn holes where the rivets had been.

The boat rocked violently as Flint hauled himself aboard, and I dropped both items to clutch at the side.

'A *vehicle*?' I was dumbfounded. 'There's a vehicle down there! What . . .? I mean, how—?'

'Makes you wonder, doesn't it?' His voice was flat. He tossed his hair back, squeezed water from his face with a flattened hand and donned his hat. 'I'm sorry, Lisa, but we need to go back now. I'll have to report it.'

'But how did it get there?' My mind couldn't deal with his discovery. 'And when? I mean, if you're up here all year—'

'My guess? From the top of the bluff there. It's pretty near a straight drop. There's only a metre or so of space between the cliff and the water. It'd sink like a stone if the windows were opened, and only something like the flood we just had would shift it. It was you who said the water must've come through the gorge at ninety knots. That'd do it, I reckon.'

'Yes,' I said feebly. 'I suppose it would. Which doesn't tell us who or why.'

He nodded at the number plate. 'But that will. Once the cops have traced the registration.'

I looked up, studying the gorge's sheer cliff – maybe ten or twelve metres high. 'It doesn't explain how a vehicle could get up there in the first place. You surely couldn't drive it up!'

'Actually,' Flint said, 'you could. Picture it as a hill chopped in half. This is the cut side, the other is just a high ridge with an easy slope. A four-wheel drive would make nothing of it. It's why only those using the river ever see the gorge – from the other side, you'd never guess it's there.'

Which meant that the vehicle, or whoever had driven it, must be local. I had a horrible thought but as I opened my mouth, Flint slanted his eyes at Lisa and gave an infinitesimal shake of his head. I swallowed the question and said instead, 'Well, at least we've got something for dinner. Do you think we should invite our guide to help eat it, Lisa?'

'Of course.' She grinned happily. 'Can we go out again sometime, please, Flint?'

*

Back at the landing point, Flint left the boat tied up and drove us home before carrying on to the police station. Cleaning the fish while Lisa filled Angus in on our day, I wasn't surprised when she darted out the back to inform me that the police vehicle had just driven down to the river.

'I expect the sergeant wants Flint to take him back up to the gorge.' I held up the cleaned and scaled fish. 'What a beauty! Do you want it grilled or in batter?'

She hesitated. 'What do you think Flint would like?'

'I have no idea. Grilled is good though, with veggies and a mornay sauce?'

'What's that?'

'Like a white sauce, with mustard and cheese.'

She nodded eagerly. 'I'll help. Then can I tell Flint I made it myself?'

I swallowed a sigh. The man was a positive magnet for impressionable girls. 'I don't see why not. Particularly if you chop up the onion and grate the cheese yourself. They're the messy bits.'

Dinner was a great success, with Lisa basking in her role as chief provider. Flint complimented her on the sauce and said he'd taken a buoy up with them to mark the position of the submerged vehicle.

'However will they get it out?' I asked.

'Airbags. It's how they salvage wrecks at sea. Raise the vehicle, empty it out, then tow it to shore.'

I raised my brows. 'It doesn't seem likely that Greg would have the necessary equipment.'

'No, the bags'll have to be brought in. He'll need a compressor too, and a boat. He did sort of imply that it was my public duty to lend mine, but I told him I owed a greater duty to my creditors – that he could hire it and me, or find another solution.'

'Well, there are a few other boats in town.' But their owners were neither as reliable nor as discreet as Flint. 'By the way, are we sworn to secrecy about your find?'

'It wasn't mentioned, so I guess not. I figure the cops in Hamilton will match the number plate and be looking at historic crimes for an answer. They'll have scope enough. Land Rovers must've been around since the fifties at least. We had one when I was a kid.'

'So did we,' I said.

Angus nodded. 'Flavour of the month. Wasn't till about the seventies that Toyotas took over in the bush.'

When the washing up was done and Lisa had gone off reluctantly to bed, Angus refused coffee, saying there was nothing he wanted to watch on the goggle box, so he'd turn in too. I raised my brows at Flint, who nodded. 'Why not? I'm always good for a coffee. And a cuddle,' he added, patting the sofa he'd shifted to.

'Let me get the jug on first.' Lightning played beyond the windows and I could hear the steady whine of mosquitoes above the frogs. 'I don't think it'll be long before the rain's back.' The chorus of amphibian sounds that filled the background of the night was so common that I normally barely registered it, though it always seemed to increase before a storm.

'The Met office happens to agree with you,' Flint said. 'So, I reckon the cops'll have a plane in here tomorrow with the gear. They won't wanna risk losing the vehicle.'

I handed him his mug and nestled in beside him. 'Yes, I've been waiting to ask. What did you see down there? You looked awfully grim after.'

'Did I? I had reason. The vehicle wasn't empty when it went in, Penny. There was a heap of bones inside. Not animal bones. The skull was upside down on the front seat, but there was no mistaking that it was human.'

I yelped as my mug slipped, spilling the coffee over my hand. He caught the cup up immediately and set it down on the low table before us. 'Sorry. Stick that under the cold tap.'

I did so until the smart eased.

'Better?'

'Yes,' I answered distractedly, sitting back down. 'God, is this town Murder Central or what? That's so awful! I wonder who . . . It couldn't have been an accident?'

'No way, my heart. Nobody accidentally drives off that cliff. Suicide? Possible, I suppose, though I can think of easier ways. No, your first reaction's probably on the money. Banner's already got it pegged as murder.'

'But – *Southbend*?' I was incredulous. 'It's not exactly Chicago!'

'It's an old town. Been here, at least the pub has, since about the 1860s. Old towns have their sins and secrets.'

'Maybe. Well! So this is life in the peaceful countryside?'

He slipped an arm around me. 'Is that why you came here?'

'No. It was for a fresh start, to forget the past. Like you.'

'In that case, this might help.' He pulled a flash of colour from his pocket and handed it to me. 'Made with a great deal of sweat and swearing, but I think I've got it about right, this time. Those findings you told me about were a big help.'

'Oh, it's lovely, Flint!' It was a bracelet, a series of small enamelled copper squares with a fine chain linking both sides of each square, and with a closed hook and eye clasp. The enamelling, gold on a brilliant blue, depicted a series of tiny infinity signs that must have taken a very steady hand to achieve. I offered my wrist for him to fasten it in place, then held it up to admire. 'Thank you! It's beautiful. I love the colours.'

'Ah.' His eyes laughed at me. 'Gold for your hair, blue for your eyes and the sign is to show that my love for you is infinite.'

'Poetry, too!' I swallowed emotion, feeling my eyes prick. 'You are so talented, Flint. I wish I was only a quarter as clever.'

'You're perfect just the way you are.' The words were lost in a kiss but presently he moved his head back, a glint in his hazel eyes. 'You think we might take this into the bedroom?'

And recklessly, no longer minding who knew, I murmured, 'Why not? Come on, then. What are you waiting for – a written invitation?'

Chapter Twenty-six

Flint left me with a kiss at daybreak, creeping out of the house before the others stirred. 'Don't want to scandalise the neighbours,' he murmured.

'Of course,' I agreed ironically, thinking of all the unmarried – at least to each other – couples in town. Still, I was setting a bad example to Lisa. I wondered at the change in myself, I who had refused intimacy with Michael until we were married, thinking that a ceremony would protect my love. Instead I had got a sham union that had ultimately hollowed my heart with grief and, yes, a degree of fury because his death left no one to vent it on. That selfsame heart was a strange, contradictory organ. Was it Fodo's example, with her acceptance of life as it came, or the discovery that my mother hadn't abandoned me that had opened mine again to the risk inherent in placing my trust in another? Or was it just time?

Not only my trust, but my love, I admitted silently. Because I did. I loved, wildly and madly, a man whose first name I didn't even know.

*

Flint was right about the speed with which the police moved. A light plane arrived over the town a little after nine o'clock, and by ten the police troop carrier, towing a packed trailer, had collected Flint from his place and driven off. Greg Banner, I reflected, couldn't have been this busy since I'd arrived and was probably heaping curses on his absent constable, who was still, I assumed, convalescing in Hamilton.

Word had spread about the drowned vehicle. Lisa would have told Roseanne and Meadow, and it was a short jump from there to the rest of Southbend. Only Flint and I knew about the bones, so the interest was more historical than morbid, the old hands in town being canvassed for their opinion of likely ownership. Marlene, calling in to return a CD, predictably asked me for 'all the details' and was disappointed to learn that I had none. I'd seen nothing and only heard the oar clunk against a solid object under the water.

'Ask Flint,' I suggested, knowing he was absent on the river. 'He was the one in the water.' She left, unsatisfied, as did Muriel and even Sue, who came, breathing heavily, to plump herself down on a large, upturned earthenware pot and ask about it.

'All I know is that it's a vehicle. Could be an old wreck – somebody getting rid of junk.' Which was plainly ridiculous. I switched the topic. 'Any idea how our plans for refurbishing the cemetery are going?'

'Well, actually, I rather think that what's happened there is helping our cause.' Sue swished the large leaf of a philodendron, in a pot beside her, like a fan before her heated face. 'The media have been all over the *mystery skeleton*, as they've billed it, and the ongoing police investigation, so even an old dinosaur like Bob Page has got to see that the first lot of tourists through will be wanting to view the murder ground.' She grimaced. 'Sorry. We all know it was your mum, Penny. What I mean is, it's now definitely in the council's interest to have the place done up. At the very least they'll have to re-fence it.'

'Fiona Reilly may get her wish after all,' I said. 'Maybe I should hint to Marlene that bicarb soda might be a good investment. For the headstones, you know. There's not much it won't clean, and the carving on them is just about lost to mould.'

'Good idea.' She heaved herself up. 'If this weather holds—'

'I doubt it will,' I said. 'It's nice today, but I fancy we've a way to go before the Wet's over.'

'Can't come too soon for me.' She waddled away and I returned to work, wondering how the salvage job was going in the river.

Lunchtime came and went. Succumbing to curiosity, I walked across to the pub, carrying a jar of my rosella jam as an excuse. The place looked spruce, I thought, latching the gate. Zim and Fodo had obviously thrown their backs into the job. The lawn was mown, the path raked and along the verandah's edge several small drums had been cut down, painted green and decorated with flower images to serve as plant holders. Zim was behind the bar, his only customer Ollie, the town's perennial barfly. Catching the former's eye, I held up my offering. 'Fodo?'

He beamed at me. 'In the behind. You go there.' He gestured at the door. I nodded and smiled and went through into the short passage that led to the kitchen. I found Fodo chopping meat into cubes in the spacious room with a large gas range and even larger refrigerator.

'Busy?' I asked. 'I've brought you some of my jam. Rosella only keeps a few months and I always make more than I can use.'

'Penny, how nice.' Her hair was tied back today, and an apron cinched her trim waist. 'Did you say rosella?'

I grinned. '*Not* the parrot, if that's what you're thinking. It's a northern fruit, cousin to the hibiscus. You pluck the sepals that wrap the seed pod and use them. It's delicious. Makes great pies too. So, how are you finding life in a real house?'

'Thank you. It sounds like a lot of work and what a lovely colour. I'm sure we'll enjoy it. And living here – it's not too bad, actually.' She finished her task and rinsed her hands. 'Fancy a cuppa?'

'I've not long had lunch, but thanks.' I nodded at the table with its generous helping of meat. 'That'll make a lot of dinner.'

'Four extra tonight – we've got our first guests,' she said. 'They came in on the plane this morning, on account of the vehicle in the river. There's an underwater salvage guy and a couple of others. I don't know how long they'll be staying, but first impressions, you know? A good meal always goes down well with men.'

'Feed the brutes,' I agreed. 'How's Meadow?'

'Oh, she's loving it, being here. Fixing up her room, titivating the place. She did those.' She nodded at a fan of dried flowers in a little plaited holder affixed to the wall. 'She's always collected bits and bobs and made stuff from them. She's very artistic, my daughter.'

'It's lovely,' I said sincerely. 'Is the holder made from strips of cabbage palm? How clever!'

'The planters out front were her idea too,' Fodo said. 'At least it's stopped her moping around and'—she shook her head, smiling—'I rather think the young salvage guy may have made an impression, though she only saw him for ten minutes. He *is* rather dishy though, so I can't fault her taste.'

'Oh well, her age,' I said excusingly, but I was glad to hear it. Teenage crushes could be as short lived as they were violent.

'Yes.' She looked at me. 'Our visitors do seem very determined to recover this vehicle. What's that about? I mean, of course rivers shouldn't be used as dumping grounds, but it's a lot of expense, I would've thought. It's not as if there's much traffic along the Rainsford.'

'No, well, I suppose there'll be an explanation someday,' I said evasively. 'Have you heard from Agnes lately? How's Bev doing?'

'He's in rehab now, but I think it'll be a while yet before they let him out. He's got no movement at all in his arms, which is terrible to think about.' Fodo shuddered. 'And he's not coping well, according to Agnes. Well, I'm sure I wouldn't be either. To be so dependent on another.'

'Fortunately she seems devoted to him. Though I'd never have guessed before. I used to think she was like a sheepdog, driving him every which way. It just shows, when the chips are down . . .'

'Mmm.' She was looking at my wrist. 'That's a very pretty bracelet. New? Wherever did you find it?'

'Oh.' I felt myself colour and closed my other hand over it. 'It was a gift, and yes, it is lovely. Simple but striking.'

She smiled. 'So you are seeing him, then? Lisa showed me her pendant and she said he was potty about you. I had wondered myself, ever since the pair of you saved Meadow. I'm glad for you. Flint seems a nice guy. Attractive too.'

'He is,' I said stiltedly, and she laughed.

'Go for it, Penny. I'm only surprised he's still available. You too, for that matter. There's not what you'd call an overabundance of young women up here, so I'm really astonished that you're still single.'

Perhaps it was time to stop hiding the past. I said, hoping I wouldn't regret it, 'Actually I've been married. But he died, some years back. So—'

'Oh, I'm sorry.' Along with the words came a swift glance from those green eyes. 'Well – but you're over it, yes?'

'It didn't end well, so yes, I am.'

'Good for you. We all have to move on in life. And your niece seems happy about you and Flint.'

'She is now,' I agreed. 'Until recently I wasn't aware she even knew.'

'Kids'll pick up on the slightest thing,' Fodo said cheerfully. 'Especially girls. I'm sure there's antennae under their hair that pop out at puberty and there's not much that gets past them. The boys, bless them, rarely have a clue.'

Not much wiser, I returned home, resigned to waiting on Flint for news. The clouds were building again and the birds seemed extra restless. Perhaps it was down to the wind that had arisen, but by mid-afternoon, screeching flights of corellas and galahs had swept in across the town to the shelter of the river trees, where their silhouettes constantly rose and descended upon the foliage there. The plovers that haunted the sodden verges of the roads seemed super active too, their plaintive clinking calls piercing the afternoon's heat.

'Gonna storm,' Angus said. He rubbed his nose, faded gaze on the river. 'They don't get that vehicle outta the river today, she might be five miles downstream this time tomorrow.'

It was spitting by the time Lisa got home from school, and a drenching downpour arrived on the heels of Flint. 'You'll stay for dinner?' I asked, kissing him to the sound of falling rain.

'Love to. I dunno what's in my fridge, so yeah, that'd be great, thanks.'

'Good.' A blast of wind blew the rain in on me and I shivered. 'Come inside. Looks like it's setting in. So did they get the job done?'

'Yep. Thanks, Angus,' he added, taking the offered beer. 'They brought a scientific bod for the bones and some sort of army engineer with underwater experience to handle the wreck, and another cop. For muscle, I guess.'

I nodded. 'Fodo said she had four guests. The fourth must be the pilot. Where do you suppose they got the army fellow from so quickly? Incidentally, you're safe from Meadow now. He's apparently the poster boy of the moment.'

'Ah, good to know. The engineer was up on a training gig for the boys in the CMF in Hamilton – the weekend soldiers,' he clarified, seeing my confusion. 'They train with the regular army now and then, and learn from 'em.'

'Oh well, lucky chance then. Was there anything else in the vehicle?'

'Yeah. A bag, pretty well rotted, and some other stuff. Dunno if it's enough to identify her by though.'

'You said "her",' I pointed out.

'Slip of the tongue on Greg's part. I've a feeling the cops already have a good handle on her identity – they just weren't telling. I reckon the number plate's come through for them.'

'So we get to wait to hear it on the news?'

'That's about the strength of it.' He cocked his head towards the thunder on the roof. 'The way it's raining, it might be a while. I don't see them getting out of here in a hurry if this keeps up.'

I smiled. 'Meadow won't mind. Come to the table. Let's eat.'

Chapter Twenty-seven

The rain continued through the night and morning radio brought news of a low-pressure system in the Gulf. The sky was a dull heavy grey, the clouds all but resting on the tree tops, and intermittent spatters of rain blew across the town.

Lisa, who had heard the weather report, looked apprehensive. 'Is there another cyclone coming?'

'Not necessarily, sweetie. Sometimes lows are just rain depressions. And even if it should develop into a cyclone, it doesn't have to come here.'

'It still might.'

'Well, anything's possible.' I abandoned the topic. 'What are you going to do today?' It was a Saturday. 'It's a bit wet to be going out.' Another shower rattled on the roof as I spoke.

'I don't know. Cooking? Maybe we could try a new recipe?'

'Why not? See if Roseanne wants to come over. What about you, Angus?'

'Me?' He seemed startled to be asked. 'Ah, dunno. Might weld a coupla braces onto them shadehouse frames. There's a bit of steel left over from that last job. Been thinkin' about it for a while. Another blow could bring 'em down. Flint comin' over? He could give us a hand holdin' stuff.'

'I expect so,' I said lightly. There was plainly no point pretending; it seemed the whole town was aware of our situation. Why should it matter anyway? We were both adults, free to do as we pleased. A little thrum of excitement at the thought of him went through me as, humming, I set about my daily chores.

The following day, the radio delivered the news that a 69-year-old man had been arrested in Augathella in connection with an historic murder of a woman whose remains had been unearthed in a small Gulf Country community. The arresting officers had returned the man to Hamilton, where he had appeared before a magistrate. Bail had been denied while further investigations were undertaken.

I put down the plate I'd been drying and looked across at Angus. 'They're talking about Walter.' My hands, I saw with surprise, were shaking. I clenched them to still the tremors. 'I wonder what he was doing in Augathella? Have you ever been there?'

'Passed through once.' Angus was clearing the table. He shoved the cereal box into the cupboard, picked up the marmalade pot and, before he could slam his hand down on the lid of the butter, my nerves cracked.

'Don't!' I shrieked. 'You do that every time. And every time I expect to see butter all over the table. Can you just please put it on gently?'

His bristly brows rose in pained astonishment, but he lifted his hand before it made contact. 'You all right, lass?' My eyes filled at the concern in his gaze and I gave a gasp and next minute found myself hugged against his chest, sobbing into his withered old neck.

'I'm sorry. I don't know what made me snap at you like that. It *is* an annoying habit, but I don't mind what you do with the damn butter. Truly, I don't.'

'Hush,' he said gruffly. 'You'll be fine, lass. Looks like they've got their man, which means you'll be able to put all this behind you and get on with your life – wherever it's goin'.'

A sudden insight into the worry he had concealed made me pull back to see his face and say, 'You mean Flint, don't you? He won't make any difference to our partnership, Angus. You and Lisa are my family. We go together, so he will just be joining us.' Or not, I thought. Flint had never indicated that he wanted a permanent relationship. Perhaps he regarded our situation as just a dalliance to help pass the doldrums of the monsoon? I immediately banished the thought. It wasn't that. I loved him and I was as certain as I could be that he returned the sentiment. Hadn't he said, 'My love for you is infinite'? Where, I wondered, was the old me, the one who had been emotionally disengaged and wanted love locked in and secured by the key of marriage? I would follow Flint anywhere, barefoot, content with any scraps of attention he could spare . . . I gave a little snort of amusement at the change the man had wrought in me and Angus stiffened.

'You sure you're okay? I could get him over if you want.'

'Dear Angus.' I kissed his whiskery cheek. 'You haven't shaved this morning. I can get him myself, you know. No, I just . . . After all these years I've found my mum again and now maybe there's a chance of justice for her too. I guess it just got on top of me. Women, you know,' I said, trying for flippancy. 'We cry at anything, whereas men poker up and grow ulcers instead.'

'If you say so.'

'I do. Well.' I sniffed and gave myself a mental shake. 'I suppose we could start getting the seed trays set up in the shed today. By the time this lot of weather's over we should be ready to plant the annuals – supposing a cyclone doesn't develop, of course. That'd delay things a bit.'

'Right. I better clear the work bench then. Same quantity as last year?'

'Maybe an extra tray or two of flowers. They sold out quite quickly last time. The veggie seedlings aren't such good value, or maybe more people grow their own.'

'You're the boss,' he said amicably and, catching sight of Lisa who had just come in, added, 'Wanna help your old grandad, Squirt?'

'Depends.' Lisa eyed him suspiciously. 'Is it anything stinky this time?'

'No, nothing like that. Besides, shovelling a bit of manure never hurt no one. We'd just be handlin' pottin' mix, filling trays.'

'Okay then. I'll help – till Roseanne gets here, anyway.'

They went off together and I heard Lisa squeal as a sudden shower caught them halfway to the shed. March was the wild card in the Wet pack. It could bring the heaviest rain or taper off and end altogether as soon as the wind shifted and the south-easterlies began to blow. Seeds planted now would be up by April, which was the beginning of the growing season for gardeners in the north, and town folk with those aspirations mostly bought their started annuals from the nursery. Heavy rain now would put everything back by weeks.

But there was nothing I could do about that. I finished the housework and, after a quick tidy before the mirror, went out and down the street to tell Flint about the arrest of the suspect in my mother's murder case.

Nothing came of the low in the Gulf; it travelled east to fragment over the western side of Cape York and within a week the showers tailed off into dry days with streaky wind clouds.

'Wet's over,' Marlene announced, casting an experienced eye at the heavens. 'My bedroom window was rattling this morning, which means a south-easterly wind. Give it ten days and we'll be seeing the mail truck from Goola again. I'd best be getting an order ready. The shelves are getting awfully empty.' She glanced across at the back of the police station. 'I saw Greg leave this morning. The troopie looked well loaded – he had those steel tracks they use for bogs tied on up top. Like he was trying for Hamilton.'

'He might be lucky,' I said. 'Wouldn't the creeks still be up in the limestone country?'

'I expect he can sit and wait on 'em running down. Maybe the young fella – Whitberry, that's it; I'll forget my own name next – is ready to return to work. He's been gone a good three months or more.'

'It was a nasty crash, though,' I reminded her. 'He's really lucky to be alive.'

'Have you heard anything more about the vehicle they pulled out of the river?' She dropped her voice dramatically. 'Barry Lacey reckons there was a skeleton in it.'

'Really?' Of course it was bound to get out. I wondered if I was still supposed to hold my tongue on the subject. 'Who told him that – or was it reported somewhere?'

'Somebody from *The Leader* rang up asking him if it was true. Do you know if it is?'

The Leader was Hamilton's local rag. 'Sounds a bit unlikely,' I said. 'Didn't they print a story about a traveller who'd sighted a UFO last year? Anyway, why would I know anything?'

'Well, I thought perhaps Flint . . . Him helping the cops out – they might have said something.'

'You'll have to ask him yourself.' Determinedly I changed the subject. 'If the rain's over, the CWA ought to be able to meet pretty soon. Maybe we can get the cemetery project started? Only Fiona won't make it in for a while yet.' The roads to the stations further north were always the slowest to dry out.

'Ah,' she said with guilty satisfaction, 'that's what I meant to tell you. Sue asked me to pass it on. She's organising a teleconference for the members so we can have the first meeting in our own homes. That way we can get started now. It's not too long till Easter and there're the sports trophies and food, not to mention the working bees, to organise. Stan was down at the racecourse yesterday for a look. He said there's dried mud caked all over the food stall floors and walls from the flood. It's going to take a bit of cleaning, I can tell you. He said a firehose wouldn't go amiss – pity we don't have one.'

'What a good idea of Sue's,' I said. 'Let me know the day and time. Now I really must go. See you, Marlene.'

'Yes.' Suddenly distracted, she wrinkled her brow. 'I have to – oh, yes. Tell the other members, that's right. God! My memory . . .' Marlene was the CWA secretary. 'I'll go ring Muriel and the rest of them while I'm thinking of it. Honestly, sometimes I wonder if I'm getting Alzheimer's.'

Later, alone with Flint in his workshop, I passed on Marlene's news, adding, 'Do you think the reporter will try and follow it up?'

'Yeah. It's what they do. Can't see why the cops would worry about it getting out, anyway. She's dead and whoever did it is long gone. I'd've thought a bit of publicity could only help.'

'Mmm.' Watching his hands move rhythmically as he planed a piece of timber held in a padded vice, I brooded on the dead girl's fate, rousing myself at last to ask, 'What are you making?'

'A what-not stand for a corner. A small set of triangular-shaped shelves,' he elucidated. 'The sort of thing that might hold a vase of flowers and a doodad or two. I was thinking of maybe carving the brace work at the back – a fern design. What do you reckon? It'll probably be my last piece before the roads open up.'

He would be too busy then for woodwork. 'Doodads?' I teased. 'What're they when they're at home? Ferns sound lovely. Do you dream about your designs, Flint, or just dream them up?'

'Both.' He grinned at me. 'Don't tell me you don't dream about your plants.'

'Of course not.' I rose and shook a handful of curled shavings from my skirt. 'Only about you,' I said, and kissed him and left.

Chapter Twenty-eight

The teleconference worked well, nobody's connection was lost (a minor miracle) and the lines were clear, but Sue as convener had to be ruthless, cutting short long-winded discussions to allow everyone a voice before the time ran out. At the end of the session it had been arranged who would manage the different tasks needed to ready the sport's grounds and food stall and which station would provide the meat for the inevitable barbecue, and the members' approval had been attained for discussions with the council over the cemetery project. Then, just before our time ran out, Sue issued an invitation to those who could make it for afternoon tea at hers.

Leaving Lisa in charge of watching out for customers, I changed my blouse, put some chocolate muffins I'd made on a plate and walked the two streets over to the low-set house where the Harts lived on a spacious block that included a goat yard down the back.

Sue had set up a table on the verandah, one end of which was crammed with plants. A miniature cumquat in a terracotta pot struggled for space amid a plethora of ferns, potted geraniums and dumb canes. The flat leaves of baby's tears had colonised the pots, and various succulents strove for their share of light amid its smothering form. Seeing me looking, Sue asked, 'So what do you think? Doing well?'

'Very. Whatever you're feeding them is certainly working. You need to clear that ground cover though.' The plant was a positive pest and spread like flu germs.

'One of these days. Oh, here're the others. Come in, Marlene, Phyllis. Does anyone know if Muriel's coming, or Sandra?'

We didn't. 'Was there something we missed in the meeting?' Phyllis asked. She was a council worker's wife, a hard-bitten, scraggy-looking woman with twin boys, her thin hair scraped back in a pony tail and a skin like leather.

Sue smiled. 'Just doesn't seem like a meeting without a cuppa, that's all.' She had put out her good china and a scrumptious-looking sponge topped with cream. We added our offerings to the table and sat down, our hostess sighing with content as she plied the teapot. 'Nothing like tea and a good gossip. And now we have consensus on how to proceed, I thought we might rough out a schedule for the cemetery restoration. I could go along to the next council meeting and present our case, but I think having it on paper's the better idea.'

'True,' Phyllis said. 'Once it's in the minutes, it ain't so easy for 'em to pretend it never happened.'

'Speaking of gossip . . .' Marlene went on to relate the tale of Barry Lacey and the reporter, only to be upstaged by Sue.

'It was on the late news last night. A historic killing, they called it, saying that a twenty-year-old disappearance was now solved. I've never heard about it but apparently a young woman vanished in the seventies from somewhere around here. She never turned up in Hamilton and people just assumed that she'd changed her mind and headed north instead. But the vehicle Flint found in the river was registered to her, and the bones in it belong to a woman . . .' She lifted her plump hands, letting us draw the inference.

Phyllis paused a bite of cake to widen her eyes. 'So they reckon somebody done her in?'

Sue shrugged. 'Hard to see how she'd get there otherwise.'

'God!' Marlene said avidly. 'This is unbelievable. *Another* murder! First your mum, Penny, and now this one. I wonder how many more are out there waiting to be found?'

'Just the two, that I know of,' I said. 'Skeletons, that is, not murders. Some foreigner got bushed, way back and perished in the Big Scrub. And years ago a stockman died on Rainsford Downs. They found his horse but not his body – somewhere back in the range country, I believe.'

'You could lose an army back there, let alone one man.' Marlene nodded sagely. 'I bet there's bits of it still that nobody but the old blackfellas have ever set foot on. This is lovely cake, Sue. Is there another cup in that pot?'

'Well, the story's out,' I told Flint that evening. 'Sue heard it on the news last night. So the body in the vehicle officially belongs to that young woman Colleen. I imagine Greg'll be like a dog with fleas with two murders on his plate, even if they've already arrested someone for my mother. How was your day?'

'So so. Got my first booking for the season, party of four looking to get here on Good Friday. And the mail truck's gonna try the road out tomorrow.'

'How do you know that?'

'Oscar rang to find out if anyone was moving up here yet. I told him Greg had headed out and, far as I knew, had arrived, so he reckoned he'd give it a go.'

'Good,' I said. Oscar Hayman had been driving the Goola mail ever since I'd returned to Southbend and possibly for years before that. 'Why should he ring you though?'

'Well, he tried the cop shop and got no answer there, so he rang the pub and must've decided Zim either wouldn't know or wasn't a reliable judge. I was his next choice.'

'Makes sense,' I agreed. 'The CWA met today and the bad news is that we're going to need manpower to ready the facilities down on the course to have them shipshape for the Easter sports. I suppose you wouldn't like to volunteer yourself?'

'Oh, yes,' he said. 'Doing what exactly?'

'Getting the water pump set up, scrubbing the flood residue out of the buildings, carting wood for the copper and the barbie, setting up the grounds for the bending races and that sort of stuff. It won't all be on you. Some of the station blokes will help.'

'How could I refuse? I suppose you'll be chasing the local businesses to donate prizes too?'

'Not me – that's Marlene's department. She's the secretary. Fortunately, from my point of view, nobody seems to think that pot plants are any sort of prize. They hit me for a cash donation instead. But Sports Day's an institution round here. I won my first ribbon on a borrowed pony at the Southbend sports.'

'Really? Doing what?'

'Musical chairs. Just like the normal game, only this time you're bareback on a pony and have to get off to claim your chair. It's kids only, of course, and some of the nags were quite tall.'

'What was yours like?'

'His name was Snow. I never got to take him to the sports. Walter wasn't into wasting time and effort on such things. So, I only rode if somebody loaned me a mount. My mum tried to change his mind, but it didn't work.' I shrugged. 'I really don't know why he even went. He never seemed to enjoy it.'

'A killjoy.' Flint nodded. 'There was a bloke like that back home – Les Morris. He had three boys and you could hear him carping at 'em at every event. How much it was costing him, how much time he was losing on the job being there . . . I expect your dad was the same. Made your mother feel guilty for going, but was too controlling to let her go alone.'

'He wasn't my dad,' I said far too vehemently, 'but yes, looking back I think you're right. She was always on tenterhooks in his company.'

'Have you ever been back since you moved here?'

'To the Park? No. I know the Moronis, and Gwen's asked me, but I just haven't got round to it.'

'Then what about a visit tomorrow? C'mon,' he said, seeing me hesitate. 'You've been stuck in town since before Christmas, and there's no danger of getting bogged. This wind'll see to that. It's only what – twenty kilometres?'

'Thirty.' The distance rolled automatically off my tongue. 'Well, an outing would be nice, but why?'

'Because I want to know everything about you, Penny. Including where you grew up. Everyone is the sum of their parts, and your childhood has contributed to the person you are today.' He touched my curls.

'Even though it wasn't a particularly happy time for me? Though that's not really fair . . . I *was* happy at the Park. I mean, Walter was the bogeyman but the rest was wonderful. Life only got lonely and awful after Mum went and I was sent away.' I shivered. 'Mind you, I wouldn't have wanted to stay without her. I wonder if they've changed the house at all.'

'We'll see tomorrow.' He stretched until his shoulders cracked. 'We'd best make the most of the next few days, love. I'm betting this time next week we'll be rushed off our feet.'

Flint had been right about the power of the wind now blowing constantly from the south-east. It wasn't a raging gale, just a steady movement of air, but enough to firm the ground into a crust that saw the vehicle leave only the lightest tracks on the unsealed road. The river sparkled beneath the bridge, the pellucid water showing every pebble, and the morning light washed the trees in a hundred shades of green. Already the feed on the far bank was yellowing where the seeds had ripened and fallen, while a clear pale sky fit above us like an inverted bowl.

The narrow, once-familiar road to the Park had changed. It was wider, formed up with gravel and buttressed with table drains. I had expected the paddock gates to have been replaced with cattle grids, and they were. Beltane Creek, then a rocky crossing pocketed with deep holes, now had its own bridge with a sign showing its name, and there were culverts over the smaller tributaries.

'It's all so different,' I said. 'That was the boundary, that last grid. Widening the road has changed everything. I hardly know where I am.' I stared at the low scrub, a mixture of turpentine, beefwood and yellow-jack with a smattering of smaller shrubby growth, conkerberry and turkey bush. It, at least, was the same. I remembered the huge orb spiders that had spun their webs between them, the sticky strands catching on Snow's nose as he pushed his way through. 'The mailbox should be around the next bend, I think.'

'Pretty flash,' Flint said, pulling up at the gate beside it. It wasn't the old 44-gallon drum we had used but a neatly made mini garage with a roller door set atop the welded metal chain that supported it.

'Isn't it just?' I opened the gate, closed it again and pointed up the track. 'It's about two kay from here – unless they've straightened the road.'

The homestead looked much the same, wrapped in a wide verandah, the kitchen joined to it by a short walkway. The shade trees around it were far larger than my memory had made them, and the outbuildings had increased, though the old meatshed with its pyramid-shaped roof was unchanged.

'There used to be a fowlhouse,' I said as Flint pulled up. 'I remember making friends with the dearest little chicks. We had a half bantam hen, very tame, and she'd let me pick them up. There's Gwen.' I waved and the woman came over.

'Well, hello stranger! Our first visitors for the year.' She greeted Flint and beamed at us. A short sturdy woman, with freckled skin and fading auburn hair under a ratty straw hat, she wore long sleeves, carried a garden digger, and had a fingerstall on her left thumb.

'Hello, Gwen. How are you?' I nodded at her hand. 'What happened there?'

'Ken and I were butchering a beast and the knife slipped.' I winced and she nodded. 'Yeah, deep cut. It's inconvenient but it's fine. Come in and I'll put the kettle on.'

'Where's Ken?'

'Rode out to check a bore. Country's a bit wet yet for the Toyota. Silly man bogged it down the paddock day before last. Said he won't be trying that again for a bit. So, what's the news in town?'

We chatted over the tea and I commented on the growth of the garden.

Gwen sighed. 'I do my best and it's looking good now because of the rain, but things start to go back as soon as I have to use the bore water. Some stuff thrives, but there's other plants can't hack it.'

'Maybe try succulents or cactus,' I suggested. 'They're tough as old boots and there's plenty of choice. I don't carry much in that line but I could show you some catalogues.'

'That's what Jenny said.' Jenny was her daughter, presently at boarding school along with both her brothers.

'Do you mind if I have a look? Professional interest.' I smiled and left them at the table, making my way across the verandah towards the garden gate. The vehicle shed was still there, looming large; they must have added an extra bay or two, because weren't things supposed to look smaller to adults returning to childhood scenes? But that was where she would have backed out from and turned, while I sulked in full view, next to the mango – now a truly enormous tree. If only seeing me had made her relent and take me too, as I had hoped for, then perhaps she would be alive today. Or possibly I, too, would be dead? The thought made me shiver.

I squeezed my eyes shut trying to recreate that moment in time. The world blue and bright as the skies were here in mid-winter and the old green Land Rover. She had been wearing – what? I pictured the type of dress she had favoured, collared with a neat belt, but couldn't get the colour. Blue, was it – or green? A hat, of course, straw with a ribbon, the one she always wore. Her shoes I remembered clearly because I'd been staring down, refusing to meet her eye – black court shoes with a low heel and a shiny buckle across the front, already smudged with dust. You couldn't take a step on the Park without kicking up the fine red dust. I saw again the way it had spurted from under the wheels as she drove off, until the back end of the vehicle was shrouded in a drifting mist of red. Driving to her death, and the disintegration of the only life I had known.

I turned away and, when Flint and Gwen finally emerged from the kitchen, was pretending an interest in a partly shaded corner.

'You could try cannas there,' I suggested. 'They wouldn't mind the shade.' An enormous rain tree was providing that and killing off a good part of the lawn. 'It would be perfect, a nice patch of colour, and that dripping tap would keep things moist. Cannas love water and they multiply like rabbits.'

'You think so? Okay, then. I had hibiscus there, then a geranium, but even it died.' She laughed ruefully. 'Ken reckons I've got black thumbs.'

'Maybe you'll surprise him yet,' I said as she accompanied us out to the vehicle. 'Get the cannas, then have a look for aloes or agave – something equally tough that likes the dry – then plant them down that sunny patch of fence. Thanks for the cuppa, Gwen. It's been really nice seeing you. I've been meaning to come for ages and this was my only chance. We think the roads'll be open next week. No days off after that!'

'Nor here. We'll be into the mustering before you know it. I'll see you at the next CWA meeting then, if not before for the cannas. Bye, Flint.' She waved as he let in the clutch and I settled back in my seat with a huff of breath that was partly relief.

'All right?' Flint asked.

'Yes. It's just . . . strange, coming back. I almost expected to find Walter glowering at me from the shed. And I can't properly remember what my mother wore that day. Only her shoes. I should've taken more notice. If I'd known . . .'

'How could you?' he said reasonably. 'This paddock—'

'It's the horse paddock.'

'Okay. Is it where you kept your pony?'

'Yes. Dear old Snow. I suppose Gwen's kids might have ridden him,' I said doubtfully, doing the sums, then shook my head. 'No, couldn't have happened. He'd have been twenty, if he lived that long, before they were out of nappies.'

'So they're the next owners, after your fa—Carter?'

'Mmm. I wonder what's happening with him? There's been nothing more on the news since we heard about his arrest.'

'Well, the arrest. He wasn't identified. But we could always ask Greg,' he suggested.

I loved him for that *we,* but snorted as he braked for the gate. 'And a fat lot of good that would do. God, look at the time! Home, James, and don't spare the horses. Lisa'll be thinking I've run off with you and I swore to her that I wouldn't do that.'

'Pity,' he murmured, but put his foot down and sped us on our way.

Chapter Twenty-nine

The dream came again that night, vivid and disturbing. My heart broke as dust shrouded the disappearing vehicle and I heard myself sobbing as I ran after it, legs pumping, breath desperate, until Flint shook me awake.

His arms were around me, his voice reassuring in my ear. 'It's okay. It's okay, love. Just a dream. Shh, come on. You're safe now.'

My cheeks were wet, my heart hammering from the rush of adrenalin the dream had caused, and I couldn't seem to catch my breath.

'What was it?' With what light the window afforded, I could just make out the concern on his face as he kissed my forehead.

I touched his chin and felt the growth of new whiskers there. 'I tried to stop her. I was running, because I knew if she left, she was never coming back . . .'

'Oh, Penny.' He smoothed my curls, cradling my head against his body. 'I'm sorry, I shouldn't have talked you into that trip to the Park. It's brought it all back.'

'It has,' I agreed, sniffing, 'but I've had the dream before. Ever since I found her, it keeps recurring, so don't blame yourself.' In a small voice I added, 'I misjudged her for so long, thinking she'd abandoned me. It's almost like I deserve to have the dream.'

'No, you don't,' he said firmly. 'You were a kid, and they lied to you. What else were you supposed to think?'

I pushed myself up on the pillows, scrubbing at my wet cheeks as my heart slowed. 'It's crazy, isn't it? I haven't thought about her in years and now she's always at the back of my mind, even when I sleep. Was it like that for you when your wife died?'

He turned over onto his back and reached for my hand. 'For a year or three, yes. I was like a madman, still hunting for Sammy and so angry at Alice. I was a mess, grieving – and furious that I had to do it alone. But I think having a funeral helped put her to rest, and in time I was able to forgive her. Suicide is such a selfish act, but she was hurting so badly . . . It was different with Sammy. Weeks and months and years passed, and there was no news, no body, no closure. In the end the wound scabs over and you learn to live with it, but it never heals. Even now, I catch myself thinking that she's out there somewhere, when common sense and logic and the statistics of snatched children all tell me she's long dead.'

'I'm sorry,' I said inadequately.

He sighed. 'It's history, Penny. Not the one you'd write for yourself, but like I said, shit happens. It's an immutable law of life. Something that, sooner or later, we all learn. You and I both drew the short straw in that regard, but there are compensations. I've found it's best to concentrate on them, to take what's offered in the way of happiness, even if the shadow of the past is always there.'

'You're right, of course.' I settled my head on his shoulder, feeling the overhead fan stir my hair against his chest. I kissed the hard ridge of his collarbone and his hand came over to caress my head. I relaxed against him and presently sleep stole back to take me again.

The following morning brought Muriel to the nursery only minutes after my official opening time. She had driven over in Barry's work Toyota, both doors emblazoned with *Fuel, Spare Parts & Lacey's Mechanical Repairs* to match the sign on his workshop. I was planting a tray of grow pots with kohlrabi and cabbage seeds and carried on to the last pot before looking around.

'Morning, Muriel. You're early. What can I do for you? As you can see, the veggie seedlings won't be ready for a week or two yet.'

She waved my words off. 'When have I ever bought seedlings, Penny? No, I just wondered if you knew he was back in town, that's all.' I must have looked puzzled because she hurried on. 'Your dad – he's here. They've got him at the police station. Didn't the cops let you know?'

'What?' I sat down abruptly on the bench next to a bag of potting mix. She nodded, confirming what I'd just heard, and I said, stupidly, 'But why?'

'Because he's a suspect in your mum's murder? Maybe they think that bringing him back here to the crime scene will shock him into confessing?' She followed this with a snort of disbelief. 'Shows how much they know of him. Walter Carter wouldn't tell you what he ate for breakfast unless he wanted to. Never knew a man so close mouthed.'

Her words had given me an instant in which to recover and to wonder what her purpose was in coming. I said coldly, 'And why exactly are you telling me this?'

An expression I couldn't read flashed momentarily across her features. 'I know you think I'm a meddling old fool with a love of gossip, but I came to tell you because I knew damn well the coppers wouldn't. Blow-ins! What do they know about this town and the people in it? Walter always was a nasty piece of work and I don't reckon he's changed. But it isn't your fault you're related, so you deserve to be warned. That's why.'

She turned away and I sprang up, calling, 'Wait! Muriel, please.' She turned back and I went to her. 'I'm sorry. I shouldn't have doubted you. It was kind of you to come, and I do appreciate it.'

'That's all right, Penny.' A wry look crossed her plain face and, unexpectedly, her gaze softened. 'You don't remember me at all, do you? Of course, I wasn't married then, so I had a different name . . . I was your mother's best friend when you were a child. We were the same age and both with our problems. We'd meet when we could and talk, so I know better than any what her life was like with that man.'

I goggled at her. 'Really? Why didn't you say something earlier? I've never met a friend of hers before.'

Her smile was rueful. 'The gossipy old bag from the fuel depot? Who'd have believed it? Not you, for a bet. Anyway you had your own issues, losing your husband and starting up a new business.'

I gaped at her. How had she known about Michael?

As if she had read my mind she added, 'His death and all the rest of it was in the *Country Life*, you know, and with the nursery and the timing of your arrival, I just put two and two together. Anyway, Imogen was long gone and I didn't want to upset you. It was plain you didn't remember me. I'm just glad to see there's none of your dad's darkness in you. Your mum'—she gave a fond smile that lit her eyes and momentarily diminished her ugliness—'she was all light. I was never pretty but I loved her because she was, and for her happiness and sparkle . . . when he let her be that way, that was.'

I pressed her arm. 'I know what you mean. I do remember that much. And you have something better than looks, you know – a caring heart. I remember what you did rescuing Zim's horse.'

She harrumphed, embarrassed. 'That was simple enough. I always got on with animals. They don't judge you.'

There had probably been a lot of that when she was young, I thought compassionately. She must have suffered agonies as a girl with her large frame and coarse skin, big nose and mannish chin. I wondered how many dances she had sat through in the old Southbend hall, in her lonely seat with the young men inviting every girl but her to a turn on the floor.

I said impulsively, 'Did my mother ever tell you that Carter isn't my real father? Did she say who was?'

Her eyes widened. 'He isn't?' She shook her head slowly. 'I didn't know that. Did she tell you so?'

'No. I heard them rowing in the bedroom one night. He shouted it at her. I didn't know what he meant until I was older. It was just before she died. She and I . . . we never talked about them – the rows, I mean. I was too young, I suppose, so even if I'd understood . . .' A bit late, I wondered whether I should have mentioned it, for she did like to gossip.

'You can be glad,' she said bluntly, 'though I suppose it does help explain what he did.' Then, as if she had divined my thoughts, she patted my arm. 'Don't worry, Penny. I might like to know what's going on, but I can keep a secret too.'

'I'm sure,' I said, hoping she hadn't picked up on my momentary uneasiness. 'And thank you for bringing me the news. Do you grow kohlrabi at all?'

'It's one of the veggies I put in each year. Barry prefers them to turnips.'

'Here, take a tray.' I gave her one. 'You'll get about twenty from that if they all come up. Give them a week and don't let the mix dry out.' I gave a little laugh, anxious now for her to leave. 'Sorry, habit. You know all that.' I pulled off the plastic apron that protected my clothes, glancing across the way to check that Flint was home, and saw that his vehicle was in the yard. 'There's somewhere I have to be.'

'No worries.' She had a little smile on her face. 'You could do worse, Penny. He's a decent bloke. I think Imogen would've liked him.' She gave a little wave and went, carrying the tray carefully out to where the Toyota waited.

The following morning, Sue Hart rang me.

'Penny,' she said, 'great news! I'm calling all the members to let them know. Bob Page has agreed, in principle, to the refurbishment for the cemetery. The first council meeting is next Monday and he wants us to send in a plan for it.

Sally will be in school, but I'm going to ask her for a drawing to scale – maybe those of us in town could meet later today to pool ideas for that? And I wondered if you could make a list of suitable shade trees, maybe a few hedgy-type plants, depending on what design we come up with. And cost them, of course. I'm going to ask Ellen to get some input from Tom about the price of fencing. I believe they divided a paddock, or built a new one at Rumhole last year, so he ought to be up to date on the price of wire and posts.' She broke off, breathless. 'I'd like to wait until all the members can get in and hold a proper meeting, but it's too good an opportunity to miss.'

'Strike while the iron's hot,' I agreed. 'If it gets pushed to the bottom of the agenda because we don't get the paperwork in, it could be months before we get a written agreement from them – and the CWA state division will want that, won't they? Do you want to meet here or at your place? What time?'

'Oh, here, I think. Half three? If we can raise a quorum, that is. And I thought we might ask that new woman at the pub to join. It'll help with the numbers and it looks like she'll be staying a while. Shall we say two o'clock? Would that suit you?'

'Yes. And I'll go see Fodo – that's her name. She knows me and Marlene, and I think she's met Muriel too.'

'Would you? Thanks. I'll call the rest of the ladies. And maybe when we're done, we can fax whatever ground plan we come up with around the station members to get their feedback so they're not excluded from the decisions we make.'

'Good idea. See you then.' I hung up and went immediately to inspect the cake tins. We'd need afternoon tea, so I'd have to bake. A simple Victoria sponge would do, and maybe, while I was on the job, a batch of biscuits for tomorrow's smoko.

I returned from the meeting to find both girls and Flint at home enjoying afternoon tea. Lisa had the biscuit tin open on the table and offered hospitably to fetch another mug for me.

'I've just had a cuppa, thanks, sweetie, but I do think if you've a guest you should put out a plate, not the tin,' I suggested. 'It was good of you to make the tea though. Where's your grandfather?'

'Oh, Flint doesn't care,' she said. 'And Grandad's got his. He took it out the back; said he wanted to finish a job.'

'Ah. How was school then?'

Roseanne wriggled in her seat – the action always a preface to an announcement. 'Mrs Price said the cemetery project was on, and me and Lisa have been talking about that. What if'—she paused dramatically—'the school was to help, Miss Carter? All the big kids, or as many as want to? We could clean up the stones and list all the names, 'cause Mrs Price said there'll be a big board telling people all about anyone special who's buried there.'

'Yeah, or extra sad, like the little baby's grave I found, or maybe a famous bushranger,' Lisa chimed in. 'Could we do that, Penny? It'll be the holidays soon, so there'd be heaps of time.'

'That's a wonderful idea, girls. But it will be hard work, you know, scrubbing all that stone until you can read the inscriptions. And I'm not sure we had any bushrangers up here. There might be a cattle duffer, I suppose.' I was certain there wasn't, at least not a named one, but didn't want to dash their hopes.

'And we could paint in the writing again with black paint so it's easy for the tourists to read,' Roseanne enthused. 'Mum says bicarb soda cleans anything, so it won't be that hard.'

'Well, it's not settled quite yet, but we're working on it. Still,' I amended, as their faces fell, 'I don't see why you shouldn't make a start if your mum agrees, Roseanne. Not today,' I added hastily. 'I haven't time to take you out there. But tomorrow after school?'

'Yes.' Roseanne scrambled up. 'I'm gonna ask Mum now.'

'I'll come.' Lisa vanished on her heels and I reached over to feel the teapot. 'Maybe I will have a cup after all,' I said to Flint. 'I wonder how long their enthusiasm will last?'

'Depends on the degree of grot on the stones.' Flint pulled me onto his lap and nuzzled my neck. 'So how did the lady-fest go?'

'Swimmingly. We had Fiona Reilly on the phone listening in, and Sue recorded the whole meeting to play back to the other station women. We've got a plan of action now, and the goal is to complete it before the May races. Fence up, weeds cleared, paths laid down and trees planted, the stones either straightened or re-stood. And Roseanne's idea of a paint job where the names have vanished is a good one. It depends on the council okaying it, of course.'

'And you would like me to help?'

'I'm sure the ladies wouldn't say no to any muscle that's offered, so yes, please. I'll check with Sue, but maybe you could clear the old fence away for starters?'

'Your wish, et cetera, my lady.' His bantering tone dropped as he added, 'Been meaning to tell you. I went by the cop-shop this arvo. Couldn't get much out of Greg, but he didn't deny that Carter was in the cell. And he said when Walter was arrested he had two rings on a chain about his neck.' I stiffened. 'That's not proof of anything, of course, but one was too small for a man's hand, Greg said. From what I can gather, they've only circumstantial evidence against him. Reading between the lines, I'd say they're hoping to shock a confession from him. I reckon that's why they've brought him back.'

'That's not going to work, according to Muriel. She was my mother's friend – I just found out.' For some reason it still seemed surprising, as if Imogen had lived in a bubble containing only the two of us. I couldn't remember visitors ever coming to Bracton Park, save on business to do with the station, and those whom we met on our irregular outings had made little impression upon me.

'Well, they've no proof that I can see. Mind, I got the feeling Greg sorta likes him for the girl in the Land Rover, too.'

'Colleen Gaiter, really?' I frowned. 'Is that likely? Did he even know her?'

Flint shrugged. 'If she worked in the district, it'd be hard for him not to have at least seen her, don't you think? I mean, back then – if there was anything on, I'll bet everyone went to it, particularly a young woman stuck out on an isolated station.'

'Mmm, I suppose.'

'And if he's already killed—'

'But he hadn't. Colleen went missing a month or so before my mother.'

He raised his brows. 'So reverse it then. Let's just suppose he's already murdered Colleen – wouldn't that make it easier when it came to your mum? Maybe he had an affair with the girl, got her pregnant, perhaps? That would've been a big deal back then.'

I laughed. 'You're joking! There was nothing about him to attract any woman, let alone a young one.'

'Well'—he shrugged—'maybe he forced himself on her, then had to cover it up. Wouldn't be the first time that happened.'

'Rape?' I considered it. 'I don't know. He had a temper and he liked things his own way, but it's a big leap to something like that.'

'You never know what anyone's capable of, Penny,' he said soberly, 'till it's done. And there has to be a reason why somebody gets murdered. Killing another human being can never be an impartial act. Short of war, anyway.'

'You're probably right,' I agreed. 'But if he *is* a hardened murderer, he's not going to break down and confess after all these years just because Greg . . . what? Shows him the cemetery where he buried her?'

He shrugged. 'Not saying it's a brilliant notion, but it might be all the cops have. I guess they've gotta try.' He kissed me, a peck that turned into a passionate embrace that left us both breathless and wanting more. 'Uh-uh,' he said as he stood resolutely, shaking his head. 'I've a job to finish. See you tonight?'

'I should hope so.' I smoothed my curls and flushed cheeks. 'You'd better go before Lisa gets back. Never mind shocking the pants off poor Angus if he should wander in.'

He grinned. 'You're a wanton wench, my love. And bad for a man's blood pressure.' Dropping a kiss on my neck, he caught up his hat and went.

Chapter Thirty

The following day saw the first fisherman of the season arrive, in a mud-spattered four-wheel drive that was towing a trailer. The roof rack hosted an array of capped plastic piping in which to carry rods. He pulled into the pub, and an hour or two later I saw the vehicle, minus its trailer, halt in front of Flint's Place before heading back down to the caravan park. The season, it appeared, had officially begun.

For myself, I received three phone calls from locals ordering their supply of seedling vegetables. 'Good Friday,' I promised. 'They'll be ready by then. And you'll have the holiday to get them established.'

I planted another twelve trays of mixed greens, always the first to sell, then reminded Angus that we'd shortly need more potting mix. After that, I rang Sue to float the girls' idea of getting the older school kids involved in the cemetery project.

'An excellent notion. I'll have a word with Sally,' she said. 'We'd need the parents' permission of course. I rang the shire clerk about trying to get the thing through council by race weekend, so maybe they'll move a bit faster than usual on a decision.'

'Especially as the CWA's funding it,' I said dryly, and she chuckled. 'By the way, Flint's said he can pull the old fence down. Okay if he goes ahead with that?'

'I don't see why not. It'll show the council we're dead serious.'

'Oh, very funny.' I hung up on a laugh.

When school let out that afternoon, Lisa turned up alone. 'Where's Roseanne?' I asked.

'Not coming.' She pulled a face. 'She's got a sore throat and stayed home today. I begged her mum to let her come, but she said no. She gave me this.' She held up two five-hundred-gram packets of bicarb soda. 'I can still go though, can't I, Penny?'

I hesitated. 'It wouldn't be much fun by yourself, sweetie. Why don't you wait until Roseanne's better? Sore throats don't take long to heal.'

'They do. It could be a whole *week*,' she said tragically.

'Well, then, what about asking Meadow? The thing is, you shouldn't be way out there by yourself. What if something happened to you?'

'Like what?' she said combatively. 'A ghost's gonna grab me? Anyway, Meadow wouldn't come. She's different now she's got a boyfriend. She doesn't want to hang around with kids any more.' She brightened as a new thought occurred to her. 'I could ask Flint to help.'

'He's not home. He took a client fishing. And I was thinking more of snakes, than ghosts. All right, then.' I stifled a sigh. 'I'll stay with you. Change your school clothes first and have a snack while I fill the water drum. We'll need bowls and a scrubbing brush, and maybe a hand digger from the gardening tools in case some of the stones have sunk. Hurry up. I need to be back by five.' Plenty of time, I reflected, for her to learn how arduous a task she'd taken on.

I told Angus he'd have to make his own smoko, and we loaded up and set off, following the dust of another vehicle up the river road. This time there was nothing to prevent me driving right to the site. With a warning to Lisa to watch out for snakes and the tangle of rusty wire that had been the fence, we collected up the gear and lugged it across to the nearest headstone.

Lisa stared in dismay at the only bit sticking out through the rampant growth. 'How are we supposed to clean that? You can hardly even see it!'

'We should've brought the hoe,' I said. 'Well, we'll just have to pull what we can and dig out the rest.'

We donned the gardening gloves I'd brought and got started, hacking at the roots of the larger weeds with the digger and grubbing out whatever would shift. The black soil clung doggedly to the roots but persistence won and eventually the stone, a dirty grey mottled with black mould, lay uncovered between us. It was impossible to make out more than the final R.I.P. at the bottom of the epitaph.

Lisa, however, was undaunted. She filled a basin from the tap on the water drum, armed herself with the scrubbing brush, then opened the bicarb, which I'd transferred to a bottle.

'Just do a small section first,' I said. 'Let's see how it goes. Maybe we could try vinegar too. That's also supposed to kill mould.'

The bicarb helped but its qualities were less than magical and a good deal of scrubbing ensued. With half the stone cleaned, Lisa leaned back and dropped the brush, resting her aching arms. Bits of hair clung wetly to her face as she turned to me. 'How many stones do you think there are, Penny?'

'Oh.' I sprinkled more bicarb and took up my brush again. 'Maybe twenty? I think the cemetery's been here as long as the pub, and that's had its centenary. But nobody's been buried here for at least fifty years – maybe longer.'

'I can believe it.' Her shoulders drooped despairingly. 'I thought it would be easier.'

'Let's have a break.' I glanced at my watch. We'd been at it for an hour, and at this rate it would take till Christmas to finish the job. 'Why don't we clear a bit more, see if we can get a count of the stones?'

What the task really called for, I reflected, was a high-pressure hose. Barry probably owned one, but there was no water out here, and transporting the goods to be cleaned was out of the question. 'In the meantime,' I said, grabbing the bicarb packet to spread the rest of its contents liberally over the uncleaned area of the stone, 'We'll let it sit and see if it helps. It works on burnt saucepans, after all.' I moistened it slightly to encourage it to do its work.

The surface of the ground had dried sufficiently so as to resemble concrete, so pulling the yellowing vegetation was hard work. We persevered with the hand digger for a bit, then Lisa tossed it aside. 'It's too little. We need a shovel.'

'There's one in the vehicle,' I suggested. 'But I think the ground'll be too hard to dig.'

Hands on her hips, she said, 'Or we could set fire to it.'

I shook my head. 'We definitely could not. If there was a firebreak cleared around it, then maybe, but that grass out there belongs to Mount Ixion and we're not setting it alight. So I'm afraid we have to do it the old-fashioned way.'

She gave a tragic sigh and marched off to the vehicle while I concentrated on a particularly tough root. I could feel a blister starting on the inner part of my thumb and thought that Sally's pupils would quickly tire of the project. An hour would probably do it for them. Lisa had lasted well, considering, but she seemed to have given up, for she hadn't returned from her errand. Perhaps I should call it a day too. I rose and stretched my back, glancing down at the stone we'd been working on and, to my surprise, realised that my method had worked. A splash of water revealed a pristine patch of granite where the bicarb had been. Pleased, I rinsed off the rest and called to Lisa.

'It worked. Come and see. If we had a bucket of that stuff, we'd get the lot done in one day.'

A stick crunched behind me and I turned, 'It looks brand n—' The words died on my lips as I took in the sight of Lisa in the grip of a grey-haired, unshaven man. He was propelling her towards me with what looked like a pair of handcuffs pulled taut across her throat. She was as white as bone, her hands pulling ineffectually at the arm holding her as he pushed her along. Her terrified eyes held mine in mute appeal as she tried to speak, but managed only a frightened croak, the words blocked by the pressure on her larynx.

'What . . .? Who are you? Let her go!' My blood seemed to freeze and a hundred unuttered questions darted through my mind. Who was this man? Where had he come from? I had heard no vehicle on the track. And most important of all, what did he want? I took a step towards him, snarling, 'You hear me? Let her go this instant.'

For a moment I thought he would for he seemed to be nodding, but then I realised, mainly from the savage look on his face, that the movement was a habitual tic.

'Save your breath,' he said. 'I'm not lettin' her go. She's coming with me, dead or alive, don't matter much which, so don't do nothin' stupid. Where's the keys?'

I gaped at him, disbelieving the nightmare I had suddenly found myself plunged into, and Lisa croaked imploringly, 'Penny—' then gagged as the man pulled the cuffs tighter. The action released my brain from its paralysis and I made the connection with the vehicle that had preceded us up the road.

'What have you done to Sergeant Banner?'

The man's eyes narrowed but the distracting head nodding, slight though it was, continued. I took an involuntary step backwards, recognising his expression more than his actual features, which had thinned over the years. 'You're Walter Carter. They arrested you for murder. Have you killed him too?'

He bared his teeth at me. 'Hello, daughter – not that there's one drop of my blood in your veins. Fancy finding you back here. And not a hundred feet from where I planted your stupid bitch of a mother.' The cuffs dropped away from Lisa's throat, but before she could move, the fingers of his left hand wrapped about her upper arm, the handcuffs dangling to her elbow. I remembered then that he was lefthanded. His free hand went for the pocket of his pants and I saw a slight betraying tremor before it vanished to emerge with, of all things, a table knife. He swiped the air with it, his eyes fixed on mine. 'Don't think it's not sharp. I could cut her throat in an instant.'

He had Parkinson's, I thought, as his hand continued to tremble. What could I do? How could I stop him? *Keep him talking*, my brain screamed, and I repeated my earlier question. 'Where's Greg? Have you killed him too?'

His expression darkened. 'The cop? Forget him. He won't be worrying us. Where's the keys to your vehicle?'

'They're in it, aren't they?'

'Don't mess me around, girl,' he roared. 'You know bloody well they're not.'

'I don't know, then!' I cried, not having to act the fear I felt. I patted frantically at my thighs, feeling the empty pockets of my jeans. 'I haven't got them! Maybe they fell out? I thought I left them in there.' I looked helplessly around, scuffing aside the pile of weeds and debris we'd shifted to get at the headstone. The keys were in my hip pocket and I hoped that the tail of the overshirt I wore covered the bulge there. I'd ditch them at the first opportunity – if one arose. In the meantime, I had to keep him talking. 'Why did you do it? Why did you kill Mum?'

'What?' He yanked Lisa closer, raising the knife, and she whimpered imploringly, her eyes on me. 'Where are those keys?'

'I'm looking, I'm looking. They could have fallen anywhere! We've been here two hours or more. I just want to know why you'd do that. You could've just divorced her. She was forgiving and kind, far more than you deserved—'

'Yeah, and nosy,' he cut in. 'Asking about that girl, and where I'd been the day she left. I could see where that was headin'. The little slut had it coming, anyway. Gave the eye to any man that looked at her. Just asking for it. But your mother knew. Musta worked it out, Christ knows how. It was an accident anyway. I gave her a slap to shut her up, that's all.' My hands clenched at his words, as he frowned in an almost thoughtful way, 'How was I to know she'd crack her goddammed head open on that rock?'

A picture of the boulders at the river bed, which helped anchor the bridge supports, flashed through my head and partly from unsteadiness I sat down heavily on the cleaned headstone, letting one hand slip behind me to catch myself. The keys slid easily from my pocket to the hole beside the stone, where we'd dug out a small rattlepod bush. Pushing myself up again, sniffling and wiping my eyes, I made sure to grind my shoe into it, burying them.

'She was my mother!' I shouted, tears – genuine this time – on my cheeks.

'And she never learned her damn place,' he yelled back angrily. 'Now, find them bloody keys or I'll cut your kid's throat an' you can add that to my tally.'

'Don't hurt her,' I pleaded. 'Look, take me with you if you want a hostage, just let her go.' A flash of light caught my eye back on the river road and was lost again in the timber. A vehicle? It might as well have been a million miles away. I said desperately, 'Can't you start it without the keys? Don't you strip the wires and join them, or something? Car thieves don't have keys, for God's sake.' He'd have to release Lisa to do it, and maybe I'd have a chance to – what? I had no idea but I would try anything. I had no illusions about the fate of whoever he took with him. He had murdered twice by his own admission, three times if the hapless sergeant was dead. One more victim would hardly bother him.

'Two minutes,' he said, 'and you'll see blood. *Hers.*' He shook the terrified girl and she started to sob as he jabbed the knife's point into her throat hard enough to elicit a thin trickle of red. 'I got nothin' to lose.'

'Don't cry, sweetie, it'll be all right,' I promised. 'I'll find them. Don't hurt her,' I begged him. I would have to produce them, I thought. I could stall no longer. There was a chunk of stone, the broken tip of an angel's wing, near my foot. A comfortable size to throw, I thought. If I threw the keys at him, would he take the knife away long enough for me to clobber him? If he let go of Lisa's arm, she could run . . . That was supposing she was capable of movement; I knew too well how fear froze even the flight instinct. I had never run from him as a child but had stood like a rabbit caught in the glare of his hate-filled gaze.

'One minute,' he growled.

With a desperate lunge I stooped, grabbing at the stone and scrabbling through the soil to produce the buried keys. 'Don't hurt her, I have them! Here!' I threw them forcefully, deliberately wide, and as I had hoped he released his hold on Lisa and made a sudden grab to catch them. 'Run!' I screamed at her as the keys fell beyond his reach. Winding back my arm, I flung the stone with all my strength.

Lisa darted away from his side and stopped – waiting for me, I realised. 'Go!' I yelled, but still she waited.

'Come on, Penny!' she shrieked. She wasn't shifting and my heart sank as I saw that my missile had missed its target, doing no more than graze Carter's arm.

His face was wreathed in fury as he started towards me. 'Bitch! You'll pay for that.'

I looked frantically for another bit of broken granite but every headstone my fevered gaze swept was whole. It was vastly unfair considering that I'd earlier noted at least three of them in pieces. Scrabbling backwards, my heel caught on the edge of the stone we'd cleaned and I fell. I heard Lisa scream my name, then she was running at him, a blur of fury that he backhanded away, the swinging handcuff catching her across the cheek.

I scrabbled backwards trying for space enough to rise as he swung a fist at me, then, miraculously, seemingly out of nowhere, an arm hooked around his neck, jerking him backwards, and Flint snarled, 'Would you then, you bastard? Well, have a go at me instead.'

Chapter Thirty-one

I could only gape, having no idea where he'd sprung from. Then Lisa, up again from where she had fallen when Carter hit her, cannoned into me, her arms grasping desperately at my middle as she sobbed my name over and over.

'It's all right, sweetie,' I soothed, shaken to my core. Carter was on the ground with Flint on top of him. 'You're okay . . .'

The tableau before us abruptly changed as Carter buried his teeth in Flint's arm. Flint roared and jerked back, and Carter was back on his feet, Flint bounding up behind him. Carter made to flee and Flint punched him in the kidneys, doubling him over.

'I thought he was gonna kill you,' Lisa sobbed, her clutch tightening. 'Who is he? Where'd he come from?'

'Tell you later.' I prised at her imprisoning arms. 'Did you see where the keys went? We have to find them.'

She turned her head, sobs suspended on a hiccup as she watched the two men fight. Carter swung viciously at Flint's head with his left, more intent upon using the whistling steel of the handcuffs than his fist. We both gasped as Flint caught hold of them and yanked. Carter, dragged off balance, fell and Flint was once again on top of him. I didn't see what happened next but heard a strangled yell of pain, then saw Flint astride him, wrenching one arm up behind the man's shoulder blade. Carter thrashed impotently then gave up, spitting smothered abuse into the grass. Somewhere in the course of all this the knife had come to lie upon the fallen headstone and Flint now reached to toss it across into the tangled mess of old wire, without once loosening his hold on the other man's arm. Only then did he look towards me.

'Got a minute, Penny?' he gasped, chest heaving. 'Can you go through his pockets for the key to the cuffs?'

I did so, my hands shrinking from contact with the captive. 'Got it,' I said.

Flint nodded shortly, still catching his breath. 'Good.' He tugged Carter's other arm up. 'Open the cuff and slip it on. Make sure it's tight.' A trickle of blood ran from his nose and there was a red line across his jaw where an earlier swing of the metal cuffs must have caught him. 'Are you okay? And Lisa?'

'Yes,' I said shakily. I was trembling like a leaf in a gale, my legs barely able to support me now that the danger was gone. 'Where on earth did you come from? I think . . . I think he would've killed us.'

'You're safe now.' He rose and hugged me, holding out his spare arm to Lisa, who burrowed into him as if she would never let him go. 'How did he get here? I thought he was locked up.'

'Oh, my God! Greg.' My hands flew to my mouth in consternation; I'd temporarily forgotten him. 'We have to find him! He might be badly injured —' Or dead. But I didn't want to voice that thought in front of Lisa.

'Right. Well, first thing is to secure this heap of shit. Lisa'—she looked up and he smiled gently at her—'can you do something for me, kiddo? Whoa! That's some welt.' Gently he fingered the raised weal on her cheek. 'Does it hurt?' She nodded, and he grimaced. 'So does mine. Do you think you can find my big pliers? They're in my toolkit. The vehicle's just up the track a bit.' She nodded eagerly and ran off. 'I've got the boat trailer on,' he explained. 'That's why I walked in. Thought I'd use your station wagon to drag all that wire out.'

Of course; he'd been coming to dismantle the old fence. It said something for my state of mind that I'd completely forgotten that. I said, 'Greg was ahead of me on the road – where does that track actually go?'

'To a fishing hole, but if he went up that way I'm guessing he was headed for the back of the bluff, the one that makes the gorge wall – where the Land Rover went into the river. I told you I thought he liked this bastard'—he toed Carter's leg and got a glare in return—'for Colleen too.'

I rubbed my arms, feeling the goosepimples under my thin cotton overshirt. 'He'd be right then. It's the reason he killed my mother, because she was asking questions about Colleen. Both Lisa and I were witnesses to what he said.'

Carter began to swear at me in a torrent of filthy oaths, his head nodding weirdly. Flint raised his right foot in its serviceable workboot and said, 'Shut it. Unless you want a gobful of this.' The threat worked, then Lisa came running back with the pliers. Flint cut a length of rusty wire from the tangle amid the gravestones and secured Carter, or at least his handcuffs, to a nearby tree. 'That'll hold him. Right, let's go. You want to wait in my vehicle, kiddo?'

'No!' Lisa's eyes widened in panic. 'I'm coming with you.'

'Let's go, then.' I held out a hand and she rushed to my side to grasp it. 'If it's bad when we get there, you don't have to look.'

'Christ!' Flint sounded horrified. 'I never thought – I mean, he was after your vehicle, right? But the copper had one. You don't think he's dumped him, and it, in the river, too?'

I swallowed. 'I don't know. Carter just said something like "you don't have to worry about him", or "he won't be bothering us" – I can't remember exactly.'

We stopped briefly at Flint's vehicle so he could put a quick call through on the radio transceiver he had mounted in the cab.

'Who did you get?' I asked, as he returned and drove around the other vehicle with its attached trailer and boat.

'Message to the copper in town, for him to organise to collect the prisoner. And to request they alert the flying doctor. That way he'll be ready if . . .' He didn't finish the sentence. Dead or alive, Greg would need transport, either to the morgue or the hospital in Hamilton – unless he and his vehicle were at the bottom of the river.

Flint's guess as to the sergeant's destination proved to be correct. We followed the fresh tracks of the police vehicle and, sure enough, they left the road just before it angled into the river, heading bush instead.

'So, I was right,' he grunted, driving carefully between the scattered trees. The black soil had given way to red, which now became a gravel slope where the tracks all but disappeared, visible only in the flattening of the short yellowing grass.

He shifted into four-wheel drive and we climbed the back side of the stony hill.

'There!' I cried, pointing ahead as the sun glinted on duco. Straining to see clearly through the scattered boulders and the low-growing snappy gums with their orange-streaked limbs, I said, 'Well, at least he's not in the river. Stay here, Lisa.' I unsnapped my seatbelt as Flint pulled up. 'We shan't be long.' Flint gave her a reassuring smile as he got out, then jogged towards the police vehicle while I followed more slowly, dreading what I might see.

It was immediately clear why Carter had attempted to hijack my vehicle. The front of Greg's had encountered a boulder that had torn open the radiator. The sergeant was slumped over the wheel, his head, when Flint gently moved it, glued to the plastic with dried blood. It had run down his neck and soaked the collar and shoulders of his shirt. I watched Flint slide two fingers against the man's neck and my voice came out higher than I intended. 'Is he dead?'

'No . . . I think – I've got a pulse but it's pretty faint. Can you get the vehicle over here, Penny? We'll have to drive him back. Looks like he's been hit with something. A rock, maybe. Half the blood's come from the back of his head. And there's a pretty good welt across his forehead. That'd be the steering wheel.'

'Okay. We can lie him on the back seat.' I turned and ran.

'What's happening? Is the policeman dead?' Lisa demanded as I slammed the door and turned the key, accidentally revving the motor in my agitation.

'No, but he's in a bad way. Get in the front when I stop. We'll have to budge up, because he'll need the back seat to lie on. And have a look, will you – see if there's a pillow or a blanket back there we can use for his head.'

Getting the dead weight of an unconscious body transferred wasn't easy. Flint took Greg's head and I struggled with his heavy legs until Lisa added her small strength to the battle.

'What's wrong with him?' she whispered, as if afraid he might hear.

'He's had a bang on the head,' Flint answered, 'a bad one. And I was right. It was done with a thumping great rock. I've got it for the cops. God, I'm sorry, Penny. He's gonna bleed all over your seats. You haven't got anything to wrap his head in?'

'No.' Lisa had found a stack of small bags, the type that open to make a square plastic pot for nursery plants, but that was all. 'It can't be helped. Can you hurry? I can't hold him much longer.'

'Right.' With difficulty given the angle of the door, he backed himself into the car and heaved and Greg's front end followed, one flopping arm catching where the door curved into the floor. 'Shit! Lisa, can you go round and lift his arm in? That's it. Okay, one more big effort, girls, and we've got him.'

I winced as the body thumped down on the seat. The far door jerked open and Flint all but fell out as I folded the sergeant's legs to allow the one on my side to shut.

'Good job!' Flint dropped a bloodstained rock onto the floor near the driver's seat. 'Don't touch – it might have prints on it. Right, let's get him back to town.'

Flint drove to the pub, because, I suppose, it was the closest building. Zim, Fodo, Meadow and a lone drinker in the bar came out upon hearing my gabbled explanation and the men got the unconscious sergeant out and hauled him into the verandah's annexe, where Meadow and her mother had spread a sheet over the day bed, a towel waiting on the pillow. Fodo had already called the doctor who was, she said, en route. She had described the patient's condition to him.

'What did he say?' I asked.

She shrugged. 'Not to move him, in case there were neck or spinal injuries. I said the advice was a bit late but you'd had no choice.'

'True enough. He's lucky to be alive as it is, which I'm sure was an oversight on Carter's part.'

'So what happened?' She was sponging the blood from Greg's face and tilted her head towards me enquiringly, the light catching the odd grey streak in her hair and glinting off a battered-looking silver band on her wrist. 'You look a bit fraught, Penny, if you don't mind my saying so.'

'I'm not surprised.' I glanced down at the unmoving figure she tended and felt for the pulse on his wrist. 'Do you think it's all right to leave him? I could *really* do with a cuppa. And I'm sure Flint would benefit from a stiff drink.'

'Meadow can watch him,' Fodo offered, picking up the bowl and bloodied cloth. She called the girl in and Lisa followed, obviously in the middle of detailing her experience at the cemetery. I was glad to see it; perhaps it would help exorcise the trauma of the event. Better to talk it out with a friend than to keep it bottled up, breeding nightmares for months to come.

Her face had swollen into an angry red bar of flesh and I touched it gently. 'That looks awfully sore. We'll be just inside, sweetie. I'll get you some Panadol. Come and tell us if anything changes. Where's Flint?'

'He went with Zim to find a bag. For the rock. To save the fingerprints,' she elucidated. 'I can't see why. We *know* that man tried to kill him.'

'Yes, but fingerprints are proof. Otherwise it's only our word against his. It's how the justice system works. Do you want a drink?'

'No, thanks. My face aches but I'm not thirsty.' She swallowed the painkiller Fodo provided, too wound up to think of her body. I smoothed her hair and followed Fodo through the bar into the kitchen. As on my first visit, the woman's touch was again obvious and had been added to, for as well as the dried posy on the wall, chimes now turned in the breeze in the window, and there was a decorative tree branch on a shelf that sported feathers, and shells and other objects, attached in a haphazard but pleasing way to the pale timber.

'My memory stick,' Fodo said, noticing the direction of my glance. 'The eagle feather's from the mountains; the shells are from different coasts.'

'And the blue bead? It looks like lapis lazuli.'

'That came from a satin bowerbird's bower. The speckled egg is a plover's – so tiny to contain life – and the dried flower's from a gymea lily.'

'Some people just take photos, but I like this. And the wood itself?'

'Driftwood. Whitened by the salt and smoothed by the seas.' She smiled reminiscently. 'I've seen a lot of beaches,' she said, filling the kettle. 'But never mind that. Sit down, Penny.

I want to hear all about whatever's been going on. Because something plainly has.'

Greg had still not regained consciousness by the time the flying doctor arrived. Constable Whitberry, back on duty, was at the hotel by then, his prisoner safely locked back in his cell at the police station, and reinforcements to return him to Hamilton were on the way. The constable wanted statements from both me and Lisa as to the afternoon's events and by the time that was done and the doctor's plane was overhead, the daylight was almost gone. The patient was strapped to a stretcher, his neck immobilised with a padded collar, and Flint followed the police vehicle out to the airstrip to add his headlights for illumination once doctor, pilot and patient had been transferred from vehicle to plane.

Lisa and I waited for Flint's return, as his own transport was still out at the cemetery. 'You can go home if you want,' I told her. 'Angus'll be wondering where we've got to.' The day was dying in paling light, cut by the harsh cries of a flight of black cockatoos winging to rest in the river timber. From where we stood on the pub verandah, I could see a thin spiralling of dust from a cattlepad near the bridge, where a line of stock were walking in, head to tail, to drink.

'I want to wait with you,' she said.

She was standing very close and I pulled her in for a hug. 'It's okay, Lisa. He's locked up and he'll be gone by tomorrow. You'll never have to see him again.'

Her hair was a mess, and her eyes big behind the untidy fringe. 'Was he really your dad? He said you weren't his daughter but—'

'I'm not. He was just married to my mother, that's all.'

She shuddered. 'He was horrible – creepy. He kept nodding his head all the time like some weird sort of robot.'

'I think he might have Parkinson's. That's a disease that affects the brain and makes you shake. How's your face feeling?'

She fingered the angry welt across her cheek. 'Sore. It hurts to open my mouth.'

'You can have another Panadol before bed to help you sleep. You probably won't want to chew, so I'll make you some soup for dinner. How's that?'

'Thank you.' She leaned against me. 'Are we going back to the cemetery tomorrow?'

'We might give it a few days and then have Flint come with us. How's that sound?'

She nodded vehemently. 'Yes, and Roseanne too.'

I smiled at her. 'Safety in numbers, eh? And just think, we now know the trick to cleaning the stones. All we need is a tonne of bicarb. And here's Flint coming. Let's go rescue his vehicle and then we can all call it a day.'

Later that evening, with the dishes out of the way, and the day's events exhaustively hashed over again for Angus's benefit while he bristled with impotent anger at the danger his granddaughter had faced, Flint and I finally found ourselves alone on the couch beneath the ceiling fan. Both Angus and Lisa were in bed, and I had gently vetoed the idea of him staying over.

'Lisa will probably wind up in with me. She tends a bit towards nightmares, and after today I think one's a certainty tonight.'

'And you, Penny? Will you be all right?'

'I guess I'll have to be.' I shivered, remembering. 'It's strange. In a way he hadn't changed and yet I'm not sure I'd have recognised him if we'd passed in the street. He was smaller than I remembered, but the same nastiness was there, just underneath.' I struggled to explain the flare of savagery I'd seen in Carter's eyes. 'You know when you see a snake gliding through the grass and it doesn't necessarily look dangerous? But if it should be a brown and you poke it, then all bets are off. Carter's a bit like that – deadly. I think he could have killed us both with no more thought than a brown snake would give to biting whoever disturbed it.'

Flint's arm tightened about my shoulder. 'Then thank God I turned up when I did. How the hell did he get his hands on that knife anyway? He was supposed to be in custody.'

'Carelessness at the police station,' I said. 'Had to be. Carter was in the lock-up overnight, maybe longer, so they had to have fed him. I suppose out here they don't necessarily have those disposable plastic ones on hand, so they gave him one of their own and forgot to check they got it back.'

Flint snorted. 'Leave a drunk in charge . . . It was probably child's play to get away from Banner, even in handcuffs. It's a good thing the cops out here don't carry guns.'

'They probably keep one locked up in the vehicle,' I said, 'just not on their person. Carter mightn't have known, or stopped to look. Just as well I've never gotten into the habit of leaving my keys in the car.'

'Maybe it'd have been better if you had.' He hugged me to him, face grim, and I put up a hand to smooth the wrinkles about his eyes, which had deepened with his frown.

'Then what would be the chance of me ever seeing it again, eh?'

He shook his head vehemently. 'I'd swap six top-of-the-range models for you, any day. Incidentally, my love, you throw like a girl. That stone damn near hit me.'

'Well,' I said, sitting up indignantly, 'what do you expect? I am a girl. A woman, anyway. And it did hit him, so there!'

He smothered a laugh. 'Only just. She's a terrier, young Lisa, isn't she? There was no way she was leaving you to him, even though she could've run and saved herself.'

'Yes.' A surge of feeling welled within me, a mixture of pride and love. 'It's strange. She was a duty at first, but now I think of her as my own, and worry accordingly. And,' I pretended insult, 'did you just say six vehicles? *Only* six? I think I'm worth at least ten – and Range Rovers at that.'

'Well, maybe I should check again,' he murmured, bringing his lips to mine. 'Find out if I've underbid.'

Chapter Thirty-two

In the morning Lisa's face had swelled and darkened. I was sore myself; as well as my bruised elbow, I'd discovered a large discolouration on my hip from where I'd fallen over the headstone.

'We're a sorry pair,' I said. 'What would you like to do today?'

'Nothing. It's too sore. Even opening my mouth hurts.'

'I know,' I sympathised. 'But it will improve. More soup then, and perhaps some jelly? You won't have to chew that. You could try holding a frozen packet of something on it to numb it a bit.'

I left her curled up on her bed with a packet of peas from the freezer and went out to the shadehouses. Roseanne, her throat apparently improved, arrived just before smoko to hear of the adventure. Her obvious awe and dismay at the tale perked Lisa up enough for her to agree to go swimming and, as they left for the river, the two were making plans to return to the cemetery the next day. The idea was led by Roseanne, partly, I thought, for the vicarious thrill of visiting the crime scene.

'Not just us though,' Lisa stipulated. 'Flint's gonna come too, isn't he, Penny?'

'I'll ask him,' I agreed. 'Have fun, and don't forget to use the sunscreen.'

Plans, however, often go astray, as did that one, because the second item on the news that night was the murder of a police officer in north-west Queensland. I dropped the bowl in which I was mashing potatoes into the sink and ran into the living room to catch the item on the screen, just as Angus called, 'Hey, Penny. Come and see – it's Greg.'

I caught a brief glimpse of a younger, uniformed Banner, before the image was replaced by the newsreader. '. . . the vicious assault,' he was saying, 'led to a haemorrhage on the brain. He was airlifted to a Townsville hospital by the flying doctor last night for urgent treatment, but died en route. The police are treating his death as murder and his alleged killer is currently in custody in Hamilton.'

'Dear God!' Sudden death was shocking in its impact. Hand pressed to my mouth, I sank onto the couch beside Angus. 'Poor man. I didn't like him but—'

'Yeah.' Angus patted my knee. 'It's a bugger, all right. Carter coulda just knocked him out, or left him cuffed or somethin'. One thing at least,' he said, brightening, 'is they've got the bastard now. Greg's murder's a surer thing than your mum's. I mean, after twenty years an' no evidence. He'd have to confess to it—'

'He did,' I said heatedly, 'to me, and Lisa. She heard it too.'

'Yeah.' His gaze was wise with the knowledge of humanity. 'But the coppers didn't. It's your word against his, and you just a little kid at the time. She was your mum and you always hated him. No jury's gonna swallow that, lass.'

He was right, of course. Carter had called it an accident. Taking him to trial for it might well end up in a dismissal due to lack of solid evidence or, at best, a charge of manslaughter. I couldn't see any hope of pinning Colleen's death on him either, despite him as good as admitting to it. But he couldn't wriggle out of Sergeant Banner's killing, and I was fiercely glad that Flint had thought to preserve the rock that must carry Carter's fingerprints. Ideally, traces of Greg's blood would also be found on Carter's clothing to further cement the charge.

The following morning the phone rang while we were still at breakfast. It was Constable Whitberry from the police station, his young voice tight with a subdued excitement. 'Ms Carter,' he said, 'good morning. I take it you've heard about the sergeant?'

'That he died? Yes, I'm sorry,' I said formally.

The young voice hardened as he corrected me. 'He was murdered. The reason I'm calling is that a couple of homicide detectives will be in town sometime this morning. They'll need to interview you, so I'm asking you to hold yourself available for them.'

'But I've already given you a statement. We all did.'

'And they'll have questions for you all. I'll be ringing Flint in a moment to tell him the same. They should be here by ten.'

He hung up, leaving me to work out that to make it by ten they must have left Hamilton at five am, so some urgency obviously attended the matter.

Lisa, hearing the news, sighed. 'But we were going to the cemetery.'

'Maybe after lunch,' I said. 'Do you want to ask Meadow if she'd like to come?' And, I thought, I'd give Muriel a ring, see if she was interested. I had not previously made much of an effort with the older woman, thinking her a tiresome gossip better avoided, but she had been my mother's friend. She could tell me things I didn't know about her, help flesh out the few poor memories of her that my younger, angry self had striven to forget.

It was past ten and we were still waiting for the detectives to turn up. Five tourist vehicles towing vans had beaten them to town, passing the nursery on their way to the caravan park. Watching the rear of the last dust-covered van vanish up May Street, I heard the gate click and turned to see Flint, carrying a bulky crate, coming towards me.

'It's started.' I nodded after the disappearing tourist. 'I expect from now on I'll have to make an appointment to see you.'

'Yep,' he agreed. 'My phone's running hot with bookings. You'd think the Rainsford was the only river with a fish left in it.'

'Good for business. Of course,' I teased, 'it could have something to do with the fact that the only place you can get a line into it, apart from a boat, is on the bridge.' This was scarcely an exaggeration. Save where the cattlepads ran down to water, there were few natural openings in the barrier of practically impenetrable scrub lining the river's banks.

And much of it was saw-toothed pandanus, which prevented enthusiasts from attempting to chop their way in. Hiring Flint was costly, but much the easier option.

'Could be,' he agreed. 'No sign of those cops yet?'

'Still waiting. It's driving the girls mad. What have you got there?'

'It's for you.' Preceding me through the door, which I opened at his nod, he carried the crate into the kitchen and deposited it on the table. 'I just hope it's still in one piece. Barry picked it up for me while he was in Hamilton.'

'I didn't know he'd been in. What is it, Flint?'

'You'll see.' He smirked at me. 'Got a screwdriver?'

'You are a maddening man!' But I fetched the tool and watched as he pried the top from the large crate, then removed armfuls of airbags and bubblewrap from the interior.

'Ah, perfect.' He stood back to let me take his place.

'Oh, Flint!' I raised a hand to my cheek as I beheld the finished circular mirror set within its carved border of plants and birds. The oiled wood gleamed, showing up each feather and stamen and the curl of every leaf. The inset mirror had been finished with a strip of what looked like copper and I touched it gently, smoothing its satiny finish.

'Copper shim,' Flint said. 'You like it?'

'It's wonderful. Thank you so much, Flint. It's so precious. Not just the gift, or the weeks you spent making it, but that you thought of me in the same breath as your art. I am truly honoured.' I flung my arms around him and kissed him.

'Well, that's all right then,' he said, but I could see by the slight flush on his cheek that he was pleased by my reaction. 'Where would you like to hang it?'

'Oh, I don't know. Above the couch in the lounge – no, you couldn't see into the mirror from there. What about the side wall?' I walked through to tap a spot, just as the front screen door rattled to a sharp knock.

'Ms Carter?' a man's voice called.

'Damn,' I muttered, 'that'll be them. Just when you don't want them they turn up.'

'It's okay,' he murmured. 'We'll hang it later. You gonna let them in?'

'I suppose I'll have to.' I went to the door and held it wide. 'Hello. I'm Penny Carter. You're later than I expected. You'd better come in.'

The two detectives introduced themselves as Craddock and Marsh. They accepted the offer of tea and, crunching on biscuits, took Flint and me back through the events that had culminated in Greg Banner's death.

'So how did Carter come to find you, out at this cemetery?' the one called Craddock asked. He had a fine line of moustache on his upper lip, making it easier to distinguish between them; both had hard-looking faces and sceptical expressions, like men accustomed to being lied to.

'He must've seen my vehicle. He wasn't a stranger to this country, you know. He used to own a property up here, so he knew the distances and that he'd need a vehicle, and seeing Greg's was wrecked . . .'

'That's right, he was your father, wasn't he, Ms Carter? So had he been in touch prior to this?' Marsh asked.

I bristled. 'He wasn't my father. He married my mother – and killed her, don't forget. And before our meeting in the cemetery, I hadn't spoken to or set eyes on him in twenty years. And before you ask, he admitted to killing her. He said it was because she was asking questions about where he was when Colleen Gaiter disappeared a month or so beforehand. It's why Greg – Sergeant Banner – had him out there with him in the first place. Taking him back to the site where the Land Rover went into the river, because Greg believed Carter was responsible for the crime. And seeing the police vehicle got wrecked, Carter needed another. That's why he tried to steal mine.'

'And how did you happen to be on the spot to prevent it, Flint?' Craddock asked. 'Lucky that. Is Flint your first name or your last?'

'It's my name,' Flint replied levelly. 'What I'm called. I was there to get rid of the old fence. The cemetery's being reclaimed from the ruin it is and I'd offered to help. I had customers on the river, so I was late getting there. In one sense that is. In another, I was just in time.'

'And the child you say he grabbed – your daughter, Ms Carter?'

'No. She's my business partner's granddaughter, who lives with me.'

'Right, well, we'll need to speak with her too. Would she be about?'

'She'll be with her friend Roseanne, at the shop. I'll ask her to come home.'

'Before you do.' He paused to fish a plastic bag from his pocket and handed it to me. 'Ever seen these rings before?'

I smoothed the material flat and saw two rings, one a plain wedding ring that could have belonged to anyone. 'Are they my mother's?' Craddock didn't reply, so I opened the bag and tipped them both out. The second was a silver signet ring with a tiny stone that might have been a diamond set within a bar of two joined half circles. I puzzled over it for a moment, then realised it was two letters, a C overlaid by a G. It was the bar of the G that held the stone.

I showed it to Flint. 'It's hers,' I said. 'Colleen Gaiter. Plain as the nose on your face.' Looking at Craddock I said, 'You do see that, don't you?'

'That's as may be, Ms Carter,' he replied, holding out a hand for the rings to be returned. 'Could you get the kid back here now, please?'

I rang the shop and Lisa returned, but the detectives didn't spend much time with her. After a few general questions about when she'd first seen him, they asked her about the knife and whether Carter had actually cut her with it.

'Yes, he jabbed it into my neck and it bled, but not very much.' She almost sounded regretful, and I guessed that the wound, slight though it had been, had made a big impression on Roseanne. 'He did this too,' she said, touching her fingers to her bruised cheek. 'And he tried to punch Penny, only Flint stopped him. *And* he said he killed Penny's mum. Are you gonna hang him?'

'No,' Craddock replied. 'We don't do that any more.'

'Oh.' She switched her attention to me. 'I asked Meadow about going back out there, but she said she's working and can't come. And Mrs Bentley gave us all the bicarb in the shop. She said she'll send a bill to the CWA. Roseanne's got it in her bag. When are we going?'

I glanced at the clock. 'After lunch. Which is about ten

minutes away,' I said pointedly. Surely the detectives were nearly done with their questions. 'Tell Roseanne she can join us if she wants, and that she needs a hat for later.'

The detectives rose, thanked me for the tea, and Flint showed them out just as Angus came in from the back.

'Who was that?' He hung his hat and glanced around, noticing Flint. 'Mornin', boy, how's it goin'?'

'Cruising speed,' Flint replied. 'Just a brace of coppers. Heading back to the pub now. The force are certainly contributing to old Bev's profit line this month.'

Muriel, whom I'd contacted earlier, arrived just as we were cleaning up after the meal. She wore jeans and a man's shirt and pulled a hoe from the back of her vehicle. 'Thought it'd be useful,' she said, greeting me. She also had a cake tin tucked under her arm. 'I hear the cops are back in town. Pretty shocking about Greg, eh?'

'Yes. Poor man.'

'But you're all right?' She peered at me and for the first time I saw the concern behind the inquisitiveness in her eyes.

'Yes, I'm fine, thanks. And Carter's back behind bars. Oh, Muriel. He told me Mum's death was an accident. He said he hit her and she fell against the boulders down there where the bridge supports are, and that's what killed her. He said it like he was peeved – as if dying was her fault.'

'Bastard!' she muttered, and I felt the fleeting touch of her big hand on my arm, the clumsy act of someone awkward or unfamiliar with casual intimacy. 'You're safe though, and the young 'un, and he's where he'll do no more harm. So – we ready to go?'

'Just about. Angus has decided to come too. He'll give Flint a hand with the old fence.'

'Right.' She scratched her cheek. 'You do know the council hasn't actually given us the nod for this yet?'

'Yes,' I said tranquilly. 'I also know that today might be our last chance. There're five vans in the caravan park already. There won't be too many volunteers available once the tourists really start moving. Besides, we're only clearing the area. Nobody could object to that.'

'True enough,' she said gruffly. 'I'll ride with your lot then, if there's room?'

'Yes, of course. We'll take the work vehicle. Angus can come out with Flint when he finishes what he's doing.' The two men were engaged in hanging the mirror, so I stuck my head back inside to call, 'Come on, girls, we're going. Don't forget the thermoses, Lisa. I've got the bicarb.'

Chapter Thirty-three

Once at the cemetery we organised ourselves, Muriel and I tackling the overgrowth with her hoe and the tomahawk I had brought for the tough bushes that had, over the years, invaded the areas between the graves. The girls concentrated on the headstones. I kept my eye on Lisa, who had woken screaming in the night from a nightmare about Carter. It was the second night in a row for her. I had tucked her into my bed and told her she didn't have to come today unless she wanted to, but her fears seemed to have blown away with the morning's breeze. I reasoned that returning to the place of trauma with the security of friends about her was probably the best cure for her night terrors.

Roseanne, I thought, had no true understanding of the danger her friend had faced, but her awed admiration of Lisa's participation in an event that had made the national headlines was actually helping Lisa to cope. I had expected she would never want to revisit the place of her ordeal again, and yet here they both were, chattering away over their efforts with no shadow of care. The subconscious world of sleep was, of course, a different kettle of fish, and the bad dreams would probably continue for a while.

We had made good progress by the time the men arrived but had to stop work while they hooked onto the old wire and hauled it away, taking most of the already fallen timber with it, including the single standing post from the erstwhile crime scene. Once the rusty tangle had been compressed into a manageable size for loading, they returned to look at the stays on the old gate supports.

'Might as well take 'em too,' Angus said. 'There oughta be a crowbar in me vehicle.' He fetched it and Flint took it from him to begin loosening the buttressing timbers, before towing them from the ground.

I called time out for smoko and went to see how the girls were getting on. 'It's like magic, Miss Carter,' Roseanne said, flushed from energetically scrubbing the sides of the headstones. 'We can't soak this bit, 'cause the water just runs off, so it's not as good, but the rest is easy.'

'The front's what matters, and it looks brilliant,' I said. 'You've both done a great job.'

'We've cleaned six already,' Lisa said. 'It's gonna be harder with the standing ones though.'

Muriel seemed contemplative during smoko; she glanced around her, ears cocked to the hum of cicadas and the distant cries of cockies on the river, and gave a little sigh that I took to be of content. 'It's not a bad place, really. Peaceful like. I wouldn't mind it for when I go. No reason I can see why it can't be opened for business again. The town's growing, after all.'

'Well, if I get permission for my mother to lie here, maybe that can happen.'

'I hope you can. Imogen loved the quiet places, you know. She wasn't much of a one for crowds. This place'd suit her better than some big cemetery in town.'

It helped explain their friendship, I thought. Muriel wasn't much of a mixer either. I could see them both relishing the placid serenity of the river, far away from the demands and expectations of their world.

'She liked music, Imogen,' Muriel said softly, 'and flowers. Those window boxes I've got? She started them for me.'

I nodded. 'I remember the music. We always had the radio on when he was away. She'd sing . . .' The words almost caught me by surprise. 'Do you know I'd forgotten that? She'd sing "Liza Jane" and "Jeanie Marie" – oh, lots of the radio hits.'

As if on cue, a butcher bird carolled above us. Muriel lifted her face to the sound and smiled. 'There! Perfect, isn't it?' She heaved herself up. 'We'd best be getting on, I expect. Barry'll still want his tea tonight.'

We drove home in the same order we had come, Muriel in the cab with me and the girls up the back, well satisfied with the effort we'd put in. The ground around the graves had been cleared and you could now see right across the quarter-acre area with its two mature bloodwoods and at least seventeen marked graves. I knew there were more, but the flood had taken timber crosses from earlier ones, while the first to be interred had only ever had their plots marked by wooden railings outlining the shape of the grave. White ants had hollowed out some of these and the rest had been swept away. Four of the headstones were in irreparable pieces, most of the names and dates gone along with them. Perhaps, I thought, one of the station men might make a metal plaque that could be erected in their place, to at least show that a body lay beneath.

'We need some more bicarb, Penny,' Lisa said as we dropped Roseanne off at the store.

'I'll let Sue know and she can organise it,' I promised. 'But for now, home. There's dinner to cook and you need to get things ready for school tomorrow.'

Flint and Angus had taken the old posts and wire straight to the dump, which left only Muriel.

'Let me know for next time,' she said, collecting her hoe from the vehicle's tray.

'I will, and thank you. We'd never have got it cleared without you.' I waved as she left, then turned to Lisa. 'I think we've earned ourselves a treat tonight. What about apple pancakes and ice cream for dessert?'

'Yummy! Can I make the pancakes, Penny?'

'You may,' I said, 'but boring stuff first, like veggies.'

The council met on the following Wednesday. Neither Flint nor I could spare the time to attend the public session, so it was Sue who, puffing her way up the steps to bang on the door, brought the news that the CWA had been given the go-ahead on their plans for the cemetery.

'And the works department will be purchasing a tank and poly pipe to lay the water on.'

'Really?' I raised my brows. 'Wow, I'm impressed. No, seriously. It means we don't have to skimp on vegetation if we're able to water it. We can have more than a couple of shade trees. A hedge around the perimeter, maybe? Or something planted over the graves themselves? I'm thinking bromeliads, or—'

'Make a list of ideas and possibilities,' Sue recommended, 'and we'll put it to the next meeting – which is tomorrow by the way. And the shire clerk will be writing to you. They've agreed in principle to your mother's remains being reburied there, properly this time. I thought you'd probably like to know now, rather than wait on the mail. I think the wretched man saves the correspondence up and sends it out once a month. Can't think of any other reason why everything takes so long.'

'An economy drive on postage?' I suggested, and she snorted.

'On energy, maybe. His! Well, Fiona will be pleased. Simon was in for the meeting, so she'll have the news tonight.' Simon Reilly from Wildhorse Creek was Fiona's husband, a quiet, middle-aged man with two grown sons and a younger one who would soon be finishing high school.

'Getting a fence around it will be the next thing then,' I said. 'No point planting the trees until they're safe from the stock.'

'I thought we might discuss that tomorrow. One of the station wives should be able to get the info we need from their husbands – how much wire, what number of posts we'd have to buy, and where to order it all. Not forgetting a gate. Who knows,' she said with a grin, 'some of the men might be moved to organise a working bee, once we have the material, and stand it for us.'

It was how most community projects were completed, with everyone donating their time and skills. As Angus had once said, 'Bloody sight easier than raisin' the cash to pay someone, seein' we'd be the ones shellin' out for it anyway.'

Thursday, the last day of the first term, was Parents Day at school. Lisa handed me the leaflet when she got home Wednesday afternoon, ten minutes after Sue left and for once without Roseanne in tow. She stood watching me read it, before asking abruptly, 'You gonna come?'

'Well, of course, if you want me to. And I'm sure Angus will too.'

She visibly relaxed. 'Good. Well, us big girls are supposed to make biscuits and stuff to serve for the afternoon tea Mrs Price is putting on for the parents. What should I make, Penny?'

Mentally canvassing the contents of the cupboard, I said, 'What about a coconut slice? That's quick and easy, and if you use the biggest dish it will cut up into quite a lot of servings.'

'Okay.' She dived into the cupboard and from its shelter said gruffly, 'Thanks, you know. For everything. I love being here with you and Grandad, Penny. I don't ever want to leave.'

'You needn't, sweetie,' I said, 'until you're all grown up and ready to try your wings.' She emerged flushed in the face, made shy by her admission. Appreciating how difficult it had been for her to tell me that, I changed the subject. 'What's Roseanne making for tomorrow?'

'Biscuits, with sultanas. Lana and Julie' – they were the other eleven- and twelve-year-olds – 'didn't say. I think they don't cook much at home.'

'Well, I'm sure you and Roseanne will do us proud.'

*

The following afternoon, Angus and I turned up at the school to inspect the pupils' work, listen to a long recitation in verse of the school's history, written by the children themselves, and enjoy the afternoon tea provided. It ended when the class let out and the three of us walked home together, Angus carrying the empty cake tin.

'It's Good Friday tomorrow,' Lisa said, skipping along beside him. 'Are we going to the sports day on Sunday, Grandad?'

'Course we are, lassie. And to the dance that night, 'n' Monday we'll be pottin' trees. There's five hundred little 'uns arrived on the Goola mail truck today. Every one of 'em busting outta their pots.'

'And can we go out in Flint's boat again while the holidays are on?'

'That depends on how busy he is.' I pointed at the caravan park with its cluster of customers just visible beyond the line of houses. 'See how many vans there are? Most of them will want to try their hand at catching a barra. Flint will probably be rushed off his feet.'

'Oh.' Her face fell. 'He should get another boat and somebody to work for him, then he'd have more time.'

'He already has that, and a man to run it, but the customers keep coming. I've been thinking, Lisa. Maybe you'd like to work at the nursery while the holidays are on? Helping Angus and me, and minding the place when we're not around. We're coming into the busy time of the year now and we could do with a hand.'

'Really?' A speculative gleam shone in her eye. 'Would I get paid?'

'Yes. Mind, you can get sacked too, so it would be every day, not just when you felt like it. Starting Monday. Of course, there'd still be time for you to see Roseanne on the weekends.'

'Cool.' Then she was dashing off, hollering back over her shoulder, 'I'm gonna tell her now.'

'Good idea,' Angus said, watching her flying figure disappear up the road. 'A bit of pocket money an' some responsibility. Won't do her no harm a-tall.'

'Which reminds me,' I said, turning in at our gate, 'I had a call from Mount Ixion this morning. They want fifty advanced trees to plant on the banks of a dam to hold it together. They'll pick them up over the weekend when they're in town for the sports, was what he said. So we'll have to sort them out tomorrow. The dam's in their red country, so I suggested eucalypts. Have we that many advanced ones, do you think? They'd suit best and he left the choice to me.'

'Dunno. I'll have a count. If we're short we could throw in a few whitewoods. Fifty! Must be a big dam. They ain't gonna squeeze that many onto a Toyota tray. They got this dam fenced?'

'I assume so.'

'Oughta work then,' he grunted. 'I'll check what we've got.'

Chapter Thirty-four

On Friday afternoon, Fodo dropped in for a visit. I hadn't seen her since the last CWA meeting. She had come to check, she said, what would be a suitable offering for the dance supper.

'Well, anything.' I was surprised by the question. 'Doesn't have to be fancy. Have you not been to one before?'

'Only balls at home when I was a girl. And they were all catered and rather grand.' She wore the usual floaty dress and had her hair in two long plaits with a bright headband, like something from a seventies film, but on her it looked okay. She immediately spotted Flint's mirror and walked across to run a careful hand over the carving. 'Oh, that's beautiful, Penny! Such fine work. Wherever did you find it?'

'Flint made it for me. He's got a bit of a name for the workmanship of his special pieces. They fetch very high prices with the high-end dealers on the coast.'

'I can believe it. Just look at the detail in that bottlebrush! If ever a man put his soul into something . . . So,' she said, turning to me with a knowing smile, her profile mirrored in the glass beside her, 'he really cares for you then. That's a gift of love if ever I saw one.'

I smiled back, my heart buoyed with joy. 'I know. He's wonderful. I'm so lucky. And Lisa likes him too. It could've been awkward but he's really good with her. He treats her like—' I was going to say the daughter he lost, but that was his story to tell. 'Well, like a person rather than a child, and she responds to it.'

'Fortunate,' Fodo observed. 'Nothing like step-kids to cruel romantic prospects and wreck marriages. Will it come to marriage, do you think?'

I didn't even hesitate, so far had my heart travelled from its earlier fortress mentality. 'If he asks me. Anyway, have you heard from Agnes lately? Any word on how Bev's doing?'

'Mmm, that was my news – I just got sidetracked with the supper problem and then your love life.' I blushed and she laughed. 'It looks like they won't be back in a hurry. Agnes asked if we'd stay on for the rest of the year. She says by Christmas she'll have a better idea of whether she'll ever be able to bring him back. Apparently there can be all sorts of problems associated with his condition, and most of them seem to be potentially fatal, particularly with lungs and blood pressure, if something goes really wrong.'

'God! How awful. As if total paralysis wasn't bad enough. And Zim's okay with this idea? He's not wanting to hare off over the hills, I mean?'

She nodded. 'I think he's having a gradual change of heart. It's always been the open road and leaving troubles behind with him, but even Zim has to face the fact that we're growing older. He'll be sixty-five next month. I think he can see that a steady job and a permanent home is better than the freedom of the road when it's coupled with old age and an uncertain future. I expect he'll grumble now and then when he feels the road calling him, but he'll think of Meadow and me and stay.'

'Well, I hope so. You must give me Agnes's address. I'd like to send Bev a get well card.' I grimaced at the words. 'Well, you know what I mean – a "we're thinking of you" card. It must be lonely for him.'

'I'll do that. So, a butter cake then for Sunday night?'

'Perfect,' I agreed. 'I'll see you at the dance if not before.'

It was a busy Easter weekend. With the hand trolley we used to shift the extra-large pots about, Angus and I got the fifty chosen trees corralled off to one side where they could be more easily accessed when the station men came to pick them up. We then needed to move the next largest lot into the space they'd vacated and so on, until we had a bare length of bench to house the new seedling trees we would be repotting on Monday. I had ordered a new little dress for Lisa, which arrived on the same mail as the trees, and between baking for the dance, then weeding, and digging over my display bed in the front garden, I got Lisa to try it on. It was a simple waisted dress in dusky pink with a sweetheart neckline, just a little too long in the skirt.

'Well, that's easily fixed.' I measured and pinned the skirt, then Lisa washed up after the baking while I raised the hem. 'There, that's done. Try it on now.'

She did so, twirling to bell the skirt out. 'It's lovely. Thank you, Penny.' She smoothed the bodice, saying sadly, 'But I'm all flat in front, not like Roseanne.'

'Oh sweetie, you won't be for long. Everyone grows at their own pace. Give it another twelve months and you'll see.'

'Really?'

'Yes,' I said firmly. 'It's just bit by bit at first, then next thing you know you'll be needing a bra.' I gave her a hug. 'People are like plants – they can't stop turning into what they'll be, because the imprint is in their genes. You just have to wait on nature. And Lisa, if there's ever anything you want to know about stuff, like bras, or getting your period – the sort of things you'd go to your mum about if she was still here – you know you can always ask me. You must miss her and of course I'm not the same, but I will try my best to fill in for her.'

Twisting a lock of hair about her finger, she looked fixedly at the floor and said, 'I know.' And then in a rush with a little sideways glance at me, gruffly, 'I'm glad I've got you, Penny. I think Mum would've liked you.'

'Well, I'm glad we've got each other,' I said. 'Now, while the cake's in the oven I'm going to plant out the front bed. Petunias and marigolds, with carpet-of-snow alyssum for the edges. You can help me if you want. Customers are inspired to spend by the sight of a pretty flowerbed.'

'You mean they look at it, then they go and buy your plants to make one like it themselves? Sneaky,' she said admiringly.

I flicked her cheek gently with a finger. 'It's called advertising. Hang up your new dress and we'll get started.'

On Saturday, a new police sergeant arrived in town. I heard the news from Angus, who was home from a drink at the pub where he'd got it from an agitated Zim.

'Come to check up on me. So many questions! All the same, your policemans.' Angus repeated his words faithfully, though without managing the accent.

'It's understandable he'd be alarmed,' I said. 'God knows what sort of a fascist state he grew up in. But they didn't waste any time, finding a replacement for poor Greg.'

'Huh,' Angus agreed. 'This 'un could be better, anyroad. Had himself a soft drink, accordin' to Zim.'

'He might be married,' I mused. 'Maybe he's got a family? I wonder how they'll like it here.'

Angus cast up his eyes at this entirely reasonable speculation. 'You don't even know who he is, an' now he's got a family? Women!'

I said, 'Well, he might have. In fact, it makes sense – couples are more likely to settle and stay than a single man. And another family in town would be great.'

'Have it your way then.' He shook his head and stumped off.

Sunday was a kaleidoscope of bright-shirted riders and flighty horses in a whirl of dust, and endless hamburgers made by half-a-dozen of us manning the food stall, serving teas, slapping steak on buns or savs onto bread slices and making change at a furious pace.

The impromptu bar alongside the food stall did a roaring trade with a commensurate amount of noise, which added to the considerable din of children chasing about, shrieking and falling, seemingly in imminent danger of death from moment to moment by restless hooves. It was exhausting and exhilarating, catching up with station friends unseen since the Christmas dance. Ellen Howard's little Tommy, going on four months old, lay peacefully asleep in his cot in a corner of the kitchen, oblivious to the bustle around him.

'Are you sure he isn't deaf?' I asked his mother.

She laughed. 'Don't wake him or you'll wish you were. He's got a roar on him like a mad bull.'

When the noon rush was over, Flint presented at the kitchen door, wearing jeans, workboots and a vaguely western shirt patterned in blues. 'C'mon,' he said. 'I've got our lunches and a filled thermos. Let's find somewhere quiet and eat.'

'Thank God. I'm ready to drop.' I pulled my apron off and exchanged it for my hat. 'Have you seen Lisa?'

'Yep. Angus bought her lunch. They're in the stands. You've got sauce on your blouse.'

'Really?' I pulled the front out to look and wet my finger to scrub at the stain. 'Damn. Bound to happen. The lunch rush is always a madhouse. What about you? Having fun yet?'

He grinned. 'I've been busy. Also I met our new sergeant. Seems a decent bloke. His wife and son'll be coming to join him next week. I asked him about Carter. He's been charged with Greg's murder, so the sergeant will be coming round sometime Monday to see you. You and Lisa will be witnesses for the court case, if it should come to that.'

I was vaguely alarmed. '*If?* There's no if about it! We know he killed him.'

'Of course. It'll only go to court if he doesn't plead guilty. But I can't see how he won't.'

'Oh right, I get it. And what about the rest? My mother and Colleen?'

'Ah. Well, Harry – that's his name, Sergeant Harry Fisher – was pretty noncommittal there. I gathered that the cops would prefer to go with a murder charge they can prove, with evidence and eyewitnesses, rather than historic cases where they have neither.'

'But he confessed to killing her!'

'But he also said it was an accident. If he didn't get off altogether, that's manslaughter, at best. As for Colleen, they've nothing to prove he knew a thing about it. No matter what you claim he said.'

I fired up immediately, lunch forgotten. 'There's no *claim* about it! It's the reason he murdered my mother, because she asked him . . . And don't forget the ring—'

Flint raised a hand to stem the rush of words. 'I believe you, my heart. I do. I'm just looking at it the way they will. The ring's circumstantial too, no direct link, you see. But see their side for a moment. Better a slam dunk with Greg's case than a couple of wobbly indictments he just might wriggle out of.' He raised the thermos. 'I snagged a couple of proper mugs from the kitchen. Tea?'

'Yes, please.' I stared glumly at my food then took another bite, suddenly ravenous. I'd had nothing since an early breakfast and seemed to have been running ever since. 'At least he'll be in jail,' I said grudgingly. 'That's something. I suppose I'll just have to settle for that.'

Chapter Thirty-five

The sports day finished late in the afternoon, the children's races the last events. All the usual contests were included, three-legged and sack races, egg-and-spoon and foot races. Lisa dropped her hard-boiled egg but won a ribbon and five dollars in the sprint, her lithe form leaving even the competing boys for dead. Around the course horses were being loaded, or in the case of the most far-flung properties, taken back to the temporary camps that had sprung up through the timberline beyond the racecourse.

Some of the volunteers would continue to man the food stall to provide a barbecue meal before the dance, for those who were staying. More than half of the station contingent attending had come with their swags and tuckerboxes for that very purpose.

'You get off,' Sue said, bustling in to interrupt my stint at the sink. 'I'll finish up here. You've done enough for today. See you at the dance?'

'Thanks,' I said. 'Yes. Good day, wasn't it?'

She nodded. 'The CWA will have done well from it. Off

you go then.' The Association always catered for the social events in Southbend and raised good money from them. As our president frequently pointed out, everyone had to eat.

Back home I prepared a salad for the four of us and showered and washed my hair, wondering what I should wear. It seemed incredible that I had scarcely given the last dance a thought, when Flint was no more to me than a helpful neighbour. Now I found myself studying my small supply of dresses and wishing that I had something new to dazzle him with. I clasped his bracelet around my wrist and was still pondering before the open wardrobe when Lisa knocked at the door.

'Can I come in?'

'Yes. What is it?'

'Can you do my hair, please? Like before.' She handed me her comb and clips. 'What are you going to wear, Penny?'

'I haven't decided. Come, stand still. I can't—' but her eye was caught by a colour and she darted to the line of dresses, pulling one out by the skirt.

'Ooh, this one. Such a pretty blue. I'll bet you look great in it. A swishy skirt too. Just put it on, Penny, and let me see. Puh-lease,' she wheedled.

'Okay.' Perhaps it would do, I thought, slipping off the light robe I'd donned after my shower and pulling the dress over my head. It was a long time – four years, maybe? – since I'd worn it, but it fit perfectly still. It was sleeveless, with a scooped neckline and a smooth figure-hugging top above a dropped waist. The three tiers of the skirt flared out from the hips and, studying myself in the mirror, I smiled at Lisa. 'You're absolutely right. Just the thing. Right, let's get your hair up. Is Angus getting ready?'

'Polishing his shoes. Did you know he's had the same pair for *fourteen* years?'

'Well, they don't get out much. Hold still now, I'm just going to trim your fringe a bit.'

The hall had been swept out, the kitchen stove lit and the supper tables prepared when we arrived at the dance. I took my offerings to the kitchen and handed them over to Muriel, who seemed to be in charge there. 'They might need the fridge if they'll fit. The icing's a bit soft. Sue not here yet?'

'She twisted her ankle. Said Tony'll bring her along later. He was going to the clinic rooms to find a wheelchair when she rang.'

'Oh, poor thing!' In the hall someone had started the music. I said hastily, 'I hope it's nothing worse than a sprain. How're you, Muriel?'

'Grand.' She grinned, her features lightening up. 'You're looking very fine yourself, as my dad would've said. He had Irish blood, you know, liked to bung on the blarney.'

'Thank you! I didn't know that, actually. Catch you later.' Flint was in the doorway beckoning.

'G'day, Muriel. Come on, Penny,' he said and, catching my hand, pulled me onto the dance floor.

Most of the district was there. Taking in the crowd as I circled the room in Flint's arms, I hoped we wouldn't run out of food. Flint pointed his chin at a man who was standing chatting to Stan Bentley by the open door. 'That's Harry Fisher.'

The new sergeant was a serious-looking man whom I judged to be in his late thirties, and as different from Greg

Banner as could be. He was a trim, fit-looking fellow with a good head of hair and a pleasant face, who seemed to be making himself agreeable. I heard Stan guffaw as we swept past. Lisa, I saw, had no need of Angus's help this time. She and Roseanne were dancing together, perfectly in step the way I had taught them. I sent them a smile that both girls returned, young limbs flashing into a quicker pace as the music segued into a gypsy tap.

The pub was closed, as was traditional, for the sports committee was running a bar out the back, so Zim and Fodo had come to the dance. She looked very dashing in a white peasant-style blouse and flared red skirt with a magenta sash. She wore her hair up tonight, the bulk of it woven through with what seemed to be white plastic daisies. Zim was trim and moody in a shimmery black shirt, his face unusually stern. I wondered why, then realised he was watching his daughter.

Meadow was certainly worth the notice, and most of the younger station men seemed to think so too, judging by the way they were cutting in on each other through successive dances. I could see she was enjoying the attention, her eyes sparkling and the flush on her cheeks adding to the sheer picture of perfection she presented. At first I thought it was just the light, then realised there was a tiny sprinkling of glitter in her hair and just a touch more where her cheekbones gave way to the delicate skin about her eyes. She fairly glowed with youth and happiness, the dark cloud of her hair the perfect foil for her heart-shaped face. Her dress was a modest drift of floaty mauve in which I detected Fodo's taste, but it suited the girl well.

'She'll break hearts in a few years,' Flint murmured in my ear. 'Her dad already looks look like he's preparing to repel boarders.'

'Mmm. The joys of parenthood. Did I tell you they're staying on at the pub? Agnes doesn't know when, or even if, she and Bev will ever be back.'

Somebody tapped Flint's shoulder at this point, a signal to change over, but he tightened his grip on my hand and shook his head. 'You'll have to find your own, mate. This one's mine.'

I giggled, watching my would-be partner turn away. 'That wasn't very polite.'

'Bugger politeness,' he said, as the music slowed and stopped and Barry Lacey, who was emceeing that evening, called a halt for supper. Flint slid his fingers through mine as we turned towards the kitchen and slanted me a private smile, the corners of his eyes crinkling. 'I could kiss you right here with the whole town watching, but I'll settle for a cuppa instead.'

We had barely started work on Monday when the new sergeant turned up, walking in from the back entrance to introduce himself.

'Didn't think you'd be open, Easter Monday and all, but I couldn't make myself heard from the front.'

'Sorry about that, but the locals all know to come round to the nursery section during business hours,' I said. 'And plants don't recognise holidays. They need attention when they need it. This is my partner, Angus McCloud, and his granddaughter, Lisa.'

Lisa muttered a hello and continued to scoop potting mix into empty containers, shooting curious glances at the policeman.

Angus wiped a hand on his pants and offered it. 'This gonna take long? We've got five 'undred trees to pot.'

'Just a bit of a chat with the ladies. Probably unnecessary; Carter will plead guilty, but just in case.' He took us through the sequence of events that had led to our finding of Greg's unconscious body and our attempt to save him, and probed a few of our answers. When he had finished I said, 'I don't want Lisa in court. If it comes to that, can't she give her evidence privately to the judge, or in a video link, or something? And what about my mother's case – the skeleton in the cemetery? Will you be charging Carter for that, too?'

'Not at present,' he said firmly. 'And I'm fairly certain neither of you will have to appear over the other business. A nice-looking layout you've got here,' he added abruptly, the interview plainly over. He gazed at the packed benches before him and nodded. 'I'll have to steer my wife this way. She's a mad keen gardener, a real green thumb, and God knows the station's yard could do with some work.' In Southbend, the police station and residence shared the same ground, a fenced weed-grown tract with a skinny coolibah tree in one corner.

'I look forward to meeting her.' So Flint was right. The police would go for the charge most likely to stick and nail Carter for it. It was justice of a sort. However they got him there, the man would still be in jail. I would have to be content with that.

*

We finished potting the trees and sat down to a late lunch just as Flint arrived. I got up as he came in to fetch another plate but he shook his head.

'I've had mine, thanks. I've done with clients for the day and wondered, seeing as it's a holiday and all, if Lisa wanted to go fishing?'

'Oh, yes please. Can we, Penny?'

I fixed her with a stern look. 'You do remember you're working now?'

'Oh.' Her face fell ludicrously, then brightened. 'I could make it up next Saturday – weeding, potting, even that yucky blood and bone,' she promised recklessly.

'Well,' I said, pretending to consider it, 'all right then. Thanks, Flint. Have a cuppa while we finish here and wash up, then we're all yours.'

He grinned and gave me a wink. 'Good to hear.'

By the following Wednesday morning, Sue had dispensed with the wheelchair in favour of a walking stick when I found her seated on a stool in the shop talking to Marlene.

'Hi, Marlene, Sue. How's it going then?' I said, nodding to the bandaged ankle.

'Getting there slowly. I'm just too heavy for it to mend quickly.' Sue sighed, mopping her damp brow with a man's handkerchief. She eyed my hair. 'You're about due for another cut.'

'I know.' I pushed at the combs securing the curls up off my neck. 'I'll be round when I get time. I've met the new sergeant. He's got a gardening wife and, I understand, a son. So what's your news?'

'I was just telling Marlene. The material for the cemetery fence arrived Saturday and some of the blokes have organised a working bee for the weekend. They reckon half a day's work will see it stood. They'll be using Barry's posthole digger and Barry himself has offered to weld up a gate. We'll pay for that, of course. And the sign. I thought he could make it too and perhaps'—she twinkled at me—'you could ask Flint to paint it for us? We'd compensate him for his time, of course, and the materials. He's an arty fellow and really, just imagine how much we'd save not having to freight the thing from Hamilton and paying some designer to do it for us. Would he be interested, do you think? It'd be just a matter of dates, some history and maybe a bit of art. The Shire logo perhaps and a bird or two.'

'I'll ask,' I said, careful not to promise anything on his behalf, 'though he's going to be pretty busy now the roads are open. But the rest is wonderful. I can't get the trees planted until the water's laid on, but maybe we should get a little bee of our own going to clean up the rest of the weeds and see about standing the falling stones? What about next Saturday, if we feed the men?'

'Definitely.' Marlene nodded. 'Least we can do. Should I ring around, find out what people can bring?'

Sue clapped her hands. 'Excellent suggestion. I'll talk to Fodo. We should have it at the pub and tell her that we'll provide the meal. That way they'll sell a few drinks. And, by the way, the council men are installing the tank as we speak. I saw the truck going out with it on my way here.'

'In that case, I can plant on Saturday too. As soon as the ground's cleared and the paths are marked out. Angus and

I will do that. So, everyone who owns one should bring a hoe along because there's a bit of chipping still to do, despite us getting a lot of the woody weeds out last time.'

'Well,' Sue said as she heaved herself up and took her purchases, 'hopefully I'll see you in the cemetery.' She laughed, a surprisingly girlish giggle. 'Sounds like the title of a thriller, doesn't it? Don't forget to come for a haircut.'

'Actually,' Marlene said, once she was gone. 'I rather like the way you're wearing your hair now. You're so lucky to have natural curls.'

'That's what everybody thinks. But you've only got one style and that's curly. Where's Roseanne?'

'Gone to Goola with Stan to get the frozen supplies. I'm surprised Lisa hasn't been over looking for her.'

'She's working over the holidays,' I explained. 'Have you any desiccated coconut, Marlene? I'm right out.'

'Last packet.' She fetched it for me, saying thoughtfully, 'I might ring Ellen Howard first. If Rumhole can provide the meat for the meal, it'll make it easier for the rest of us.'

'Good idea.' I paid and grabbed the coconut. 'You could try the Park too. Then we'd only need the veg and a dessert. I've got to go, Marlene. Catch you later.'

Chapter Thirty-six

Flint agreed to paint the sign with the caveat that it might take a while. I had packed a lunch and stolen half an hour from my day to meet him at the river, where he'd been finishing up with his latest clients.

'Finish before the May races?' I pressed. 'That's our deadline.'

He sighed theatrically. 'For you, my lady, anything.'

I kissed him as a thankyou, saying, 'It's not a freebie, you know. We CWA-ers honour our debts.'

'I should hope so. It won't be a two-minute job. Does anybody have a final version of how it should read?'

'Sally was doing that bit. Will you join us Saturday? There's a working bee on at the cemetery.'

He sat up on one elbow, hoisting his brows in pained surprise. 'Just who do you think arranged for that, hmm? After your little adventure, I'm not dead keen on you making any more solitary trips out there. Getting the job over with seemed the best way to prevent that. Hence the working bee.'

'You're a marvel,' I said, staring at him with frank wonder.

'You saved my life and Lisa's, you've organised this for me, you share my bed, and I don't even know your first name. How can that possibly be?' The dappled shade of the ti-tree moved on his face, shadowing the hollows of his eyes and making patterns on the rug spread beneath us.

Furrowing his brow, he appeared to think about it. 'I could tell you, I suppose,' he said at last, 'but you'd have to marry me if I did. And then I could forbid you to repeat it.'

For a moment I didn't believe I'd heard him correctly. His words had been uttered in that casual half-teasing way he had, but his eyes belied his unconcern. I saw again the little flecks of gold I had noticed the first time he almost kissed me. Keeping it light, I pursed my lips in pretend thought and offered, 'Okay, I'll risk it. So, what *is* it?'

He grinned. 'I'll hold you to that, mind. Come closer. Closer still,' he commanded as I leaned towards him, intrigued. When his lips were right at my ear, and the pounding of my heart made me think I wouldn't hear anyway, he whispered a name.

'No!' I reared back, feeling a laugh ready to break forth. 'It can't be . . . No mother would . . . Oh my God! No wonder you just go by your surname.' I couldn't suppress my horrified giggle.

He frowned. 'Well, now you know. And a bargain's a bargain. We are engaged, my dear one. And you are never to repeat that name. When I die, my grave should just read something like: *Flint, who adored the woman who loved him.*'

'Don't talk about dying!' But the quick horror of my response was replaced by a slow burn of pleasure. 'Do you really adore me?'

'With every fibre of my being, my heart. Come here.'

'I love you too,' I said, 'quite frantically,' and then the world disappeared into his kiss.

When Saturday arrived, Lisa seemed to regret her promise to work off the free afternoon she'd had during the week. 'I couldn't, like, do it next Saturday, Penny?'

'No,' I said, adding reasonably, 'Both your grandad and I have jobs to do out there. Somebody has to mind the shop and water the outside stock and that somebody is you. Paid work is just that, you know. You do whatever it is you signed up for.'

A little after eight, we loaded the equipment we needed, along with the trees, and set off. We'd settled on rosemary to make a hedge for the entrance, African mahoganies for shade, and a tulip tree, flamboyant when in bloom, to go beside the sign when it was finished. The place was already busy when we arrived with half-a-dozen men including Flint, Stan Bentley and Tom Howard working on the marked fenceline. Barry's tractor was there and a stack of wire coils and fencing posts. The gate, a sturdy affair of steel, was propped against a coolibah to await instalment.

By the time the other volunteers arrived, the corner posts and their stays were in, and Barry was ramming the earth on the gateposts. Flint came across to help Angus bar out the holes for the trees, and put a steadying hand on the barrow when I wheeled it over.

'Here, let me.' He upended it, pouring the mixture of compost and potting mix into the cavernous hole; it would ensure the trees got off to a good start in their new home.

'Thanks. Looks like we'll have no trouble finishing today.' Somebody was using a dropper-driver on the steel posts, and Tom and Stan were heaving the fallen headstones back upright, having first dug a deep channel to slide them into. I heard Muriel chase them away from the one she was working on, snapping, 'Come back when it's clean.'

We still had to paint in the words incised into the granite, I remembered, but that could be done with the stones in position. The fibreglass tank sat unobtrusively outside the fence on the far side from the river and had been filled. I connected our hose and watered the new plantings in. Then, working from the plan that Sally had made copies of, Angus and I plotted out the paths between the graves, taping the marker pegs with red plastic.

'What's that for, miss?' a boy, one of the three school children who had accompanied Sally, asked.

'It's where the paths will go. If you like,' I said, for he was carrying a hoe, 'you could chop the weeds between the pegs. We'll be laying plastic down later to stop any more growing.'

'Cool.' He hoed away with enthusiasm while I turned to the next job, just as the shire clerk arrived in a council vehicle. He'd come, he said, to see how the work was going and seemed impressed by our progress. He asked the same question about the pegs, and Angus, who was passing at that moment, answered for me.

'Paths. Your average tourist ain't gonna fight his way through weeds. Wouldn't hurt the bloody council none to fetch a load of gravel down to lay on 'em.'

The clerk harrumphed, spoke to Sue, who was ensconced on a drum in front of a trestle table laden with a promising selection of smoko gear, then drove off.

'Pen pusher,' Angus said in a tone of disgust. 'He ain't soilin' his 'ands with actual work. I figure we oughta peg the area where the sign's gonna go, too. Lay a bit of sheeting there. Nothin' looks worse than a sign risin' outta a sea of weeds.'

We downed tools for smoko and I was glad to stop for a rest. The days were still quite warm. We splashed grubby hands in water drawn from the tank and sat under our hats, as there was no actual shade apart from the skimpy bit thrown by the leggy bloodwoods. Flint brought me a cuppa and we sat back to back for support, sipping and eating the baked goods Sue had supplied.

'Be nice when the trees are grown,' I murmured. The men had the wire run out, though not yet strung and strained, but the posts gave definition to the area, and with many of the fallen headstones now upright, the paths made more sense.

'Peaceful,' Flint observed. There was only a small breeze through the bushes and the soft cadence of the others' voices. A blue-capped wren and his mate appeared, then a second pair, like tiny patches of fallen sky, to drink at the puddle beneath the tap, then flirt up onto the closest post. Endemic to the area, their brilliant colour always startled the eye.

'Something for your sign,' I said, pointing out the birds. 'Think we'll finish by lunch?'

'Pretty much. Just need to strain up the fence and tie it, straighten a few more headstones, fix the gate. Barry's made the gudgeon pins and once they're in, it's only a matter of drilling the holes and fixing the bolt on the opposite post. Looks like the weeds are under control. What are you doing with the paths?'

'Laying plastic as a weed suppressant. Nobody's decided yet what to put on it, so that and the sign will be all that's left to do. Sue thought woodchip or pine bark, but I'm not so sure that'll work. The next Wet would probably shift it and another flood certainly would.'

'I'm sure you'll work something out,' he said. 'You're a resourceful lot, you women.' He groaned and stood. 'Well, back to the salt mine.'

'Think of the lunch you'll be getting after at the pub,' I quipped. 'That's got to be worth a bit of sweat.'

We were finished and home in the early afternoon. Fodo and Meadow had organised a delicious buffet lunch with the food the CWA members had provided. At the end of it, Sue rose from her place to thank all the volunteers and invite them to the formal opening, which, she said, would take place sometime during the May race weekend. After that everyone collected the bowls and pans in which they'd brought the food and dispersed.

'See you later,' Flint promised, heading for his own vehicle, 'when we break the news to the family.'

'You think I should say something to Lisa first? I know she's fond of you, but she still seems a bit insecure, though I've told her I'll always keep her.'

'Whatever you think is best,' he said, which was no help at all.

Angus and I found both girls in the nursery, raking patterns into the damp soil of the shadehouses. Roseanne, putting up her rake, said, 'Hi, Ms Carter. This is okay, is it? Hello, Mr McCloud.'

I smiled at her. 'It looks very nice. Sort of zen-nish. How did it go, Lisa?'

She grinned widely. 'I sold two pot plants! And a lady wants to come back and talk to you about something she's trying to grow. I told her Monday – I said we didn't open Sundays.'

'Very good. Well, you're off work now. Did you have lunch?'

'We made some sandwiches,' Roseanne said, adding hastily, 'And we cleaned everything up after.'

'I appreciate that.' I glanced across at Lisa, but now was not the time for a private conversation.

'Did you finish at the cemetery, Grandad?' she asked.

'Sure did, lassie. Looks good enough to be buried in to this tired old man. I'm gonna have a shower an' a lie down. Rest me back for a bit.'

'You do that,' I said, 'and I'll be right behind you for the shower.' In the meantime, I needed to think about dinner. Something a bit special to mark the occasion. I wished that I had made time for that haircut, but then I reflected that I could ask for Lisa's help to pin up my wayward curls. It would be an excellent time, in the intimacy of my room, to tell her about my engagement. Hopefully she wouldn't be too upset. And there was Angus. He knew how I felt about Flint but a bit of reassurance there, to let him know that his future wasn't about to change as far as the business or living arrangements went, couldn't hurt either.

He was resting after his shower when I told him. I tapped on his door then entered the room to find him stretched out on his bed. 'Don't get up,' I said as he heaved himself into a sitting position. 'I just came to give you my news. Flint's asked me to marry him.'

'Did he now?' He rubbed his nose. 'You gonna do it? Course y' are.' A grin split his face. 'Good on yer, lass. He's a great bloke.'

'I'm glad you approve.' Sitting down beside him, I gave him a hug. 'He'll move in with us, but nothing else will change. Flint'll run his business, and we'll run ours. I just hope Lisa's going to be okay with it.'

'Course she will be. Thinks he's Christmas, she does. I couldn't be 'appier for you both, lass. You deserve it, and I reckon Lisa'll see it that way too.'

I had my doubts but when the moment came, I was surprised to find that she was delighted.

'That's so cool.' She abandoned the comb she'd been attempting to place and plumped down on the bed behind me. 'I sort of guessed you were gonna get married, because Roseanne said he would. Ask you, you know. I bet her mum told her so.'

I swivelled the stool around to face her. 'Then you don't mind that he'll be with living with us for good? Not just dropping in now and then?'

She shook her head. 'Course not. It'll be like having a proper dad. I mean, Grandad's great but he's old . . . How did he do it – did he kneel or just, you know, say like, "You wanna marry me, Penny?"'

I smiled. 'Not quite. You know Flint has his own way of doing things. Tonight's dinner's a bit special, so I thought we'd make a pretty table with some flowers and napkins. You could wear a dress and I'll put your hair up, just like for the dance. Okay?'

'Super.' She bounced off the bed heading for the door,

leaving me to tend to my own curls. 'I'll have my shower right away.'

Later that evening after dinner, sitting on the verandah in the dim glow cast by the light in the living room, Flint's hand rose to brush my shoulder just as I was about to bring up the subject I had been thinking about all evening.

'You're very quiet tonight.' His breath was warm on my ear. 'Penny for 'em, Penny. Not having second thoughts, I hope?'

'Of course not. Just thinking. Did you enjoy your dinner, by the way?'

'You bet. Two great feeds in one day. A man could get fat around you, my heart. So what are you thinking about?'

'About adoption,' I said baldly. 'How would you feel about us formally adopting Lisa? I know it's a big ask, but it was just something she said when I told her we were getting married – I asked her if she'd mind, and what she said was that it would be like having a proper dad again. I mean, Michael was only ever there for her part time. I think she'd jump at the prospect of feeling she really *belonged* again. But would you want that degree of responsibility and expense? It's life-long after all. And,' I hesitated, 'what about Sam? Would Lisa be too much of a reminder if—'

His breath went out on a little laugh as he interrupted me by nuzzling my neck. 'Dear Penny, I have spent fourteen years learning to overcome the loss of just that. Lisa's not Sam, and she wouldn't be a replacement for my own girl, because no one ever could be. But she could be another daughter to me. She's a likeable, spunky kid. I have a great admiration for her and what she's survived, and I would be honoured beyond words to have the chance of standing in as her father, if that's what you both want.'

'Then it's settled,' I said, turning to kiss him. 'Thank you, Flint. I'll ask her in the morning.'

'You do that. Are we going to set a date, by the way?'

That, too, had been on my mind. 'How do you feel about next month, the week before the race weekend? That'll be a busy one for both of us. It's not much time but I don't need a fuss. A marriage celebrant and just the four of us, then a nice meal somewhere afterwards. Stay the night and home next day?'

'Suits me, though it would mean we won't get a honeymoon,' he pointed out. 'We can't leave our businesses in the middle of the season.'

'No, but we could always have a holiday next Wet. We could take your work to the coast and go on from there, for a week or three.'

'Sounds like a plan. Meantime,' he said, pulling me to my feet, 'come along, my bride to be. It's time for bed.'

'Oh, yes.' Lovingly I palmed his cheek. 'With all the trials you'll face as a new dad, you'll need lots of comfort and guidance. Luckily, I think I can provide that.'

Chapter Thirty-seven

I didn't attend the opening of the cemetery on the race weekend, though both my menfolk did, Angus representing the nursery and my husband his own business. A reporter from Hamilton, out for the event, turned up to take a photo of the action, showing the new fence and now gravelled paths (courtesy of the council's Works Department) and catching the moment when Bob Page cut the ribbon and lauded the improvements to the historic site as 'a community project led by the council'.

My own turn came a fortnight later when my mother was laid to rest in a private ceremony conducted by the flying padre. A Uniting Church man who made periodic visits to the scattered stations and tiny towns across the north-west, he arrived at the Southbend airstrip with the coffin containing my mother's remains. Barry Lacey dug the grave with the council's front-end loader, and Muriel, clutching an armload of bush blossoms, a mixture of beefwood, wattle and silver oak, laid them on the refilled surface once the coffin had vanished. There was no headstone, just a short steel frame into which

Flint's offering slotted – a carved slab of hardwood depicting a pair of hands opening to release a dove, and her name and the dates of her life beneath.

When that was done, Muriel, quite unexpectedly, began to sing 'Amazing Grace'. She had a surprisingly deep, melodic voice to which the padre joined his. Flint and I stood in silence in air scented with carbeen and wattle bloom until the song ended then I pulled her into a heartfelt hug.

'Thank you, Muriel. That was beautiful.'

She flushed a little and sniffed. 'She loved to sing, Imogen. And she was my friend.' Then, resuming her normal abrasive attitude, she continued, 'And wherever she is now, I hope she knows that bastard's in jail for what he did.'

Carter had been sentenced and locked away when he pleaded guilty to killing Sergeant Banner, not my mother, but it wasn't worth correcting her.

'Anyway,' she said as she brushed pollen and wattle dust from her arm, and gazed around at our peaceful surroundings, 'I'm glad she's here. Thanks for asking me today. It means a lot. And I never got to congratulate you on your wedding.'

'Thank you.' I smiled. 'It was very simple. A marriage celebrant in the River Park. Just us four and two witnesses we borrowed from the courthouse. Lisa was happy – she got a new dress and a bag of rice to throw. I shouldn't be surprised if the lawn there grew a crop of the stuff next Wet.'

Barry, who had removed the machinery, now returned to join us. 'Time we was going, old girl,' he told Muriel. They left in their vehicle, and we returned the padre to his plane and watched it taxi down the strip, then rise like a bird and dwindle away to a silver spot in the blue.

'That's that,' Flint said. 'Now there's only the adoption papers to come through. Maybe next week?'

'Or next month, or the one after that . . . Doesn't matter, as long as it happens. What now?'

'Home,' he said firmly, taking my hand in his. It was my left, the one wearing his ring, the magic circle that had held my mother in chains of fear, unlike mine, which cradled me in bands of love.

'Where the heart is,' I said. 'Oh, yes. Right now, I can't think of a better place to be.'

Acknowledgements

I would like to thank the great team at Penguin Random House, in particular Ali Watts and my amazing editor Amanda Martin, who applies the polish to my words. Also a shout of appreciation to all my faithful readers, who make it possible for me to continue to pound the keyboard.